# Praise for Richard Herman, Jr.

# DARK WING

From the heights of heroism . . .
to the depths of hell

**Colonel Matt Pontowski III**—Once as reckless as he was gifted at the controls of a high-performance fighter, he has now accepted the burden of command. Heading up the men and women of the 303rd, he will enter a deadly conflict in which the fate of his fliers—and the whole world—is at stake.

**Victor Kamigami**—Long listed as MIA, he has been freed from his southeast Asian prison by Chinese rebel leader Zou Rong; now, his hard-edged fighting expertise—learned both in war and in captivity—could prove invaluable to Zou Rong's fight. But this is a different kind of war, one that requires him to choose between devotion to his people—and a woman's love.

D0465785

---

**General Kang Xun**—The growing civil unrest in China has unleashed in full force his lust for power. He has formulated one simple solution to all his military and political problems: slaughter the enemy. His primary aim is the domination of Asia. His primary obstacle: the fliers of the 303rd squadron.

**Brigadier General Mark Von Drexler**—Sent by the Pentagon to meet with Zou Rong, Von Drexler is driven by a single motive: the enhancement of his own career and public image. But his strategies could have fatal consequences for the pilots under Matt Pontowski's command.

---

**Shoshana Pontowski**—Matt's beautiful, Israeli-born wife has suffered through every battle he has fought. But this time the war will come to her . . . with an impact neither she nor her husband ever imagined.

**Mazie Kamigami**—Victor's daughter, the gifted Japanese-American sits on the staff of the American president's national security advisor. Her colleagues may underestimate her, but her insights and advice will have a dramatic impact on the China crisis—and on the fate of billions of people.

**Books by Richard Herman**

Dark Wing*
Call to Duty
Firebreak
Force of Eagles
The Warbirds

*Published by Pocket Books

# DARK WING

## RICHARD HERMAN J. R.

**POCKET STAR BOOKS**

New York   London   Toronto   Sydney   Tokyo   Singapore

This book is a work of fiction. Names, characters, places and incidents are products of the author's imagination or are used fictiously. Any resemblance to actual events or locales or persons, living or dead, is entirely coincidental.

A Pocket Star Book published by
POCKET BOOKS, a division of Simon & Schuster Inc.
1230 Avenue of the Americas, New York, NY 10020

Copyright © 1994 by Richard Herman, Jr., Inc.

ISBN: 0-671-53493-9

First Pocket Books printing February 1996

10  9  8  7  6  5  4  3  2  1

POCKET STAR BOOKS and colophon are registered trademarks of Simon & Schuster Inc.

Front cover illustration by Brian Bailey

Printed in the U.S.A.

*In memory of my father,*
**Richard Herman**

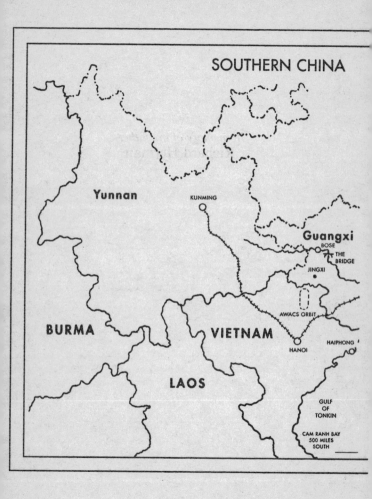

SOUTHERN CHINA

Yunnan

KUNMING

Guangxi

BOSE

THE BRIDGE

JINGXI

AWACS ORBIT

BURMA

VIETNAM

HAIPHONG

LAOS

HANOI

GULF
OF
TONKIN

CAM RANH BAY
500 MILES
SOUTH

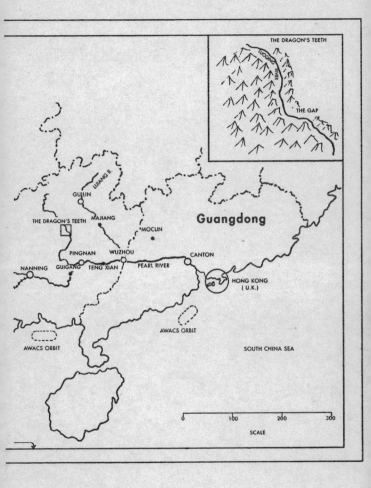

THE DRAGON'S TEETH

WUJONG RIVER

THE GAP

GUILIN

LIJIANG R.

MAJIANG

THE DRAGON'S TEETH

MOCUN

Guangdong

PINGNAN     WUZHOU

CANTON

NANNING   GUIGANG   TENG XIAN   PEARL RIVER

HONG KONG
( U.K.)

AWACS ORBIT

AWACS ORBIT

SOUTH CHINA SEA

0        100        200        300

SCALE

# THE BEGINNING

The Pontowski saga began long before Matt Pontowski, the protagonist of this story, was born. Matt carried the same name as his father and grandfather before him, and like theirs, his destiny was tied to the profession of arms as practiced by men who would fight and die in fighter aircraft.

The first Matthew Zachary Pontowski was born in Oakland, California, on November 11, 1918, at the exact time the armistice ending World War I was declared. Not too much is known about this particular bloodline of Pontowskis in the United States, and Zack, as the first Matthew Zachary was nicknamed, would only say they were of good peasant stock and were always a tight-lipped and lusty lot.

Zack Pontowski was drawn to airplanes from the first time he saw one, when he was three years old. As a teenager, he learned to fly from a barnstormer who had flown with Eddie Rickenbacker in World War I. Early on, he realized the war against Hitler and fascism was his war, and he volunteered to fly with the Royal Air Force in 1940. His experiences flying the Mosquito, the RAF's "Wooden Wonder," how he met his wife, Tosh, and why he entered politics is chronicled in the book *Call to Duty*.

The last major crisis during his term as president of the United States is also found in *Call to Duty*. As an old man, Zack Pontowski ordered young men to execute a dangerous rescue mission in the Golden Triangle of Burma. The memory of when he was on the cutting edge of combat in World

War II sharpened his sense of responsibility as he made the crucial decisions about who would live and die.

Zack and Tosh's only son, called Zack Junior, died in Southeast Asia when his F-4C Phantom fighter crashed into a hillside in North Vietnam. The earlier book *Firebreak* relates how it fell to Zack and Tosh to raise their headstrong and willful grandson, Matt. Matt followed in his father's and grandfather's footsteps and became a fighter pilot in the United States Air Force.

But Matt was a throwback to an earlier age when fighter pilots were expected to be devil-may-care characters disdainful of all duly constituted authority. Only the influence of his famous grandfather, now president of the United States, saved him from being thrown out of the Air Force because of his wild and irresponsible conduct.

*Firebreak* tells how Matt was molded by one of the best pilots ever to strap on a high-performance fighter— Lieutenant Colonel Jack Locke, a squadron commander in the Forty-fifth Fighter Wing. It fell to Locke and the men and women of the Forty-fifth to teach Matt the true nature of leadership and responsibility. But it was the crucible of combat that ultimately changed Matt and bound him to the tradition that places service, sacrifice, and obligation over the individual.

The way of leadership and the obligation for service that Matt had to learn was formed in the past, when air combat was still in its infancy. It was passed to him through Jack Locke and the Forty-fifth Fighter Wing. The first two books of this series, *The Warbirds* and *Force of Eagles,* tell the story of the Forty-fifth Fighter Wing and of the men who made it a legend.

*The Warbirds* described how Anthony "Muddy" Waters assumed command of the Forty-fifth, a wing of obsolete F-4E Phantoms and poorly trained fighter jocks. And among them was a superb but irresponsible young pilot—Jack Locke. Waters transformed the Forty-fifth in time to deploy to the Middle East to engage in a devastating action that ended in an "Arab solution." But in the political fallout, the Forty-fifth had to fight its way out of its base at Ras Assanya.

In the inferno that engulfed the base, Waters fought to save the Forty-fifth, and in the final stage of the battle, moments before he was killed, he passed the mantle of leadership to Jack Locke. It fell to Locke, now the new Wolf leader, to lead the last of the wing's fighters to safety.

In *Force of Eagles,* Jack Locke reached maturity as part of the team that rescued from captivity the men and one woman left behind at Ras Assanya. The legacy of Muddy Waters was safe with Locke, who had become that rarest of individuals—a man others will follow willingly into combat, even at the risk of their own lives.

Now it is Matt Pontowski's time.

# PROLOGUE

**Monday, November 6**
**The Pentagon**

Only his eyes betrayed the grief that still bound Lieutenant Colonel Matthew Zachary Pontowski III as he walked briskly down the main concourse of the Pentagon, heading for the relative quiet of his office. His athletic gait matched the flow of the crowd and a small cone of silence surrounded him as people deliberately cleared a path for him. Only a dunce would not have immediately recognized him—or someone who did not watch TV, listen to gossip, or play at office politics. And there were very few of those left in the Pentagon.

TV cameras had made Pontowski an instant celebrity, capturing his lanky six-foot frame and barely controllable shock of brown hair for national consumption when he had delivered the eulogy for his grandfather, Matthew Zachary Pontowski. The nation had shared in his mourning for the elder Pontowski, a former president of the United States who had died quietly in his sleep, a revered and much-honored statesman.

Every person watching the funeral service at the cathedral had been struck by the physical similarity of Pontowski to his grandfather—even if the TV commentators had not repeatedly drawn their attention to it. His piercing blue eyes and hawklike nose were Pontowski trademarks the late president had engraved on the national consciousness. Matt

1

Pontowski's statuesque wife and two-year-old son had also bewitched the TV cameras. Most of the viewers found the common description of Shoshana Pontowski as a "raven-haired Israeli beauty" totally inadequate and many mothers envied the calm and unobtrusive way she controlled their bright and rambunctious son.

More than one power broker on the national scene had reviewed the videotapes, read the newspapers, consulted his inner oracles, and mentally calculated what it would take to develop Pontowski as a successor to his grandfather.

One of the rare lieutenants assigned to the Pentagon broke the impromptu protocol of silence that had sprung into place around Pontowski and said, "I'm sorry, sir." Pontowski nodded in reply and turned down his corridor.

The civilian secretary stood up when he entered the office. Unbidden tears filled her eyes. "I'm so sorry, Colonel, so sorry." They looked at each other for a moment. Pontowski again nodded, a gentle look on his face, and she sat down. She faced her computer and pounded on the keys, trying to exorcise her own sense of loss.

Before Pontowski could reach the safety of his own office, his immediate superior, Brigadier General Mark Von Drexler, the chief of Foreign Sales, walked in. Von Drexler looked like a TV soap opera's version of a general and artfully rode that image as he made his way up the ladder of promotion. "Matt," he said, "please let me extend the sympathy and condolences of the entire staff." Von Drexler had rehearsed his words in front of a mirror, making sure his facial expression matched the tone in his voice. "I know words are inadequate at a time like this. The passing of your grandfather, one of our great presidents, is a momentous loss to our country and marks the end of a chapter in our nation's history."

"Thank you, sir," Pontowski responded. Again, the head nod worked and he was able to retreat into his office, closing the door behind him.

Von Drexler turned to leave. "I wonder how the 'golden boy' is going to make it on his own now?" he asked himself aloud. "Without his grandfather around to run interference." He didn't expect an answer. The secretary said nothing and mashed the keyboard harder. The brigadier gave a snort-like laugh, his sign of contentment when things were going well, and left.

"No good looks can hide the fact, General VD," the woman muttered under her breath, the tears still flowing, "that you are one rare bastard."

Inside his office, Pontowski hung up his overcoat, unbuttoned the coat to his uniform and looked out the window. The eulogy had forced him into a reflective frame of mind that had turned into a deep inner search. During the process, he had discovered many things about himself. Well, Grandpop, he thought, you're still making me learn. And Von Drexler spoke the truth when he said we've reached the end of a chapter—especially my chapter here at Fort Fumble.

The thirty-two-year-old lieutenant colonel knew he had reached a crossroad in his life and was about to discover what he could do without the far-reaching influence of his grandfather clearing the right-of-way. He had heard the rumors about his below-the-zone promotion to major and then lieutenant colonel. He wanted to prove them all wrong. He was not someone who owed his rank to political influence.

He sat down and stared at one of the photos on his desk, the one with his grandfather, Shoshana, and Little Matt. The president was smiling at the baby cuddled comfortably in the crook of his right arm. Pontowski focused on Shoshana's image. The photo didn't reveal any marks of the fire that had scarred her. Only her missing left earlobe and two fingers from her left hand that reconstructive surgery could not repair were still visible, but they were hidden from the camera's lens. But I know the other scars you carry, he thought.

Looking at the photo helped ease the dull ache that was tormenting him. "I miss you," he murmured to himself. His grandfather and grandmother, the elegant and loving woman called Tosh, had raised him since he was three, and he could not remember his parents.

Pontowski's father had died in a fiery crash when his F-4C Phantom had slammed into a hillside in North Vietnam in 1968. His mother never recovered from her grief and joined the antiwar protests in Berkeley, California. Unfortunately, she had also turned to the counterculture movement. Drugs and poor hygiene destroyed what was left of her frail physical and mental state. In the vague reaches of his memory, he could remember attending her funeral when he was five years old. It had fallen to Tosh to make him understand that his parents had both been casualties of the horror that was called Vietnam. During the last year of his grandfather's presidency, the ugly disease lupus had claimed Tosh. Now his grandfather was also gone.

Matthew Zachary Pontowski picked up the first folder in his in-basket, glanced at it, and then threw it back into the basket. It could wait. Okay, he told himself, decision time. Be honest. You love the flying but can't stand the bureaucracy and the ambitious assholes who stalk the halls of the Pentagon. So what are you going to do? Do something now, while you can still get an assignment to a front-line fighter squadron.

But Pontowski had seen how political influence exerted its power and he knew that any request for reassignment submitted now would be instantly given the inside track. He sensed the unfairness of it all. He would be taking a flying slot away from another jock who was committed heart and soul to the Air Force and trying desperately to make a career in the scaled-down service that was emerging after the end of the Cold War. He wanted to be considered on his own merits. Yet he knew the tinge of political influence would plague him no matter what he did. Still, every instinct told him that he had to escape from the paperwork side of the Air Force or get out.

He picked up the phone and jabbed at the buttons, calling his old back-seater, Ambler Furry, who had found a home at the Air Reserve Personnel Center in Denver managing the Air Force Reserve. Furry alone would play it straight with him. "Yo, Amb," he said, "can you help save an old buddy?" Ten minutes later, he hung up and called Shoshana to ask how she felt about taking a new assignment to Whiteman Air Force Base in Missouri. It would mean his resigning from the regular Air Force and joining the reserves.

But there were compensations.

**Thursday, December 28**
**Hanoi, Vietnam**

"I want to see him. Now."

The four guards stared at the teenager, surprised by the steel and command in his voice. "Of course," the older sergeant said, suddenly anxious to do the boy's bidding. He motioned for the other three guards to stay back, afraid that one might let the ancient hatred the Vietnamese held for the Chinese break through. That could only mean trouble, as his superiors were treating the boy as an honored dignitary. Besides, why this Chinese whelp was interested in the American they had held captive for over a year was not his concern. The sergeant led the way down the dark corridor, automatically counting the thick wooden doors on the left.

It puzzled the sergeant why he, a hero of the Vietnamese people, should be groveling around this slender boy. The sergeant was, after all, a combat veteran who had fought the Americans in the Ia Drang when he was no older than the lad he was now escorting, butchered scores of South Vietnamese during the Tet offensive, and marched into Saigon with a victorious army in 1975. Now, twenty years later, he was all but bowing to this Chinese boy who was marked only by expressive eyes and a commanding voice. Kill the bastard, he told himself. But just as quickly, he discarded the thought. There was too much involved. "In here," the sergeant said, stopping in front of the fourth door. He turned the key in the lock, pulled the heavy bolt back, tugged the door open, and swept the cell with his flashlight. A giant of a man was sitting yoga-style on the concrete shelf that served as a bunk. His Oriental features were composed and calm, oblivious to his dank surroundings.

"Pig!" the sergeant shouted. "You know the rules. Sit at attention on your bunk, feet on the floor." The prisoner only blinked at the bright light. The sergeant made no attempt to enter the cell. Aware that the boy sensed his fear of the man, the sergeant pointed the beam at the floor, illuminating the spot where he wanted the man's feet, and showing that he was in charge.

Slowly, the man swung his bulk around into the required position. A rat scurried across the floor, running along the base of the bunk and behind the prisoner's bare feet. With a speed the boy could not believe, the man's right hand snapped out and tweaked the rat behind its neck, snapping it. With a graceful motion, he threw the dead rodent into the far corner. The flashlight panned across the cell onto a pile of dead rats. "This is the way he amuses himself," the sergeant said.

The boy studied the American. The reports had not exaggerated—he was at least six and a half feet tall, and even in his emaciated condition, had to weigh two hundred pounds. "Bring some decent food," he told the guard.

"That would only give him strength," the Vietnamese replied.

"I want to talk to him. Alone."

"That is against the rules." The boy only stared at the guard. "I'll bring some food," the sergeant finally said, withering under the intense look. He turned and retreated down the hall, locking the cell door but leaving the light on.

"They tell me you speak some Cantonese," the boy said in that language. "I've come to free you."

Silence. Finally, the man turned and looked at the newcomer. "Thank you, I'm grateful." His voice was amazingly soft and gentle, totally at odds with his bulky body, and barely audible as he fumbled with his limited Chinese vocabulary. "You're not Vietnamese."

"No," the teenager replied in English. "And the way you torture your words tell me you're not Han."

The man shook his big head. He saw no reason to tell the boy he had been born on the island of Maui and that his heritage included both Hawaiian and Japanese bloodlines. He was not Chinese. But a strong instinct warned him to be very candid about the matter that had brought this strange teenager to this prison in Hanoi. He was not what he seemed at first glance. "If I get out of this cell, I'll try to escape."

"That won't be necessary," the boy smiled. "You'll be set free as soon as we are out of Vietnam."

"Why should you go to all this trouble? You don't even know me."

"I am seeking the help of the Vietnamese in a cause much like their own," the young Chinese replied. "An official

6

mentioned you during an ... ah ... conversation. I thought perhaps you might also be willing to help us."

"Who is 'us'?"

How much should I tell him about our cause? the young man thought. He is an American by birth and not Chinese. What will it matter to him that we must try to claim our own fate and again throw our lives against the power of a corrupt government? Perhaps the simplest answer is the best for now. "My people, the Chinese."

"And if I won't?"

"Then you're a free man. We'll get you to Hong Kong."

A long silence came down. "What is your name?" the American finally asked.

"Zou Rong."

A smile played across the man's face. "I thought he died over ninety years ago in jail—when he was nineteen."

"I'm surprised that an American would know the name," Zou said. "I adopted his name because mine means nothing and I resemble his photograph. But I am nine years older."

"You had me fooled, Mr. Zou." The American came to his feet in an easy and fluid movement, a decision made. "I am grateful for you getting me out of here but I need more information before I decide to help you."

"That is only wise," Zou said. Then he added, "You've never told the Vietnamese your name. Must it remain a secret?"

The man's face was impassive as he considered his answer. "Victor Kamigami."

"You were in the American Army?" A brief nod of Kamigami's head answered. "Your rank?" There was no answer.

## Monday, January 8
## The Executive Office Building,
## Washington, D.C.

The woman slipped into the conference room early and found a seat at the far end of the table. Mazie Kamigami was short, overweight, and as usual, dressed in a comfortable but very drab gray suit. She settled her short body into the chair, her feet not touching the floor. Her round but pretty face mirrored her frustration. It's the Japanese in my blood that did this to me, Mazie Kamigami thought. She often wished the powers that be realized short people also worked in Washington, D.C.

Still, she decided, this particular seat was perfect for watching the delicate steps the staff members were taking as they jockeyed for position around the newly appointed national security advisor, William Gibbons Carroll. Mazie had seen the intricate minuet before as old staff members danced around a new appointee. James Finlay, the veteran chief of staff Carroll had inherited, entered the room surrounded by his little bevy of cronies. That's a swarm of wanna bees, she decided.

They ignored Mazie, since her chair was safely outside the inner orbit where the national security advisor sat during staff meetings. Her geographical position relative to the president's most trusted advisor wasn't something Mazie worried about. But the rumor that Finlay was calling her "the Frump" had cut deeply. One of Finlay's aides threw copies of the meeting's agenda on the table, not bothering to distribute them. Mazie squirmed out of her chair and placed one at each position.

More staffers filed in and the room rapidly filled. Wentworth Hazelton was the last to enter. He surveyed the table, unhappy that all the prime seats had been taken. He gave an inward sigh and took the last vacant chair, beside Mazie. Hazelton had all the right credentials for the National Security Council. His lineage was impeccable: main line establishment that blended the best families of Boston and Philadelphia, old money, master's degree in Middle Eastern Studies from Georgetown, a closet of Savile Row suits, old but well-brushed shoes, and an ambitious mother.

His mother took pride in her son's rangy good looks and mass of dark hair cut to the Kennedy image. She was certain that he had a future. Wentworth agreed and saw only two obstacles in front of him. One was his age—twenty-five was considered young for the NSC. The other was much more temporary—he had to sit next to the Frump. "Do you have anything for Mr. Carroll today?" Hazelton asked Mazie, trying to be sociable and show that he was willing to associate with the less important members of the NSC, even ones that were rumored to be on the way out.

"I'm last on the agenda."

"Oh," he said. "Nothing important then." It was a smug pronouncement.

"Who knows?" Mazie said. She smothered what she really wanted to say. What a bunch of idiots, she thought. Bill Carroll knows what's important when he hears it. True, her division, the Far East, had been given a low priority lately. But Mazie trusted Carroll and was certain he would listen to her when events needed his, and by implication, the president's attention.

"It's going to be fun watching this," Hazelton continued, now adopting the easy manner of the informed insider. "Finny"—he used the nickname the prickly Finlay hated— "should have gotten the appointment, not Carroll. Our Mr. Carroll is in over his head and isn't going to know what hit him. The poor bastard."

"Do you really think so?" she asked.

"I know so." It was another smug pronouncement. "Finny will run staff meetings exactly the way he'll run the NSC. He'll decide who talks to Carroll and when." Like the other members of the NSC staff who had come on board with the current president, Hazelton seriously underestimated Mazie, dismissing her as a lightweight, totally out of her element. He personally attributed her presence on the staff to tokenism—a female of Oriental descent to keep the scales of equal opportunity in balance.

The veteran staff members, and more important, Bill Carroll, did not suffer from any such illusions.

Finlay stood up. "Before Mr. Carroll gets here," he said, "let me reassure you that my staff meetings have not changed. The agenda is prioritized and we will follow it. Mr. Carroll has a very full schedule, so if we run short of time, I'll call the meeting to an end and save what isn't covered for the next time." One of the old heads gave Mazie a knowing smile.

Hazelton glanced at the agenda. "Finny's out to score some points," he said. "Supposedly Carroll's forte is the Middle East. We'll play to that today."

"Maybe it's not smart to tell someone what they already

9

know," Mazie replied as the new national security advisor walked in and sat down. Hazelton dismissed her with a condescending look. He was the Middle East expert who had prepared most of the material on the agenda.

"I wish he at least looked the part," Hazelton complained. It was the only point they agreed on. The slender, athletic, dark-complected Carroll looked more like a high-school football coach in his mid-thirties than a former major general in the Air Force.

The meeting started, and as Hazelton had predicted, they stayed glued to the latest instability coursing through the Middle East. Many of the questions were funneled to Hazelton, and he found that being at the bottom of the table among the nobodies highlighted his importance. He casually explained that the situation was taking a new turn as the tide of Islamic fundamentalism engulfed the countries of North Africa.

Mazie listened, and since that part of the world was not her area of concern, concentrated on the reaction of the staff. She felt Hazelton stiffen when he realized Carroll was asking for much more than a cursory discussion of problems. He wanted hard analysis followed by workable solutions. Hazelton and a few other Middle East "experts" would be spending many late nights at work patching up their bruised egos with hard work and the creation of a new briefing book for the president.

"What else is on the agenda for today?" Carroll asked. It was a question no one wanted to answer.

"Sir," Finlay said, "we've covered the important issues."

Mazie raised her hand as Carroll stood up to leave. "For Christ's sake," Hazelton whispered, "what are you doing? Finny will rip you a new one."

Carroll looked down the table. "What do you have, Mazie?"

Finlay glared at Mazie, willing her to evaporate. "We're running late, Mr. Carroll," he said. "You're scheduled to appear before the Senate Select Committee on Intelligence in twenty minutes."

"The PRC is going after the Fourth Dragon," Mazie said. Her eyes sparkled, belying the passive look on her round face.

Carroll sat back down. "I didn't need to hear that, Mazie," he said. "Lay it out."

"The senators . . ." Finlay whispered. He motioned at the door.

"Send my apologies and tell them I'll be fifteen minutes late, Finny. We wasted too much time on the obvious."

## Thursday, January 11
## Near Bose, Guangxi Province, China

The old man and girl approached the river from the southern hills, not seeing it. The girl walked silently, and occasionally she would glance at her grandfather. They had been walking since five-thirty that morning and she was thirsty. But they had drained their water bottle hours ago and she hoped they would stop. Only the flip-flop of his ragged sandals broke the silence of the unusually warm and muggy afternoon. "We're almost there, child," the old man said in Cantonese. His voice was weak and raspy, a suitable match for his bent and worn body. Still, he spoke in a pure Cantonese, a master of that difficult language with its five tones.

The girl nodded, glad that this part of her journey would soon be over. This was the furthest Li Jin Chu had ever traveled from her village in the southern hills of China and her lithe body ached with fatigue. The girl shifted her grip on the heavy cord that bound her bag. Her grandfather offered to carry it but she shook her head. Everything Jin Chu claimed as her own was in the bundle and it was only proper she carry it. Another glance confirmed her suspicions. Li Jiyu had passed his fifty-eighth birthday two days before and was tired to the point of exhaustion. He looked and acted as if he were eighty years old.

"Oh," she gasped, when she saw the river and the bridge at the same time. Li Jiyu smiled. He had planned it that way. His eyes never wandered from his granddaughter's face. He had seen the river before and would see it again before he died. But he would never see his granddaughter's face again. It was one of the pleasures of his life to see her come alive with surprise or happiness. Now he was going to

11

lose that. But it had to be if Jin Chu was to bring honor and wealth to her family.

The girl stopped and set the bag down. A gust of wind plastered her damp shirt against her body, outlining her small and immature breasts. With one graceful motion, she lifted the straw hat away from her head and let her long dark hair fall free. Li Jiyu had seen it before as Jin Chu became one with her physical surroundings. Wind and water, even the earth, the hills, and the heavens were joining with her. Only fire, thunder, and rain were not visibly present. But she would feel their influence, the old man reassured himself. He did not break her trance—he knew how fragile it was.

The wind caught at Jin Chu's hair and whipped it around, outlining her face. Such a beautiful face, Li Jiyu thought, it captures the best of our people, the Zhuang.

How many times had he tried to determine the bloodlines that had formed his granddaughter? Every race would want to claim his granddaughter's beautiful dark almond-shaped eyes, the glowing black lustrous hair, and the delicate facial structure with her high cheekbones. It was all there, he thought, Chinese, Thai, Malay. But it was also the curse of the Zhuang, for the Han Chinese distrusted all foreigners, even the Zhuang, who were as integrated into the main-stream of China as any of the minorities. Over his lifetime, Li had seen the Han, who made up 94 percent of the Chinese, alternate between amused condescension and tole-ration to outright hostility toward their minorities.

Li Jiyu tried not to worry about the journey his grand-daughter was making to Hong Kong. It isn't that far from Guangxi Province, the home of the Zhuang, he reassured himself. Besides, he reasoned, his granddaughter had to go to Hong Kong to develop her gift. "Jin Chu," he said, "we must hurry and not miss the bus."

Jin Chu studied the Pearl River below her, understanding it. The river spilled out of a gorge and onto the broad plain that formed the heart of Guangxi Province. She could see far to the east and traced the Pearl's path as it meandered on its gentle way toward Guangzhou, the city westerners called Canton, and the sea. "I'll remember this time," she told him, "when I first saw the Pearl River."

Slowly, Jin Chu's gaze focused on the bridge below them. It was a single-span structure supported by a curved arch of steel girders anchored in solid concrete footings on each side. A single traffic lane on top allowed vehicles of all descriptions and foot traffic to cross the gorge and enter Yunnan Province to the west. It was the main land link between the two provinces but it jarred the harmony and beauty of the land. The girl's slender frame tensed as she watched the stream of trucks, foot traffic, and bicycles on the bridge. "Grandfather, did foreigners build this bridge?"

"I was told engineers from Beijing built the bridge. Some foreigners helped them, but I don't know where they came from. They were white."

"Are people from the north considered foreigners?"

"They are Han and some would say yes." The old man could not contain his curiosity. "Why do you ask?"

"Because they built it in the wrong place and there are many angry dragons here."

The old man shuddered at the thought of how much bad luck a single angry dragon could bring down. And Jin Chu had clearly said there were many dragons present. "The stories say that a *feng shui* man, a very powerful geomancer, came from Canton to select the site for the bridge."

"He was wrong, Grandfather."

"Are the dragons angry at us? the Zhuang?" he asked.

"No. Only foreigners. Let's walk across and catch the bus on the far side."

Li Jiyu did not argue with his granddaughter. There might be foreigners on the bus and he saw no need to chance a dragon's anger.

# PART 1

DISSIDENT MOVEMENT CONFIRMED IN SOUTHERN CHINA. Independent sources now confirm the existence of a dissident movement in the Guangxi-Zhuang Autonomous Region (Guangxi Province) of southern China. The leader is reported to be a young, charismatic individual operating under the assumed name of Zou Rong. The exact strength of the dissidents is unknown but informed analysts see no threat to the political stability of the region at this time.

# CHAPTER 1

**Friday, January 12**
**Knob Noster, Missouri**

"Knob Noster?" Shoshana asked, not able to control the humorous disbelief in her voice. She shook her head in dismay as they drove through the small Missouri town near Whiteman Air Force Base.

"Don't blink," Pontowski said, "or you'll miss it." Silence. He chalked it up to the long drive from Virginia. He reached over and stroked her cheek, stealing a glance as she caressed his hand. It amazed him that she could remain so unruffled and serene after wrestling with Little Matt for the thousand-mile drive from Washington, D.C. He automatically glanced at the trip odometer. Actually, 983 fun-filled miles, he thought. How many times had his grandfather said he was simply getting his comeuppance for all the trouble he had caused when he was young? He glanced back at the latest member of the Pontowski clan, who was now curled up asleep on the backseat of the minivan. I don't believe it, he thought. He looks like an angel when he's sleeping.

"Knob Noster," he explained, "is pretty much your standard midwestern farm town. It's little more than a village."

"I didn't know Missouri was considered part of the Midwest," she said.

"Depends on who you talk to."

"You Americans can never make up your mind about basics."

He could hear a trace of humor behind her words. "I guess so," he replied.

"Just like you." Now there was definite amusement in her voice. Shoshana had been perplexed by his decision to resign his regular commission for one in the reserves in order to become commander of the 303rd Fighter Squadron. But she had not protested and humorously reminded him about his earlier comments on the aircraft the 303rd flew, the A-10 Thunderbolt II. Her esthetic sensibilities had been thoroughly assaulted when she first saw one. "No wonder you call it the 'Warthog,'" she had said. "Why do you want to fly one of those?"

It was a question he could not answer, especially since the Warthog was being phased out of the inventory and the 303rd was one of the few squadrons still flying the beast. But Ambler Furry, Pontowski's old backseater from F-15Es, had convinced him the jet still had a few good kicks left and that it could be an interesting tour. After talking to Shoshana, he had filled out the paperwork and sent it up through normal channels.

Not once did he make a phone call to let a well-placed friend know of his interest in the assignment. In the end, he got the job because the name Pontowski still carried weight and very few qualified pilots were interested in commanding a lame duck squadron whose aircraft would be consigned to the boneyard at Davis-Monthan Air Force Base in Arizona in a few years. The competition would have been intense if the 303rd were slated for a follow-on aircraft. But like the Warthog, the 303rd was also destined for the scrap heap.

Still, it was a flying assignment that would last for a year or two. After that, it would be time to look for another career, free of politics and the Air Force. Pontowski consoled himself with the old truism that flying fighters is a young man's game. He would be pushing that envelope in a few more years and believed that it was always best to quit a winner. Shoshana knew the truth of the matter, even though she would never tell him unless he broached the subject. It was very simple: The love between Matt Pontowski and the Air Force had died.

"I suppose," she ventured, "you'll be going to work tomorrow, even though it's a Saturday."

"This weekend is what the reserves call a UTA—Unit Training Assembly. It'll be a good chance to meet the troops."

"You Americans are funny. You work during the week and play at soldiering on the weekends."

"At least we come home horny."

"You don't have to tell me that."

## Friday, January 12
## Kansas City, Kansas

The principal's secretary collared John Leonard before he could escape from the teachers' lounge and reach the parking lot. "Mr. Leonard," she called, "the principal wants you in his office immediately." She looked up and down the deserted hall like a conspirator. "It's not about what you think. They haven't selected the new English department chairman yet. You're still in the running. It's the Ratloffs and they've got a lawyer with them."

John Leonard glanced out the door and to freedom. The old urge to escape from his cares at Green Valley High School, one of Johnson County's more prestigious high schools, swept over him. He knew the lawyer and Ratloffs meant big trouble, probably a lawsuit. "Is Troy with them?" he asked.

The secretary shook her head. "No one can control that young man." She paused for a moment. "What did you do that got them so riled?"

"I asked Troy when I could expect his term paper, which was due two weeks ago. Troy's answer was a memorable, 'It's none of your fucking business. I can flunk if I want and no dumb, sorry-ass shithead is going to tell me what I can do on my own time.'" Leonard found the secretary's silence encouraging. "Not a good way to influence the teacher."

"And what did you say?" The elderly woman was circling the problem, homing in on it.

"I said, 'You can smoke dope, sniff coke, knock your girlfriend up, and wreck two cars if you want on your own time. But a can of rocks has got more smarts.'"

The secretary's mouth pulled into a little pout. "Troy has covered all those bases this semester and he is dumber than a June bug. Unfortunately, truth isn't in high demand these days." She sighed. "I suppose the lawyer means a lawsuit. If you want, I'll say you've already left. It's us Christians versus the lions again."

Leonard considered the woman's offer. At least it would give him the weekend. "Well, the early lion always gets the fattest Christian," Leonard told her.

"You are a delectable morsel," she said, trying to give him a little encouragement. John Leonard felt crushed. Over the last few years he had grown pudgy and potato-shaped. His face had lost its lean and hungry look and had become round and soft. At least his dark hair was all intact and only a few wisps of gray were showing at the temples. A look in a mirror would have confirmed what the secretary had said— he looked like choice lion meat.

He glanced out the open door and to freedom. The old urge to cut and run was back. But he had never run from a confrontation in his life. Then his decision was made. "Thanks. I'll see you Monday." He darted out the door.

Sara Waters stood in front of the full-length mirror in her bedroom, carefully appraising her appearance. Waters was not a vain woman or overly concerned about her looks. She just wanted to be sure her new uniform fit properly. Her mother had altered it so the light blue blouse tapered perfectly to her waist and the dark blue skirt hung straight and did not show a panty line. The only concession to vanity was the hemline. It was a little higher than 35-10, the dress regulation, allowed. But it did show off her legs.

"You look great," Melissa, her ten-year-old daughter, said. "Much better than those 'widow's weeds' you've been wearing."

"Widow's weeds?" It was hard not to be amused by the girl's comments. "I've never worn widow's weeds, Melissa. Wherever did you hear that term?"

"I was reading one of Gram's 'bodice rippers.'"

That made sense. Melissa had a voracious appetite for books and read everything she could get her hands on. It was almost a full-time job for Waters and her mother to monitor Melissa's reading. Martha Marshall, Sara Waters' mother, was the only grandmother Melissa had known, and the older woman loved to read historical romances that she laughingly called "bodice rippers." "Have you been going into your Gram's room uninvited?" Waters asked. She knew her daughter would tell her the truth.

"Of course not, Mother." There was a faked exasperation in her voice. "I know the rules," she proclaimed, the injured party now. She should be an actress, Waters thought. "Gram told me I could read it," Melissa said, her defense complete. Waters and her mother were both widows and had lived together since Melissa's birth. Theirs was a comfortable relationship and they had blended their talents to raise the precocious little girl. Sometimes Waters thought they might have been too successful, for Melissa was growing up too fast.

The girl looked at her mother, doing one of her periodic evaluations, giving her a grade. Sara Waters stood exactly five feet eight inches tall and had an outstanding figure kept young by constant exercise—although the girl thought her breasts were too large, but only slightly so. There was no gray in Waters' blonde hair and Melissa approved of the way she kept it a shade lighter than natural. Only the little crow's-feet at the corners of her luminous brown eyes hinted at her forty years. Melissa decided her mother rated at least an A. No, she corrected, Mom's still an A plus.

"They don't deserve you," Melissa said as she bounced out of the room. Waters only shook her head as she finished packing for the Unit Training Assembly at Whiteman Air Force Base. So far, she had no regrets about joining the Air Force Reserve and picking up the pieces of her old career.

As Melissa had grown older, Waters had found herself with more and more free time. At first she had volunteered to serve on a number of local charities in Kansas City, but Martha and Melissa had conspired and urged her to join the Air Force Reserve where she could make better use of her talents. Actually, they were hoping she would meet a more "interesting" type of man. Both were convinced that she had been a widow too long and was only meeting "dud dudes," as Melissa described her mother's infrequent dates.

Waters had hesitated at first. Then long-forgotten memories of her days in the Air Force came surging back, demanding her attention. Time had not dimmed or altered them. She remembered the pain as well as the joys.

Sara Marshall had been a captain assigned to the Pentagon when she met Anthony "Muddy" Waters, an over-the-hill fighter pilot. Their relationship had been slow developing and Muddy had held back, worried about their age difference and haunted with memories of his first wife and child, killed in a car accident years before. She had broken through that barrier by seducing him. In more honest moments, she would admit to herself that she had actually dragged him to bed and then proposed marriage to him. Someday she would have to tell Melissa about their courtship, but she hoped that could be postponed for another ten years.

Their marriage marked a turning point for Muddy, and in short order he found himself in command of the Forty-fifth Tactical Fighter Wing, a wing made up of young hell-raising jocks and aging F-4E Phantoms. The names had come back, unbidden and strong, vivid personalities that breathed with life. They were all there, including Bill Carroll and Jack Locke. Muddy had been given the job of whipping the wing into shape and turning it into a fighting machine. It had been a torturous process and she had watched her husband age under the responsibility. Her being pregnant with Melissa had helped, and Muddy had never lost his bearings or humanity. She was in her seventh month when Muddy had led his wing into a short, brutal war and then died getting them out.

It had fallen to Jack Locke to bring the last of the F-4s out of the burning base that consumed her husband. Just before Locke had launched, Muddy had given Locke his call sign and Locke had become the new Wolf leader. In quiet moments, Waters often thought of the phoenix, the giant bird of mythology that was consumed in the fire of its nest only to rise again, born anew. What rubbish, she had scolded herself. Muddy, Jack Locke, and all but Bill Carroll were dead. But the names were back, all of them, not letting her forget.

Waters had finally called Bill Carroll to ask his advice. He had answered by stopping over in Kansas City and taking her out to dinner. Melissa had approved of him from the first and immediately started working out romantic connections. Waters had to set her straight—Bill Carroll was a happily married man. Melissa was very disappointed. Carroll had told Waters about a number of possibilities, including an executive officer slot that was open with the 303rd Fighter Squadron, a reserve unit at nearby Whiteman Air Force Base in Missouri. The more she thought about it, the better it sounded. Slowly, the tug of the Air Force drew her back and she joined the reserves. The obligation for service had again established its claims.

"You do look nice," Martha Marshall said from the doorway, bringing Waters back to the moment. Martha Marshall was a sixty-three-year-old woman bustling with energy, good health, and common sense. "Your new commander should be impressed."

Waters snapped the small suitcase closed. "I imagine he'll be more impressed if I'm a good executive officer."

"First impressions, dear," Martha replied, "are still very important. Have you heard any names yet?"

"I haven't seen anything official. But there's a rumor that it's Lieutenant Colonel Matthew Pontowski."

"Isn't he the grandson who gave the eulogy for President Pontowski?" Martha asked. "The one who was on television?"

"Yes, that's him."

Martha keyed on the tone in Waters' voice. "You sound worried."

"I am. He's the pilot who killed Jack Locke."

John Leonard's nine-year-old clunker groaned as he turned up his driveway. Rust and Kansas City winters had gotten at the subframe and the car was ready for the junkyard. "One more year," he begged the car, "just one more year and then

23

an honorable burial." He was surprised that Marcy's new Jaguar was in the garage. His wife normally didn't get home on Friday until well after seven. He sat in the car for a few moments, going over the words that would smooth what he needed to say. It doesn't matter what you say, he thought, she won't like hearing it.

He dropped his briefcase in the kitchen and opened the refrigerator for a quick raid. Rhonda, their maid, had scrubbed it clean and thrown out the leftovers, forcing him to settle for a beer. Pulling his tie loose, he wandered toward the stairs. As usual, the restored Victorian house was immaculate, thanks to the attentions of Rhonda. It was a showplace, too pristine for his taste, and he longed for a more livable home with clutter and comfort.

But it was an old argument he could not win. More and more, he felt like a kept man, the indulgence of his wife, a very successful plastic surgeon. How many tummy tucks did it take to rebuild the foundation? he thought. How many breast implants to remodel the front room? The house was an obsession with Marcy. He heard the clank of the Nautilus from the exercise room upstairs. Marcy was also obsessed with her body. He climbed the stairs and the old weariness was back.

"I'm almost finished," Marcy said when she saw him standing in the doorway. "Did you get it?" She was working on her legs, straining at the weights.

Leonard didn't answer. He felt the familiar urge in his groin as he watched her exercise. His wife did have a great body, still capable of stirring the old lust in him. Now even that was going. "The subject didn't come up," he finally answered. "There's another problem . . . some parents came in . . . they had a lawyer with them." He told her about Troy Ratloff.

"Correct me if I'm wrong," she said, her exasperation and anger breaking through. "I thought the idea was for you to become head of the English department—not get fired." Leonard took a long pull at the beer and didn't answer. "Don't you want to be the principal? How much longer can that old fart last? Getting the English department is the stepping-stone to . . ." Her voice trailed off. They had been over the same ground countless times before. "You don't want the job, do you? You just want to stay in that damn classroom and fly every weekend you can sneak away."

"It's not like that," he protested.

"The hell it's not!" She stood up and stormed into the sauna, pulling her leotard off. "Look, let's not argue now. I've got a seminar this weekend in St. Louis and Michael has offered me a ride over tonight."

"In his King Air?"

"Of course." She stood in the doorway naked, looking at him. "You're jealous, aren't you? It really gets to you that Michael can afford his own plane and use it whenever he wants."

Leonard wanted to tell her that Michael didn't have a clue about how to use an airplane. He had flown with the doctor before and watched him sit in the left seat and play pilot while his professional copilot did all the work. "I just wish he'd quit using my wife," Leonard said. He was tired of the charades they had been playing.

"What does that mean?" Marcy snapped, not moving from the doorway.

"Come off it. You two have been screwing like bunnies. At least have the honesty to own up to it."

Marcy looked down at her body and then back to Leonard. "He does nice things to me." She turned and opened the door to the sauna. Pausing, she looked back at him, more sad than angry. "I think we've reached an end, don't you?" As always, she was in control. "Why don't you go play in your Warthogs this weekend and we'll discuss what we're going to do on Monday."

## Saturday, January 13
## Whiteman AFB, Missouri

Early Saturday morning, Pontowski angled his van into the reserved parking spot in front of the headquarters building at Whiteman Air Force Base. He could see a small group of people waiting for him inside the double glass doors. The reception committee, no doubt, he mused to himself as he got out of the car. Sergeant Lori Williams, a tall and willowy twenty-year-old African-American, held the door open and the group filed outside and lined up.

"Some hunk," Lori told Sara Waters. "Nice buns. TV didn't do him justice."

"Please try to remember, Lori," Waters said, her lips barely moving, "that he's your commanding officer and not a sex object."

The squadron's operations officer, Major Frank Hester, a middle-aged man with thinning blonde hair and pale blue eyes, called them to attention. They saluted in unison when Pontowski reached the top of the stairs. Pontowski returned the salute with an easy motion and the introductions went smoothly. Waters was impressed as he seemed to know the basics of each one's career. When he was introduced to her, he shook her hand and said, "I understand you spent some time at Fort Fumble in the Watch Center."

It caught her off guard. She had expected him to mention Muddy, her late husband, not her tour in the Pentagon. "Yes, sir. But that was a long time ago."

"Wasn't 'Sundown' Cunningham chief of staff then? Did you ever brief him?" The crusty old general had a reputation that still lived on after his death.

He knows the answer, Waters thought. "Yes, sir. He was and I did."

"Legend has it that he ate briefers alive."

"Only if they hadn't done their homework," she answered. And you've done yours, she thought. "You never wanted to go in unprepared." Pontowski nodded and Hester, the ops officer, continued with the introductions before they went inside.

"Please try to remember," Lori parroted as they trailed in after him, "that he's your commanding officer and not a sex object."

"Don't be stupid," Waters snapped. She was positive she had been formally correct, cool, and reserved. Or had she?

The morning turned into a whirlwind for Waters as she followed Pontowski on a tour of each office in the squadron. After each brief visit, he would rattle off some questions he wanted answered. By eleven o'clock, they were back in his office and she was certain he had sensed the underlying mood of the 303rd. "Captain Waters," he said, as he settled into his chair for the first time, "how long have you been the executive officer here?"

"Five months, sir." She deliberately kept her voice stiff and formal.

"Lighten up, Captain," he grinned. "I'm not the beast sent from the Pentagon to devour the innocent."

"Well, sir," she said, not bending in the least, "you did come as a surprise to most of us." She was certain he got the message.

He leaned back in his chair. "Captain Waters, how do you see your job as exec?"

"Oh, well . . ." She hadn't expected that response. "My job is to run the administrative end, take care of the paperwork, make sure we meet all our deadlines."

"It's more than that," he said. "You're my eyes and ears. You're the one who should know what our people are thinking and feeling, what their problems are, what's hurting them." She didn't answer. "I want you to come to work full-time."

"I really don't think that's necessary," she said. "You have a full-time civilian secretary and we've always functioned smoothly."

"I can't do this without your help," he said.

"I am sorry, sir. I don't understand. Do what?"

He looked at her, his face impassive. "The morale of the 303rd is in the dirt. I want to turn it around and I can't do it without your help."

Waters stifled a sigh. "It's a combination of many things," she explained. "Everyone knows we're going to be deactivated."

"And?" he asked.

She took a deep breath. He cuts right to the heart of the matter, she thought. "Well, most of the pilots think the ops officer, Major Hester, should have gotten the squadron."

"I see," Pontowski said. "Please arrange a commander's call for fifteen hundred hours this afternoon with the pilots."

She started to protest that a commander's call would

disrupt the training schedule. But an inner voice warned her that his decision was not open to discussion. "Yes, sir. I'll get right on it." She wanted to leave.

"Schedule it for the squadron lounge," he told her. "I'd like to keep it informal and casual, a chance to meet the jocks. We'll get morale turned around," he reassured her.

"I don't want to sound defeatist, but I don't think you—" she paused for effect, "can turn it around."

"I see," he said. His voice was calm and measured, with no sign of stress or emotion. "I'm part of the problem."

"Some would say so, sir."

He smiled. "Now you're doing your job."

"Is there anything else?" she asked.

"No." She turned to leave. "Captain Waters." His voice stopped her. "You knew Jack Locke."

"Yes, sir," she said, half turning around. "He was with my husband at Ras Assanya." There, she thought, now it's on the table. Ras Assanya was the base where her husband had died.

Again, his voice was cool and composed. "I served under Locke. He was a good man."

"One of the best, Colonel." She forced an iron clamp on her emotions and hurried back to her own office. John Leonard was waiting for her.

He handed her a form. "Personnel tells me I need the colonel's endorsement on this."

Waters glanced at the form. It was an employment application to work full-time as an Air Reserve Technician, ARTS, the reserve's version of being on active duty. "I thought you had a full-time teaching job," she said.

"I'm resigning," Leonard told her.

A warning flickered in her mind. It was little more than a niggling glimmer of trouble. Should she ignore it? "Colonel Pontowski will probably ask why," she said.

"It's simple enough," Leonard told her. "Teacher burn-out. Happens all the time."

The warning light sparked. During her short tenure as exec, Waters had processed other requests from pilots to go full-time. In half the cases, the pilot was looking for a way to escape from the emotional wreckage of a failed marriage or career. If the problems were too traumatic, the previous commander would disapprove the request and pass the word to Frank Hester to keep an eye on the pilot's flying. Flying a fighter, even one as slow and forgiving as the Warthog, demanded the best from a pilot. Accident investigation files were full of cases in which the pilot had killed himself because of the weight of emotional baggage.

"Are you having marital problems?" she asked. She hastily added, "The commander will want to know."

"I'll be glad to discuss this in private with him," Leonard replied.

Personal problems, Waters concluded. "Perhaps that would be best," she said. "I'll get you on his schedule." She scanned Pontowski's appointment calendar. "Can you be here at fourteen-thirty hours today?" He nodded and left.

After Leonard had left, she called Hester for his recommendation. The ops officer's reply was a terse, "Leonard's been having some personal problems lately. Nothing serious . . . it's only temporary . . . he'll get over it." She typed a cover memo with his remarks and sent it into Pontowski's office.

At fourteen-thirty hours sharp, Leonard reported to Pontowski with a snappy salute. The lieutenant colonel waved him to a chair and quizzed him briefly about his request. Leonard thought the interview was going well and started to relax. "What problems need fixing?" Pontowski asked.

Leonard had been expecting that one. "There are a few maintenance problems on the ramp, mostly with B Flight. Probably because we're starting to phase down. A good line chief could fix that one in a heartbeat." He paused, thinking. Maintenance was not his bailiwick. "We still need to sort some bugs out of LASTE. Mostly software glitches." The last modification on the A-10s had been a new computer weapons delivery system called LASTE, low-altitude safety and targeting enhancement. LASTE was a relatively cheap modification at one hundred thousand dollars a copy and had great potential.

Then Pontowski hit him with a question right off the wall. "As a flight lead, how do you feel about women flying Warthogs?"

"Oh . . . ah . . ." he stammered, "you mean Skeeter."

First Lieutenant Denise "Skeeter" Ashton was the first woman pilot assigned to the 303rd. What do I tell him? Leonard thought. Like most fighter pilots, Leonard harbored deep-seated feelings about women flying in combat. He didn't like it. "Skeeter's got a ways to go," he finally said.

"How does she compare to other lieutenants with the same amount of flying experience?"

Leonard hedged his answer. "I'd say about average, maybe slightly above." He couldn't bring himself to admit that Skeeter Ashton was an excellent pilot.

"I signed off next week's flying schedule. You're slated to lead a four-shipper to the gunnery range next Saturday."

Leonard brightened at the mention of flying. "Great! I was hoping to sneak on the schedule."

"Ashton's the deputy lead," Pontowski told him, watching the pilot's face for a reaction.

Disappointment registered on Leonard's face. "Well, she is a fully qualified lead," Leonard answered. The basic fighter unit is a pair of aircraft called an element, which is made up of a flight lead and a wingman. A four-ship formation is made up of two elements. The deputy lead flies as number three in the formation and takes command of the formation if the leader has to abort. "No," Leonard conceded, "that won't be a problem."

"So she can hack it?"

"She has so far."

Pontowski checked his watch. It was time for his first meeting with the pilots. "I'm going to put your request on hold until I get my feet on the ground." He stood up. "Time to meet the troops." He led the way to the squadron lounge.

"Room. Ten-hut," Sara Waters called when he entered. The pilots were all there, standing at attention in front of chairs neatly arranged in rows in front of a podium.

He gave Waters a sideways look, a sign of his disapproval. It wasn't what he wanted. He stood to one side of the podium and leaned on it, trying to create an easy and relaxed atmosphere. Most of the pilots were in their mid-thirties and could have been fresh out of a Kiwanis or Rotary club meeting. According to their files, about half were pilots with commercial airlines and commuted from as far away as Las Vegas, Nevada, to fly with the 303rd. The other half were a melange of lawyers, stockbrokers, and engineers, with one pig farmer mixed in.

He had no problem finding Skeeter Ashton. She was the college girl sitting in the third row. Her dark-brown hair was pulled back into a French braid, accentuating her pleasant but plain face. Her neck muscles revealed the effects of constant exercise, a necessity for fighting the *g* force a fighter generated when it maneuvered. A neat and trim young woman, he decided. Nothing spectacular.

After talking for a few minutes, he could sense an invisible wall between him and the pilots. "Okay, I know most of you are convinced that we're on the way to the scrap heap, another casualty of the peace dividend."

"Shit happens, sir," came from one of the pilots in the last row. It was the break he had been waiting for. In any fighter squadron with good morale, there was a constant and easygoing flow of barbed comments, ironic quips, and deft character assassinations.

"Yeah, it does," Pontowski conceded. "But things have a way of changing, and we're not dead yet. So until we turn out the lights, we're going to make shit happen." Did he sense a crack in the wall? He gestured toward the bar at the far end of the lounge. "Time for some beer," he said, bringing the meeting to a close.

The room rapidly emptied, leaving him alone with Waters. The wall was rigidly in place. "This isn't what I wanted, Captain," he said, looking at the chairs.

Waters looked at her new commander. She wanted to support him and be a good executive officer. But so much stood in the way. The shadow of political influence tinged his appointment as commander. She wanted to give him the benefit of the doubt, to let him prove himself. Yet he was the only survivor of the midair collision that had claimed Jack Locke's life. Jack Locke, she thought, remembering. Muddy had passed the torch of command to him at Ras Assanya. Not the formal, ordered, rank-conscious assumption of command that the Air Force held dear, but the moral imperative of leadership that demands a true leader be one with his men and still able to inspire them to willingly follow him into the crucible of combat. Even knowing it could be at the cost of their own lives. Few men, very few, had that ability. Muddy Waters and Jack Locke had it. Now Pontowski was aspiring to it.

Much against her will, she relented. "Sir, Major Hester told me that he'd take care of the details."

"I didn't expect this," Shoshana said. She stopped at the bottom of the stairs that led to the main dining room on the second floor of the Officers' Club and waited for Pontowski to join her. "I never would have guessed." The Officers' Club was luxurious in the extreme.

"Stealth bombers are wonderful things," Pontowski told her. "The club got a major facelift when the Air Force decided to base the B-2 here." Waters had told him that the club was the best place to eat on a Saturday night and Pontowski had called Shoshana to ask her to join him for dinner. She had jumped at the chance to escape their temporary quarters when Waters had arranged for a babysitter for Little Matt. "I asked Major Hester and Captain Waters to join us," he explained. He hoped that Shoshana didn't notice the quiet place they occupied in the crowd of reservists streaming into the club. Most had changed into casual clothes but he could see a smattering of uniforms.

"Your Captain Waters is most efficient," Shoshana said. "I'm looking forward to meeting her." She studied the formal portraits that lined the wall.

"I'm sorry I'm late," Waters said as she joined them. "I had a last-minute phone call from Major Hester. He sends his regrets that he won't be able to join us."

Shoshana turned and froze. Like the club, Waters was unexpected. She had let her hair down and changed into tight blue jeans and cowboy boots. The loose, bulky-knit sweater that hung to her hips hinted at the figure underneath. Shoshana felt matronly in her simple print dress, and her spirits sank as Pontowski went through the introductions. They climbed the stairs to the dining room.

After dinner, Pontowski decided to call it an early evening, since Sunday would be a full day. "Tired?" he asked once they were in the van.

"A little," Shoshana answered. Silence. "They're avoiding you."

"I got that too," he admitted. "The few people that did talk to us seemed more interested in Waters."

"Can you blame them?" He could hear the tone in her voice that warned him not to discuss the matter. He had learned from hard experience when to shut up. But Shoshana wouldn't let it go. "Those jeans."

He smiled. "You've got a few pair just like them, if I remember right."

"I'm going to burn them," she promised. "All of them."

"Why? You look great in—"

"I'm too old to wear crotch-cutters," she interrupted.

"What do you mean? Waters has got ten years on you."

She hit him on the shoulder. Hard. "You're just like all the others. You were all undressing her."

"Come on," he protested.

"What do you mean, 'Come on'? Tell me you haven't looked at her. Do you have any idea of what she's done to the hormone count on Whiteman?"

Pontowski knew better than to answer.

Shoshana disappeared into the bedroom when they reached their temporary quarters in guest housing. Pontowski sank onto the couch and rubbed his forehead. Women! he thought. A few moments later, Shoshana walked out of the bedroom barefoot, wearing a tight pair of jeans and a short tank top that bared her midriff. She sat on his lap, nuzzled his ear, and deliberately wiggled and twisted until she felt him grow hard. "Am I in trouble?" he asked.

"You had better be," she answered, a deep throaty promise in every word.

# CHAPTER 2

Sunday, January 14
Canton, China

"Sit down," Zou Rong ordered. He motioned Kamigami away from the ramp that led from Canton's train station to the parking lot and pointed to a spot near a noodle vendor's cart. Kamigami's size was drawing too many stares and he hoped they would be less conspicuous sitting down. He told his driver to buy some food from the vendor for the American and the two Chinese waited patiently while Kamigami shoveled food into his mouth.

Zou Rong used the time to run his mental abacus, calculating the contribution Kamigami could make to his cause. Behind Zou's boyish facade lay the heart of a born rebel with the ambition of a Napoleon. He wanted power. But equally, he wanted to free his people from the yoke of the oppressive and corrupt government that ruled China from Beijing.

Sensing the discontent of the people of southern China, he had adopted the name Zou Rong, in honor of the young student who had written the short book *The Revolutionary Army* in 1903. The original Zou Rong had urged the Chinese to seize their own destiny, unite, and struggle together in a new army. For his audacity in challenging the status quo, the Manchus had thrown him in jail, where he died a year later at the age of nineteen.

Now the new Zou Rong was organizing a rebellion,

tapping the discontent, disobedience, disorder, chaos, and even barbarism that boiled beneath the calm surface of China. The nucleus of his rebel government was taking shape at Nanning, the capital of Guangxi Province, 325 miles to the west. But he needed a general to lead his army, someone of near-mythical stature to give leadership to his soldiers. It had to be someone, preferably a foreigner, he could cast into oblivion when he needed to tame the same soldiers who had made his rebellion a success.

He was certain he had found that man in Victor Kamigami.

But the big American had not committed and Zou could not waste much more time convincing him. He slid the counters of his mental abacus, first adding, then subtracting the effect of all he had shown Kamigami. Zou's instincts warned him that he, born of a different culture, did not see the world the way Kamigami did. Still, he was coming to understand this quiet man. But would he be able to understand other Americans? He had little experience with foreigners and wished he had studied or traveled in other countries. Perhaps that was why he was drawn to Kamigami, a feeling his soldiers would also share.

Zou's one big asset, that he had freed Kamigami from his Hanoi cell, had been offset at the border, when the Vietnamese border guards had decided their travel papers and exit permits were not in order. The hard look the lieutenant in charge had shot at Zou was ample warning, at least for Zou, that the Vietnamese had decided not to support his rebellion and were going to play another game in which he was the prize.

After making a phone call, the lieutenant had apologized profusely, begged their forgiveness for not letting them pass into China, and asked if they would please return to the headquarters building a mile back from the border to straighten out the confusion. One of the guards was told to escort them, since it was night. But the guard had telegraphed the same warning to Kamigami when he held his battered AK-47 at the ready. Kamigami had walked quietly outside with his head bent, a sign of surrender and subservience to the Vietnamese.

The darkness outside the guard shack was enough. Kamigami stumbled into the guard, and before the man could recover his balance, snatched the AK-47 out of his grasp and punched him in the throat. Kamigami then swung the stunned man around, threw an arm lock around his neck, jammed a fist against the left carotid artery and twisted. Ninety-five seconds of silence and it was over.

Kamigami cradled the AK-47 in one arm, picked up the body with the other, and walked back into the guard shack. He dropped the body on the lieutenant's desk and announced that their papers were in order. The lieutenant took one look at Kamigami's face, quickly agreed, and escorted them to the Chinese barrier.

The sums are in balance, Zou decided as Kamigami finished eating. "Why do you want to see the train station?" Zou asked.

A steam train rattled and smoked its way into the station. "I like your trains," Kamigami said.

"They're a symbol of our country," Zou replied. "Very sturdy, hardworking, but hopelessly old-fashioned and in need of modernization."

"I heard many soldiers are coming in," Kamigami said.

Zou smiled at him. I didn't tell you that, he thought, so you must understand more Cantonese than I thought. Is that a good sign? "You are interested in soldiers?" Kamigami said nothing and only gazed at the people, much like a tourist. Zou's eyes narrowed as he swept the growing collection of vehicles in the parking lot. "Most of the drivers are soldiers," he said.

A crowd surged out of the station. Most of the men were wearing rumpled olive green cotton uniforms. "No weapons," Kamigami muttered.

"The People's Liberation Army," Zou explained, "can't make up its mind whether it's an expression of proper socialist principles or a modern fighting force. But these are combat soldiers. You can tell by the good boots they are wearing."

A squad of armed soldiers marched out of the station and cleared a path to the street. A gleaming black sedan drove up and a sharply dressed officer jumped out of the front passenger seat and snapped the rear door open. No command was given, but the soldiers visibly stiffened and came to attention. The noisy, clattering hustle that marks a Chinese city tapered away and a rare quiet fell across the crowd. "Someone big is coming," Kamigami said.

"Be quiet," Zou commanded.

For a moment, nothing happened. Then less brave souls at the edge of the crowd scattered, frail leaves being chased by an invisible wind of fear. A strange sixth sense that Kamigami had only experienced in combat drew him to the vortex of that fear. A heavy-set man, perhaps five feet ten inches tall, was walking down the ramp leading out of the station. Kamigami guessed his age to be in the late forties or early fifties. His uniform was immaculately tailored and freshly pressed, showing no signs of travel. Thick, wire-rimmed glasses gave him an owl-like stare as he slowly looked left, then right. For a fraction of a second, he focused on Kamigami before moving on—a predator looking for more valuable prey. He descended the steps and disappeared into the waiting sedan.

On cue, the noise was back, as if the entire crowd had taken a collective deep breath. "Who was the general?" Kamigami asked.

"Kang Xun," Zou answered. "Did you feel the fear?"

"I saw it," Kamigami replied.

"But you didn't feel it?" Zou was incredulous.

"No. I didn't feel fear."

"Ah," Zou probed, certain that Kamigami was masking his own fear. "What did you feel?"

Kamigami didn't answer and only looked at the soldiers still moving through the crowded station. He turned and looked at Zou, his face impassive. "I felt sorry for you." He stood up. "I need to see more."

The four men sprawled on the grass in the small playground near Canton's Baiyun Airport. To all appearances, they were taking *xiuxi,* the time-honored afternoon nap. But on this particular day, they were working. "Have you seen any cargo planes?" Kamigami asked.

Zou translated the question for the teenager whose team

watched the airport. After listening to his reply, Zou explained that every plane that had landed in the past five days had been carrying passengers and that not a single military or cargo aircraft had been seen.

"Ask about truck traffic," Kamigami said. Zou again repeated the process. This time the old man answered.

"Less than a hundred military trucks have been counted," Zou said. "They even checked suspicious trucks to see if they were hauling supplies for the PLA." Zou gave a snort of laughter. "They were smugglers. Black market. Mostly cigarettes—Marlboros."

"Nothing at the air bases, so that means the PLA is being supplied by rail," Kamigami said. Zou translated.

The old man rattled off some numbers. "I got it," Kamigami said before Zou could translate. "Perhaps ten boxcars earmarked for the PLA."

"Is this important?" Zou asked.

"I estimate," Kamigami said, "that over fifty thousand PLA troops have come into the area around Canton within the last week. It doesn't track. We're seeing too many troops for the supplies coming in."

Zou had to translate. "What does this mean?" he asked.

"This is an army that lives on the local economy."

A torrent of words gushed from the old man when he heard the answer. He had lived through that before. "He says the farmers will suffer greatly," Zou translated.

"I got most of it," Kamigami said. He thought for a few moments. He had come to like Zou and the Chinese he had met. Still, he wanted to return home and see his daughter, the last of his family. But I owe Zou for getting me out of jail, he reasoned. "I want to see what it's like in the countryside," he finally said.

Zou fell silent. He had spent too much time with Kamigami and needed to return to his headquarters in Nanning. Still, he was learning much and needed to gauge for himself conditions in the countryside. "I'll go with you," he said.

**Friday, January 19**
**Washington, D.C.**

The two Secret Service agents were warmed up and ready to go when the national security advisor came out of the White House. Like them, he was bundled up for an early morning run. "You two ready to do some serious running today?" he called.

"You better believe it, Mr. Carroll," Wayne Adams, the taller of the pair, answered.

A boyish grin spread over Carroll's face, making him look younger than the two agents, who were in their early thirties. "That's what Chuck said last night," Carroll said, going through his stretching exercises.

"Not fair," Chuck Stanford complained. "So I cramped up."

"At least it didn't hurt your elbow," Carroll said. He liked to drink beer with the people he ran with and they had dispatched a few the night before. Stanford was still suffering from a hangover.

The two agents jogged in place, ready for the challenge. They were the only two currently assigned to Washington who were up to the drill. There were three other agents who would run with the national security advisor when Chuck Stanford and Wayne Adams weren't available, but they couldn't match Carroll's pace. "Is this going to be another marathon?" Stanford asked.

"Not enough time today," Carroll answered. He checked his shoelaces and headed for the East Gate of the White House.

"Thanks for small favors," Stanford mumbled. The two agents fell in beside him. Outside the gate, the two backups were waiting on their mountain bikes with the heavy artillery safely hidden away in the saddlebags. A helicopter hovered over the Potomac and copied the message that William Gibbons Carroll was out and running. Like a well-oiled machine, the various units checked in, ready to guard and protect the president's assistant for national security affairs, as he took his daily run.

Carroll turned right when they reached the Mall and

headed for the Potomac River, letting Adams set the pace. They looped behind the Lincoln Memorial and circled the Tidal Basin before turning eastward. The two agents ran in silence, keying off Carroll, not anxious to break his silence. Carroll was working a problem and when he had a solution, he would start talking and running much faster. Until that happened, the agents kept a constant scan going, looking for anything unusual.

They had run about three miles and were approaching the Air and Space Museum when Carroll stopped dead in his tracks. "I'll be damned," he muttered. Pieces of the puzzle were coming together and the shadowy movements going on inside China were making sense. "Maybe," he said under his breath, "you're not so inscrutable."

Then he smiled, pleased with himself. "Do you think our bikers have been getting their money's worth this morning?" He turned and looked at the two Secret Service agents on the mountain bikes.

"Why am I certain they're about to?" Adams asked, breathing easily.

"Oh, no," Stanford groaned, knowing what was coming next.

"Right," Carroll laughed. "It's hurtin' time." He erupted like a sprinter at the sound of the starter's gun. "Gentlemen, we've got a race." The two Secret Service agents hurt all the way back. "Enjoyed it," Carroll told them when they reached the East Gate of the White House. "Sorry it's too early for a brewski." He disappeared through the gate.

"Thanks for small favors," Stanford puffed.

"You know who Carroll is?" Adams asked.

"Yeah. The guy who's gonna give us a heart attack."

Before he headed for the showers in the basement, Carroll told Margaret, his secretary, to set up a meeting with Finlay in an hour and have Mazie Kamigami in his office soonest. Mazie was waiting for him when he came back. "Thanks for coming over so quickly," he said, settling into his chair.

"Margaret said it was urgent," Mazie said, still panting from the run from her office in the Executive Office Building across the street. The word had gotten out that Carroll liked hustle.

40

"Mazie, how serious is the problem in China? Are we looking at a civil war or something a lot bigger?"

Mazie thought for a few moments, organizing her words. It was a question she was paid to answer. "Bigger," she answered. "Much bigger."

"That isn't the answer I wanted," Carroll grouched.

Then don't ask the question, Mazie said to herself. But Carroll was waiting for an explanation. "The problem is Kang Xun," she began.

"Isn't Kang Xun the general who fancies himself the new Mao Zedong of China?" Carroll asked.

"Indeed he does," Mazie replied. "Kang Xun is the son of Kang Sheng and he's every bit as bloody." Carroll nodded. He was one of the few westerners who had studied the career of Kang Sheng and how he had created China's secret police for Mao Zedong. Kang Sheng had created a system that systematically tortured and terrorized millions while he exterminated hundreds of thousands of his fellow Chinese.

"General Kang Xun," Mazie continued, "thinks and acts more like his father than Mao. He has a simple solution to most problems—slaughter the enemy. He learned that from his father. He has stated repeatedly that China is destined to rule Asia and Japan is the enemy."

"That could be an economic policy statement," Carroll said.

Mazie shook her head. "It doesn't read that way in the original. It loses something in translation."

"Like *Mein Kampf*," Carroll added. "Hitler gave us fair warning."

"And like Hitler," Mazie continued, "Kang is exploiting internal problems. A drought has decimated the wheat and sorghum crops in northern China. Combine the drought with the massive overpopulation of the rural areas and you've got severe food shortages. That has led to riots."

"How does the PLA get involved in all this?"

How to explain the strange mixture called the People's Liberation Army? Mazie thought. She didn't have enough time and decided to keep it simple. "The PLA is controlled mostly by hard-liners led by Kang and they blame the central government for the current mess. Kang is the hard-liners' favorite son because he's in command of Guangzhou Military Region next to Hong Kong.

"To appease Kang and the hard-liners, the central government has agreed to split control of the country. The PLA under Kang controls China south of the Yangtze River and the central government controls the northern half. Supposedly, this is being done in the name of 'emergency measures.' But it is a power struggle for control of China in every sense of the word."

Carroll was like a bulldog that kept worrying a bone. "Last week you made a convincing case for the PLA going after the Fourth Dragon. Finny thinks you're way out in left field on this one and claims time has proven you're wrong."

Mazie knew that she was in trouble with James Finlay, Carroll's chief of staff, and didn't answer at first. There were four emerging economic powers on the rim of Asia that, combined, could challenge the economic might of Japan. The first three dragons, Korea, Taiwan, and Singapore, were safe in their nests. It was the Fourth Dragon, Hong Kong, that was in danger.

"The British," she said, carefully choosing her words, "lower the Union Jack for the last time on July first, 1997, and the colony reverts to the Chinese. The people are getting out now, while they can, and they're taking their money and skills with them. We're seeing a mass exodus from Hong Kong."

"And since Kang is the commander of the military region next to Hong Kong, you think he will . . ."

"Seal off and then take over Hong Kong early to save its wealth."

"So, it's a combination of the 'Berlin Wall' and 'nationalize the Suez Canal early' schemes," Carroll said.

"For Kang," Mazie said, "southern China and Hong Kong are only stepping-stones to power. Next, he'll take over the central government in Beijing. Then he'll go after two of the other little dragons—probably Taiwan and Singapore. That will give him the industrial and military base he needs to take over Korea. Japan is next."

"Which," Carroll said, "is the crux of the problem. At that point, war would be inevitable. We need to stop him now, while we still can." He fell silent, considering how much he should tell Mazie. "Tell me about the Pearl River basin."

"It's the heart of southern China. Agriculturally, it is very productive. The people there are mostly Zhuang, not Han Chinese. The Zhuang are a fairly large minority, maybe twenty million. Racially, they are Mongoloid and get along well with their neighbors. They've been well integrated."

"But not totally?"

Mazie shook her head. "That's the reason the Chinese government didn't make the Pearl River basin a province. They call it the Guangxi Autonomous Region. Most Americans think China is a monolithic culture. It's not."

"When was the last time the Zhuang tried to declare their independence?" Carroll asked.

Astonishment and wonder crashed over Mazie like a full-blown thunderstorm. She knew what Carroll was thinking. It was all she could do to name the year. "Nineteen-sixteen."

"Tell me about Zou Rong," Carroll said.

"Oh, my God," she whispered. "You're going for the Soviet Option."

"In this case," Carroll said, his voice icy cold, "call it the China Option. If China is going to threaten its neighbors, we're going to help it come apart."

James Finlay, Carroll's chief of staff, was in his office in the Executive Office Building closeted with Wentworth Hazelton when he heard that Mazie was with the national security advisor. "Damn it," Finlay sputtered, "I control access to Carroll. How in the hell did the Frump get in there without me knowing?"

"She seems to be a loose cannon," Hazelton said.

Finlay didn't like Hazelton's answer because it was the truth. He liked even less the implication that he was not in control of his staff. Normally, Finlay would have cut a junior staffer down to the janitorial level for being so observant, but that was a luxury he couldn't afford with Hazelton. The kid's mother had intimated that she would be most appreciative of any boost he gave to Wentworth's career. Since she had the money and influence to help any career in the rarefied atmosphere of Washington politics, he had decided to sponsor Hazelton.

"Went," Finlay said, "this is a fine opportunity to demonstrate what you can do. When we go in there, keep Carroll's attention focused on the importance of the Middle East. Other than Japan, the Far East is a sideshow."

Hazelton looked at his shoes. Rumor had it that Finlay wanted Carroll to make a horrendous mistake. "Kamigami does make a strong case, sir."

"That's for me to decide," Finlay snapped. He was still smarting from the staff meeting at which Mazie Kamigami had upstaged him at the last minute and was determined to give her a lesson in corporate loyalty. He wanted to fire her. But it amazed him how Carroll hung on every word the dumpy little woman said, not that she ever said much. He checked his watch and stood up. It was time for the meeting. "Just give it your best shot," he said. He stood and marched over to Carroll's office in the White House.

He's a fast learner, Carroll thought as he listened to Hazelton summarize the situation in North Africa and the Middle East. The analysis presented by the young man was cutting and concise. "Very good," Carroll said when Hazelton had finished. Even Mazie was nodding in agreement. "Here's my problem," Carroll continued, "we have two potential hot spots either of which could flare in the near future. I can tell you from personal experience the president does not like surprises. But he likes idle speculation even less. So what do I tell him?"

This was the opportunity Finlay had been waiting for. "I don't think there's a choice," he said. "A serious disruption in the flow of Middle Eastern oil to Europe and Japan means economic disaster for our two most important trading partners. The Middle East must remain our number-one concern. Compared to the situation there, China is an insignificant sideshow worth a few well-timed press releases."

Carroll looked at Mazie. "Your thoughts, please."

"Mr. Finlay is right," Mazie said. "The Middle East must remain our top priority. But any disruption in the flow of oil will boomerang. The oil-producing countries need

44

petrodollars to stay afloat and meet the rising levels of expectation of their own people. Shut off the money and the Arab masses may decide it's time for new leaders. Problems in the Middle East will not last long."

"As usual," Finlay snorted, "Miss Kamigami doesn't grasp the big picture. Before that could happen, the economy of Europe would be in a shambles and that means serious problems here. The president does not need to get sidetracked and drawn into an Asian cesspool when the Middle East is coming apart."

No sign of emotion flickered across Mazie's face. "We cannot disengage or ignore events in China because Europe is having problems. We're talking about over one billion people, one-fourth of the world's population. Millions can die—"

"Of what?" Hazelton interrupted.

"War," she answered.

"You're not paid to be melodramatic," Finlay snorted.

Carroll turned to Hazelton. "Went, your thoughts."

The young man shot a furtive glance at Finlay and stared at his shoes. He understood Mazie's argument for a coherent and active China policy. Another glance at Finlay and he decided to hedge his answer. "The Far East is outside my area of expertise." Silence.

"Well then," Finlay said. "I think it's obvious where we need to concentrate. China can go on a back burner."

"Mazie, Went," Carroll said, "would you please excuse us?" The two stood and left while Carroll's fingers drummed a tattoo on his desk. "Finny," he began, "I agree we must give the Middle East top priority. But"—Carroll stressed the word—"we cannot ignore developments in China."

Finlay snorted. "I don't believe all the bullshit Kamigami has been pushing about Kang what's-his-name."

Carroll stood and walked to his window. Outside, a winter's day played out in stark beauty. In front of him was a world at peace. Was it like this when Hitler first came to power? he thought. How many mad, vicious men like Kang had taken the stage to be casually dismissed by the world? How many countries had been devastated, how many people sacrificed because no one believed a man could be so evil? "Finny, we can't afford another Hitler. Mazie has put all the pieces together and is giving us fair warning."

"You make her sound like a Cassandra," Finlay protested. "She's not a prophet."

"She's a first-class intellect," Carroll told him. "No one can match her track record when it comes to predicting trouble. Use her."

Finlay nodded. He understood his boss and knew that he had received firm marching orders. "I'll start working the problem." The meeting was at an end and he left, now determined to get rid of the woman.

## Saturday, January 20
## Cannon Range, Missouri

The range control officer at Cannon Range noted the time off range in his log when the four F-16s departed to the south. Absolutely shitty scores, he thought, making another notation in his log. The veteran fighter pilot had a commanding view from the top of the sixty-foot control tower abeam the run-in to the strafe target, and the F-16s had not impressed him.

Automatically, he scanned the quadrant to the northwest with his binoculars, looking for the next flight that was scheduled on the bomb range. The Warthogs should do better, he thought. He dropped his binoculars against his chest when he saw four specks on the horizon and picked up the microphone. John Leonard's voice crackled over the UHF radio. "Cannon Range, Toga flight three minutes out."

"Toga flight," the range controller transmitted. "You're cleared onto the range. Altimeter, two-niner eight-four."

John Leonard repeated the altimeter setting back as he dialed the setting into the barometric scale on his altimeter. "Cannon, do you have our numbers and events?"

"Rog, Toga," the range controller replied. Then a grin cracked the corners of his mouth. "Check this out," he told his assistant. "They're flyin' fingertip tryin' to impress the home folks." Normally, Warthogs entered the range in a route formation. But Leonard had them in a fingertip with his wingman, Toga Two, on his immediate left. Toga Three, Skeeter Ashton, was welded to his right wing. Ashton's wingman, Toga Four, was on her right wing.

"Echelon right," Leonard transmitted. Ashton and her wingman slipped in unison further to the right, opening a space for Toga Two. Toga Two slid smoothly underneath Leonard and pulled into the open space. Ashton closed up onto his right wing and Leonard had to admit that the young flight lead had done it smoothly.

The four A-10s crossed the range in a tight echelon formation with the nose of each set slightly back from the aircraft on the left. They peeled off to the left at eight-second intervals to take spacing for their first circuit on the range. The timing was critical if the four Warthogs were to enter the rectangular pattern correctly. The idea was for one jet to be at each corner once they were in the circuit. Leonard radioed, "Toga One, base," when he turned base leg. He checked his formation—all were in sight and spread out perfectly behind him. Everything's fucking perfect today, he thought as he rechecked his switches for the first pass.

The altimeter was rooted on twelve thousand feet as he made the final turn. "Toga One's in," he radioed, rolling onto the target. The first event was a forty-five-degree dive bomb, the steepest wire they would fly in dropping bombs. From the cockpit, it looked as if he was going straight down rather than at forty-five degrees. The symbols on the HUD (head-up display) in front of him flickered. What the hell is wrong with LASTE now? he thought.

LASTE was the low-altitude safety and targeting enhancement system that gave the Warthog a highly effective gun and bombsight. A sophisticated computer integrated inputs from the inertial navigation system, autopilot, and radar altimeter and projected everything the pilot needed to know onto his HUD. A pilot never had to take his eyes off the target and look down into the cockpit to check his instruments. When LASTE was peaked and tweaked, it made the Warthog super-smart, not the bombs.

Leonard's decision was automatic. "Toga One will be dry, systems," he radioed. He double-checked his instruments as he came down the chute. The airspeed was accelerating through 375 knots, the altimeter was frantically unwinding, and the symbols on the HUD were telling him exactly what they should.

The pipper dot was approaching the target, which was inside the bombing reticle circle as the altimeter touched seven thousand feet, the release altitude. "Toga One's off dry," he radioed. He honked back on the stick, loading the A-10 with four gs in two seconds as he pulled off. It had been a perfect sight picture and except for that strange flicker on the HUD, a perfect pass. And of course, he reminded himself, the decision to go through dry. Probably a queer electron, he thought. He turned crosswind and checked his flight. A Warthog was at each corner. Crisp radio calls filled the radio.

"Toga Two's in." His wingman was turning final and rolling onto the target.

"Toga Three's base." Ashton's voice was cool and quick as she turned onto her base leg. Toga Four was at "coffin corner" and no radio call was required.

The three members of his flight all scored a bull on their first pass, impressing the range controller. They're going to be tough today, Leonard told himself. Toga flight continued to circle the range, working down to the lower-altitude events. The LASTE in his bird worked as advertised and his scores were good. He grudgingly noted that Ashton sounded good on the radio and flew better.

After twelve minutes, they were to the event he liked best—strafe out of a pop maneuver. It suited his nature to fly the pattern at one hundred feet above the ground and then pop up to eight hundred feet before rolling 135 degrees and pulling the nose down to the target. They practiced to minimize exposure time on final and tried to keep their run in to five seconds. He would root the airspeed on 325 knots as he came down the chute and the pipper in the HUD marched to the target. At 2,250 feet slant range from the target, his finger would twitch on the trigger and the GAU-8, the seven-barreled, thirty-millimeter gatling gun that was designed to kill tanks, would fire, giving out a deep growl. He loved it.

"Toga One's in," he radioed.

"Cleared," the range controller answered.

Leonard rolled out and lined up on the "rag"—an old drag chute that was strung between two telephone poles. The analog range bar that rotated counterclockwise around the inside of the HUD's gun reticle circle was passing the five o'clock position. He was inside five thousand feet slant range of the target.

The range controller watched the Warthog as it approached. A cloud of smoke erupted from its nose, followed by a sharp crack as the bullets shattered the sound barrier passing his observation tower. Then a harsh, angry growl shook the glass windows, the sound of the gun firing. The sand in front of the left pole exploded as Leonard walked his burst wide and to the left. The middle of the telephone pole disappeared in a wooden cloud as the rounds shredded it. Damn! Leonard raged. What went wrong? It looked like a good pass.

The range controller's lips compressed into a tight grimace. Four of his Range Rats would spend half a day replacing the pole. "Toga One," he radioed, "you got the pole. Go to a backup event." The other A-10s would not get their chance to use the gun.

"Rog," Leonard answered. "Toga flight, this will be a pop to a low-angle bomb on the timber trestle bridge." The controller pulled a face. He couldn't see the bridge his Range Rats had built in a shallow valley on the far end of the range. He picked up his binoculars as Leonard led his four-ship formation around the pattern at one hundred feet above the deck.

"One's in," Leonard radioed as he started his pop.

"Cleared." The controller studied Leonard's pop. "He's a little close and apexing high," he mumbled to himself. Being too close to the target and high, Leonard would have to dive bomb at a steeper angle than normal. The controller held the mike to his mouth, ready to call Leonard off. Then he thought better of it. The pass was in parameters.

The Warthog rolled sweetly as Leonard apexed at exactly two thousand feet and brought the nose to the bridge in one smooth motion. The HUD flickered once and he double-checked his instruments. His airspeed was approaching 325 knots and the dive angle was at seventeen degrees.

A little steep, he thought, but nothing to worry about. He

made a mental note to pickle high so he would have plenty of altitude to pull out. He had seen this before on the first pass. That queer electron is a persistent little shit, he thought. Rather than go through dry, he maneuvered the Warthog so the target was moving down the projected bomb impact line and into the bomb reticle on his HUD. Looking good.

He could clearly see the trestle bridge in the valley and the low treelined ridge immediately beyond it. Unconsciously, his feet danced on the rudders and the Warthog responded. A tickle at the back of his mind warned him the sight picture was wrong. He ignored it and concentrated on the target, totally oblivious to everything but the bridge he wanted to bomb. The pipper was approaching the target. His thumb started to depress the pickle button.

Suddenly, the target blurred as the ground rushed at him. Target fixation, the curse of every fighter pilot, was trying to kill him. Bitching Betty, the computer-activated woman's voice in the ground collision avoidance system, bitched at him. *"Pull up! Pull up!"* It was ninety-five decibels of imperative he couldn't ignore. He had gotten too low to the ground and at his speed and dive angle, he needed about 150 feet to pull out. He wasn't sure he had it. He honked back on the stick until he got a steady tone in his headset, telling him that he was max performing the jet. The Warthog responded and he pulled out of the valley, barely clearing the ridge line. Gonna make it, he thought.

The A-10 was climbing steeply and Leonard had cleared the ridge line by twenty feet when his left wing struck a tree. The tree took a chunk out of the wing, severed the hydraulic lines, and bent the outer nine feet of the left wing up at a thirty-degree angle. The Warthog rolled to the left as Leonard fought for control, still maintaining a climb. But he couldn't stop the roll. He jerked at the ejection handles at the sides of his seat.

The ACES II ejection seat fired as the Warthog rolled past ninety degrees. An eleven *g* kick sent him out of the cockpit three-tenths of a second after he pulled the handle—on an angle toward the ground below him.

Skeeter Ashton had rolled out onto her base leg when the canopy flew off Leonard's Warthog. For two seconds she watched horrified as the ejection seat shot out of the doomed jet on a shallow downward trajectory. He needed 150 feet of altitude to get a full parachute. The drogue chute streamed out from the seat and deployed the main chute. He was jerked out of the seat just as it disappeared into a tree.

"Toga flight," she transmitted, "Toga One is down. Climb to three thousand feet, stay in the pattern, and maintain visual contact." She had taken command of the flight.

A better idea came to her. "Toga Two, climb and orbit overhead to establish contact with home plate for radio relay. Toga Four, RTB. Repeat, return to base. Cannon Range, Toga Three is almost overhead Toga One. His chute deployed and there was seat separation. Standby." Now she could see the parachute. "I have the chute in sight, hanging in a tree. No movement observed."

"Rog, Toga Three," the range controller acknowledged. "SAR Crash Rescue is on the way. Can you direct them to the pilot? It's real hard to find anybody in all that foliage."

"Can do as soon as they come up this frequency," Ashton told him. "The jet crashed just beyond the SCUD mobile launcher. It's starting to burn. Send the fire wagon."

Sara Waters was standing at the scheduling counter in squadron operations talking to the SOF, the supervisor of flying, when the UHF radio came to life. "Groundhog, Toga Two. How copy?" The transmission was scratchy, barely readable.

"Toga Two, Groundhog reads you two by," the SOF answered. Waters glanced at the Plexiglas-covered boards on the wall behind the SOF. According to the schedule, Toga flight should still be on Cannon Range.

"Toga . . ." A cracking sound drowned out the transmission.

"Toga Two, say again. You're unreadable." the SOF radioed. "He's either got radio problems or out of range," he told Waters.

More crackling and spitting from the radio. ". . . crash on Cannon Range."

"My God!" the SOF shouted. "Get the boss."

Waters bolted out the door and made the short run down

the hall to Pontowski's office. "We've lost a plane at Cannon!" she blurted.

Pontowski was out of his chair. "Name? Call sign?" he asked as he rushed past her.

"It's a Toga," she told him.

"Shit!" he blurted. Visions of Skeeter Ashton charred to a grisly, unrecognizable lump in the mangled cockpit of a Warthog flashed in front of him. He skidded through the door and pushed his way through the small crowd that was already lining the scheduling counter.

"It's Toga One," the SOF told him. "John Leonard. He ejected and his parachute is in the trees. No word on his condition. Crash Rescue is almost to him now. Pretty thick trees and foliage. Skeeter's vectoring 'em in from overhead. She stacked Toga Two above the range as a radio relay and told Toga Four to RTB."

Pontowski nodded. Skeeter Ashton could obviously do the job and had done everything right. "Good work," he said. He pointed to the scheduler, who was standing next to the SOF. "Call the tower and have them do an accountability check on all airborne aircraft. Tell the command post so they can verify with the range control officer at Cannon and start on the messages. Call wing headquarters and make sure they know. Get the flying safety officer ASAP."

"Well, Colonel," a voice said behind him. "It looks like we're making shit happen now."

Pontowski turned to the speaker. It was his operations officer, Major Frank Hester. His face was an impenetrable mask.

"This wasn't what I had in mind," Pontowski growled.

# CHAPTER 3

The crash of Toga One at Cannon Range triggered a finely honed response by the Air Force. It was a reaction learned, refined, and reinforced over the years for one purpose—to discover the cause of the accident to prevent it from happening again. That task fell to a safety investigation board, commonly called an SIB. Hard experience had taught the Air Force two hard lessons: Act fast and do not use the results of the safety investigation board to punish.

Within forty minutes after learning of the crash, the wing at Whiteman Air Force Base had convened an interim SIB. The vice wing commander was appointed the acting board president, and he was in a helicopter with the chief of safety heading for Cannon Range with one objective—to preserve the evidence for the regular SIB.

The job was made much easier because the pilot, Captain John Leonard, had survived with minor bruises. Crash rescue would not have to gather parts of the body or scrape off human remains that had welded to the wreckage. There would be no small lump lost in a green body bag, and the wing commander and chaplain would not have to tell a wife she had lost her husband.

Before noon, Colonel Charles A. Tucker, the vice commander of the 552nd Air Control Wing, received a phone call at his quarters on Tinker Air Force Base eight miles southeast of Oklahoma City. It was his boss telling him that he was the president of an SIB being convened at Whiteman and to get moving. Three hours later, Tucker was flying to Whiteman Air Force Base to take the reins of the investigation. Within twenty-four hours, his board would be completely formed with five other voting members: an investigating officer who was an expert at investigating accidents, a pilot member who was qualified in A-10s, a maintenance officer, a flight surgeon, and a commander's representative from the wing. They would be supported by three nonvoting members of the board—two egress and life support NCOs and a recorder.

Colonel Charles A. Tucker was a thin, balding, slightly hunch-shouldered, and irascible individual who had served on four other SIBs as board president. He had earned a reputation for being ruthless in gathering evidence, demanding the best of everyone involved, and ferreting out the truth. He spared no one and his nickname, "Tucker the Fucker," traveled with him. But in the end, he was totally impartial and fair.

Because of men like Tucker, the system worked.

Sara Waters was in the small kitchen off the squadron lounge drawing a fresh cup of coffee when she heard two men talking in the lounge. She immediately recognized the voices of Major Frank Hester, the squadron's ops officer, and Hal "Snake" Bartlett. "He's such an asshole," Bartlett said. "He proves it's who you know, not what you know that counts."

"There's good news," Hester said. "We have to provide a commander's representative to the SIB and Pontowski asked me to select a pilot. Will you do it?"

"Sure," Bartlett said. "Isn't the commander's rep a spy for the commander?"

"Yeah," Hester answered, "everybody knows that. But in this case, I want you working for me. Make sure the SIB hears that Legs called the week before the accident asking for a recommendation about Leonard. I'll lay it all out for 'em if I get the chance. Pontowski should've grounded him."

Waters blushed brightly when she realized the "Legs" they were talking about was her. Everyone in the squadron was given a nickname they called a tactical call sign, some earned, others given by common agreement. Then a hot indignation swept over her—the nickname given her was sexist. She heard a low-pitched belly laugh from Bartlett. "When Tucker the Fucker hears that, he'll nail Pontowski to the wall for not acting on his own ops officer's recommendation."

"Yeah," Hester said. "We'll hold the record for having a commander with the shortest time on base."

"Great," Bartlett said. "Absolutely fuckin' great."

Waters slipped out of the kitchen, shaking with fury. She hurried back to her office, infuriated with the nickname they had given her. Slowly, she calmed and reasoned it through. If I make a case out of "Legs," she thought, they'll just cut me out of the pattern. Damn, she swore to herself, cut me out of the pattern—I even use their jargon. She scanned the squadron roster that included everyone's tactical call sign. It helped her control her anger when she saw First Lieutenant Rod "Buns" Cox. Sergeant Lori Williams, her administration clerk, had given him that nickname and the squadron had stapled it to the lieutenant as his personal call sign, ignoring his protests.

"Men," she fumed to herself. At last, she was able to think clearly and remember what else the two men had said. Her anger started to rise again and she checked her notebook. Her notes detailed the ops officer's recommendation on Leonard: "Hester—Leonard's been having some personal problems lately. Nothing serious . . . it's only temporary . . . he'll get over it."

That lying bastard, she thought. She sank into her chair and sipped her coffee, thinking. Damn him. Hester didn't say to ground Leonard. In fact, his recommendation was worthless. Then it came to her. Hester was covering for his men. But would the safety investigation board get to the truth of the matter?

The injustice of it all ate at her. Pontowski wasn't responsible for Leonard's crash on the range. If anyone was responsible, it was Hester, for not giving Pontowski the advice he needed to make good decisions during the first days of his command. Would Hester tell the board the truth? Her stomach soured as she realized she would never know, because testimony taken by the board was confidential and never released.

Methodically, Waters evaluated the individuals involved with the crash and made a decision. It was time to choose sides. Pontowski had only asked two things of her—to do her job and to be his eyes and ears. She rose from her desk and went in search of Lori Williams. She found the girl in Public Affairs. "Lori, I've got a job for you."

Ten minutes later, Lori reported to the captain acting as the recorder for the SIB and told him that she was the administrative clerk temporarily assigned to help the board. The captain was relieved to have competent help and set her to work typing.

That night, Lori shoved a manila envelope under the door to Waters' BOQ room.

Two days later, Waters steeled herself with the knowledge of three reports Lori had back-doored to her, walked over to her commander's open door, and knocked twice. Pontowski looked up from the pile of paperwork that greeted him every morning and motioned her to take a seat. She closed the door and sat. Pontowski leaned back in his chair. "I take it the door means this is close-hold," he said, grinning at her.

"Yes, sir, it does." Last-minute doubts ate at her. How is he going to react to what I'm going to say? she wondered. He may be competent, composed, quiet, and good-looking, but he is an unknown quantity. She took a deep breath. "Two items for you, sir," she began. "One's relatively minor, the other important." He said nothing and waited for her to continue. "I overheard the nickname the men have given me and I don't like it."

"I hadn't heard," he said. "Do you want me to do something about it?"

She blushed. "They're calling me 'Legs.' I'm not sure it would do any good for you to get involved. But I wanted you to know."

"Let me work on it," he said. "And the other item?"

"Major Hester is giving the safety investigation board

misleading information." The look on Pontowski's face warned her that she was on dangerous ground.

"Two questions," he said, his voice very even and measured. "Is he lying to the board?"

"I wouldn't call it lying," she answered. "But he claimed his recommendation to you about Captain Leonard should have been enough to ground Leonard and you should have acted on it."

"How were pilots grounded before I got here?"

"It was my experience that Major Hester always handled it."

Pontowski allowed a slight smile. "The SIB will discover the truth," he told her.

"Sir, Colonel Tucker hates your guts." Lori had also relayed the gossip she heard while working with the SIB.

"Tuck and I go back a long time," he said. "He hates everybody's guts. But he's fair."

"I hope so." Waters stood, ready to leave. "Will there be anything else?"

"My second question, Captain. How did you learn what Hester told the SIB?"

"Don't ask, sir." He nodded and she left, leaving his office door open.

## Wednesday, January 31
## Washington, D.C.

The hard shadows of anguish and doubt that darkened Mazie Kamigami's life faded as she read the report. For the first time in over a year, the faint glimmer of hope that flickered at the back of her existence burned brightly. Are the dark months of this winter finally over? she thought. For a moment, she could hardly breathe as she stood in the corridor outside her office.

"Finny did say you would be interested in this," Wentworth Hazelton said, surprised by her reaction. He waited impatiently while she read the report again. He had signed for the secret document and would have to give it back to his secretary for safekeeping and accountability. The safeguarding of classified material was a fact of life on the third floor of the White House Executive Office Building where the staff of the National Security Council spent their days.

She can't be more than five feet tall, Hazelton calculated as he looked down on her. He was ten inches taller. Slowly, she lifted her face and looked up at him. "Yes . . . thank you . . ." Both her face and her words carried a warmth that amazed him. Until this moment, he had dismissed Mazie as an inscrutable, career-driven woman. Then he saw her tears. Mazie was anything but inscrutable.

"Ah . . ." he stammered, "would you rather go into your office?" The open show of emotion embarrassed him. What would people think if they saw him standing with the Frump while she had a good cry?

"Please . . . but I don't want to keep you."

An unfamiliar feeling pulled at him. He wanted to help. Was it because Mazie looked so vulnerable? "It's quite all right." He nodded encouragingly and followed her into the cluttered office. It astonished him that she could find anything in the stacks of documents and reports that littered her cubicle. She sat down and again read the report, more slowly this time. With it committed to memory, she handed it back to him. "I didn't know you tracked MIAs," he said.

"It's not part of my job," Mazie explained. "But my father is listed as missing in action."

The simple statement came as a shock to Hazelton. He had never met anyone who had a relative or loved one classified as an MIA. In his circle, that always happened to "others." His mother would consider it in very bad taste to be listed as an MIA. "After all," she had repeatedly told him when he was enrolled in Navy ROTC, "Hazeltons are only lost at sea."

The logic of it appealed to him. "Lost at sea" tied everything up in a neat package with no loose ends to entangle one's life. Hazelton's life had been a series of neat, tightly wrapped bundles, starting with the "proper" day school, then the "proper" prep school, and then Harvard. Maman—he gave the word a French pronunciation—had definite ideas about what was proper. She had always stressed that Hazeltons only became corporate directors, diplomats for the State Department, Episcopalian ministers, or, if they were wildly irresponsible, naval officers. "Proper Navy," she had said, "not the wretched flying type." Maman had been very upset when he told her that he wanted to work on the National Security Council for James Finlay.

"May I ask how it happened?" Hazelton ventured. This was turning into a revelation for him with one surprise piling on top of another.

"Perhaps," she began, "you remember the rescue of Senator Courtland's daughter? Out of the Golden Triangle."

He nodded, recalling the time he had met Heather Courtland. The senator had ideas about her marrying into the Hazelton family, but Maman had dismissed Heather as "an unfortunate, poorly adjusted child." That was her code for "a piece of trash."

"My father," Mazie continued, "was part of the Delta Force team that rescued her."

"I do remember reading about that," Hazelton said. "But the papers only said there were light casualties."

"One killed, two wounded, and one missing in action," Mazie recited.

"And there was no trace of your father?"

"There was one unconfirmed report that he had been captured in Laos and turned over to the Vietnamese. Apparently, he was searching for a former Binh Tram commander."

"Binh Tram?" Hazelton asked. He had never heard that term.

"During the Vietnam War, the Ho Chi Minh Trail in Laos was broken down into operational areas called Binh Trams. A Binh Tram was run like a private fiefdom, and one of the Binh Tram commanders was infamous for hacking up any prisoner of war his people captured. My father was in Special Forces during his third tour in Vietnam. He was leading an insertion team on the trail when they were captured. You can guess by whom. He was the only one to escape. He saw his team executed."

"So you think he was settling some old scores?"

"My father would do that," Mazie said.

"And this report about an incident on the Sino-Vietnamese border?"

"The description fits my father."

Hazelton glanced down at the report that related how a huge American of Oriental descent had strangled a border guard. He briefly wondered if any boys had been brave enough to date Mazie in high school. Probably not, he decided. Then it came to him. Mazie Kamigami was a very lonely person, and this report had given her hope. He could see it on her face and hear it in every word. Was it the same for all the families of MIAs? Could he live with the uncertainty, the not knowing, year after year? It was a type of bravery beyond his experience.

"Well, you must excuse me." He stood, ready to leave.

"Thank you, Wentworth." He could still hear the warmth and hope in her voice.

"That was stupid," Mazie grumbled to herself when she was alone. Her imagination let her hear the clink of glasses, the aimless chatter and the buzz of networking in progress at some late-afternoon cocktail party. And in a corner, she could hear Hazelton's well-modulated Bostonian accent as he related the incident of the Frump's tears for the edification and enjoyment of her coworkers.

## Thursday, February 1
## Near Mocun, Guangdong Province

The driver of the heavy truck coasted to a stop on the wide shoulder of the paved highway two miles east of the town of Mocun, seventy-five miles due west of Canton. It had taken longer than planned to reach the fertile farming area and he was tired. But the driver had learned from past encounters with farmers that early morning was the best time for their lessons in "patriotic support in the fight against western imperialism."

The man in the passenger seat jerked awake and straightened his dirty olive green uniform. Only the distinctive gold shoulder boards of an officer of the People's Liberation Army were clean and presentable. "Perhaps that village, Lieutenant," the driver offered. "We missed it last time." The lieutenant rubbed the early morning sleep from his eyes and tried to see the village through the mist rising off the rice paddies. "It's nearer to the road than it looks," the driver said.

The lieutenant grunted and pulled on his wire-frame glasses. Now he could see the low mud-colored buildings in the distance. "Yes," he decided, now fully awake, "we will educate those farmers. Get the men ready." The driver walked around to the rear and dropped the tailgate with a sharp clang. "Be quiet, you fools," the lieutenant hissed as the four soldiers clambered out.

The echo of the falling tailgate reached through the orchard on the other side of the road and woke Victor Kamigami. For three seconds he didn't move and only listened. Then he rolled onto his feet and into a crouched position, shedding his blanket. It was a reaction born of countless days spent in combat and again, he listened, his sharp sense of hearing searching for clues. It was the familiar sound of armed men, but they were on the far side of the road and moving away from him. Satisfied that they posed no immediate threat, he woke Zou Rong and the old man. "Soldiers," he told them and pointed to the vague image of the truck in the morning mist.

"They are raiding the village for food," Zou said. "We need to leave before they find us."

"I want to see how they work," Kamigami said. "So far, I'm not impressed." He rolled up his blanket and moved toward the road.

Zou said nothing and followed him without hesitation. Zou Rong and the old man had accompanied Kamigami on a reconnaissance of Guangdong Province to observe the PLA. Originally, Zou had intended to keep the big American out of trouble. But shortly after they had started the journey, he and the old man had become eager followers and students. Zou and the old man were careful to move forward using available cover, exactly as Kamigami had taught them.

"A mistake," Kamigami said when they reached the road. "They left their transportation unguarded."

"Then we should disable it," Zou said.

"Go," Kamigami ordered. Zou moved silently across the road and lifted the hood of the truck. He quickly reversed the two wires on the coil as Kamigami had taught him. It was a fault easily corrected, but it would need a mechanic to find it. He lowered the hood and scampered back across the road.

"They are stupid," Zou said. "A single man should guard the truck and protect their rear. If they abandoned the truck, we can have it running in a moment." Kamigami nodded, pleased with the young man's progress. He motioned them across the road. The three men were little more than silent, moving shadows as they followed the soldiers down the rutted path into the village. They took cover behind a tomb in the vegetable garden in front of the village and watched as the soldiers forced the villagers to open a storeroom.

The lieutenant stood in the center of the threshing floor where the villagers winnowed rice and snapped out orders. "Search the village. Bring the truck in from the road."

"Now the complications begin," Zou whispered as the driver ran for the road.

"What do you see?" Kamigami asked.

"Five soldiers, one officer. All armed. This is the first time they have raided this village for food," Zou replied. "They will take all the food in the storerooms because they know the villagers have hidden more away."

"Will they search for that too?" Kamigami asked.

"Not this time. If they come back, they will."

"They are taking more than food," the old man told them. He pointed to a soldier carrying a TV set out of one of the hovels. "These are not soldiers," he growled contemptuously. "Under Chairman Mao, the PLA protected the people and soldiers moved among them like a fish through water. I wish we could stop them—teach them a lesson."

Zou gestured at the old man. "He was born in a village much like this one," he explained.

Kamigami's hands flashed in a series of movements—silent commands for action. Zou moved off to the left while the old man retreated to the road. Kamigami darted forward and crouched behind a low stone wall. He had picked a vantage point from which he could easily see and hear what was going on.

A soldier flushed a group of children out of a small shed and onto the threshing floor in front of the lieutenant. The children huddled for protection around a slender girl standing in their midst. Her head was held high and her face calm as she stared at the soldiers. Kamigami had a clear view and judged her to be no more than eighteen years old. Her features were different from the villagers', more finely drawn, with high cheekbones, a definite bridge to the nose, and wide luminous eyes. Where did she come from? he thought. She's beautiful.

"Why were you hiding?" the lieutenant barked, also intrigued by the girl.

"For safety," the girl replied calmly.

"For safety?" the lieutenant repeated, confused. "Do you always hide at night?"

"No," she replied.

"Ah," he said, "then why were you hiding now?"

"Because you were coming."

"You knew we were coming?" The lieutenant smiled as he pushed through the flock of children surrounding the girl. They scattered like leaves before a foul wind. "What else besides the children are you hiding?" His eyes squinted as he looked at her. Only silence answered him. He reached out and pulled the girl's thin shirt open, exposing her small breasts. She modestly folded her arms across her breasts, not moving.

The lieutenant turned to one of his soldiers. "What have we found here?"

"It is said that General Kang pays well for maidens like this one," came the answer.

"Yes," the lieutenant breathed excitedly, "this could be most fortunate. The general does offer certain rewards." He pushed the girl's hands away and stroked her breasts.

Kamigami's hands moved, ordering Zou to fall back. Zou's contract when they maneuvered was to keep Kamigami in sight. Together, they moved back to the road. "I wish we had weapons," Zou said.

"We will in a moment," Kamigami assured him.

Their older companion stepped out of the shadows. "The driver is trying to fix the truck," he said. Ahead of them, they could see the back of the driver as he bent over the engine.

"His weapon?" Kamigami asked.

"A submachine gun," came the answer. "A Type 85, I think. It's in the cab."

Kamigami walked quickly, never slowing. He motioned the two men to guard his rear while he closed on his victim. He slammed a fist between the driver's shoulder blades and drove him headfirst into the engine compartment. He grabbed the man's neck with his right hand and squeezed, cutting off his wind. With his left, he hooked the back of the driver's belt and lifted. Then he drove the man's head into the engine block, much like a battering ram. Twice more his arms moved like pile drivers before he dropped the body over the fender, its head still in the engine compartment.

"What now?" Zou asked.

"We wait until the lieutenant sends another man to find out why the delay."

"Will he only send one?"

"More than likely. They are not very good. Do you want to take him out?" Zou hesitated. He had never killed a man before. Then he nodded. "Do it there." Kamigami pointed to a clump of bushes set back from the road next to the path. "Do you know how to use a garrote?" Zou shook his head no and Kamigami quickly demonstrated how to use a length of wire to strangle a man. Zou grunted and moved into the bushes.

"He's never killed before," the old man said.

Kamigami pointed toward the village. "Now's his chance." As expected, a lone soldier was coming to check on the truck. Kamigami moved into the shadows near Zou and waited. The soldier had passed the spot where Kamigami was hidden when Zou made his move. He stepped silently up behind the soldier, threw the wire garrote over his head and pulled. But the wire caught on the soldier's chin and he was only jerked backward. Kamigami stepped out of the shadows and chopped at the man's Adam's apple, crushing his larynx. "Do it again," he commanded.

Zou slipped the wire down onto the soldier's neck and

twisted. He turned around so they were back to back and pulled the man's head over his shoulder with the wire. The doomed man's arms flapped helplessly for a moment. "I'll do it right next time," Zou promised.

They moved fast. Kamigami told Zou to drive the truck to the edge of the village. While Zou ran for the truck, Kamigami and the old man, now armed with two submachine guns, moved back to the stone wall on the edge of the village. The truck was grinding up the path to the village when Kamigami reached his position. Zou stopped the truck fifty meters short of the threshing floor where the villagers had piled bags of rice. The lieutenant, irritated by the delay, strode angrily toward the truck. The three remaining soldiers were watching the lieutenant as Kamigami and the old man stepped out from behind the wall. A sharp command and the soldiers raised their hands. The villagers quickly stripped the soldiers of their weapons.

The lieutenant looked confused, unable to comprehend the swift turn of events. Moments before, he had been ransacking the village, all-powerful and in command. Now, the villagers were closing in, silent and menacing. "I'm your prisoner!" the lieutenant shouted at Kamigami. "Protect me!" He looked frantically from side to side, searching for a way to run. Panic was etched on his face, and like a frightened rabbit he bolted for the stone wall. Only a woman holding a long-handled flail stood between him and the wall. She swung the flail at his knees and cut him down. The lieutenant's fall served as a signal for action, and the villagers swept over the soldiers, knocking them to the ground and stomping with their feet.

Kamigami moved to the side, watching, not fully understanding the fury playing out on the threshing floor. The girl tried to herd the children away, but they wanted to watch and climbed on top of the wall. Two of the older boys rushed at the crowd and pushed their way in.

They were saving the lieutenant for last.

The girl studied Kamigami's face for a moment. "You don't understand," she said in Cantonese. It was not a question, only a simple statement of fact. "By taking their rice, the soldiers were sentencing the village to starvation. Many would have died this winter."

Kamigami understood most of what she said. "What will they do to the officer?"

"The old women want to cut him up," the girl replied, still speaking Cantonese. "But the village elders want the cage. That way, he kills himself." She looked out over the rice paddies, seeing the future. "They will build a tall and narrow bamboo cage with a wooden collar in the top. Then they will pile stones at the bottom for him to stand on. The stones will be high enough for his neck to fit inside the collar. Each day, they will remove a few stones until he is standing on the tips of his toes. He will live three, maybe four days, before he strangles."

Again, Kamigami understood most of what she had said. "Killing should be fast," he told her.

"There is justice in it," the girl said. "Starvation is slow."

"You will watch him die?"

The girl turned to him. "No," she said in broken English, "I go with you."

The girl's quiet words rang through Kamigami with a clear, bell-like finality. It was a statement of fact, not to be questioned. "I'm not so sure you really want to do that," he said. The girl only looked at him.

Zou and the old man joined them. "I have spent too much time in the countryside," Zou said. "You have taught me many things but it is time I return to Nanning."

"She wants to go with us," Kamigami said.

"I want to go with you," the girl said in Cantonese, looking at Kamigami.

"You may go where you wish," Zou told Kamigami. "I know you are anxious to return to your home."

Kamigami said nothing, thinking. Zou had been consistent in his promise from the very first. Now it was press to test time. "I want to go to Hong Kong," he said.

Much to his surprise, Zou only nodded, a slight smile on his lips. "I expected that. I am sad to see you go. Your help would have been invaluable. But I ask one more favor of you. Will you please tell your president what you have seen here? Tell him that the old cycle of protest and repression has started again in the land of the Pearl River. Tell him that we are spilling our blood to escape our history of helplessness. Tell him that Zou Rong wants to give his people their voices. Your president will understand."

"I can try to deliver your message," Kamigami said. "But I seriously doubt that I can reach the president."

"Your daughter can," Zou replied.

Kamigami stiffened, his mind racing with the implications. Zou wanted a conduit to the president of the United States and was using him to reach Mazie.

"My people will see you safely to Hong Kong," Zou said, ending the discussion.

"Do you want to come with me to Hong Kong?" Kamigami asked the girl. She nodded. "My name is Victor Kamigami," he told her.

"My name . . . Li Jin Chu."

"Her name, Jin Chu," Zou said, "means True Pearl in Cantonese."

"It fits perfectly," Kamigami allowed.

## Friday, February 9
## Whiteman AFB, Missouri

It took almost three weeks for the safety investigation board to finish its work. When the report was typed, Tucker requested an outbrief with Pontowski to discuss the SIB's findings. He had some very pointed comments about the performance of one Major Frank Hester that were not in the report. After Tucker had left, Pontowski read the report and then asked Waters to send it to Hester. "Tell Frank to see me after he's read it," he told her. Three hours later, Hester was in Pontowski's office, report in hand.

"What do you think?" Pontowski asked.

Hester shrugged. "Pretty much your standard accident report. Pilot error. What I expected."

"And you disagree?" Hester shrugged in response. "Personally," Pontowski continued, "I think the primary cause was supervisory error, not pilot error. We should have grounded Leonard."

"We?" Hester replied.

"Specifically, you should have grounded him," Pontowski

answered, his voice emotionless, matter-of-fact, "or recommended that I ground him. You did neither."

"Didn't I?"

"No you didn't. And the SIB didn't buy your implication that you had."

"That wasn't in the report," Hester snapped, "and Tucker the Fucker shouldn't have told you. That was confidential and you know it. I'm going to the IG." He stood to leave.

"I didn't dismiss you," Pontowski said. "Please sit down." There was steel in his voice, and Hester obeyed. Pontowski hit the intercom button to Water's desk. "Captain Waters, please come in and bring your tape recorder. I need you to act as a witness and have a statement typed up for Major Hester."

A knock at the door broke the silence that ruled the room. "Come," Pontowski said. Waters entered and set her mini cassette tape recorder on his desk. She punched the start button and announced the date, the location, and who was present at the meeting. "Statement for Major Frank G. Hester, operations officer of the 303rd Fighter Squadron," Pontowski began. "I declare under penalties of perjury of the Uniform Code of Military Justice that no member of the safety investigation board revealed to me any of the testimony or proceedings of said board." He turned the recorder off and looked at Hester.

"You'll get a typed and signed copy," Pontowski said, "then you can run to the inspector general, write your congressman, or see the chaplain. Your choice."

"You'll have my resignation on your desk in an—"

Pontowski interrupted him. "I'll shoot it right back and tell you to resubmit in ninety days."

"You can't do that," Hester spluttered. "Lincoln freed the slaves."

"It's a question of flying safety," Pontowski said, "and leadership." Hester stared at him, at a loss for words. Pontowski leaned back in his chair. "I haven't got a clue about the strengths and weaknesses of my pilots. You do. True, I can get someone else to do your job and the squadron might, just might, muddle through without anybody else bustin' their ass. But I'd rather bet on your past record." A voice from his own past came back, pounding at him with a meaning he had only partially understood at the time. Now his turn.

"When I was a lieutenant," Pontowski said, "Jack Locke was my squadron commander." He could tell from Hester's look that the name meant nothing to him. "Jack Locke was one of the best sticks who ever strapped on a fighter. He taught me that without leadership, a fighter puke isn't worth shit. And the key is a sense of responsibility—I didn't have it then." Pontowski's voice was filled with pain of remembering. "Do you have it now? Or are you going to desert your men?"

"You could solve the problem by resigning," Hester grumbled.

"I know who was the second choice to get the squadron," Pontowski told him. "How would you support him?" Hester looked sick. He had assumed that he would have gotten command of the squadron if Pontowski had not applied. "The ball's in your court," Pontowski said. Hester still did not answer. "Look," Pontowski said, "stay and do your job for ninety days. If the squadron has another accident during that time, I'll resign."

"Why?" Hester asked.

"It all comes down to leadership. As the commander, I'm responsible, and if we have another accident, I'll have blown it. Ripper here heard it all." He nodded at Waters. "You've got a witness."

Hester stood up. "You've got ninety days." He saluted and left.

"Ripper?" Waters asked, disbelief in her voice.

"As in 'Jack the.' Do you like 'Legs' better?"

Waters understood. Pontowski had defused the issue by simply giving her another nickname, hoping his would stick. "Will there be anything else?" she asked. He shook his head.

Outside, she leaned against the wall, holding the mini cassette to her chest. Her own memories were back, demanding a price. Jack Locke had learned that same lesson on leadership from her husband, Muddy. Where had Muddy learned it? Was it as painful for him? Is this some kind of torch they pass down? She walked slowly to her desk, certain that she had made the right decision. She would give

Matt Pontowski her undivided loyalty and be the best executive officer she could.

Lori Williams was waiting for her, fingering a message. "This just came in," she said. "We've been deactivated. We get chloroformed in six months."

The 303rd Fighter Squadron was a casualty of the peace dividend.

# CHAPTER 4

A sudden jerk and light snore from Matt's side of the bed woke Shoshana. She glanced at the clock—five minutes after two. Her husband was having a restless night and sleep was impossible. She sat up and got out of bed to check on Little Matt. As usual, he had kicked his blankets off. She tucked him in and returned to bed. "Are you okay?" Pontowski asked.

"I'm fine," she answered. "Little Matt kicked his blankets halfway across the room." She gave a little laugh. "He had an erection."

"At his age?"

She snuggled against him. "It's a Pontowski trademark," she said. He could hear amusement in her voice.

He switched on the light to look at her. Her long black hair cascaded across the pillow and her face glowed. "You are beautiful," he said as he rubbed her back.

"Go to sleep." She recognized his intention.

"No way," he said, still caressing her.

"You put goats to shame," she scolded as she turned to him and returned his caresses.

Later, she arranged the pillows, propped herself into a sitting position, and started to brush her hair. "Okay, talk. What's bothering you?" Shoshana knew her husband too well. He only had trouble sleeping when he was wrestling with an intractable problem.

Silence. "This isn't fun," he finally said.

"Did you expect it to be?"

"No," Pontowski answered. "But I was hoping to have a year or two with the squadron . . . a chance to do something. Now . . . six months. It changes everything." He paused, thinking about Leonard's accident and what Tucker had told him during the outbrief. In many ways, the informal meeting was more valuable to Pontowski than the accident report. Tucker had told him the unvarnished truth based on his own observations—none of which could be proven and included in the accident report.

"You can already feel a 'who gives a damn' or 'why worry about the future when there isn't one attitude in the squadron. I know it's affecting their flying and it's only a matter of time until another one of those swingin' dicks prangs. I've got to keep them from doing something stupid until the squadron stands down from flying." He had reached the heart of the matter.

"So what must you do?"

"I'm not sure. Probably start grounding a few of them."

"And you don't want to do that."

"No. That's not the way to end a squadron like the 303rd. These guys have a great record. They've gone to Gunsmoke and blown the big boys with their electric jets off the gunnery range." Shoshana braced herself to again hear about the exploits of the 303rd at Gunsmoke, the biannual tactical bombing competition held at Nellis Air Force Base outside Las Vegas, Nevada. The squadron was always among the top contenders, and one of their pilots had once taken home the coveted Top Gun trophy. But he said nothing and turned out the light.

"Don't let your feelings rule your head," she said, her voice a soft comfort in the dark. "Do what you have to and put your personal feelings aside." She reached out and touched him. "But always remember where you hid them."

Pontowski tried to go back to sleep. But it wouldn't happen as the irony of it all bore down. He had wanted a chance to prove himself, free of the influence of his famous grandfather, and shake the "golden boy" image. Instead, he was contending with the very real dilemma of how to preserve the lives of people he barely knew and who didn't like him.

He was alone with the agony of command.

"Please have a seat," Sara Waters said. She motioned John Leonard to a chair next to her desk. "You're early," she told him, "and Colonel Pontowski hasn't returned from a meeting with the wing commander." She watched him fidget until she couldn't stand it. "Lighten up, Captain. He's not the beast from the Black Lagoon."

"That's easy for you to say, Ripper," Leonard replied. "He's not after your ass."

Waters arched an eyebrow. So now I'm Ripper, she thought. The boss's nickname had stuck. She decided Leonard deserved a break. "He's not after your ass."

Leonard's expression was a mixture of disbelief and relief. "I . . . I was certain," he stammered, "that he was going to permanently ground me because of the accident."

"I don't think so," Waters said. "At least, I haven't seen any paperwork to that effect. I know that he is worried about your—"

"Home life?" Leonard interrupted. "That's sorted out. I left my wife and moved into an apartment." He warmed to the subject, glad to have someone listen. It was an emotional release. "So far it has been a relief. I guess our marriage has been over for some time but I didn't have the courage to face it."

She liked the sound of his voice and gave him a little nudge. "And your job?"

"I've got a handle on it. My principal gave me a leave of absence and says he wants me back when I get my feet on the ground."

She could hear satisfaction now and liked that. "Will you go back?"

"Probably. I like teaching. Besides, there won't be much else to do after the squadron shuts down."

Pontowski came through the door and motioned for Leonard to follow him into his office. Leonard came to attention in front of his desk and snapped a sharp salute.

"Captain Leonard reporting as ordered, sir." Pontowski waved a salute back and told him to sit down.

He came right to the point. "Are you ready to start flying again?" The look on Leonard's face made him want to smile.

"In a heartbeat, sir," Leonard said. "May I ask a question?" Pontowski nodded a reply. "Why are you doing this? We're nothing but a bunch of lame ducks and there is no reason to give me a second chance."

Pontowski forced a hard look. "Captain, until we turn out the lights, the 303rd is going to look like a fighter squadron, talk like a fighter squadron, smell like a fighter squadron, and fly like a fighter squadron. You ready to do that?"

"You bet."

The tone in Leonard's voice was exactly what Pontowski wanted to hear. "Good. I'm looking for volunteers to be our flying safety officer. You interested?"

"Yes, sir. I'll be the best flying safety puke who ever strapped on the title."

"You've almost got the job," Pontowski told him. "What will be your number-one priority?"

Leonard thought for a moment. "I'm going to change the 'I don't give a shit' attitude that everybody is wearing around here."

Pontowski nodded and punched at his intercom. "Captain Waters, please come in." Waters appeared in the door holding her notebook. "Please cut orders making Captain Leonard the squadron's new flying safety officer."

"My pleasure, Colonel," Waters replied.

From the tone of her voice and the look on Leonard's face, Pontowski was certain he had at least two allies. "That's all," he said. Leonard stood and saluted while Waters waited for him to leave. "One more thing," Pontowski added. "I want the squadron to go out in style. You two see if you can come up with some ideas." He watched them leave. Style my ass, he thought. He wanted a reason for the squadron to fly safe.

Waters kept circling the table in her office, looking first at the schedule of events, then at the publicity posters, then at the map that outlined the different areas. She glanced out the window, surprised that it was dark. Even though she was tired, she couldn't contain her enthusiasm. "This is brilliant, John, absolutely brilliant." She bestowed a radiant smile on the pilot, who had collapsed on a comfortable couch. "I think the boss will like this."

"You deserve a lot of the credit," he told her. He moved his pudgy body into an upright position and watched her move. Like a cat, he thought. He caught his breath when she bent over the table and her dark blue uniform skirt stretched tight. The Air Force blouse strained at the seams and could not hide her figure. A shot of hormones drove a very lustful feeling into the lower regions of Leonard's abdomen that was rapidly replaced by the more comforting realization that his ex-wife had not emasculated him. "Look, he said, "we've been at this for three days and it's late. Why don't we knock off for the night. I'll lock up."

Again, she smiled at him, revitalizing the blood vessels in the lower part of his body. "Thanks. I want to call my daughter before she goes to bed. I haven't seen her in four days. Maybe tomorrow I can get home for a few days."

"Four days is too long," the schoolteacher in Leonard said. "Kansas City is too far to commute, so why don't you move her here?"

"I wonder if it would be worth it for six months," Waters replied, considering the possibilities.

"I think it would," Leonard told her. "You can rent a house."

She gathered up her coat, hat, and handbag and headed for the door. "I'll think about it," she said. Leonard let out a long, low whistle after she had left and went about locking up the building.

Outside, Waters headed for her car in the deserted parking lot. Her routine was well-established and she moved quickly, keys in hand while looking for anything unusual. Nothing. She was reaching for the door lock when a dark shape rose out of the shadows behind a nearby car and rushed at her. Waters heard the quick footsteps and turned, only to have a huge hand grab her hair and bang her head on the roof. The man jammed his body against hers and forced her against the car. She could feel his weight against her back and the hardness of his erection against her buttocks.

"Scream and I'll cut your fuckin' throat," he growled. His free hand stripped her coat and handbag away.

"Don't hurt me," she pleaded. "Take the purse. I won't scream."

"That's fuckin' smart," he said. He knocked her hat off and pulled her away from the car. Now she had an idea of his size—he was huge, well over six feet and close to three hundred pounds. Her hope this was a mugging vaporized when he kicked her handbag under the car and forced her toward the open field that backed the parking lot.

Tears streamed down her face from pain as he held her head back and his right hand grabbed her breasts. The hand moved lower and grabbed at her crotch. She fought against it by walking faster. "In a hurry to do this?" he rasped in her ear.

"Please, don't hurt me," she whispered. She was vaguely aware that she was still holding on to her car keys.

"You gonna like this." He threw her down onto the grassy bank of a ditch and covered her, using both his hands to hold her wrists above her head. He forced his legs between hers and kicked her feet apart. He freed her right hand when he reached down to pull up her skirt. She swung blindly at him, still clutching the car keys. But he caught her arm before she could hit him and jammed it back against the ground. The car keys flew out of her grasp. "Bitch!" he growled. "Don't move. You gonna like havin' a man."

He held both her wrists with one hand. "My wrist," she gasped. "The right one. It's broken. Please let go." It was a lie.

"Sure, bitch. But don't move or I'll twist it off." He released her right hand and she could feel his hand move down between his body and hers, pulling at her skirt. She groped for the keys while he unzipped his pants and laid his penis against her. Then he hit her in the face. Hard. "You dumb bitch. I told you don't move." She didn't move until he grabbed his penis. She tried to distract his attention by wiggling and twisting her left arm, which was still in his grasp, while she groped in the grass with her right hand, searching for the car keys.

He dropped his penis and hooked a blunt finger under her panties and ripped them away. His breath was panting in her right ear and she could smell his sour odor when her hand grasped the keys. She clamped them in her fist, with the point of one key sticking out between her index finger and forefinger. She felt the head of his penis move against her inner thigh as he tried to guide its penetration. Adrenaline surged through her and she bucked against his body. She drove her right fist into his face and buried the key in his left eye.

The man's pain filled the night with a primeval shriek. Waters shoved him away and came to her feet. But his hand reached out and grabbed her leg. A demonic fury possessed her as she kicked free. Again, she kicked at him, this time feeling her high heel break off when she made contact. Another scream, this time more animal than human, and she was free. She ran for the building, stumbling once. Ahead, she could see a man coming out of the entrance. It was Leonard. He ran toward her.

"What happened?" he shouted.

Waters swung at him, wildly, out of control. "Get out of here!" she cried. "Let me alone!" He grabbed her shoulders with both hands, holding her at arm's length. She half-swung at him. "Get out of here," she moaned. "Please let me alone." Her knees gave out and she collapsed.

Gently, he guided her to sitting position on the ground and stood back, sensing she didn't want him to touch her. "It's okay," he told the sobbing woman. "It's okay." He draped his flight jacket over her shoulders and ran back to the building entrance. He broke the outside fire alarm, figuring that was the quickest way to summon help. He ran back to her, sensing, rather than knowing, what had happened. An unfamiliar rage captured him and for the first time in his life, he wanted to kill. "Where is he?" he said. She pointed at the field just as a security police car turned into the parking lot.

"Over there!" he yelled at the squad car and pointed at the field. A second car came into the parking lot, followed by a fire truck and a crash wagon. Within moments they were safely surrounded by concerned faces. A woman paramedic helped Waters to her feet. Slowly, her breathing returned to normal as she told them what had happened. Waters straightened her skirt and tucked in her blouse. Standing there barefoot with his flight jacket over her shoulders, Leonard was struck by her composure. She had been assaulted, mauled, and terrified. Now she was reclaiming her dignity.

The paramedic escorted her to the crash wagon, helped her inside, and closed the door behind them. A security cop from the first car walked over to them. He held a plastic evidence bag with the remnants of Waters' panties. "This is one rape suspect who won't get away," he said.

The chief master sergeant who was acting as on-scene commander took the evidence bag. "You found him at the scene?"

"No," came the answer. "He had crawled into the bushes."

"He'll claim he was sleeping off a drunk." There was a disgusted resignation in his voice. He had seen too many suspects convince juries they were innocent on such a minor point.

"Not this time, Chief," the security cop said. "He's still got a key buried in his left eyeball with Captain Waters' key ring attached and the heel of her shoe planted an inch and a half deep in his left armpit. Let him explain that to a jury."

Leonard watched the crash wagon pull out of the parking lot and disappear into the night. "Pontowski named her right," he said to no one.

Pontowski drummed a tattoo on the security police report with his fingers. "You didn't have to come in today," he told Waters.

"There's work to do," she replied. He was amazed by the woman's composure as she stood in front of his desk. Other than the ugly, fresh bruise on her left cheek, which no amount of makeup could hide, she seemed perfectly normal. "Besides, I want to make a point."

"Which is?"

"No miserable son of a bitch messes with my life."

"Have you heard the reports from the hospital?" Pontowski asked. She shook her head. "They've identified him. He's lost his left eye. It seems you stepped in animal dung in the field and he's got a bad infection from whatever was on your heel." He let that sink in. "By the way, he claims he's innocent."

"Really?" Waters replied, her voice icy cold.

"There's one thing that isn't explained in the report," Pontowski said. "Exactly what were you and Tango working on that kept you here last night?"

It was the first time Waters had heard Leonard called by that name. What was Pontowski doing? Renaming the entire squadron? The name does fit, she conceded. "We were working on a way for the squadron to go out in style," she explained. For the first time, she became animated. "John . . . ah, Tango . . . came up with a great idea. He thinks we should put on an open house. It would be a farewell gift to the community for all their support. He says they are the stockholders and we should show them what they got for their money."

Her enthusiasm broke through the frosty look on her face and she smiled. "John thinks the open house should be timed to coincide with our last day of flying before we stand down. We could put on an air show with the Warthogs. The closing ceremony could be the retirement of the colors with a flyby. Why don't I get him in here to explain the details?"

Her enthusiasm was contagious and Pontowski told her to call him in ASAP. He watched her rush out of the office. An open house with an air show, he thought. It might do the trick.

Five minutes later, Leonard was in the office, laying out the details for his commander. His excitement about the project matched Waters'. He finished his pitch by telling Pontowski, "The motto around here will be to 'Wow the crowd.' We can have a competition to see who will be on the aerial demonstration team and then to see who will do the flyby. Everybody will want a piece of the action and will be bustin' their butts to look good. No one will want to screw up."

"Have you got a title for all this?" Pontowski asked. "One that we can go public with."

"We'll call it 'The Flight of the Thunderhogs.' We'll make the Thunderbirds jealous as all hell."

Pontowski smiled at the two officers. By all accounts, both of them should have been emotional basket cases. But for some reason, both were coping and getting on with their lives. "Let's do it," he told them. "One thing, troops . . . let's not end up being called 'the Thunderturds.'"

## Thursday, February 15
## Kowloon, Territory of Hong Kong

The nine-mile run across Mirs Bay from mainland China to the New Territories of Hong Kong had taken twelve minutes in the boat the Chinese called a Tai Fei. It had been a wet and pounding ride in the converted Cigarette offshore racer used for smuggling between Hong Kong and China. The skipper had assured Kamigami that he could have made the crossing in nine minutes if a woman had not been aboard.

The two were still damp when they reached the outskirts of Kowloon, and Jin Chu was shivering from the cold wind blowing off Victoria Harbor and bringing winter from the mainland. "We need to find a room and dry out," Kamigami said.

"Perhaps," Jin Chu said, "we should buy different clothes." Kamigami agreed, for she was drawing stares from every person they passed on the crowded street. Jin Chu's black trousers, padded jacket, and sandals marked her as fresh from the country and a newcomer to Hong Kong.

They turned down a side street lined with well-stocked shops occupied only by worried-looking owners. Near the end, he selected a small clothing stall owned by two Indian brothers. While a young girl helped Jin Chu, Kamigami watched the Hong Kongers flowing past the stall. "It is more pleasant in here," he said to the older of the brothers.

The man smiled. "Ah yes," he said in the distinctive singsong English spoken by Indians. "We do not have the worry. If you look, you will see most of them carry cellular telephones. That is because of the worry." Kamigami said that he did not understand. "Ah yes," the Indian explained. "They worry about reversion a year from July. They want to leave before Hong Kong becomes part of China. They do not trust their new masters. They carry the cellular phones to learn quickly of new opportunities to leave. There are many rumors."

"Do you have a cellular phone?" Kamigami asked.

"Ah no. You see I have a passport from India. We can leave any time we wish. We do not have the worry."

People were starting to hurry down the street, telephones clamped to their ears. Shouting drifted up from the main street. "There must be a new rumor going around," Kamigami said. The Indian stepped onto the sidewalk and looked down the street. People were now pushing and running. He darted back into the stall and called to his brother. The two young men quickly moved their sidewalk displays inside and pulled down the steel shutters at the front that worked like a garage door.

"Ah yes," he panted. "You should stay here now. It will be dangerous on the streets." He turned on a radio and dialed an English-language broadcast station. The noise outside subsided.

Jin Chu came out of the back room where she had been trying on new clothes. The young assistant beamed with pleasure at her handiwork. She had outfitted Jin Chu in tight designer jeans, a jade green scooped-neck sleeveless blouse, and low-heeled boots. Jin Chu's hair was pulled loosely onto the back of her neck and held in place by a matching green bow. The girl handed her a short jacket to wear and smiled. "Very pretty," she said.

Kamigami could only stare. Changing clothes had not solved the problem, perhaps only compounded it, for Jin Chu still demanded attention. Then it came to him. It was her, not the clothes. Jin Chu was one of the world's truly beautiful women. For a moment, there was only silence in the stall. "You do not like?" Jin Chu asked hesitantly, not sure of his reaction.

"I like," Kamigami smiled at her, feeling like a fool and, for the first time in his life, understanding why older men made idiots of themselves over young women. Someone started banging on the steel shutters at the front with a pipe or crowbar, and he could hear fresh shouting coming from the street. The older of the two brothers motioned them to silence and turned off the lights.

"Perhaps they will go away." They moved to the back of the store and huddled around the radio.

". . . the riots that started in Tsuen Wan have now spread south into all of Kowloon," the news reader on the radio announced in a crisp English accent. "Authorities are urging all foreigners to remain inside until order is restored. Meanwhile, leaders of the Chinese community say the situation is beyond their control and that order can only be restored if Her Majesty's government vigorously rejects the latest proclamation by the People's Republic of China. The same leaders are urging Her Majesty's government to let the people of Hong Kong determine the future of Hong Kong and not impose an agreement negotiated without their participation."

Kamigami's eyes narrowed as he listened to the radio detail the violence, burning, and looting sweeping the New Territories. The latest bulletin reported scattered rioting on Hong Kong Island. "Apparently," he said, "that proclamation by the PRC was the spark that started all this. Do you know what it said?"

The two Indian brothers shook their heads in unison. The banging on the steel shutters grew louder. The young shop assistant pulled a telephone from under the counter and punched at the buttons. They watched her panic turn to terror as she listened. She dropped the phone. "Very bad," she whispered. "Beijing says that Hong Kong is now part of China. No one can leave until the new government has taken over. Very bad, very bad."

The People's Republic of China had seized the crown colony of Hong Kong seventeen months ahead of schedule.

The girl was crying. "Chinese riot and are killing whites and some of us," she said. The "us" she was talking about were Indian merchants.

Angry shouts were coming from outside and Kamigami smelled smoke. He looked around for Jin Chu. She was gone. A surge of panic clamped his chest until she came out of the back room, dressed in her old clothes. "It is time to go," she said. A deafening crash rocked them as the steel shutters bowed inward. They heard an engine race and gears crunch, followed by squealing tires. Again, a deafening crash hammered at them as a pickup truck smashed into the door. A hand reached through a gap at the side of the door and felt for the latch.

Before the shop assistant could scream, Kamigami was at the door and grabbed the arm at the wrist. He twisted until a bone snapped. He didn't let go as a loud scream echoed outside the shop. Kamigami lifted the arm above his head, dragging the man on the outside up until his feet were off the ground. He forced the man's palm open by pressing forward on the back of his hand, and with a hard slap, impaled the palm on a jagged shred of metal at the top of the door. He left the man hanging on the outside, shrieking in pain, a warning siren to the rioters that danger lurked inside. Kamigami had bought them a little time to escape.

The older of the brothers showed them out the back and into a narrow alley barely wide enough for Kamigami to squeeze through. Jin Chu surprised Kamigami by asking the merchant, "Where is the nearest temple with fortune tellers?" The Indian gave them directions to Wong Tai Sin. "You must leave now," she cautioned the young man.

"Ah, but we must stay," he told her, "and save what we can. It is all we own." He rushed back into the stall.

"Please," Jin Chu said, "we go to Wong Tai Sin Temple." Kamigami understood it was not a request and led the way down the narrow alley. He didn't see the tears in her eyes. Fifty feet from the end they collided with a burly young Chinese pushing a dolly loaded with a bundle of Oriental rugs going in the opposite direction. The man pushed at them and yelled for them to back up. Kamigami pushed on the rugs and forced the man to back out of the alley, protesting loudly in indecipherable Cantonese. All traffic on the main street was stopped and the crowd was moving in the direction they wanted to go. Kamigami used his bulk as a battering ram and they reached the temple forty minutes later.

The temple's courtyard was an island of tranquility in the maelstrom of madness outside. Jin Chu led the way to a long, single-story arcade set against a back wall. The sign above the entrance announced that fortune tellers and soothsayers were inside. Every stall was occupied and people were lined up two and three deep to have their fortunes told and seek advice. Jin Chu walked slowly down the arcade listening to the voice of each fortune teller. Then she stopped and joined a line behind four other people. She had heard the voice she wanted.

The fortune teller was an old man Kamigami gauged to be in his seventies. He was dressed in a western-style suit with a carefully knotted silk tie. He looked up, his lined face expressionless, and saw Jin Chu standing in line. He stood and waved the crowd aside with a shaking hand, his face suddenly animated. His eyes never left Jin Chu. A silence that Kamigami could feel hung over the small group. "You must forgive me," the old man said. "I do not know your name." He motioned her to come forward and the woman sitting at the fortune teller's small table willingly gave Jin Chu her seat. "I am not the one to tell your fortune so how may I help you?"

Jin Chu spoke in a language Kamigami did not understand. The old man only listened and nodded. When Jin Chu was finished, the fortune teller produced his cellular phone and punched in a number. Much to the bystanders' surprise the call went through immediately. Now the old man spoke Cantonese and Kamigami could follow the drift of the conversation.

When he had finished, the fortune teller turned to Kamigami. "You must take Miss Li to Cheung Chau Island." The tone in the old man's voice carried a deep respect when he said "Miss Li." Kamigami would hear it many times in the future, always spoken in the same tone of voice. The old man sketched a map showing Kamigami how to reach the ferry to the island. "The Mass Transit Railway is still running. Take it to Hong Kong and get off at Central station." He was shaking. "Be careful."

Two of the bystanders escorted them out of the temple and to the nearest Mass Transit station. Kamigami hesitated when he saw the mass of people pushing into and out of the underground entrance. "It is dangerous," Jin Chu warned him. "But we must go."

"Hold on to my belt," Kamigami said. The strength of

her grasp reassured him and he plowed into the crowd, using his bulk to bulldoze a path to the boarding platform. As they waited for the next train, a man tried to shove Jin Chu aside, yelling at her. Kamigami spun the man around, grabbed him by his shirt collar and belt, and threw him six feet back over the heads of the crowd. All pushing and shoving stopped until the train pulled into the station.

Total chaos ruled when the doors hissed open. People tried to push out of the train while the crowd on the platform tried to board. Kamigami braced his hands against the sides of the open door and blocked the crowd behind him while passengers got off. When he let go, the dammed strength of the crowd catapulted him and Jin Chu into the car and against the opposite door. His left foot bumped against a small bundle. He looked down and saw the body of a child that had been trampled to death. The train started to move and an eerie silence settled over the car. The pungent aroma of urine drifted past him.

Kamigami studied the map the Mass Transit authorities had posted on the wall. His lips compressed into a tight line when he realized they had to go under Victoria Harbor. He decided to get off at Tsim Sha Tsui, the last station before they crossed under the harbor, and take a Star Ferry across to Hong Kong. But the engineer did not stop and the train rushed through the smoke-filled station. A hail of bullets cut into the train and shattered windows, plowing into the hapless passengers.

He clutched Jin Chu to him and tried to shield her with his own body. The screams of the wounded quickly died out as they were pushed to the floor. The sudden rise of heads above the crowd announced who was standing on a fresh body. Kamigami felt the train start a gradual descent into the Victoria Harbor tunnel. They were plunging into the depths of hell.

The train was on the level when the lights flickered and went out. The train coasted to a stop. Panic swelled in the darkness and the madness that had been held at bay only by the train's forward motion swept over the living. The emergency lights came on and the noise in the car reached a crescendo of shouts and screaming. A new odor, faint and different, reached him. Before he could identify the smell, it was gone. He stiffened, remembering Vietnam. A faint odor had often been the only warning that danger was at hand.

Years of experience had taught him not to ignore the warning. But what was it? It would have to come back stronger for him to smell it again. Then it was back and he knew what it was. Brine. And the only possible source was the harbor above their heads.

Jin Chu would never understand a shouted command in the hysteria that ruled the car. Kamigami grabbed her shoulders, spun her around, pinned her against the door with his body and dug his hands into the rubber gasket that sealed the doors closed. He heaved. Nothing. The crowd pushed at his back and he felt a sharp pain in his lower right side, just above his belt. The man behind him tried to cut him down with a knife to clear the way. Kamigami twisted around and fixed the man with a hard stare. In the instant Kamigami jammed his palm into the man's nose with a sharp upward motion, the man knew he had made a mistake—a very bad mistake. He crumpled to the floor.

Kamigami ignored the pain in his back and threw all his strength against the doors. They started to open. The smell of sea water was much stronger and the crowd caught it. He heard the sound of breaking glass as windows were shattered for escape exits. The shouting and cries were deafening. Slowly the doors moved open and with one last heave, they parted.

The pressure of the crowd shot the two out of the car and slammed them into the tunnel wall, stunning Jin Chu. The doors snapped closed, trapping a woman, her body a wedge holding it open. A man stomped her down the crack and crawled over her and onto Kamigami's back. Kamigami drove an elbow into the man's stomach and forced him back against the train. He reached for Jin Chu and in the dim light saw water in the track pit below the car. He guided her hand to the back of his belt and felt the reassuring pressure of her strong grasp.

The emergency lights in the train went out and they were submerged in total darkness as screams echoed in anguish. He moved forward along the narrow cement ledge that served as a catwalk. The power cables anchored on the wall gave him a handhold. Twice, he had to push free when someone tried to crawl out of a window onto them. When they were clear of the train, he moved faster, becoming more confident in the darkness as they left the swirling vortex of screams and death behind.

"Stop," Jin Chu commanded. She guided his right hand to the pain in his side. He could feel blood pouring from the knife wound. He ripped off his shirt, tore a large piece from the back, and jammed it into the wound to stop the bleeding. Then he spun the shirt into a long twist and tied it around his waist, holding the makeshift compress in place. He had been wounded before.

They started to move along the catwalk as the rising water lapped at their feet. Ahead, Kamigami could hear a ventilation fan. The emergency generators were keeping the ventilation and water pumps on-line. The water level had reached their ankles when he felt the slope rise. They were starting out of the tunnel. The screams coming from the train died away as death ruled the stalled train. "Hurry," he commanded when he heard the sound of the fans stop. "With the electricity off the water pumps will stop." They were almost running when Jin Chu slipped and fell into the track pit. Wildly, he searched for her in the water and came up with a fistful of hair. He dragged her back onto the catwalk. She was unconscious. He threw her over his right shoulder and moved forward, but the water had risen to midcalf and slowed his progress.

It was a race against the rising water in the tunnel. He felt dizzy. His mind registered the change—carbon monoxide buildup or loss of blood. The resistance of the water and the weight of Jin Chu worked against him and sapped his strength. He fought against the water as it reached his knees. He focused what was left of his strength and drew short, sharp breaths with each step, slogging ahead. For the first time, he doubted he could make it. He drove himself forward one step at a time, refusing to give in to defeat. The water reached his waist.

Ahead, a glimmer of light broke the darkness. "Put me down," Jin Chu said. He let her slip off his shoulder as he gasped for air. Her hand was against the small of his back and she pushed. It was enough to get him moving. The air grew fresher and the light brighter. Four more steps and the water started to recede. They were coming out of the tunnel into a lighted station.

Jin Chu pulled herself onto the passenger platform and grabbed Kamigami's hand. She threw her body back and pulled until he was beside her. He lay panting while she checked his bandage. "You're still bleeding," she said in Cantonese. She ripped off a leg of her pants at the knee, wrung it out and pressed it over the first compress. She retied the bandage, cinching the compress tight. Slowly, Kamigami came to his feet and she helped him up the stalled escalator into a swirling mass of Hong Kongers.

He collapsed outside. Jin Chu grabbed him under the shoulders and tried to pull him to the side of the walk, away from the rushing crowd. But his weight was too much for her. She looked around for help but knew that no one would stop. Then she saw it. One of the rickshaws in which old men pulled tourists around for an exorbitant fee was partially hidden behind a pile of cardboard boxes. She ran over to it and called for the driver. When there was no answer, she pulled the rickshaw free and trotted over to Kamigami. She half-rolled and half-pulled until she had him in the two-wheeled cart. She picked up the poles and threw her weight forward until she picked up speed and was trotting down the elevated concrete esplanades that fronted on Hong Kong's harbor.

A mass of humanity blocked the entrance to the Cheung Chau ferry terminal. Jin Chu screamed and tried to barge her way through the mob but was pushed aside by a heavy-set woman. Four young boys, high-school students returning home, surrounded her and started shouting and pushing, forcing the rickshaw through the crowd and up the gangway onto the ferry. Surprisingly, once on board, the temper of the crowd changed and willing hands helped lay Kamigami on a long table while the four boys dumped the rickshaw overboard.

An old man materialized out of the crowd and demanded a first-aid kit from a crewman. "I am a doctor," he told Jin Chu. With skilled but shaky hands, he cleaned Kamigami's wound and sewed it up. "Luck is with you," he said. "The blade missed his kidney. But he needs a shot of antibiotics to fight infection. It is a bad wound." In the way of the Chinese, they talked, exchanging personal information that a westerner would never reveal to a stranger. When Jin Chu mentioned the name she was seeking on the island, the doctor shook his head. "He will never see you."

An hour later, the ferry coasted through the breakwater at Cheung Chau and entered a time warp, with old-fashioned junks and fishing boats anchored side by side in long rows. The harbor front was quiet and people went about their business as usual, unaffected by the madness sweeping Kowloon and Hong Kong. The four boys helped Kamigami to his feet and propped him up while the doctor led the way down the gangway. The doctor stopped, his mouth open. A bearded old man, bent with age and dressed as a fisherman, was standing in a deserted circle, surrounded by a quiet ring of people. "It is Zhang Pai," the doctor whispered, awe-struck.

The old man hobbled forward on his staff. "Miss Li?" he asked. She nodded in reply. He cocked his head to one side and studied Kamigami, surprised by the man's size. "Your companion served you well," he allowed. "But then, Ronald said he would." He smiled at her confusion. "Ronald is the fortune teller at Wong Tai Sin Temple who called me. I was expecting you." He turned to the crowd and pointed to Kamigami. "Please help this man to my home. He saved my adopted daughter." He smiled at Jin Chu. "You will become my daughter, you know." He spoke so the crowd could hear him. "They say you are a *feng shui* woman of great power. I will make you a master."

Kamigami was confused. He had heard of the ancient mystical art of Chinese geomancy called *feng shui* but didn't believe in it. "I thought only men practiced *feng shui*," he said.

"That is mostly true," she replied, her voice modest and pleasing to his ear. "But some women have the gift. I have a little of it." She captured his eyes with hers. "I can also see the future. Not always clearly."

"And what do you see?" he asked.

"For now, you and me." He liked her answer.

## Monday, February 19
## Washington, D.C.

The rumor exploded in the NSC offices like a large firecracker, deafening everyone except the subject—Mazie Kamigami. In the way of rumors; she never heard it and was the last to be told of the staff meeting in the main conference room. She hurried down the hall, her legs flashing. She pushed through the door into the crowded room. Wentworth Hazelton motioned for her to join him at the foot of the table where he had been holding a seat.

"Thanks, Went," she said, wondering why Finlay's protégé was being so considerate. There hadn't been any feedback from the episode in the hall, and judging from the way the more glamorous staffers and secretaries made themselves available whenever he was around, she wasn't being subjected to the "only available woman" syndrome.

Bill Carroll and Finlay walked into the room. It was rare for Carroll to attend a staff meeting of the working troops. "Oh, oh," Mazie whispered, "something big has hit the fan." Hazelton's smile was a contrast to Finlay's sour look.

"If you haven't heard," Carroll said as he looked around the room, "we got an 'atta boy' from the president this morning during the cabinet meeting. The chief hates surprises and we were ahead of the Hong Kong crisis. So it was really an 'atta girl,' thanks to Mazie."

"Carroll gave you all the credit," Hazelton whispered as Finlay took charge of the meeting. She barely heard the discussion that recounted how the State Department's quick counter to the People's Republic of China's attempt to nationalize Hong Kong early had contained the crisis.

"There are problems," Carroll said, taking the meeting away from Finlay. "We still haven't got the Chinese to totally back off. But they are not sounding so belligerent and the riots in Hong Kong have stopped. But we are not out of the woods yet. It gets complicated because of the Middle East. We are seeing signs that it is about to flare, maybe even torch, if the Islamic fundamentalists consolidate their power in North Africa. In short, we could be looking at two MRCs." He paused for effect in the stunned silence. Because of the spread of nuclear weapons, a single MRC, major regional conflict, could escalate into a nuclear exchange. In the strange calculus of geopolitics, two MRCs did not double those odds—they quadrupled them, because of the shifting alliances and power vacuums that surrounded each conflict.

"So," Carroll continued, "what recommendations, military included, should I send up? Keep in mind that the so-called 'peace dividend' and the drawdown of our armed services have taken many of the president's military options off the table. But we should not abandon China." He turned and quietly outlined a few instructions for Finlay before he left the meeting.

"That's why Finlay is pissed," Hazelton whispered. "He wants to put China on a back burner."

"It's hard to ignore one-fourth of the world's population," Mazie countered.

Finlay was much more confident after Carroll had left and went around the table, tasking different individuals. Mazie listened carefully as he gave detailed instructions on what he wanted done. Grudgingly, she had to admit that Finlay was an excellent administrator and was covering all bases. Then it was her turn. "Miss Kamigami," Finlay was pointing at her with a pen, "I want you to do a detailed analysis of what's-his-name . . . the PLA general . . ."

"Kang Xun," Mazie told him.

"Right," Finlay said, flustered. "I want it on my desk ASAP. No later than next Monday."

Mazie mentally scanned the study she had recently completed on her own time—the physical profile of the fifty-one-year-old general, his health, education, training, experience, politics, family, friends, and so on. She had reviewed every shred of information the intelligence community of the United States had on the man. She recalled the interview of one of his former mistresses conducted by the Air Force Special Activities Center. It always amazed her how that outfit of oddball con artists managed to reach so many key people and convince them to talk. Then she considered Finlay. Should she tell him that she had anticipated his directions? Probably.

"Sir, I already have something that might be usable."

Finlay's heavy eyebrows shot up. He had learned the hard way that Mazie was the master of understatement. The "something" would be a detailed and fully documented dossier. "What kind of person are we dealing with here?" he asked.

"Absolutely ruthless," Mazie answered. "He butchers the opposition."

"A Chinese version of Saddam Hussein," Finlay said from the head of the table. Every head turned to Mazie, waiting for her reply. The exchange resembled a tennis match as the subject Kang was batted back and forth.

"Only in that one respect," she answered. "Unlike Hussein, he is well-educated and considered a competent military tactician."

"What's his political base?"

It was a question Mazie had expected. Finlay was a political animal and never strayed far from his home turf. "He operates within the traditional Chinese political structure," Mazie explained, "family, friends, favors, connections, bribes, bargains, and tradeoffs. While the system is unbelievably corrupt, Kang is austere, vicious, and with one exception, quite puritanical. He is the perfect tool for implementing the grim repression that follows protest of any kind in China."

"You mentioned an exception?"

"He's a sexual deviate."

Finlay shook his head. "Let me see what you've got before the close of business."

"Good show," Hazelton told Mazie as they filed out of the conference room.

Carroll glanced at his watch. It was time for his run. Chuck Stanford and Wayne Adams, the two Secret Service agents detailed to run with him, would be waiting at the East Gate of the White House. He tied the laces to his running shoes and glanced at Mazie's report on Kang Xun, still lying on his desk. It had been a frightening read. His stomach hurt, and for the first time since he had come out of Iran years ago, he started to shake. My God! he thought, I haven't had this reaction since I was in the dill in Iran and being shot at.

Outside, the two agents did mild stretching exercises as Carroll went through his warmup. They recognized his preoccupation and relaxed, certain that it would be an easy run. They were wrong. From the first stride, Carroll was pounding hard.

"You'd think the devil was nipping at his ass," Adams complained. That was the last time he had the breath to talk. Both agents were still in trail when they finished and even the two agents detailed to follow on mountain bikes with radios and submachine guns hidden in the panniers were breathing and sweating hard.

"Goin' for a new record today?" Stanford asked.

"No," Carroll replied. "I was just thinking." The two agents waited. They knew how the national security advisor worked. "What do you know about Churchill and Hitler?"

"Wasn't it like a personal feud between them?" Adams replied.

"Or a duel," Stanford added.

"Yeah." Carroll nodded. He turned to go back to work. "I don't think we'll be hitting the brewskis for a while," he told them as he disappeared inside.

"What do you make of that?" Adams asked.

"Beats me," Stanford shrugged. "Maybe he's got a fight on his hands."

"Or thinks he's Churchill," Adams speculated.

"Churchill never ran that fast in his life."

# CHAPTER 5

Sunday, February 25
Kansas City, Kansas

The ten-year-old girl sat on the packed suitcase listening to her mother. "Melissa, quit trying to out-negotiate your grandmother on homework. I'll be calling every night to check on you and should be home late Friday afternoon."

Melissa was listening carefully, not to the words but to the tone of her voice. The little girl's sensitive internal barometer was finally at rest after charting the emotional weather changes that had been going on inside her mother. Everything seemed normal, so it was natural that her fertile mind considered other reasons, all right out of her grandmother's romance novels, for a pilot driving her mother to the base. "Who is he, Mother?" she asked.

"Just a friend, Melissa," Waters replied.

"Friend?" Melissa replied. She didn't want to believe it.

"You've got to learn the difference between being friendly and being romantic," Waters told her.

The doorbell rang and Melissa bolted down the stairs. "I'll get it," she shouted. She was back in a flash. "Oh, Mother. Not him! He's an overgrown teddy bear." John Leonard was waiting at the door.

"I do appreciate this," Waters told Leonard as she slid into the front seat for the seventy-mile drive to Whiteman Air Force Base.

"No problem," Leonard smiled. "Besides, it will give you

a chance to read the plan before we take it to the boss." He handed her the thick operations plan titled OPPLAN STAND DOWN.

It was the first time Waters had seen the air show spelled out in detail. While she had been occupied with her assailant's trial, Leonard had created an exciting program that made the spectators part of the flying routine by setting up large video monitors in the main hangar. By tying into video cameras at different locations, the audience could follow the pilots through the briefing and launch of A-10s on a mission to the gunnery range. Two screens would be devoted to the range and the crowd could watch the Warthogs in real time as they dropped bombs and strafed targets. On the last screen, they could watch the debrief in the squadron and see videotape that was recorded through the HUD from the mission they had just seen.

For an added touch of realism, the audience had to go outside and watch the Warthogs fly an overhead recovery pattern—the traditional landing pattern flown by fighters returning from combat. For the show's finale, Leonard was proposing that five A-10 pilots fly an aerial demonstration like the famed Thunderbirds or Blue Angels. He was calling it "The Flight of the Thunderhogs."

"This is fantastic," Waters told him. "I hope Colonel Pontowski buys it." Leonard smiled, nodded, and concentrated on driving. Waters sank back into the seat and closed her eyes, feeling warm and safe.

Major Frank Hester was waiting outside the deputy for maintenance's office building when Pontowski arrived. He snapped a salute. "Ripper said to meet you here. She didn't say what about." There was a hard undertone in his voice.

"Have you read STAND DOWN?" Pontowski asked. A sharp nod in return. "We need to find out how maintenance can support the air show." Hester was silent as they walked into the deputy for maintenance's office.

The room was packed with every maintenance officer and NCO who could think of a reason for being there. The excitement was contagious as the wrench benders and gun plumbers told the two pilots what they wanted to do for the air show. Corrosion control, the section responsible for painting the jets, wanted to paint every Warthog's nose with teeth and eyes like the famous nose art from the Flying Tigers.

"The regs," Hester blurted, "don't allow nose art."

"To hell with the regs," a gruff old NCO growled. But the idea died a quick death.

An excited junior captain promised them, "We're going to have LASTE peaked and tweaked on every jet. Every bomb you drop is going to be a shack. We're talking nasty LASTE time on the range."

Twenty minutes later, the two pilots were walking back to the squadron. "It looks like the wrench benders have bought into the air show," Pontowski said, pleased with Maintenance's response.

"Is all this necessary?" Hester groused. "The damn air show is still five months away. Hell, it doesn't make any sense. Why fly so damn many missions to the range on the last day of flying? When the last plane lands, that's it. The squadron is kaput, finished."

"What would you do, Frank?" Pontowski's voice was flat.

"Just fly the time line out." The time line was the number of flying hours the squadron was allocated to fly each calendar quarter.

"That's not in the cards," Pontowski told him. "We're going out in style with an open house and one hell of an air show. Maintenance will be ready. Will the pilots?"

Hester shrugged. "I'll tell 'em."

"I want more than that," Pontowski said, a trace of anger clipping his words.

"I can't perform miracles," Hester shot back.

Pontowski walked in silence for a few moments before he decided to take the gloves off. He started on a low key. "Until we stand down, I've got three simple objectives: motivate, motivate, motivate. The 303rd has been too damn good for too long to go tits up at the very end. I want the squadron to go out with flags flying and every swingin' jock alive and well.

"You've kept your end of the bargain so far and I appreciate what you've done. But damn it, Frank, you're digging your heels in on this one and not giving me other options. So right now, you've got three choices—lead, follow, or get out of the fuckin' way. Be in my office in an hour with your decision." Pontowski surprised the major by throwing him a salute and then turning and marching off. A very confused major waved a half, and very hesitant, salute at his commander's back.

Hester arrived fifteen minutes early for the meeting with Pontowski. Waters told him to have a seat and she would get him inside as quickly as possible. "There's no hurry," Hester told her. "Ah . . . Ripper . . ." He hesitated, searching for the right words. "You're behind him all the way, aren't you?"

"He's my boss."

"Is that the only reason?"

"No," she answered. "It's because he cares and lets nothing get in the way of real accomplishment. He's going to make a difference here."

"With only five months to go? What can he do in that short time?"

"You haven't been listening, Major. He means it when he says he wants everyone alive and well when we turn out the lights. But he wants something else." She took a deep breath, knowing that what she was going to say sounded trite and corny. "There will be no doubt in anyone's mind that the United States Air Force just lost its best fighter squadron."

Hester nodded, his decision made. The intercom on Waters' desk buzzed. "You can go in now," she told him. Three minutes later, Hester walked out, his face unreadable. Pontowski followed him into the outer office and watched him disappear.

"Surprise, surprise," he told her. "He says if I'll keep him, he'll give it his best shot."

Waters recalled her own feelings when she had made the same decision. "You can believe him," she said.

Pontowski shook his head and smiled. He had three allies.

# Tuesday, March 5
# Cheung Chau Island, Territory of Hong Kong

The faint gold of the rising sun outlined the gray mass of Lamma Island five miles to the east as Kamigami sat alone on a rock keeping his early morning vigil. The cloud-laced sky slowly streaked with red and gray and then rushed into brighter hues of red as the sun lifted above the horizon. But Kamigami was oblivious to the panorama playing out above him and kept scanning the sea for the fishing boat that would bring Jin Chu back to him.

The ache of worry grew heavier in his chest. I should have gone out on the fishing boat, he berated himself, not her. Since food was scarce, she had insisted she had to help the islanders and nothing he could say or do changed her mind. But for the first time, his body had failed him and he was still weak from the infection that had ravaged his massive frame. The knife wound and the polluted waters of Victoria Harbor had almost killed him.

How clearly he remembered when his fever was consuming him and he had lost the will to fight. All else was lost in a vague fog but Jin Chu. She had stepped out of the mist, her nude body glowing in the half-light of early dawn, and had crawled into bed beside him. She had only held him, speaking in a language he did not understand, and stayed with him until his fever had broken. After he had slept for over twenty hours, she had returned and gently bathed him with a sponge. Then she dropped her clothes onto the floor and slipped into bed beside him. She sat astride him as they made love and he knew from her pain that she was a virgin.

"They will return," a voice said. Kamigami turned, surprised to see Zhang Pai standing behind him. He shot to his feet and motioned to the place on the rock where he had been sitting. Like everyone on the island, Kamigami deferred to the old man they called "the Master." And like Jin Chu, the old man sensed what Kamigami was thinking.

"She is *ho wan*"—good luck—"and the fishermen trust her. The catch will be good because she is with them. Perhaps," Zhang Pai continued, "you can help us in a different way. There are reports of gangs raiding the islands for food. Soon they will come here to take ours." Kamigami nodded. He had heard the radio and TV reports detailing the violence that followed in the wake of the embargo the PRC, the People's Republic of China, had clamped on Hong Kong.

The United Nations and the western powers had used diplomatic protests to make the PRC back off enough to avoid a military clash and force a stalemate. The colony was still embargoed but, thanks to the fishing boats, not enough to starve it into immediate submission. Trade was still going on between the colony and the Shenzhen Special Economic Zone on the mainland next to Hong Kong. In exchange for the wealth of Hong Kong, the Chinese kept supplying water, electricity, and some food to the colony. But it was a one-way exchange that would soon bleed the Hong Kongers dry. Until that happened, the gangs were going to take what they could.

"I can help," Kamigami said. Zhang Pai led Kamigami down the hill and into the town.

A cold north wind started to blow after midnight and the two boys shivered as they sat on Cheung Chau's extreme northern headland. "There," one of the boys said, pointing into the night. Seven low shapes in the water, high-speed motorboats, were moving toward them. Five of the boats stopped while two continued at a slow rate toward the harbor. "Run," the older boy told the youngest. The boy ran at breakneck speed down the path that led to the harbor. Kamigami's early warning net was working.

When the boy arrived breathless at the police station Kamigami had appropriated as a headquarters, Kamigami listened, sent him right back and initiated a silent alert.

Within minutes, every able-bodied man in the town and on the harbor was roused with the news that a raid was in the offing. "The two boats," Kamigami explained to Zhang Pai and his lieutenants, "are a diversionary attack. We'll separate them at the breakwater entrance." The men nodded in understanding and another runner was dispatched, this time to the men stringing out along the man-made breakwater that formed the harbor. More reports came in.

"This is too easy," one of Kamigami's lieutenants chortled.

"Wait," Kamigami told him. For once, he was glad that Jin Chu was out on a fishing boat.

The men on the breakwater crouched unseen on the landward side and waited for the two boats that were now accelerating for a high-speed dash into the harbor. The stern of the first boat had barely cleared the entrance when the men raised a heavy anchor chain that had been salvaged from an old freighter. The second boat never saw the chain and plowed into it going forty miles an hour. The force of the impact ripped a gaping hole in the bow and pitch-poled the boat up and over onto its back, spilling the raiders into the water. The first boat came about to rescue the men as three Molotov cocktails were hurled from nearby sampans. Only one of the flaming bottles of gasoline hit the boat and ignited. But it was enough to force the raiders on that boat into the water.

A shout from the breakwater rang out and the harbor turned into a dark boiling caldron as a swarm of sampans converged on the entrance. Lanterns were lit to aid in the search and shadowy figures leaned over the sides of the sampans, swatting the water with oars and clubs. It was over before the burning hulk of the first boat sank.

The sampans scurried for shore and shouts of triumph reached the police station where Kamigami was waiting long before the first boat bumped against the dock. He cautioned the men clustered around him to remain calm. "We still have much to do," he warned them. Shortly, two half-drowned and badly beaten men were dragged into the room. One of the guards handed over two walkie-talkie radios they had found on the prisoners. Kamigami tested them, surprised that one still worked. He thought for a moment. "What is the signal for the other boats to retreat?" Kamigami asked in passable Cantonese. Silence. "Do you understand my words?"

One of the men spat in defiance. Kamigami whirled and, with incredible speed, karate-chopped the man's Adam's apple. He watched the man gurgle and gasp as he choked to death. He turned to the second man, who was looking at him with wide, fear-struck eyes, not believing the apparition in front of him. Kamigami said, "Do you understand my words?" This time he received a nod.

Kamigami hooked his fingers under the man's jawbone and lifted him up until his feet were dangling above the floor. "You must make a choice," he said, his soft voice totally at odds with his actions and masklike face. "Tell us the signal for the boats to withdraw and live. Or you can spend the next three days dying. It will be a miserable, most painful death. You will curse your parents for giving you birth. You will wake up to your own screams. The women and children of the village will beg me to end it. When I slit your stomach and show you your own guts you will thank me and you will kiss my feet in gratitude as you bleed to death. Choose now." He dropped him to the floor.

Words spilled from the man. Kamigami nodded and handed him the radio. "You give the signal," he ordered. The man keyed the radio and spoke. When he was finished, Kamigami told the guards to put him in a cell. "Now we wait to see if he gave the correct signal."

"He didn't lie," Zhang Pai said. "I have never seen such fear in a man. Would you have done all that?"

Kamigami shook his head. "No. I wanted him to talk and didn't have much time to convince him."

"They will come back again," a man said. "They will be better prepared and stronger."

"And so will we," Kamigami replied. The same boy who had brought the original warning darted into the room with a new message: The five boats that had been standing offshore were leaving at high speed.

"We have gained some time," Kamigami told the crowded room. "Have divers salvage everything they can from the boats. Dive until you find every weapon the raiders were carrying. I'll show you how to make them serviceable." He smiled. "A little salt water never hurt bullets."

Zhang Pai spoke to the silent room. "Sun Tzu wrote that balking the enemy's plans is the highest form of generalship. We have such a general among us." He pulled himself to his feet and walked out the door.

The setting sun cast a warm glow on the island's busy waterfront as the sea turned to the color of dark red wine. Kamigami and Jin Chu found a bench at the edge of the water and sat down, the sun warming their backs. A pack of six-year-olds scurried past, jabbering and smiling at them. A sampan bumped against the dock with its load of Blue Girl Beer for the Park 'n Shop store across from them as people went about their business.

"It's so peaceful," he said, looking up and down the shops that lined the other side of the street. "Two days ago they were fighting for their lives. Now, you would think everything was normal."

"Life doesn't change," Jin Chu replied. "They are safe for now and that is enough."

"Is this what you want?" he asked.

Her answer was soft. "I want what they want. A place where my children can live without hunger or fear."

"That's an easy one," he laughed. "We leave for the States tomorrow." He felt her head move in a gentle shake. No.

"Please, you must listen." He could feel her trembling. "You are my love." She hesitated, afraid to say the next words. "But our love can only live here."

Kamigami stiffened at her words. Her tone of voice and the way she stared straight ahead warned him she was seeing beyond their immediate time and place. His western education, training, and experience rebelled at the idea, yet something deep in his Oriental background responded to the girl and would not be denied. The words of his long-dead grandfather came back. "The truth is what you believe." But did he believe her?

"What can I do?" he asked her. "I'm not Chinese."

She did not answer at first. "Look how they trust you. What you have done for the islanders, you can do for Zou Rong."

"I'm not so sure," he answered. "Defending the island against a gang was easy. They were only vicious. The PLA is a standing army." Jin Chu said nothing and waited. "You want me to help Zou?" he asked.

"Only you can decide," she answered.

"If I do, will you stay with me?"

Jin Chu turned toward him, not touching. Public displays of affection in China rarely went beyond standing close together. Her eyes were full of tears. "You are my love," she whispered.

They fell silent as Kamigami made his decision. "Well,"

he finally said, "Zou did ask me to relay a message to the president. I think I had better write a letter. But I'm not very good at putting words on paper."

"There is an old English woman who lives here," Jin Chu told him. "Years ago she taught the children English. She will help you." Kamigami remembered the bent old woman with the floppy straw hat he had seen in the marketplace. She had struck him as a true English eccentric. Jin Chu stood. "Come," she said, beaming at him. "We will find the English woman together."

Kamigami walked beside Jin Chu into the small town, willing to risk the depths of hell to be with her.

**Tuesday, March 26**
**The Executive Office Building, Washington, D.C.**

Mazie sat in her office oblivious to the commotion in the hall. Her intercom buzzed like an angry hornet demanding her attention. She ignored it. Nothing could penetrate her preoccupation with the letter tucked away in a pocket. Like every article of clothing she owned, her suit coat possessed large pockets that served as part of her filing system. The bulging pockets made her look even shorter and dumpier, but she didn't care.

"Why now, Dad?" she mumbled to herself, recalling every word of the typed letter.

Dear Mazie,
    Please forgive your old dad for not writing sooner but until two months ago, I was a prisoner in Hanoi. This is the first chance I've had to write. I am well and in Hong Kong. By the time you get this letter I will be back in China helping some friends of mine. That is the reason I'm writing to you.
    I was freed from prison in Hanoi by Zou Rong. You probably know who he is. I have decided to help him fight for his people's freedom and he has asked me to send a message to our president. Will you please do it for me? Zou wants the president to know that the old cycle of protest and repression has started again in the

land of the Pearl River. He says, "We are spilling our blood to escape our history of helplessness and I want to give my people their voices." He says the president will understand.

I have been traveling along the Pearl River and around Canton. He has the support of many people and has created an army. I will understand if you decide not to do it. I promise to write more often.

Your loving father

It was the longest letter she had ever received from her father.

Hazelton appeared at her door. "You had best move it, my dear," he said. "All hell is breaking loose and the old man is calling for your body."

Mazie forced herself to focus. "Tell Mr. Finlay I'll be right there."

Hazelton frowned. "Mr. Finlay is clearing his desk as we speak." He wanted to laugh at Mazie's confused look. "Where have you been this morning? Carroll fired Finny right after they came back from meeting with the president. Come on, snap out of it. Carroll wants to see you now."

"I hadn't heard," Mazie stammered.

Hazelton was more than willing to relay the latest hot item sweeping through the NSC. "The president had asked for options in the Far East when Finny suffered a massive attack of terminal bad judgment. He interrupted Carroll and said that some character named Zou Rong who is causing problems there isn't even worth a statement to the press.

"There's more," Hazelton continued. "Islamic fundamentalists have taken over Saudi Arabia. The Saud royal family is out and Mr. Carroll is predicting trouble, big trouble, if they can consolidate their political base. He mentioned an oil embargo, nationalization of foreign assets, renewed support of terrorists, and a huge increase of financial aid to the Palestinians. But we've got some time before that happens. So Carroll wants to stabilize the situation in China now, before all that happens. We can't handle two MRCs at one time."

Mazie caught her breath. A single MRC meant big trouble. Two MRCs meant political disaster. "Does Mr. Carroll have something in mind?" she asked. They entered the tunnel that led to the White House from the Executive Office Building and she had to hurry to keep up with Hazelton's quick pace.

"He's creating a China Action Team. Obviously, it will fall to the Far East Division." He glanced down at her. The confused look on her face surprised him. "Are you okay?" he asked. "You seem very distracted."

"Earlier today . . . Carroll asked me to head the China Action Team. I accepted. But . . . I . . . I . . ." Mazie hesitated, and for reasons she did not understand, confided in him. "I received a letter from my father." She fished the letter out of a pocket and let him read it.

Hazelton nodded, understanding. "We best hurry."

Carroll was pacing the floor of his office talking to an Air Force major general when they were shown in. The two very bright, very new stars on the general's epaulets announced his recent promotion. "General Von Drexler, I believe you know Went." The general nodded. "I'd like you to meet Mazie Kamigami," Carroll said. "She's the chief of my China Action Team, CAT for short."

Mazie was struck by the general's good looks. He could be a movie star, she thought, or in a recruiting video. I hope he's just not another pretty face. Von Drexler stood up and shook her hand, his blue eyes and wide smile captivating her.

"Mazie," Carroll said, waving her and Hazelton to seats, "what's the latest on the situation in southern China?"

She snapped out of the mental fog that had been swirling around her. "The rebels are gaining momentum in Guangxi Province and have taken over Nanning, the provincial capital. Zou Rong is very clever and has created a government and army of sorts by simply taking over what's already there. He kicks out the old leaders and replaces them with his followers." She considered showing Carroll her father's letter but decided against it. "Fighting has been reported around Canton but it appears that Kang Xun is in firm control of the city and Guangdong Province.

"It's mostly quiet in Hong Kong," she continued, "with sporadic outbreaks of gang violence. The embargo has stopped the movement of people and goods but not the electronic transfer of money. The Hong Kongers have managed to secure most of their liquid assets in foreign banks. But the PRC is forcing Hong Kong to buy water, food, and electricity from the mainland to survive."

"So," Von Drexler said, "in the long run, the PRC will get its hands on those assets anyway."

"No, sir," Mazie said. "The Chinese don't work that way. The people who control that wealth will find a way to get out of Hong Kong with their money intact. Sooner or later, Hong Kong will run out of money and goods to sell for food and water. Then food riots and violence will break out. The PRC will use that as an excuse to move in and restore peace and order. That way, they take Hong Kong over on their own terms and can disregard any prior agreements with the British."

"The president," Carroll said, "and key members of Congress want to avoid an MRC in the Far East and at the same time reestablish the status quo on Hong Kong. The betting is that the PRC will back off with a show of resolve. So we are going to up the ante in this poker game by relieving Hong Kong. The president envisions an operation along the lines of the Berlin Airlift, the main difference being that it will be civilian.

"If they don't get the message, the president wants to hit them with a series of quick responses. He has told the State Department to approach every major power and arrange for worldwide diplomatic recognition of the rebels as a legitimate government. The boys and girls at Foggy Bottom are working on it.

"If that doesn't convince the PRC to become more reasonable, we will recognize the rebels as the legitimate government and support them with enough aid to seriously challenge the PRC's control of all of southern China. General Von Drexler has been ordered to set up a MAAG mission, a Military Assistance Advisory Group, to funnel military aid to Zou's fledgling government.

"But Zou will need more than material and advisors to survive. The president is considering sending an American Volunteer Group to form the core of an air force."

"A new American Volunteer Group," Mazie mused. "An AVG just like Claire Chennault's Flying Tigers."

"Actually," Von Drexler explained, "it will be much different because the American Volunteer Group will remain under my control as the commander of the MAAG mission. In effect, I will wear two hats, one as the commander of the MAAG and one as commander of the American Volunteer Group. That will put me in a position to implement our policy in southern China."

He sounds like General Douglas MacArthur, Mazie thought. She dismissed the idea. The world had changed since World War II.

Carroll studied his two young staffers before he dropped his bombshell. "The president wants the logistical support behind the rebels to be international. The congressional oversight committees have bought into it. We will handle the political end, make the initial contact with the appropriate governments, open the right doors, that type of thing, while the China Action Team"—he pointed at both Mazie and Hazelton—"works out the logistical and financial details. You've got to twist the arms of our erstwhile Asian allies for covert support. Make them understand they've got more to lose than we do from an aggressive and expansionist China."

The look on Hazelton's face made Mazie smile. "But, sir," he protested. "My area is the Middle East and if—"

"You'll like working for Mazie," Carroll said, cutting off any further discussion.


## Tuesday, March 26
## Whiteman AFB, Missouri

Two quick knocks at the open door of Matt Pontowski's office caught his attention and he looked up from the pile of paperwork that greeted him every morning. His executive officer, Sara Waters, was standing there, trying to look cool and composed. He had sensed something was bothering her for days and wasn't surprised to see her. Sooner or later, he reasoned, she will want to talk about the brutal attempted rape that had shattered her peaceful existence. He motioned for her to enter. She closed the door and sat down.

"I take it," he said, "that the closed door means this is personal and has nothing to do with the air show."

She took a deep breath and he knew the time for talking had come. "Yes, sir, it does." All of the doubts she had about him were gone except one. Now it was time to settle that last, nagging issue. Trusting him, she took another deep breath and plunged ahead. "Something has been bothering me for a long time, sir. You knew Jack Locke . . ." Her voice trailed off when she saw the look on his face. She had struck a deep hurt.

"Jack Locke is a very painful memory," Pontowski said. It was the one subject he hadn't expected.

She felt her face redden. "I'm sorry, sir. It's just that my husband and Jack were very important in my life. I apologize. I was out of line." She rose to leave.

"No, it's okay," he reassured her. "Please sit down. I've heard the stories about Jack and Muddy." She nodded, now sorry she had broached the subject. "I've been living with the rumors about the midair collision where Locke was killed for a long time." He reached into a desk drawer and pulled out the old accident report. It was dog-eared and worn from use. "Read." He threw the report across his desk. "Make up your own mind."

Waters picked up the report and left. Outside, she leaned against the wall, holding the report to her chest. Her own memories were back, demanding a price. Why am I torturing myself with the past? she thought. She sat down and read the accident report.

It took Waters over two hours to wade through the report and she had to reread a few parts three or four times to fully understand what had happened. But the findings were clear and laid the blame squarely on pilot error when the pilot flying in the backseat of Locke's aircraft had taken unauthorized control of the aircraft and crashed into the aircraft flown by one Lieutenant Matthew Pontowski. She carefully closed the report and stared at it. A demon had been spiked in the heart and laid to rest.

The report was lying on her desk that afternoon when Frank Hester walked in with Skeeter Ashton in tow. "Can we see the Bossman?" he asked. "Skeeter here has come up with a great idea." Waters hit the intercom as Pontowski walked out of his office.

"Come on in," he said.

"Colonel," Hester said, "Skeeter has got an idea for painting the noses of the Warthogs."

Pontowski couldn't help himself. "This from the man who told Maintenance that nose art was against all regulations?"

Hester blushed. "Well, I've been thinking about it and told Skeeter, since she's studying graphic design and, well, I thought you should see what she's come up with."

"What have you got, Lieutenant?" Pontowski asked.

"It's in a hangar, sir, if you'd care to see it."

"Why do I get a funny feeling about this?" Pontowski replied. He pulled his hat out of the leg pocket of his flying suit and headed for the door. "Ripper, you want to join us?" Waters grabbed her hat and followed them out.

Two grinning NCOs from corrosion control were waiting for them outside the hangar. One hit the door switch and the massive doors started to roll back, warning bells clanging. A large group of officers and pilots were inside, all clustered around a single A-10 sitting in the middle of the hangar. Pontowski hesitated, not sure what he was seeing.

The A-10 is a big jet and only in a hangar does its size become apparent. The Warthog stands almost fifteen feet tall and it is a scramble to climb the boarding ladder into the cockpit. But no one was sitting in the cockpit. The crowd parted and made a path to the Warthog. Then he saw it. "Well, I'll be . . ." he muttered. He walked up to the nose and stroked it. Skeeter Ashton had given this Warthog a face.

On the nose of the gray Warthog, Skeeter and the NCOs from corrosion control had painted a vicious set of snarling teeth complete with tusks pointing upward toward mean-looking eyes. Instead of the traditional red, black, and white of the famed Flying Tigers, these teeth and eyes were yellow against a black background, befitting the beast the jet was named after. The round, seven-barreled muzzle of the GAU-8, thirty-millimeter "Avenger" cannon formed a pig's snout with the eyes and teeth.

"Perfect," Pontowski muttered, "absolutely perfect. A thing of beauty." He looked around at the sea of beaming faces. A hand motioned toward the cockpit. Underneath the canopy rail was stenciled "LtCol M. Pontowski." Directly below his name was painted the single word "Bossman."

"I hope we can get away with this," he said to no one in particular.

"Who's going to tell us no?" Hester deadpanned.

Shoshana recognized the symptoms the moment Pontowski came home. She had lived through it all before. He had to make a decision and would be gruff and cranky until his stubborn disposition accepted what his common sense demanded. Even Little Matt sensed the tension building in his father and played in his room after dinner. An unusual quiet descended over the house after Shoshana put him to bed and Pontowski settled into his favorite chair to read. But it was all a sham and he threw the book on the floor.

Finally, she decided to force the issue and took a shower while he channel-surfed through cable TV. She padded out of the bathroom, her nude body still glowing from the shower, and dropped a bottle of baby oil in his lap. He looked at her in surprise when she knelt in front of him and pulled his shirt off. Her fingers unbuckled his belt. "What's got into you?" he asked.

"Nothing yet," Shoshana answered. She went to work, determined to break his mental stalemate.

Shoshana was straddling him, gasping for air, when his body went limp. She collapsed against his chest until her breathing had slowed. Then she sat up, made a fist, and hit him on the shoulder. "You are a sexual pervert," she announced.

"Me!" Pontowski protested. "Who started this?"

Shoshana cuddled against him and waited. Nothing. "Talk," she finally said, tired of waiting.

"The squadron is too damn good," he told her. "They shouldn't be getting the ax."

"I imagine a lot of squadron commanders feel the same way," she said.

"Yeah, I know. But you don't go throwing quality away."

"And you want to save them," she said. He nodded a yes. "There is a way, you know. But you won't like it." They had come to the heart of the problem.

He shot her a look. "Political influence? Pull strings? I can't do that."

"You can be as stubborn as a camel," she said. Her Middle Eastern heritage was showing. "Sometimes I think you confuse being stubborn with being righteous." She wiggled around and sat in his lap. "Political influence comes with your name and you can't change that. Pulling strings, as you call it, has gone on ever since mankind crawled out from under a rock and started living together. Political influence can be either good or bad. It depends on how you use it. There are times when you must do things because they are right, no matter what the cost."

A gentle smile spread across Pontowski's face. "How come you can be so smart?"

"How come your grandfather didn't explain it to you?" she retorted.

"He probably did. I just wasn't listening at the time."

"Come to bed," she said. "My feet are cold and I need your warm body." He followed her to bed, dreading the next few minutes.

The next morning, Pontowski had Sara Waters cut a set of travel orders. He turned the squadron over to Frank Hester and caught the next scheduled flight out of Kansas City for Washington, D.C. Waters suffered no doubts or second thoughts about pulling strings. She picked up the phone and dialed an old friend, Bill Carroll.

# CHAPTER 6

Monday, April 1
Washington, D.C.

"Both sides of Asia are coming unhinged," National Security Advisor Carroll said, pacing the length of his office in the White House. He paused long enough to look at his staff. All except Mazie Kamigami were poised with pens hovering over notebooks. Mazie didn't need to take notes. Her memory was better than a tape recorder and she registered subtleties and nuances beyond the range of electronic devices.

"In the Middle East, the Islamic fundamentalists are purchasing nuclear weapons and making ugly noises. Meanwhile, China has not got the message. The Hong Kong airlift is not making a difference and if anything, the PRC has increased the pressure on the British in Hong Kong. We also have reports of heavy fighting in southern China.

"The president," Carroll continued, "has issued marching orders. The Middle East must and will remain our number-one priority. We are focusing our effort in that area. The memory of the Persian Gulf War should still be strong enough that a military buildup will douse the hotheads over there with a soaking of cold reality.

"That brings us to China. The president intends to extend diplomatic recognition to the rebels under Zou Rong in the next few days. Great Britain, France, and Germany will do the same."

Mazie noted that not a single Asian country was willing to recognize the rebels. Thanks to Carroll, she thought, the president is on top of the situation and might be able to keep the events in China from spiraling out of control. There was no doubt in her mind that the administration saw the developments in China as a major regional conflict.

"Unfortunately," Carroll said, "because of the so-called 'peace dividend,' our responses are severely limited." Carroll paused to let the last statement register with everyone in the room. "So for now, we are going to increase the Hong Kong airlift. We've offered the British a squadron of F-15s to back them up in case the PLA tries to shoot down a few planes.

"The British accepted because it makes the airlift more of an international effort without getting the UN involved. Also, it commits us to more support in the future. It's just like the Brits to get us to help save their bacon—the devious bastards." Carroll spent the next ten minutes detailing specific responsibilities to his staff. When the meeting broke up he called Mazie aside. "How's Hazelton working out?"

"So far, he's doing great," she answered. "In fact, he's at the Pentagon with General Von Drexler making sure we are all playing from the same sheet of music."

Wentworth Hazelton was impressed by the efficiency of the organization boiling around him in the basement of the Pentagon. His view of the military as a collection of stumbling and pompous officers fed by overbearing egos was taking a severe beating. What he was seeing indicated that Von Drexler was an organizational genius.

Within hours after being given the hammers necessary to make it happen, Von Drexler had appropriated the command rooms of the deactivated Watch Center, another casualty of peace, and created his own mini National Military Command Center. By raiding various offices in the Pentagon for experts, he had created the staff he needed.

"Please, be seated," Von Drexler said as Hazelton entered his office. "Your name came up in a conversation last night," he continued. "Some people whose opinions count had some very good things to say about you. I'm glad you

113

came alone because I need your advice on some, shall we say, rather delicate matters."

Hazelton felt his face blush at the unexpected compliment, but he felt himself drawn to the man, wanting to talk. "I hope I can help," he said.

"Well," the general smiled, "you've got to understand where I'm coming from. I'm an old war horse used to doing things the old way." He held up a hand, stopping Hazelton from replying. "I know I've got to change. That's why we need to talk. You see, I've never had to interface at the command level with women and Miss Kamigami is my civilian counterpart." Again, the hand was up, keeping Hazelton from responding. "I was hoping you could give me some advice before I make a fool out of myself."

"Mazie," Hazelton said, "is arguably the brightest and most intelligent person on the NSC and is an expert on China. She is not a vain person and is very approachable. Treat her like you would the head of any major office and I don't think you can go wrong." A relieved look played across Von Drexler's face, encouraging Hazelton. "She's not a militant feminist with an ax to grind," he added. "In fact, she's very human."

"I suppose it's her lack of a military background that has me worried," Von Drexler said.

"She's an Army brat," Hazelton replied, "and knows a great deal about the military." He found the look on the general's face reassuring and related what he knew about Mazie and her father.

"Thanks," Von Drexler said, "for setting me straight. I appreciate it more than you know." Von Drexler became the professional, sharing confidences with an equal. "As you well know, resources and material are always the most critical issue." He gave the young man a knowing smile. "Civilians think strategy, military professionals think logistics. Perhaps it would be most productive if you met my director of resources so you can see how we are building up our logistical infrastructure." The general buzzed for his director of resources and turned Hazelton over to him.

The door had hardly closed behind Hazelton before he was on the phone to his secretary. "Get me the file on a Command Sergeant Victor Kamigami," he ordered. "He's

listed as an MIA, but I think I may have located a deserter."
He smiled as he hung up the receiver.

The colonel escorting Hazelton was short, slender, and with just the beginnings of a potbelly. He spoke with a hoarse gravelly voice and the confidence born of long experience in logistics. "We've got serious problems," the colonel explained. "The force structure of the AVG hasn't been identified."

"When you say force structure," Hazelton asked, "what are you talking about?"

"The number and type of aircraft. We also need to know the type of ordnance, sortie rates, expected duration of employment, the total personnel package, anything that has to do with dropping bombs on the bad guys." The colonel gave a sharp snort of contempt. "We can't do squat all until that's decided."

"What type of aircraft does the AVG need?" Hazelton asked. It seemed like a logical question to him.

"Von Drexler wants cosmic jets, preferably F-16s and the Stealth, backed up by B-1s. Talk about sending elephants after pissants." The little colonel decided he could trust Hazelton. "The operations plans section is trying to identify the number and type of aircraft for the AVG right now. You need to talk to them." He led the young man into a back office.

The colonel in charge of operations plans was the intellectual counterpart of the director of resources, but he was even more opinionated. "Von Drexler is thicker than a fence post," the colonel said. "I've spent hours talking to intelligence and they say the China theater is a low-threat environment and will stay that way."

"So what does that mean?" Hazelton asked.

"Tell me the threat and I'll tell you the weapons system," the operations plans colonel growled. "It means Warthogs."

"It also means Von Drexler won't buy it," the colonel from logistics said. "Not glamorous enough, too low-keyed, not enough prestige."

Hazelton's first impression that Von Drexler was an organizational genius was falling apart. He had the firm impression that the ego of one General Mark Von Drexler was the driving force behind the MAAG.

He beat a hasty retreat back to the safe, understandable sanity of the NSC. His secretary had a message for him to go directly to Mr. Carroll's office in the White House, where Mazie was waiting for him. "What am I?" he groused to himself. "A Ping-Pong ball?" He felt better when he was ushered into Carroll's office without delay.

Inside, he immediately recognized Matt Pontowski, who was sitting next to Mazie. The other officer, a thin, slightly hunch-shouldered colonel, was unknown. "Went," Bill Carroll said, "I'd like you to meet Colonel Charles Tucker, the new commander of the 552nd Air Control Wing, and Lieutenant Colonel Matt Pontowski, the commander of the 303rd Fighter Squadron." The men shook hands.

"These two gentlemen have magically appeared out of the woodwork," Carroll continued, "claiming that we can't give a war without them. Actually, I contacted Matt here when I heard he was in town beating the bushes trying to save his squadron from the boneyard. He recommended Colonel Tucker be brought in."

"This is pure bullshit," Tucker growled. "Whatever you do in China, you need a warning and command system, which means the AWACS. But no way am I gonna let my crews and aircraft be made part of some volunteer group. That sucks."

Pontowski smiled. The colonel hadn't slowed down since he was made commander of the 552nd and was still living up to his reputation as Tucker the Fucker. "Don't pay any attention to the colonel's bark," Pontowski said. "His bite is much worse."

"As part of the deal for recognizing the rebels," the national security advisor explained, "we cut a deal with the British and deployed a squadron of F-15s to Hong Kong in case the PLA gets trigger happy and tries to shoot down a few cargo aircraft. The Forty-fourth Fighter Squadron out of Kadena is already in place."

Tucker interrupted him. "The British can handle their own air defense. Why do they need our help?"

"Because it gives us an excuse to send in an AWACS," Carroll said. Mazie caught the exchanged glances between Carroll and Tucker. Neither would continue the discussion with her, Pontowski, and Hazelton still in the room. They didn't have the security clearances and certainly had no "need to know" about the real capability of the AWACS. The pulse Doppler radar on the E-3 Sentry could reach out over the horizon more than 250 miles and track all aircraft movement deep inside China.

Tucker gave a sharp nod. He didn't need things explained to him. With an AWACS on station, they could monitor anything the Chinese put in the air and provide a vital intelligence and command function.

"You can deploy to Hong Kong as an Air Force unit chopped to British operational control," Carroll said. "I still want everyone to be a volunteer. Can you make that happen?"

"In a heartbeat," Tucker answered. "How many aircraft and crews you want?"

"Start with one aircraft and two crews," Carroll said. "I'll grease the skids with the Pentagon." He made a note before turning to Hazelton. "Went, what's happening over at the AVG?" Hazelton recounted what he had observed. "Sounds like someone has to make a decision for Von Drexler," Carroll said. "He may not like it, but the AVG's getting A-10s." He made another note.

"Matt, it gets more difficult with the A-10s since I want to deploy a full-up tactical wing into mainland China. We can always cobble a wing together, but I would rather use as much of an existing unit as possible. That way, we avoid teething problems and can hit the ground running, ready to fly and fight."

Pontowski played with the idea for a moment. "I see, you want a wing of Warthogs to magically appear out of the shadows."

Carroll nodded. "Right. If you will, a dark wing." He ran the concept of a dark wing through his set of mental filters, liking the idea. "Everyone will have to resign from the Air Force, in your case, the Reserves, and sign on as a volunteer with the AVG."

"Does that classify them as mercenaries?" Pontowski asked. Suddenly, the AVG with its dark wing didn't look like such a good deal.

"On the face of it, yes," Carroll answered. "But everyone will be enrolled on the directed assignment roster."

"The directed assignment roster," Mazie explained, "or DASR, is used for covert operations. Special units like Delta Force are carried on it for political reasons. You are still in the Air Force, paid by the Air Force, and your dependents receive full benefits if you are a casualty."

"But if something goes wrong," Tucker added, "your government will deny you exist and hang you out to dry. Count on it."

"There is a downside to it," Carroll conceded.

Mazie responded to the tone and emphasis of the men's words. They were rapidly losing interest in the project. She pulled her father's letter out of her pocket. "They have to understand what they are volunteering for," she explained.

In a few short sentences, Mazie summarized the famine in China, how the PLA general Kang Xun was consolidating power as a new and vicious warlord south of the Yangtze River, and how he was opposed by Zou Rong's rebels. "I got a letter from my father," she said, reading it to them. Silence ruled the room when she had finished.

"'The old cycle of protest and repression has started again,'" Carroll repeated, moved by the words he had just heard. "'We are spilling our blood to escape our history of helplessness . . . I want to give my people their voices.' I want to show your father's letter to the president." Mazie handed him the letter.

Pontowski stared at his hands. "I can't think of a better reason to volunteer."

"Can you get enough volunteers from your squadron to form the core of a wing?" Carroll asked.

Pontowski thought for a moment. "I can try. Let me test the waters and I'll let you know. How long do I have?"

"No firm time frame," Carroll answered. "But make it quick. The situation is very fluid in China and the president is holding off on the decision to deploy the AVG. But we've got to be ready."

**Tuesday, April 2**
**Tinker AFB, Oklahoma**

The gray E-3 Sentry taxied slowly into the chocks at Tinker Air Force Base. A low ceiling of dark clouds spit huge drops of rain, promising a deluge as a crew chief marshaled the highly modified Boeing 707 into position. The thirty-foot diameter radar dome was still rotating at 6 rpm on top of the two struts that held it eleven feet above the fuselage. The crew chief crossed his two wands above his head to signal a stop and made a slashing motion across his neck to cut engines. He looked at the nose gear and frowned: two feet right of the yellow-painted block the tires should be standing on. This pilot can't taxi worth shit, he thought.

The ground crew pushed boarding steps up to the forward entry door on the left side of the fuselage just aft of the flight deck as a crew bus pulled up to transport the crew to operations. The rain started to pelt down as sixteen officers and NCOs of the mission crew that manned the radar and communications systems on board the AWACS (airborne warning and command system) clambered down the steps and ran for the bus. The flight engineer and navigator from the flight crew were right behind them.

A huge captain appeared in the entry door and glanced over his shoulder. From a distance, he bore a startling resemblance to the movie star Arnold Schwarzenegger. Up close, the image changed—Captain Neil "Moose" Penko had a Cro-Magnon face with kind eyes. He hurried down the steps, getting soaked in the rain as he dashed for the bus.

"Hey, Moose!" one of the lieutenants called to Penko, "what's the holdup?" Moose Penko shrugged an answer. He felt the same frustration and fatigue after completing the thirteen-hour mission. "The major's talking to the pilots," he said.

"Oh, shitsky," another voice added, "what I wouldn't give to hear that."

"You're not combat ready," Penko said, "and Major Mom doesn't take prisoners." He had been on the receiving end of one of Major Marissa LaGrange's animal acts and recalled the incident only too clearly. It was on his second mission as a fully qualified weapons controller. He had been working the number-two radar console, directing two F-15s into a rendezvous with a KC-10 tanker for an in-flight refueling.

LaGrange was the MCC, mission crew commander, and was watching the radar scope over his shoulder when he turned the F-15s too early and rolled them out in front of the KC-10. He had blown the radar intercept big time. LaGrange had kicked him out of the seat and salvaged the busted rendezvous by directing the two F-15s into a tight stern conversion. It had been a virtuoso performance at the radar set. LaGrange's chewing out afterward had also been masterful. It was an experience he didn't want to repeat.

On board the AWACS, LaGrange was standing with the pilots on the flight deck. "Look, numb nuts," LaGrange barked, jabbing a sharp fingernail into the aircraft commander's chest, "when I'm sorting out a fuckup because I've got a crew full of clueless meatheads, you stay out of it. Copy?"

"Come on, Major," the pilot replied, backing away, "you were coming down way too hard."

"That's none of your business unless it has to do with flying safety. And then you call me up to the flight deck so we can discuss it in private. Got it?" LaGrange spun on her left foot and stomped down the boarding stairs, her blonde pony tail bobbing up and down. "Do it again," she called over her shoulder, "and I'll rip your balls off and feed 'em to you at happy hour."

"You'll have to sew them back on first," the pilot muttered, careful that she didn't hear him.

"Major Mom can really be a bitch," the copilot said.

The two pilots ran after her, knowing she would leave them behind to walk if they didn't board the bus right behind her. A fact of life in the air control wing at Tinker Air Force Base was that Major Mom was anything but motherly.

After debriefing the mission, LaGrange turned down an offer to join a few of the crew for a beer in the Officers' Club and headed for the condominium she called home. Once in her bedroom, she shrugged off her flight suit and kicked it into a corner. She glanced into a full-length mirror, carefully appraising her legs. Not bad, she thought, for a thirty-nine-year-old woman who stood barely five feet two inches tall. She pulled her T-shirt off, revealing the black lingerie she preferred to wear. It was one of her secret concessions to femininity and Galeries Lafayette of Paris counted her as a valuable customer. Her tummy was still flat and her breasts were firm and well-shaped. But she was getting hippy and her bottom was not as tight and bouncy as it once had been. I need to exercise more, she warned herself.

She walked into the bathroom and examined her face in the mirror. A face best described as cute with a pert nose stared back. "Girl, you're showing your age," she murmured. Worry lines etched the corners of her eyes and she had the beginnings of a double chin.

Before she could start the shower, the telephone rang. It was the squadron duty officer. "Sorry to disturb you, Major," she said. "But Tucker the Fucker is back on base and he wants to see you ASAP. He's in his office at wing headquarters." LaGrange gave an inward sigh and donned fresh lingerie, T-shirt, and flight suit. Be honest, she told herself, you're not enjoying this anymore.

Colonel Charles A. Tucker was clearly irritated by the thirty-five-minute delay before LaGrange reported to his office. He was a very impatient man. "Take a seat, Major," he growled as he returned her salute. "I've got to do something extremely stupid and ask for volunteers for a special mission. I need a detachment commander to run the show. You want it?"

"If I've got a choice, I would like to hear more details first," LaGrange answered. It wasn't the answer he wanted and the two exchanged glares. The colonel and the major had the same attitudes and approach to business but deep down, they also shared an intense dislike of each other.

Tucker slammed back in his chair and stood up. "Dammit, Major, whatever happened to standing tall, saluting, and saying 'yessir'?"

"The Air Force has changed. Besides, I'm a woman."

"Bullshit," he snapped. "If you're not a mission crew commander, you ain't shit around here."

"I never could figure out what that phrase means," LaGrange replied.

The colonel humphed and told her about the mission to Hong Kong to provide an airborne warning and control capability as well as monitor movement deep inside China. "You'll fall under the operational control of the British," he explained.

LaGrange's right eyebrow shot up. "The Air Force relinquishing operational control of an AWACS? That's unusual."

"Tell me," Tucker growled. "That's why I want a detachment commander with balls to run the show." And not do anything stupid, he mentally added.

"I can give you smarts, Colonel. But if it's balls you want, you had better get one of the weak dicks drinking beer over in the Officers' Club."

Again, Tucker humphed an answer. "Can you get enough volunteers to man two crews?"

"I can do that," she assured him.

"Anyone you specifically want?"

She thought for a moment. "Moose Penko."

"Penko?" Tucker replied. "You know he asked to be transferred off your crew."

"He doesn't like working for a female MCC," LaGrange told him. "He'll get over it."

"You got him," Tucker said. "I want two crews and one jet in place in thirty-six hours."

"I can do that," LaGrange repeated. She stood, threw him a salute and left. Tucker watched her go, his face an impassive mask. Now he had to sell his boss, the brigadier general who commanded the 28th Air Division, on his decision to give LaGrange the command of the deployment. Normally, a lieutenant colonel or even a colonel would have been designated the detachment commander. But there was no doubt in his mind that he had the right person for the assignment.

## Tuesday, April 2
## Whiteman AFB, Missouri

It was the first time Sara Waters had used the STU-III, the plug-in-anywhere secure telephone receiver that allowed top secret conversations over regular telephone lines. It was deceptively easy. Just dial or answer the phone normally, turn a key, and press a button. Matt Pontowski's voice came through with a tinny ring from the encryption but was easily recognizable. Her face paled as he talked and she jotted down notes. "I'll relay the message, sir, and have Major Hester call you as soon as he lands." Her hands shook as she replaced the receiver and deactivated the encryption circuit. Now she wished she had not called Bill Carroll.

She called for her assistant. "Lori, find Captain Leonard. It's important." Lori Williams heard the worry in her voice and misinterpreted it as panic. She rushed out of the office and returned with Leonard in tow. "The Bossman just called on the STU-III," Waters told the pilot. "He's asking for volunteers for a special mission." She read from her notes, filling in the details. "It's not firm, just a possibility," she hastened to add.

"Holy shit!" Leonard shouted. "He's got one volunteer. Me."

"Why?" she asked.

"A special mission means this could be a chance to drop real bombs on real targets. This is what Warthogs are all about. I'll get the word out." He almost ran out of the office.

Waters shook her head. "They're teenagers who grew old and never grew up." Lori agreed with her.

Waters was briskly efficient as she went about her duties during the next three days. The mother in Waters did not like the thought of combat and privately she was glad that most of the pilots had not responded with the same enthusiasm as Leonard. Only four, among them Skeeter Ashton, had signed up and the rest had held back, not willing to commit until it was more definite. Frank Hester had given a positive slant to the request because he was the operations officer, but even he had not volunteered. On the other hand, she had to agree with Leonard that it was an opportunity for the 303rd to shine.

Only in Maintenance had the response been overwhelming, and the wrench benders were standing in line to sign up. Lori said the crew chiefs were claiming, "If I don't go, I'll fuckin' A quit."

Waters was surprised when Pontowski appeared Saturday

morning, escorting a little woman of Oriental descent. "Sara," Pontowski said, "I'd like you to meet Mazie Kamigami." The two women exchanged greetings. "I hear only four pilots have signed on." Waters handed him the short list. He read it and passed it to Mazie. "Not good. I was hoping for a better response. I want the pilots to hear what Mazie has to say."

"Well, sir, this is a UTA weekend and all but two are in the squadron. I can fit a commander's call in at nine-thirty." Pontowski told her to do it.

"UTA?" Mazie asked.

"Unit training assembly," Waters explained. "We have one every month." Mazie nodded and asked a few questions about the reserves. Waters found herself drawn to the younger woman and instinctively trusted her. "We've got a few minutes before commander's call, would you like to see the squadron?"

"Is it true you've got wall-to-wall Tom Cruise types?" Mazie asked.

"Not hardly," Waters answered, taking her on a short tour. Mazie was struck by how ordinary the pilots appeared. "Most of them are airline pilots," Waters explained.

"They're not what I expected," Mazie confided. "Colonel Pontowski gave them quite a buildup. What happened to the straight teeth and crooked grins?"

"Right now they seem like normal and rational human beings," Waters said. "But something happens when they get within fifty feet of a Warthog. I can't explain it, but they change." Mazie filed that away and looked at the pilots from a new perspective. She followed Waters into the main briefing room, thinking of what she should say.

When Pontowski introduced her, she walked to the podium and stood beside it so the men could see her. She noticed the one woman pilot, Skeeter Ashton, sitting in the back row with three other pilots. They were the only volunteers. Mazie pointed to the Pearl River on the large map of China that was projected on the screen behind her.

"You've all heard what's going on in China," she began, "and that Colonel Pontowski is seeking volunteers for a possible rerun of the Flying Tigers. I suppose I could give you all the propaganda about the good guys versus the bad guys, but I don't think it would mean much. Basically it's a nasty little war along the Pearl River. You could call it a civil war, which it is. Common wisdom holds that it is very foolish for third parties to take sides in a civil war, and generally speaking, that's a true statement.

"Rather than tell you what's happening, I'm going to show you slides that were taken before, during, and after a recent battle that took place here." She pointed to the town of Wuzhou on the Pearl River, 125 miles to the west of Canton, just inside Guangxi Province. "We estimate the PLA outnumbered the rebels ten to one, yet the fighting lasted a week."

A slide of smiling young men and women holding small arms flashed on the screen. "The rebels are mostly farmers armed only with light weapons," Mazie explained. "A French photographer was with them at Wuzhou and took most of these pictures." Mazie hit the remote advance button and a series of slides marched across the screen, documenting a hard-fought battle. She said nothing. Too often, the scenes depicted a young man or woman charging a tank or machine gun nest with a flaming Molotov cocktail.

"The last pictures are courtesy of the PLA," she said. "They speak for themselves." The quality of the slides changed: These were grainy and poorly processed. They chronicled the victory of the government forces in the final stages of the battle. Slide after slide showed PLA soldiers burning, looting, and rounding up civilians. The last set of slides showed hundreds of captured rebels digging a huge ditch and then being lined up on the edge and machine-gunned. The ditch was full of bodies.

The last slide showed an obviously pregnant woman lying on the ground, on her back. A soldier was standing over her as he drove a bayonet into her stomach. The woman's face was contorted in pain as her legs curled up. Her hands clutched at the bayonet in a vain attempt to protect her unborn child as the soldier leaned on the butt of his rifle. The screen went blank.

"I only have one question," Mazie said. "What was missing from all these pictures?"

Skeeter Ashton didn't hesitate. Her words were low and carried to every corner of the hushed room. "Air power," she said.

Frank Hester stood up and walked out of the room. "What's the matter, Frank?" a voice called.

Hester stopped, his back a rigid spike. "The next time you see a dog and pony show like this one, there's gonna be a Warthog in it. Mine." He walked out of the room. Slowly, the room emptied as most of the pilots followed him. A few pulled off into a little knot and talked among themselves in the hall. They would not volunteer.

"You did good," Pontowski told Mazie.

"I think I understand them a little better now," Mazie said.

"Really?" Waters replied.

"They'd rather die than admit it," Mazie said, "but they're idealists. Besides, no fighter pilot worth his salt really wants to be an airline pilot."

## Sunday, April 7
## Wuzhou, China

"A major battle was fought here," Kamigami said. He was looking out a window of a clapped-out bus as it rattled into the outskirts of Wuzhou. Jin Chu was perched on the edge of the seat next to him, leaning forward to see around his bulk. She was wearing a padded jacket, and with her hair piled up under a cap, looked like a boy. It was a disguise Kamigami encouraged. The road outside was littered with burned-out hulks of tanks, armored personnel carriers, and trucks bulldozed to clear a single lane. Every building was gutted or destroyed and dead animals lay bloated and stinking in the gutter.

The bus driver pumped the brakes, dragging the bus to a stop at a roadblock. "PLA," Kamigami said.

A dirty soldier climbed on board and worked his way down the aisle, checking IDs and travel papers. Kamigami took a professional interest in the soldiers milling around the roadblock as he evaluated their uniforms and the condition of their weapons. Only their large number impressed him. The soldier checking identifications glanced at Jin Chu, scanned Kamigami's identification, and dismissed them with a contemptuous look.

The soldier strutted back to the front of the bus, a sour odor following him. He turned and faced the passengers. "The People's Liberation Army," the soldier said, as if reciting from memory, "has won a glorious victory freeing the people of Wuzhou from those who would oppress them and deny them the fruits of the people's revolution. Many of your comrades willingly gave their lives so the revolution may continue and justice of the people may rule our land. Do not be distressed by the destruction you see. It is a monument to the courage and dedication of the People's Liberation Army. Long may the People's Liberation Army serve!" He hurried off the bus.

Another soldier Kamigami judged to be a sergeant climbed on board. His face was frozen into a permanent scowl as he studied the passengers. "As your army has sacrificed," he said, "so must you also sacrifice. You will help your brave comrades in restoring order to everyday life." He ordered the passengers to get off the bus.

"A work detail," Jin Chu said. "It shouldn't last more than two or three days." Kamigami collected their bags from the overhead rack and followed her. About twenty of the soldiers standing at the roadblock were detailed to herd the bus passengers into town. Out of sight of the roadblock, they halted, and the soldiers descended on the passengers, searching their bags and taking anything of value.

Kamigami stood passively when a young soldier frisked him, taking what money they had. The soldier pulled Kamigami's wristwatch off and fitted it on his own arm. But the watch band was too big and it flopped down on his hand. "This one," the soldier snarled, "is a lumbering ox and will be good for heavy labor." He jabbed the muzzle of his rifle into Kamigami's stomach, bending him over in pain.

Jin Chu bent over him. "Say nothing," she whispered. "Do nothing." She helped him to his feet and the procession made its way to the far side of town. "That one is a stupid farmer from the north," she told him. "He is not of the Pearl."

"How do you know he's a northerner?" Kamigami asked.

"His features are different and he called you an ox. If he was from the south, he would have called you a water buffalo."

The soldiers led them into a destroyed part of the town that was still smoldering from fires that had been allowed to burn out. A sergeant split the group in half. Jin Chu was ordered to help collect bodies from the embers while Kamigami and most of the men were set to digging a communal grave.

It was dark before Kamigami saw Jin Chu again. She and an old woman were struggling to carry a badly burned body to the grave in a blanket. Kamigami rushed to help them. "She wasn't on the bus," he told Jin.

"Don't say anything," Jin Chu cautioned. "She lives here. She says there was no fighting in this part of town and the soldiers came after the battle was over. The soldiers looted and raped before setting fires. They threw women and children into the flames and shot them if they tried to escape. She only wants to find her family and bury them. If the soldiers discover her, they will shoot her too." Kamigami took the gruesome bundle and carried it to the grave. The old woman watched with tears in her eyes as he laid it tenderly down, adding to the endless line of bodies that filled the ditch.

The soldiers lit torches and the grisly work continued into the night without a break for rest, food, or water. Once Jin Chu managed to slip him a bottle of water. Kamigami took a sip and passed it to the next man, who guzzled it down. The night was cold and a bitter wind cut at them, but the work continued while most of the soldiers found shelter and slept.

Jin Chu carried a small bundle down into the ditch. Her face was etched in despair and streaked with tears. "It's the old woman's granddaughter," Jin Chu said. "She tried to wash her for burial, but a soldier clubbed her and then urinated on the child's body." She motioned to a shadowy figure standing above them at the edge of the ditch. "Him," was all she said.

Kamigami took the body from her and gently laid it down. "Why do you waste time, Ox." It was the same soldier who had stolen his watch. "You," he pointed his rifle at Jin Chu. "Take off your hat."

Jin Chu gave Kamigami a frightened look. "I saw the soldiers rape a woman," she said. "Then they cut her throat." She took her cap off and her hair cascaded down.

"I thought so," the soldier hissed, pleased with his discovery.

The rage that had been building in Kamigami exploded. He had seen too much, endured too much, and now an intense anger broke the dam that had contained it. For a moment, he could neither move nor speak as he struggled to control the fire that seared his soul and threatened to consume him. But his years of training and experience held, and slowly he regained control. He turned and focused his rage and anger on the soldier standing above them.

"No," Jin Chu whispered. Nothing in her experience had prepared her for what she saw on Kamigami's face in the half-light of the flickering torches. "You are not like them," she pleaded.

"Girl!" the soldier barked. "Come here." His finger twitched at the trigger of his rifle.

Kamigami nodded, not taking his eyes off the man as Jin Chu scrambled up the path leading out of the ditch. The soldier moved along the edge, toward the spot where the path ended. He never saw the large shadow that rose out of the ditch behind him. The soldier was almost to Jin Chu when Kamigami reached him. Kamigami's hands were a blur as one reached over the man's shoulder and grabbed his chin while the other clamped down on the crown of his head. Kamigami jerked once and the soldier's neck snapped. Kamigami twisted again, ripping neck muscles and ligaments apart. Then he twisted again.

Kamigami threw the body into the ditch and jumped over the edge, following it. The man who had guzzled the water was running away, fearing what the soldiers would do when they found their dead comrade. Kamigami caught him before he had taken five steps. "Bury him under the others," he ordered. "When the soldiers ask where he is, tell them that he took the girl and me into town. That's all you know." The man was too frightened to protest and did as he was told.

Kamigami stripped the rifle and equipment from the body before he climbed out of the ditch. "Hurry," he told Jin Chu. They disappeared into the night.

Above Wuzhou, the Pearl River had cut a shallow river valley less than a mile wide through the hills. The verdant hillsides had been transformed into multilayered man-made terraces and the moist subtropical climate gave the land a soft, lush appearance as the gentle Pearl flowed eastward toward Canton and the sea. In the distance, the first of the limestone buttes called karsts rose out of the green valley floor. The small, isolated mountains with their steep sides reminded Kamigami of dragon's teeth growing out of the ground.

The rhythmic throbbing of the single-cylinder diesel engine that drove their small boat westward against the current cast a lethargic spell over the two passengers and for the first time in weeks, the tension that marked their lives shredded. The frightened, trapped look had left Jin Chu's face once Wuzhou was behind them.

Kamigami spent hours sitting at the bow of the boat, studying the landscape as the boatman worked his small craft upstream into the heart of southern China. Jin Chu would lean against him, curled up like a kitten while she entertained him with stories of her childhood. Slowly, the stories became an oral history of China and her people, the Zhuang.

Jin Chu's formal education had ended when she turned ten years old, yet she had listened to her grandfather, Li Jiyu, and learned well. "There is a pattern to your history," Kamigami told her. She said nothing and waited for him to continue. It was not in her tradition to teach a man, she could only entertain and hope he saw the meaning behind her simple stories. "When a dynasty falls," Kamigami said, "civil war and chaos follow."

"The last of the Manchus were driven from the Forbidden City over eighty years ago," Jin Chu said. "My grandfather heard the stories as a child." Her soft voice lulled Kamigami as she told of the droughts, famines, and floods that wracked China before the turn of the century. "Nature sends warnings of civil war and fighting with terrible

130

earthquakes and floods," she said. "It is a sign that our rulers have lost the mandate of heaven to rule."

Kamigami interpreted her stories from a western viewpoint. He saw a simple cause and effect reaction, in which rebellion was born out of misery and poverty when the government neglected the needs of its people. Still, through her, he began to understand this strange land. And in understanding, he loved her even more.

They were approaching Nanning, the capital of Guangxi Province, when Jin Chu told him of the last of the Manchus and the empress dowager, Tz'u Hsi. Jin Chu's storytelling was dramatic and enthralling as she whispered the tale of how the favorite courtesan of the emperor had clawed her way through the corruption of the Manchu court to become the power behind the throne. Because of Jin Chu, the story became alive and real, as if it had happened yesterday.

Kamigami did not understand a single word of the language Jin Chu was speaking as they made their way through the streets of Nanning. He noticed she dropped her eyes and looked away whenever she saw a man or woman with the round, bland features of the Han Chinese approach. Yet she would talk freely with willowy and slender Chinese who shared her delicate facial features. But it was the language she keyed on. Finally, she found a man who could tell her what she wanted to know. "He can take us to Zou Rong," she told Kamigami.

Twenty minutes later, they were sitting on a bench in a quiet courtyard. The old man who had been with Kamigami and Zou when they rescued Jin Chu from the PLA appeared out of a darkened doorway. "General Zou is with an emissary from the United States," the old man said. "You must wait."

Jin Chu surprised Kamigami when she said, "I would like to bathe and change clothes. Is that possible?" The old man nodded and led her away. It was dusk when Jin Chu returned. She had changed into western-style clothes and was dressed in tight jeans, a jade green silk blouse, and white running shoes. Her hair was pulled back and held with a bow at the nape of her neck. "Like in Hong Kong," she said, waiting for Kamigami's approval.

Her transformation stunned Kamigami and as in Hong Kong, he knew that she was the most gorgeous woman he had ever seen. "You are beautiful, no matter what you wear," he told her. Her face clouded, unsure of his meaning. He laughed. "Yes, I like what you are wearing very much."

The old man joined them. "Come," he said in English. "It is time. Miss Li, you please wait here." Kamigami rose and followed him into the building. The old man led him to an ornate room where a tailor was fitting Zou with a silver-tan uniform. Kamigami looked around and said nothing. The foreign emissary the old man had mentioned, an American, gauging by his clothes, was sitting on a comfortable sofa drinking tea. A large number of uniforms were hanging on a rack. This was a different side to Zou Rong and he wasn't sure if liked what he was seeing.

"Ah, Victor," Zou said. "I am pleased to see you again. Please, let me introduce General Mark Von Drexler. General Von Drexler, Victor Kamigami." Zou was proud of himself for getting through the western-style introduction in English.

A curious look crossed Von Drexler's face. "Command Sergeant Major Victor Kamigami, United States Army?"

"Yes, sir," Kamigami replied. Von Drexler did not reply.

Zou caught the exchange between the two men and sensed that Von Drexler was telling Kamigami who was in charge. But it puzzled him why a general from the Air Force would know about a sergeant from the Army, much less talk to him. It was not the Chinese way. "Sergeant major?" Zou said. "I thought you were an officer."

"I never claimed to be an officer," Kamigami replied. "I apologize if I misled you, Mr. Zou."

"It's President Zou," Von Drexler corrected.

"The United States, Japan, Great Britain, Germany, and France have recognized my government," Zou announced. A tight smile crossed his face. Zou had established his preeminence over both of the men. "General Von Drexler," he explained, "is in command of the American military assistance advisory group providing arms and supplies for my army."

Kamigami pulled inside himself, thinking. The situation

was totally beyond his experience, yet he understood it. Zou and Von Drexler were no different from most men except for the will to power that drove them and the stubborn pride that could destroy them all. Where had he learned that? Then he remembered. Jin Chu had told him the story of a rebel general from deep in China's history. He couldn't remember the rebel general's name, but the lesson remained. "It will take more than arms and supplies to defeat the PLA," he said.

"Why do you say that?" Zou asked.

"I came through Wuzhou a week ago," Kamigami said. He quickly summarized what he had seen. "Besides leadership and training, your army is going to need close air support to offset the PLA's advantage in armor. It might have made the difference at Wuzhou."

Von Drexler drummed his fingers on the arm of the sofa. "What were you doing in Wuzhou?" he demanded.

"Passing through. We were trying to reach Nanning."

"Where had you been before that?" Von Drexler asked.

"Hong Kong."

"Why didn't you report into the American consulate?"

"I had been injured in the riots and didn't have a chance—"

"How long were you there, Sergeant Major?" Von Drexler interrupted.

"Over a month," Kamigami answered, refusing to lie.

"Did you ever consider telephoning?"

Nothing in Zou's face or actions betrayed the anger that he felt. Von Drexler assumed that he had authority over Kamigami, but Zou could not allow that, not within his domain. Reports from Cheung Chau Island had reached as far as Nanning, and Zou wanted Kamigami to train and lead his small army in much the same way. But he also needed the supplies that Von Drexler controlled. He silently cursed the general for forcing him to choose between them.

The door opened and Jin Chu entered, shattering the building tension. Von Drexler stared at her, lost for words, not believing what he saw.

Zou quickly looked away when he was certain it was the same girl they had rescued from the PLA soldiers foraging for food near Canton. At the time, the villagers had told him of her powers as a seer and geomancer. In his mind, it was no fluke that she had chosen this exact moment to enter the room. It was an ample demonstration of her abilities. Abilities that he sorely needed.

But more than that, Jin Chu's quiet beauty had captivated him and he wanted her. She was true to her name and was a real pearl. He glanced at Kamigami. Even a fool could see how the big American felt about her. It was a relationship he could turn to his advantage. And then there was the problem of Von Drexler, a man who lusted for power and control but did not understand the way things were done. Still, he needed all three of these people if he were to succeed.

Jin Chu spoke to Zou in the same language she had used in the city. Zou's face was impassive as she spoke. "Yes," he said when she had finished, "I agree." He rang a small bell on his desk. Immediately, the door opened and the old man entered. "Please find quarters for General Kamigami," Zou said. "We will talk in a few days, after you have rested." The old man bowed and ushered them out of Zou's office, leaving a bewildered Von Drexler behind.

Kamigami was equally confused. "What did you say to him?" he asked her.

"I told him the truth. I said you can help our people and they will follow because you have the face of a general."

He shook his head. "That may have been the fastest promotion in the history of the military. That's not the way to choose a general."

"It is the Chinese way," Jin Chu said.

Kamigami stood on the second-floor balcony of the house where the old man had deposited them the day before and watched the sun set over Nanning. Below him, he could see Jin Chu sitting beside the garden pond as she fed the goldfish and koi that cut the water with flashes of gold and white. Why am I so restless? he berated himself.

The feeling stayed with him through dinner and into the evening. Finally, he found a comfortable spot on an old divan near the charcoal brazier that warmed the main room of the house and stared into the coals. What more could a man ask for? he thought. Then it came to him: He was feeling guilty because he was happy. He hadn't done guilt in a long time.

Jin Chu glided silently into the room carrying a leather-bound book and curled up beside him. "Why do you feel sad because you are happy?" she asked.

How does she do it? he thought. People can't read minds, but she seems to know what I'm thinking. Am I as easy for her to open as that book? A warm feeling swept over him. It pleased him that Jin Chu was so close, physically and emotionally. You're crazy in love with a girl who is ten years younger than your daughter, he chastised himself. The guilt came rushing back. He gave her a forlorn look and shook his head. He didn't know himself well enough to answer her question.

She turned the subject away from him and to the book in her lap. "There are many legends in my land," she began, flipping through the pages. Kamigami relaxed, giving himself over to her storytelling. She found the page she was looking for. Four woodcut prints had been glued into place. Each print was finely carved and detailed, showing a highly stylized portrait of a different woman. Jin Chu pointed to each print, naming the women.

"I'll never keep all those names straight," Kamigami told her. "Besides, they all look alike to me."

"That is sad, for each was a beauty."

Kamigami looked at the prints, at a loss for words. "Somebody should talk to the artist, for I sure don't see it."

"Look with your heart," Jin Chu scolded, "not your eyes." Kamigami tried harder, but he still couldn't see what made the four women so appealing. "Each belonged to a man like I belong to you," Jin Chu said. Kamigami lifted his eyes to her face. "And each was a pearl beyond compare, filling the heart of the man she loved. Because of their beauty and loyalty, we remember the legend of the four beauties and tell it to this day."

Jin Chu's eyes filled with tears as she looked at the prints. "It was not their fate to be happy." She closed the book and reached out with her hand, touching Kamigami's chin. She turned his face toward her. "Each was given as a gift to another man: one for greed, one for lust, one for power, and one for peace."

"I'd never let you become part of a legend," Kamigami said. Jin Chu stroked his cheek, wishing he could understand. That night they made love until Kamigami fell asleep in her arms. He had never been so content.

# CHAPTER 7

**Wednesday, April 17**
**Whiteman AFB, Missouri**

This is stupid, Pontowski thought. He stood in the doorway to his office and glanced at his watch: 5:45 in the morning. Sara "Ripper" Waters and Lori Williams were already at work, arranging piles of paperwork on the long table they had brought in to help with the sudden overflow. He had worked until eleven o'clock the evening before and managed to clear the table. Now he had to do it all again. "I can't believe this," he groaned. "Where is all this crap coming from?" He knew the answer.

Waters looked up from her work. "Higher headquarters and the Pentagon," she told him. "Where else?"

He rifled through the first pile. It was from the Office of Environmental Engineering and tasked the 303rd to prepare and submit a two-part environmental impact statement. The first part would have to prove their departure from Whiteman would not adversely affect the local environment. The second part would have to prove their operations would not disrupt the environment at their new location. "I suppose," he grumbled, "that we have to prove our bombs don't dig craters."

The second pile of paperwork was from Social Actions and detailed an awareness program on Chinese culture and traditions that all volunteers would have to immediately complete. A stop action was placed on any deployment until everyone was certified socially aware.

It was the bureaucracy gone wild. During the drawdown of the armed services after the collapse of the Soviet empire, every branch of the Department of Defense had been cut but one—the bureaucracy in Washington, D.C. The milicrats, that strange combination of military and civilian bureaucrats who inhabit the woodwork of offices inside the beltway that surrounds the capital, were experts at preserving their own jobs. Unfortunately, there was very little left for them to regulate and control. Now they had a chance to justify their existence.

"Those idiots are getting in the way," Pontowski grumbled.

"There is a way to stall them," Waters said. "We shoot a message back to each office"—she waved at the piles of paperwork on the table—"and tell them we are requesting budgetary funding to comply with their directives. In the interim, can they make funds available?"

"Will that work?" Pontowski was incredulous.

"Money always works," she assured him. "By the way, Frank Hester needs to see you. He's already in." Pontowski beat a hasty retreat and headed for Operations, leaving Waters with the paperwork. "Coward," she muttered.

Hester was in his office working on the day's training schedule with John Leonard. "G'morning, Boss," he said.

"What's up?" Pontowski asked.

"Not enough pilots," Hester replied. "Only twenty-seven of our jocks have signed on." Pontowski ran the numbers through his head: Three-quarters of his pilots had volunteered. That was enough to form the core of a wing, but he was going to need twice that. "Tango here has come up with an idea," Hester continued. "He wants to advertise on the electronic billboard."

AFMPC, the Air Force Military Personnel Center at Randolph Air Force Base in Texas, used the Air Force's computer net to advertise assignment openings like a classified want ad section of a newspaper. The electronic billboard was so popular that every office with a computer constantly monitored the system. "I've got a friend who can tap into the electronic billboard," Leonard said, "without the Personnel Center knowing about it." He handed Pontowski a sheet of paper.

WANTED: Hired guns who specialize in wars fought, maidens saved, dragons slain, and other services to humanity. Volunteers for this special mission must be proficient in use of Warthogs, Mavericks, and Mark-82s. Only manly men and women who are willing to travel to foreign lands, meet strange and wonderful people, and drop bombs on them need apply. Send resume with past heroics to 303rd Fighter Squadron, Whiteman AFB, Missouri

"Are you suggesting," Pontowski said, "that we subvert one of the finest systems AFMPC has developed to advance our own nefarious ends?" He had a hard time keeping a straight face. Leonard grinned a yes at him. Pontowski gave him a sad look. "Your friend had better be one devious hacker. Otherwise, AFMPC will stomp all over your schwanz."

"She's the best criminal hacker in the business," Leonard assured him.

"What the hell," Pontowski said. "Why not? What can they do to us?"

"Make us all civilians?" Leonard deadpanned.

"Do it," Pontowski said. Leonard grabbed the want ad and disappeared out the door. "Who's his friend with the criminal instincts?" Pontowski asked.

"Ripper," Hester answered.

"That woman will be the death of me," Pontowski said. He rose to leave.

"Boss," Hester said, "thank you."

Pontowski hesitated. "For what?"

"For keeping the faith in me when I was acting like an asshole."

"Frank, if you were being an asshole, I want a squadron of 'em." Pontowski headed for his office, thinking about the gyrations they were going through. He motioned for Waters to follow him into his office. The long table was bare and only three folders were in his in-basket. He sat down and leaned back in his chair. "Ripper, what the hell are we doing here?"

"Getting ready to fight a war," Waters answered.

"It seems like it's all smoke and mirrors," he said. "Is it worth it?"

"Who knows?" she replied.

He gazed out the window. "When I was in the Forty-fifth Fighter Wing," he said, reminiscing, "Mad Mike Martin was the deputy for operations. He was a wild man—a rootin', tootin', snortin' fighter jock. Mention combat and he jumped. One time he jumped so hard he got himself killed."

"You did sign on to fly and fight," she said, thinking about her own husband. "The possibility of getting killed goes with the territory—an occupational hazard."

"I suppose it is. Thanks for letting me bend your ear." She nodded and left. Why the questions now? he thought. When I was younger, I never had a flutter of doubt. He shook his head, clearing the cobwebs of uncertainty, and picked up the top folder in his in-basket and went to work.

Matt Pontowski was part of the tradition that stretched back through Mad Mike Martin, Jack Locke, and Muddy Waters. Like them, he was a professional soldier who had made the commitment to serve, fight, and protect. The burden of command had added to that commitment. Now his decisions determined who would live and die, and he had to learn how to live with himself.

With the milicrats held at bay, Pontowski actually found time two days later to fly. What a refreshing idea, he thought, doing what the Air Force pays me to do. He looked at the flying schedule and saw that Skeeter Ashton was scheduled to lead a flight of three to Cannon Range that afternoon. He wandered down the hall to Operations to see if they could come up with a jet and turn Ashton's flight into a four-ship. He wanted to see for himself how the young woman was doing.

He found Hester standing alone behind the scheduling counter. "Can you get me into Ashton's flight?" he asked.

Hester called Maintenance to see if a fourth Warthog was

available. "It doesn't look promising, Boss," he said. "They're prepping the birds for the deployment and we've been short one airframe ever since Leonard pranged on the range. They'll try to get a jet ready."

"I want to fly with Skeeter and see how she's doing."

"Skeeter's got a ways to go," Hester said.

Pontowski heard a tone in Hester's voice he had not heard before. His inner alarm bell warned him to proceed with caution. "How does she compare with other lieutenants with the same amount of flying experience?" It was a fair question and he expected an honest answer.

Hester hedged his answer. "I'd say about average, maybe slightly above." He sat down and leaned back in the chair.

"Colonel, that's a goddamned lie. She's good." Pontowski waited for an explanation. "I've got a problem with women flying jets," Hester continued, "which, I suppose, is all due to my macho male fighter jock ego getting in the way."

The tone of his voice was light and bantering but his expression betrayed how seriously he took the matter. "Personally, I'm not convinced that women have what it takes to fly fighters. But hell, 99 percent of the male pilots I know haven't got what it takes either. Now, suddenly, every female who feels the urge claims she should have a shot at flying a fighter just because she's a woman. Screw that noise. Let them scramble for it the way you and I did. They ain't going to be worth shit in the air if they can't fight their way into the cockpit to begin with."

"Things change," Pontowski said. "I guess our job these days is to see that qualified women get a chance to join the scramble." There was no response. "One question," Pontowski continued. "I saw Ashton's personnel folder. You endorsed her application to join the squadron. Why did you do that feeling the way you do?"

"Ripper."

Pontowski raised an eyebrow. "What did she do? Threaten you with a sexual discrimination complaint?"

A pained look crossed Hester's face. "She beat me at arm wrestling."

"She what?" Pontowski couldn't believe it. Hester was a husky, well-conditioned forty-five-year-old man and outweighed Waters by at least fifty pounds.

"We had a knock-down, drag-out, take-no-prisoners argument over Ashton. I told her women don't have the right attitude to engage in combat and in most cases aren't strong enough. So Waters challenged me to an arm-wrestling match right then and there. There's a trick to it and she's stronger than she looks. No sooner did we get to it than she reached under the table and grabbed my balls. The old nomex flying suit may be great protection against fires, but it ain't worth shit against long fingernails. I came out of that chair like I had a rocket strapped to my ass and I was going for a low orbit. Anyway, she slammed my hand to the table and told me to endorse Skeeter's application."

"I can see the look on your face now. And the 303rd gets stuck with a woman pilot because Waters cheats at arm wrestling."

Hester stared at him. "There are times when cheating counts in this business." He was deadly serious.

"Thanks for telling me that," Pontowski shot back.

"You fuckin' A think I like it?" Hester groaned.

"You got her, you give her a fair break."

"Why me?" Hester desperately wanted to pass the buck.

"Because that's life," Pontowski said. "Cope." The phone rang. It was Maintenance. They had a plane ready for Pontowski to fly. "Maintenance did good," he allowed.

"All the time," Hester replied.

The mission to Cannon Range was faultless and Ashton knew it. When she finished the debrief with the traditional "That's all I have," Pontowski knew he had a fighter pilot who happened to be a woman. He walked back to his office, not sure that he liked the idea.

Waters was waiting for him. She motioned to four sergeants sitting in his office. "Sir, the first response to the ad on the electronic billboard." The four men were well-turned-out in the new class A blues, polished shoes, and fresh haircuts. He judged them all to be in their late thirties to early forties. "They're the Range Rats from Cannon," she explained, leaving them alone.

Pontowski turned to the NCOs. "Range Rats?" he asked.

One of the men, a master sergeant, stood up. He was lean, emaciated looking, and over six feet tall. "Sir, I'm Ray Byers, the NCOIC of the range, this is Tech Sergeant 'Little

Juan' Alvarez." All six-foot-six of the dark-complected and good-looking Alvarez stood up. He was the tallest Mexican-American Pontowski had met. "This is Tech Sergeant 'Big John' Washington," Byers said. Washington was an African-American built like a fireplug and about the same height. "And this is Staff Sergeant Larry Tanaka." Tanaka was a Japanese-American of average height and build.

Ray Byers, Pontowski thought. Should I know that name? "What do Range Rats do?" he asked.

"Sir," Byers explained, "we scrounge up targets for the range and keep it operational. We think we got one of the most realistic target ranges in the United States." He stressed the "u" in "united" and spoke with a southern accent. His voice was hoarse and gravelly, the throat of an alcoholic damaged by years of hard drinking.

Pontowski agreed with his judgment about the range. It was a well-maintained facility and the surface-to-air missile sites, aircraft, tanks, and trucks scattered around the range were extremely realistic. "Where do you come up with all those targets?" he asked. "They look like the real McCoy from the air."

"That's because they are," Byers answered. He didn't say where they got them. It was an answer Pontowski wouldn't like.

"In all honesty," Pontowski hedged, "I don't know why you're here. If you want to volunteer, you should be talking to Maintenance."

A sardonic grin split Byer's face. "They wouldn't know what to do with us, sir."

"What would I do with you?" Pontowski asked.

"We're procurement specialists," Larry Tanaka said.

"You need it, we'll get it," Big John Washington added. Little Juan Alvarez nodded in agreement.

"Sir," Byers said, "just give us a chance to prove what we can do." He was pleading.

"We are short one A-10," Pontowski joked.

"With or without LASTE?" Byers asked. "And when do you want it?" He was dead serious.

Pontowski couldn't believe what he was hearing. "With LASTE and we need it ASAP."

"You got it, sir," Byers assured him. The four men saluted as one and marched out of his office.

Pontowski followed them out. "This is turning into United Nations day at the funny farm," he muttered to Waters. "Byers, Ray Byers. Should I know that name?"

"He was Jack Locke's crew chief during Operation Warlord," Waters told him.

"I'll be damned," Pontowski groaned. "That Byers." Ray Byers had been in the backseat of Locke's F-15E when Locke had shot down five Iranian fighters. Byers had taken a terrible beating in the backseat of the F-15 but had held true to his contract with the pilot and constantly checked their six o'clock position. Twice he had saved them from being shot down, and somehow, he had been able to lock a Maverick antitank missile onto a MiG. The missile had tracked and speared the fighter, consuming it in a fiery blast. Locke's request that Byers be given equal credit for the kills had been disapproved at higher headquarters. But unofficially, and more important, by legend, he was recognized as an ace.

Outside, in the hall, Byers held a quick staff meeting. It was not the formal, ordered, agenda-laden meeting favored by the Air Force but a highly focused and efficient discussion of how to get something done. Big John Washington made a phone call and then rejoined them, forcing a bored expression across his broad face. "No big deal," he told them. "We got a Warthog with LASTE. My buddy at the boneyard came through." The boneyard was the unofficial name for the Air Force Material Command's Aerospace Maintenance and Regeneration Center at Davis-Monthan Air Force Base at Tucson, Arizona. "He says they're swamped with A-10s and he can diddle the paperwork so we can have one for ground training and display. But we got to take good care of it and give it back—eventually. Getting it to Whiteman is the problem."

"What we need is an A-10 pilot," Little Juan Alvarez said.

Larry Tanaka decided to take the direct approach. "My cousin works at AFMPC. I'll give her a phone call." Twenty minutes later they received a fax from the Air Force

Military Personnel Center. They had the pilot they wanted—one Captain Dwight "Maggot" Stuart.

Another phone call and Byers found himself talking to a drunken voice on the other end. The voice belonged to an extremely average-looking man: normal height, dark brown hair, and blue eyes. Three things made Dwight "Maggot" Stuart different: lightning-quick reflexes, eyeballs with a wide-angle field of view that covered 240 degrees while he was looking straight ahead, and an attitude. "I understand you're separating from the Air Force," Byers said.

"That's right," Maggot slurred back. "The fuckin' Air Farce is kicking me out. The peace dividend strikes again."

"Did you see the ad on the electronic billboard?" Byers asked. "The 303rd is looking for A-10 pilots to volunteer for a special mission."

"I've been on terminal leave and just heard about it. Too late now. Half the fuckin' Warthog drivers in the fuckin' Air Farce are looking for flyin' jobs and are lined up in front of me." Maggot was decidedly drunk. It helped to control the bitterness he felt at being forced out of the service. "Sheeit," he grumbled, drawing the obscenity out into two syllables, "nobody gives a damn if you can fly and fight anymore."

"If you help us, we can help you get on with the 303rd," Byers said.

"Who do you want me to kill?" Maggot suddenly sounded interested.

"Nothing that drastic," Byers replied. "Just fly a Warthog to Whiteman for us."

Late Monday afternoon, a single A-10 landed at Whiteman Air Force Base.


Pontowski was not surprised when the four Range Rats and Maggot appeared in his office early Tuesday morning. Maintenance had already called about the new Warthog. Waters ushered them into his office and stood in the doorway. Pontowski gave her his "go away" look but she refused to move. "I want to see this one, sir," she said. Pontowski relented.

"The documentation and maintenance records," Byers said, "for one Warthog with LASTE." He laid a stack of paperwork on Pontowski's desk. "You endorse the transfer/acceptance from on top and it's all yours." Byers pointed to Maggot. "There is one glitch, sir. He comes with it."

Pontowski surveyed the medals on Maggot's uniform. The pilot had flown his share of combat and had been wounded. "Desert Storm?"

"Yes sir," Maggot replied.

"How many hours in the Warthog?"

"Over two thousand."

Pontowski was impressed. "Go talk to my ops officer, Major Hester. Tell him I sent you." Maggot saluted and bolted out of the office. Pontowski turned and stared at the four NCOs. "I suppose you're going to hold my feet to the fire on this one," he said.

They nodded as one. "You want another Warthog, sir?" Byers asked.

"No way," Pontowski shot back. He decided it was time to even the score. "If you work for me, you're the Junkyard Dogs and the captain here"—he pointed to Waters—"is your master. She whistles, you jump and start barking. Your job is emergency requisition. Get over to Maintenance and find out what they need." He watched them file out of his office. "Why do I think I'm going to regret this?" he muttered, loud enough for them to hear.

## Monday, May 13
## Nanning, China

The nine young captains slumped with fatigue as they huddled around the charcoal fire for warmth. A flickering light cast shadows across their tense faces as Kamigami paced the large room on the second floor of his house in Nanning. He knew these nine men, the commanding officers of his nine infantry companies, were tired after two months of hard training. But were they ready for the ultimate proving ground? A successful combat operation would send morale through the roof and draw in more recruits for Zou's army.

"You have learned very fast," he told them in Cantonese,

"and you have trained your men well. They are ready for the next challenge." The young student Zou had found to serve as a translator rattled off his words in *putonghua,* the common spoken tongue. The boy ended by translating into English. The captains laughed, breaking the tension.

How well do I know them after two months? Kamigami wondered. The nine men in the room were all veterans of the battle of Wuzhou. Unfortunately, Zou's best officers had been killed in that battle. Yet during the last few weeks, each one of the captains had proved that he could lead, motivate, and train the soldiers under his command. But the same question remained—were they ready for combat? He wished Jin Chu would return so he could ask her.

He pointed to a map. "The PLA is fanning out from Wuzhou," he told them. "They are like a swarm of locusts devouring the countryside and have moved eighty kilometers up the Pearl River. Many troops, perhaps ten thousand, have occupied the town of Pingnan." He heard a slight sucking of breath from the nine young men. They understood the threat that was moving ever closer to them.

Kamigami led them to the crude sand table where a model of a village had been constructed. He pointed to the model as the boy translated. "The PLA is still moving west and wants to control all shipping on the Pearl River. Five hundred troops have been sent here as a forward outpost, four kilometers from Pingnan. That is four kilometers closer to us. Because they are so close to Pingnan, they think they are safe." He paused for effect. "But we are going to cut them off and kill them." He studied the men's faces and knew they wanted it.

"Tomorrow, we begin training for the attack. Stay with your men tonight. Make sure they are all fed and have a warm place to sleep. I will demand much of you in the next few days and you will demand the same of them."

Kamigami sat silently as the men left. Nine captains, he thought, each with fewer than fifty men in his company. My so-called First Regiment. How in the world can I build an army from such a small beginning? Can I do it? Jin Chu, where are you?

"I am here," Jin Chu said, answering his thoughts. Kamigami turned and cast his worries into the fire. Jin Chu was standing in the doorway, still bundled up against the cold. She walked across the room and touched his face. "Do not drown in the worries of the moment," she told him. Her voice was tired and she drooped with fatigue from her journey. He wanted to wrap her in his arms and shield her from the cares of the world. But he fought off the urge, knowing it would embarrass her. "Come," she whispered in his ear. "I have missed the warmth of your bed." She followed him demurely into their bedroom.

As always, Jin Chu lay on top of him after they had made love. Her cheek was against his chest and she held him inside her as the warmth of her bare body enveloped him. "I saw many things," she said, wanting to talk before they slept. "I reached Canton. The PLA is moving many men and supplies upriver."

"Are they staying to the rivers?" he asked.

"I traveled only on the Pearl River and saw soldiers there," she answered. "But I talked to many people and they told me that soldiers are moving northward up the Lijiang River toward Guilin."

The PLA was moving exactly as Kamigami expected. The westward thrust up the Pearl River was pointed at them. The northward drive up the Lijiang would secure the PLA's right flank and pacify the northern half of Guangxi Province. How far up the Lijiang have they moved in force? he wondered. How much are they moving on the roads and railroads? Damn, Zou needs better intelligence.

"The PLA is doing much building at Pingnan," Jin Chu said. Kamigami gave a mental jerk. The outpost he was planning to attack was four kilometers from Pingnan. "There are many soldiers at Pingnan," she said, "and many, many officers. But very few go beyond Pingnan."

"It all makes sense," Kamigami said. He rubbed her back the way she liked. He decided they would talk more in the morning and he would tell her of the attack he was planning on the outpost near Pingnan. Jin Chu moved, making herself comfortable but still holding him inside her, not releasing him. Slowly, he felt his penis harden and her muscles relax. "You must create the spirit of the nine," she told him. Since they were speaking Cantonese, he wasn't sure if she meant "the spirit of the nine" or "the will of the nine." But she was obviously referring to his company commanders.

"The spirit of the nine?" he repeated, not understanding.

"I have been to the village near Pingnan you want to attack," she said, not answering him.

The wrong parts of his body stiffened. How did she know I was thinking of attacking that village? he wondered. She must have seen the sand table and recognized the model, he rationalized.

"The soldiers in the village are well-led and brave," she continued. "You must not sacrifice your nine men there."

"I don't plan on sacrificing them anywhere," Kamigami said.

For a moment there was silence. "Look to Pingnan. There, you will find *ho wan*"—good luck—"and the New China Guard will prosper."

"The New China Guard?" Kamigami asked.

"That is the name of your army," she replied, her voice soft and drowsy. He said nothing and listened as her breathing slowed and fell into the rhythmic comfort of sleep.

The first light of morning spilled across the bed, waking Kamigami. He jerked awake, anxious that he was alone. In the next room, he could hear Jin Chu's soft voice. He piled out of bed and dressed. When he entered the main room, he saw the backs of the captains gathered around the sand table and Jin Chu. He could hear her but didn't understand the language she was speaking. He walked up behind them, careful not to interrupt. The model of the village had been wiped off the sand table and a new model created. It was the town of Pingnan.

Jin Chu looked up and saw Kamigami's angry face. He stared at her, afraid to speak. What could his half-trained youths do against the large contingent of PLA regulars at Pingnan? His anger grew, for no one could even tell him the PLA's order of battle at Pingnan. She spoke a few words and the room emptied, leaving them alone.

"What are you telling them?" he gritted.

"There is *ho wan* at Pingnan," she answered.

"Who believes that?"

"They do," was her only answer. She hung her head and

tears streaked her cheeks. He walked out of the room and onto the balcony. Sounds of Nanning coming to life in the early morning sunlight reached over the wall.

Two days later, Kamigami was in the field on a training exercise when a Chinese colonel in a shiny new staff car appeared with a summons from Zou. He insisted that Kamigami accompany him without delay to Nanning. The colonel was proud of his staff car and told how it had been airlifted in the day before.

They drove in silence to a large building in central Nanning. A newly mounted bronze plaque at the entrance announced "The Combined Headquarters of the Military Forces of the Republic of Southern China and the United States Military Assistance Advisory Group." Underneath, smaller Chinese characters repeated the name. Two boys were washing the staff car before he reached the door.

Very fancy, Kamigami thought as the colonel escorted him through the halls. Workers were putting the finishing touches on a major renovation and the building was full of freshly minted Chinese officers wearing the same field-gray uniform as the colonel. An equal number of American officers roamed the corridors. About half were U.S. Army and the rest U.S. Air Force. The Air Force officers were wearing the new class A blue uniforms that reminded Kamigami more of a bus driver than an officer. A small gold nameplate on the left breast pocket of each American was engraved with the same words as the bronze plaque outside.

"General Kamigami," the colonel announced as he opened the door to a luxurious conference room. He bowed Kamigami in with a click of his heels. Zou Rong was sitting at the head of an ornate table wearing his field marshal's uniform. A map of western Guangxi Province was on an easel to his immediate left. Von Drexler and his staff were sitting on one side of the long table and their Chinese counterparts on the opposite side.

"General Kamigami," Von Drexler said, "we have been waiting for you." There was a trace of irritation in his voice. "I had hoped you would have changed into a more appropriate uniform."

Kamigami stared at his muddy boots and wrinkled fatigues. How many of these turkeys have actually been in the field? he wondered. He knew he wasn't a gifted speaker and would never make a staff officer. But he was equally certain that very few of these staff officers had ever broken a sweat leading men in combat.

"We are discussing," Zou Rong said, "the First Regiment. Is it ready to take its place at the head of the New China Guard?" Von Drexler's head came up at the mention of the New China Guard. He had never heard that name before. Zou smiled at him. "That is the name I have chosen for my army," he said.

"Ah, yes," Von Drexler said, recovering. "I had a different name in mind. Be that as it may, the First Regiment has received the lion's share of logistical support." He stood up and paced back and forth, expounding on the formation of the army now called the New China Guard. He had an intimate working knowledge of every part. "It is time," Von Drexler concluded, "to discover if our expenditure of resources on the First Regiment has been warranted."

Von Drexler's performance reminded Kamigami of the stories he had heard of General Douglas MacArthur, and he marveled at how all lines of authority in the New China Guard pyramided to Von Drexler—not Zou. The man is an organizational genius, Kamigami decided. And a raging egomaniac. "I am training for an attack against a forward outpost of the PLA," Kamigami said.

"Insignificant," Von Drexler snorted. "You must think bigger, more strategically."

Kamigami's eyes narrowed. Was Von Drexler baiting him? Forcing him to commit to a bigger operation than his men were ready for? What was Von Drexler trying to do? Guarantee failure? "We need to build on small successes," Kamigami finally said.

"Given the time and material you're consuming," Von Drexler said, "I had hoped for a bigger objective than a small hamlet."

Zou made a steeple with his fingers as he watched the exchange develop between the two men. He lightly tapped his fingertips together. "Kang Xun," he said, "still commands the PLA. He will remind us that he is the King of Hell if we do not act quickly. The First Regiment will attack Pingnan."

Kamigami wanted to protest, but an inner voice warned him that this was not the place. Decisions were being made in private for reasons beyond his understanding. He needed time to think.

"President Zou," Von Drexler said, "may I ask why Pingnan?"

*"Ho wan,"* Zou answered. Every head on the Chinese side of the table nodded in agreement. Zou rose and left the room. His staff stood and followed him out, leaving the Americans to themselves. The meeting was over.

"What is this *ho wan* bullshit?" Von Drexler groused to his second in command, Colonel Charles Parker.

"Sir," Parker answered. "I believe *ho wan* is the Chinese belief in good luck."

"Does Zou make decisions based on luck?"

"Sir," Parker replied, "I can't answer that."

Kamigami knew the answer. When Jin Chu spoke, her words traveled with lightning speed through Zou's headquarters staff. Well, at least one-half of the staff, he corrected himself.

The lantern hanging from the ceiling of the ancient barn burned brightly above the small group as they crouched around the large, hand-drawn chart. The hard rain drumming on the roof was muffled by the thick tiles but a shower of leaks rained down through the cracks. Only the chart and their weapons were protected. The paved barnyard outside the door was awash as sheets of water drained into a nearby stream that fed a raging torrent gushing toward their objective—Pingnan.

"The rain," Kamigami explained to his captains, "is the cover we need to move into position." The men reacted to the confidence in his voice. It was a confidence born out of hard training and detailed intelligence. Jin Chu had been right in identifying Pingnan as the objective, not the smaller, well-fortified outpost he had originally planned to attack. The local PLA commander had reinforced the outpost with his best troops as a forward buffer between Pingnan and Zou's forces farther to the west. It would be a tough nut to crack. The soldiers remaining in Pingnan were mostly Construction Corps and staff officers. But there was a problem—one tank had been seen in Pingnan.

"There is no safety in numbers for the PLA," Kamigami continued, "but you must move quickly." They all had the attack plan memorized and he was giving the pregame pep talk. "Hide in the rain and the night." He couldn't contain what he really felt. "But don't let your men get carried away. We've got to get in and out quickly." A few last words and the men rose to their feet and disappeared out the door and into the rainy night.

Jin Chu stepped out of a dark corner. She surprised him by coming to him and letting him fold her in his arms. She was shaking, but not from the cold.

Shadowy figures emerged out of the rain, following the gushing river that cascaded out of the hills and flowed through the town before it joined the Pearl. They moved along the base of the dike that contained the river as it passed the area where most of the Construction Corps was quartered. Not a single guard challenged them as they approached the dark concrete mass of a recently completed command post. The captain of Ox Company motioned a demolition team forward as the rest of his men moved into position.

Within moments, the team had rigged demolition charges against the wall of the command post. At exactly 2:35 A.M., the captain of Ox Company made a chopping motion with his right hand and the command post erupted in a manmade hell of concrete, stone, gravel, and mud. The echo was still reverberating over the town when Ox Company rushed the breach in the command post wall.

Behind them, the night erupted in booming thunder as more demolition charges exploded and mortar shells raked the Construction Corps and the supply dumps. The bark of submachine guns reached them as four companies attacked the main compound. Inside the command post, Ox Company systematically searched for communication code books and any high-ranking officers who might still be alive.

Kamigami checked his watch and looked at the walls of

his makeshift command post, trying to visualize what was happening in the town. He stepped outside, not able to remain in the barn. The sharp, cracklike echo of a heavy weapon reached him. It wasn't his. Again, he glanced at his watch. They were six minutes into the attack and the enemy was responding. Another sharp crack was followed by the rattle of heavy submachine guns. Every instinct he possessed shouted TANKS! His operations officer called from the door of the barn that three tanks supported by infantry were counterattacking in town. Kamigami ran back inside.

The three companies he had positioned in front of the nearby hamlet to keep the soldiers there from moving in relief of Pingnan radioed they were under heavy attack. He checked his watch. Seven minutes had elapsed since the first demolition had blown the command post, signaling the start of the attack. And it was all coming apart.

Kamigami glanced at Jin Chu. She was huddled in a corner and his staff was looking at him for guidance. He fought down the urge to go see for himself what was happening and personally lead his men. His eyes narrowed into slits. "They were expecting an attack," he said to himself. "It was all too easy. Damn, why didn't I see it before. We were suckered in." He was learning the hard way how Kang Xun fought. Now he had to save his regiment.

Jin Chu appeared by his side and pointed at the map. Her finger was resting on a river two kilometers north of Pingnan. "There will be a bridge here," she said.

"There's no bridge shown on the map," he replied. "I wish there was."

"It's there," was all she said.

The more he studied the map, the more sense it made. Many paths radiated from the point in a way that suggested a bridge. If it was there, his men could retreat to the north along the minor dikes that contained the rice paddies. The tanks would have to stay on one major dike and advance single file. Once his men were on the other side, they could blow the bridge. But if the bridge wasn't there, they would be trapped and have to swim for their lives. How many of his men could swim? He didn't know.

Now, time was the only thing he had on his side. If he could get his men moving quickly enough, before the counterattack had time to fully form and gain momentum, they might be able to withdraw over the bridge. If it was there. He made his decision.

First, he ordered the one company he had held in reserve to head for the bridge. "Tell Horse Company to hold the bridge at all costs and wire it for demolition." His eyes narrowed as he studied the map and more reports came in. He ordered Dragon Company to disengage and head for the bridge. A pattern clicked into place and he sensed they could do it. His hopes soared when a squad from Horse Company reached the spot on the map and reported a sturdy footbridge spanned a raging torrent.

"Do not sacrifice Ox Company," Jin said.

He felt his knees go weak. He had made a horrendous mistake. In his hurry and preoccupation, he had lost sight of the big picture and forgotten Ox Company. By withdrawing to the north, he had left them behind on the south side of town at the PLA's command post. "Put me in radio contact with Ox Company," he rasped.

The radio/telephone operator spoke into his mike. "General Kamigami," he said, "the commander of Ox Company was killed moments ago during the search of the command post."

Kamigami knew what he had to do. He issued a series of orders to his operations officer on when the remaining companies were to break off contact with the enemy and head for the bridge. "You can do it on the run," he told the Chinese colonel. "You and the staff head for the bridge right now." He wouldn't leave anyone else behind.

"Sir," the colonel blurted, "aren't you coming with us? Where will you be?"

"With Ox Company," Kamigami answered. He motioned for his personal radio/telephone operator and weapons bearer to follow him as he disappeared out the door.

Kamigami found the lieutenant commanding Ox Company's First Platoon outside the destroyed command post. "We have the code books," the lieutenant told him, pride in every word. He pointed to two prisoners they had taken—a general and a colonel. Ox Company had done its job, now Kamigami had to do his.

"We're going to fight our way out of here," he told the

lieutenant. The lieutenant from Second Platoon joined them as he pointed out their route to the bridge. "We are going right through town," Kamigami said. "They won't be expecting that. Keep your men together, keep moving, and stay in contact." He looked up at the rain, hoping it would continue. He pointed at the two captives. "Take them with us." He picked up the body of the dead captain and snapped, "Go." He felt much better now that he was in the thick of it and actually leading men in combat.

The small size of Ox Company became an advantage as the men ran through the town. They hid in the rain and made good time. At a major intersection, Kamigami waved them to a halt as a lone T-59 main battle tank clanked past, headed for the Construction Corps compound. The turret swung onto the men, and for a fraction of a second, they froze. The First Platoon's lieutenant stepped forward, made a hurried, pointed gesture in the direction of the command post and yelled for the tank to hurry. The tank's diesel engine raced as the tank pivoted on its tracks and the turret traversed away from them. The tank disappeared down the street, headed for the command post they had destroyed. Kamigami couldn't believe their good luck. He waved his men forward.

They ran into the roadblock on the northern outskirts of town. The men pulled into the shadows to catch their breath while Kamigami and one of the lieutenants crept forward to reconnoiter the barrier. "We need to find another way around," Kamigami said.

"We can find a way," the lieutenant said. "If we have time."

In the distance, they could hear the tank returning. "I think we've run out of time," Kamigami replied. "Fortunately, they haven't got the players sorted out," he said, confusing the lieutenant. "Lots of confusion," he explained as they retreated down the street toward the advancing tank. "Do you know how to kill a tank?" he asked. The lieutenant assured him he could do it. When they reached the men, Kamigami explained how they were going to go through the roadblock.

Kamigami waited until the tank had passed by before he motioned Ox Company forward. The men moved out of the shadows just as the rain spit down in a sudden surge, momentarily reducing visibility to less than thirty feet. They fell in behind the tank and moved forward with it, exactly like supporting infantry, as it approached the roadblock. The driving rain washed over the men, drenching them, turning them into vague and shadowy figures. The soldiers behind the barrier waved the tank forward.

Kamigami's luck held and they were through the barrier before the rain let up. A soldier realized what had happened and shouted a warning. A burst from a submachine gun cut him down.

The lieutenant led three men up the back of the tank while Kamigami led a squad around to the left. The lieutenant from Second Platoon and his men cleared the right. The surprise was complete and the PLA guards broke and ran. The coaxial mounted machine gun on the tank swept the street, killing four of its own men. The lieutenant was on top of the tank and threw his poncho over the tank commander's periscope and vision blocks. Another soldier slammed his helmet over the gunner's sight and held it there while a third soldier dropped his poncho over the driver's viewport. The tank was blind as its turret traversed, machine gun firing.

The tank accelerated down the street as the tank commander popped his hatch to see what was going on. A mistake. The lieutenant was waiting and dropped a grenade down the hatch. The men slid off as a muffled boom echoed from the tank. The lieutenant had been true to his word—he knew how to kill a tank.

Ox Company quickly reformed as Kamigami picked up the body of the captain, which had become his personal burden. He would not leave anyone behind. The men ran for the bridge, now in the open and unopposed.

Kamigami was the last to cross the footbridge, still carrying the captain. He was as muddy, dirty, and tired as the rest of his men, but there was victory in his stride and bearing. The men cheered when he gave the order to blow the bridge. He totaled the peculiar balance sheet of combat with his operations officer as his regiment headed westward to safety. On the credit side: two high-ranking prisoners, captured code books, and a destroyed headquarters, supply base, and construction corps.

On the debit side: nine killed, twenty-nine wounded, and one missing in action—Jin Chu.

Zou was pleased as he flipped through the photos a spy had taken of the destruction at Pingnan. He stood and paced the deep pile carpet that covered the floor of his office in Nanning. "Here is the spirit of the nine," Zou announced to the three Americans. "It is the spirit of the New China Guard."

No movement betrayed Kamigami's reaction. To his way of thinking, the attack had been a disaster, and only the rain and Jin Chu's bridge had saved them. He glanced over at Von Drexler, who was obviously upset. But it was the other man, a heavily built, sandy-haired U.S. Army colonel, who commanded his attention.

"It was a fiasco," Von Drexler growled. "It doesn't help to put a good face on it."

"Ah," Zou smiled, "we see it as a victory. Nine captains with the luck of nine good years defeated an evil force with only nine deaths. They are saying the spirit of the nine will bring good luck."

The Army colonel had a confused look on his face. "I don't understand the 'nine good years' you mentioned," he said.

"The First Regiment has chosen," Von Drexler explained, "to name its companies after the years of the Chinese calendar, not alphabetically as I recommended. Instead of having an Alpha and Bravo Company, they have a Rat and Ox Company and so on. It sounds more like a zoo than a military organization," he groused. "The point," he continued, "is that the First Regiment accomplished nothing."

"Maybe not," the colonel replied. "General Kamigami decapitated the command structure at Pingnan and sent the PLA a message it will not forget. Kang has ordered his best troops to protect his headquarters and supply bases."

"And how do we know that?" Von Drexler asked.

"The PLA hasn't changed its codes yet," the colonel explained. "Thanks to the code books General Kamigami captured, we are reading most of the PLA's message traffic."

"We were lucky at Pingnan because of the rain," Kamigami said. "The next time, we'll need modern anti-tank weapons and close air support."

Zou paced back and forth. "General Von Drexler, you have promised me both. Where are they?" Von Drexler heard the anger in Zou's voice and promptly claimed he would have to return to Washington, D.C., to arrange it. Satisfied, Zou stared at Kamigami. "I am very disturbed by the disappearance of Miss Li. Perhaps you can find her?"

"My men tell me she crossed the bridge with them," Kamigami said. "I'll try to find her." He didn't tell Zou that Jin Chu came and went as she pleased.

Zou motioned toward the door. "I must discuss other matters with General Von Drexler," he said.

The colonel and Kamigami stood and left. Outside, Colonel Robert Trimler shook his head. "Victor, what in the hell have you gotten into?"

# CHAPTER 8

Friday, May 24
Washington, D.C.

The two Secret Service agents were jogging in place, waiting for the national security advisor to slip out the White House's service entrance for his daily run. They recognized the look the moment he appeared and started to warm up. "Not again," Wayne Adams moaned.

"Again," Chuck Stanford said, confirming the other agent's suspicions. They had come to know Bill Carroll's moods and dreaded moments like this. Carroll was an impatient man and when events forced him into a waiting mode, he gave vent to his frustration by running. The two agents fell in behind him as he started to loop around the Mall. "We'll be doing five-minute miles today," Stanford panted. Adams saved his breath.

They felt a surge of hope when one of the agents following on a mountain bike caught up with them. "Mr. Carroll," he called, "a message from your office. The Chinese have walked out of the United Nations."

Carroll's head twisted around, a look of triumph on his face. "Yo boy," Wayne Adams groaned. Carroll cut back toward the White House and put on a burst of speed with one loud, and very unusual, whoop. Before, he had been running to control his anxiety and nagging doubts. Now he ran from pure exaltation. Months before, he had convinced the president to chart a new Asian policy and against the headwind of cabinet and congressional opposition, had held true to the course. Ahead of him, he could see the landfall of success. He gave another shout and ran faster.

The two agents tried to keep up with him, but were two hundred feet behind when they reached the wrought-iron fence surrounding the White House gardens. They hung on the fence, gasping for breath, as Carroll disappeared into the mansion. "I'm transferring to the FBI," Adams announced.

"Geez," Stanford moaned, "at least do something respectable—like playing piano in a whorehouse."

Carroll's secretary was waiting for him in the hall with a towel and a folder. "The president is waiting for you," she said.

He draped the towel around his neck and headed for the Oval Office. "I'll need to see the CAT right after I talk to the president," he said as he went through the door.

Carroll stifled a grin when he returned from the meeting with the president. Mazie was sitting quietly in his office while Hazelton paced the floor. Typical, he thought.

"Congratulations," Mazie said. "It's happening as you predicted."

"Dumb luck always prevails over skill and cunning," Carroll said, depreciating his efforts. Mazie knew that dumb luck never achieved what Carroll had brought off. He had created a multipart strategy to counter the chaos, disruption, and threat of war coming from China. Part of that strategy involved using Zou Rong's rebels to force the PRC to focus inward. At the same time, Carroll had patched together a coalition of countries to apply external pressure. Now the two were coming together exactly as Carroll had planned. Not only had the United Nations passed a resolution condemning China's blockade of Hong Kong, but an unusual alignment of third world nations had called for a guarantee of human rights in China and forced that resolution through.

"China's ambassador walked out of the United Nations in a huff," Carroll explained.

Mazie's eyebrows shot up. She hadn't heard. "That leaves a power vacuum we can maneuver in," she said.

"Which opens a door for action the president intends to

enter," Carroll added. "We're turning the Hong Kong relief effort over to the United Nations. If that's successful, we're going to press for a UN resolution making Hong Kong a self-governing international zone under a US mandate. At the same time, the president wants to increase the flow of material and money to Zou Rong. But our main effort has to remain in the Middle East. Obviously, we can't make it happen all by ourselves. Like I said before, you're going to have to do some major negotiations with our allies to make it happen."

"I've been working the problem," Mazie said, "and ran some numbers by the logisticians at the Pentagon. Because of the Middle East buildup and Hong Kong airlift, we don't have the airlift capability to supply Zou. Finding the material Zou needs is easy compared to getting it to him."

Carroll sensed that Mazie was embarrassed because she didn't have an answer to the problem. Fortunately, he did. "The Vietnamese can help us," he explained. "They want to reestablish relations with us. So we play linkage. As a show of their good intentions, they let us use the port of Haiphong and the Hanoi-Nanning railroad. The rail line has been closed for years but the track is in good condition and all we need are engines and rolling stock."

"I see," Mazie said, understanding the potential. "We transship through Haiphong and use the railroad to supply Zou from Hanoi. The Vietnamese will jump at the offer." Her eyes fixed on Carroll as she mused aloud. "That will mean a diplomatic quid pro quo, which also offers some interesting possibilities."

Carroll was making notes. "I'll see what doors I can open. In the meantime, you start organizing a logistics pipeline. The State Department has made the right contacts but it's up to you and the CAT to make it happen."

"Sir," Hazelton interrupted. "My area is the Middle East and I don't see where I fit into all this."

"The China Action Team," Carroll said, feeling sorry for the young man, "needs a front man." A confused look spread across Hazelton's face. "Perhaps you had better explain it, Mazie."

"We work in the shadows," Mazie said, "and cut deals. Nothing is put in writing and everything is based on 'understandings.' The men we will be negotiating with are mostly Asian or Middle Eastern and they won't deal with a woman. You'll be the front man, I'll be your interpreter."

"I see," Hazelton mumbled. "You call the shots and if I overstep my bounds, you do a 'What Mr. Hazelton really means is' routine."

"If it comes to that, yes," Carroll said. "But you are part of the team and won't be operating in the dark. Do you want out?"

Hazelton ran the pros and cons through his mental calculator. Here was a rare opportunity to move on the world stage. It was the way reputations were made. But did he want to play second fiddle to Mazie Kamigami? What would his mother say? Suddenly, he didn't care what his mother would say or think. He had seen Mazie work and trusted her. "No, sir," Hazelton said, "I want the job."

"You won't regret it," Carroll reassured him. His tone never changed when he dropped the bombshell. "Zou Rong has formally asked the Military Assistance Advisory Group for pilots and aircraft. The president wants to honor that request but needs to line up congressional support. When that is accomplished, he'll sign an executive order creating the American Volunteer Group."

"We'll have to act fast," Mazie said, "before the Chinese realize what's happening and return to the UN and turn on the pressure against our coalition. Voting on resolutions condemning China is one thing, condoning military intervention is another. It's not a big window of opportunity."

"It's big enough," Carroll replied. "And the 303rd is ready."

Mazie almost asked if he had considered ways to disengage the 303rd should the need arise. But she decided not to raise the question since she didn't have an answer.


## Saturday, May 25
## Nanning, China

Kamigami's huge shoulders slumped as he listened to Colonel Robert Trimler recap the attack on Pingnan from his perspective. "Victor, you were lucky at Pingnan. It was a small, tight operation that you could control at the critical moment when it was all turning to shit. And the opposition was inept. Make that fucking inept. You won't be so lucky next time."

The sandy-haired colonel was a big man and moved with an easy grace. Corded muscles ran down his neck and many people assumed he was all hard lines and no brains. Under the wrong circumstances, that could be a fatal mistake. Trimler was an expert in logistics, special operations, a former commanding officer of Delta Force, and Kamigami's last CO.

Kamigami was up against the hard reality of modern warfare and he knew his limitations. It took years to train officers who could command and supply division-level units in the field. His expertise ended at the battalion level. "I know," Kamigami conceded. "I need help."

"First, don't trust Von Drexler," Trimler said. "He's got a reputation for pure slash and burn. He's only concerned with one thing—the promotion and advancement of Mark Von Drexler." He thought for a few moments. "Let me put together a staff for you. Half American advisors and half Chinese."

"I don't see that working," Kamigami said. "You don't know the Chinese. Things happen here I can't explain. Can you believe they made me a general because of my face?"

"That's quite a promotion system," Trimler dryly observed. "Look, you can give them the leadership they need and make a joint staff work. For some reason, the Chinese hold you in awe. You can lead them, I can't."

"Can you handle working for an NCO who used to work for you?" Kamigami asked.

"Hell," Trimler grinned, "I've worked for incompetent, goose-stepping assholes. You were never incompetent. Look, you call me Bob and I'll call you sir. So let's go kick some ass."

"What did you have in mind?"

"You execute a series of small raids to keep the PLA holed up and off balance while we build an army for Zou," Trimler replied. "One thing, who is this Jin Chu everybody keeps talking about?"

"You wouldn't believe it if I told you," Kamigami answered. "You'll meet her when she wants to meet you."

## Sunday, May 26
## Whiteman AFB, Missouri

The usual pile of paperwork was waiting for Pontowski when he arrived at work. Sara Waters and Lori Williams were still sorting it out and he could smell coffee brewing. Lori looked up from her desk and gave him a beautiful smile. "Coffee's on, sir," she chirped. It aggravated him that anyone could be so cheerful so early in the morning. He drew a large mug of coffee and disappeared into his office.

"He'll be better after he gets a jump start," Waters said. She waited twenty minutes for the caffeine to work before she buzzed him on the intercom. "I've got the day's schedule ready," she told him. "Number one on the agenda: a decision on the air show." He grumped an answer and told her to get Frank Hester and John Leonard. Waters disconnected. "Lori, is that decaf?"

"No way," Lori answered. "Strictly leaded."

"We need to make the first pot stronger," Waters told her. The two women had learned how to handle their boss.

Pontowski had settled into the day's routine when Waters escorted Hester and Leonard into his office. Leonard had the operations plan STAND DOWN tucked under his arm and an expectant look on his face. "I've got two questions," Pontowski said. "How's the deployment coming and is the air show interfering?"

"This is turning into a goat rope," Hester told him. "We've got twenty-four Warthogs and thirty-six pilots ready to go. Eight of those jocks are here on their own: no official status, no pay, no nothing. They're paying their own way and hope we get the word to form up before they go broke. I've got 'em flying for currency, but the shit will hit the fan if anyone finds out. We got the core of a wing here, but we need more aircraft and pilots. And it ain't gonna happen until someone upstairs gets their head out'a their collective rectum and makes a decision."

Leonard said, "Sir, we can't do both. The air show is getting in the way. It's one or the other."

Pontowski thought for a moment. Then he made his decision. "I'm betting we'll get the go-ahead to form up a wing of volunteers and deploy. Cancel the air show. But we need to get our act together and quit flailing around in the dark on this. John, you did good work on the planning for the air show. I want you and Ripper to build an activation plan. Call it OPPLAN DARK WING."

"You got it, Boss," Leonard said. "We'll have something on your desk this week."

Leonard followed Waters out of the office and threw the operations plan for the air show into a wastebasket. She pulled it out. "That's a lot of work to be throwing away," she told him.

"Screw it," he said. "Dropping bombs and killing tanks beats looking good any day of the week. Let the Thunderbirds do the glamour. We'll do the fightin'."

Waters gave him a studied look. "I'll get the Junkyard Dogs to help," she said.

"Can they write an activation plan?" he asked.

"No," she answered. "But they can steal one."

Leonard smiled. "Ripper, I got to tell you, I haven't been this alive in years." He followed Hester out of the office.

"Men!" Waters fumed to herself. "Someone needs to jump start their brains."


## Wednesday, May 29
## Washington, D.C.

"Always have a folder in front of you," Carroll said as they sat down at the witness table in the Senate committee hearing room. "Make a show of referring to it before you answer a question. Use the time to think."

Mazie did as she was told and pulled a folder out of her briefcase. She glanced at it—copies of airline schedules in the Far East. She watched the dozen or so senators and representatives as they came into the room and took their places at the committee table. It was the first time she had been invited to a closed session of the joint Senate-House Select Committee on Intelligence.

A slight commotion at the rear of the room caught her attention as the doors were being closed and locked. Major General Mark Von Drexler had just arrived from China. The dapper and aging senator who chaired the joint committee gaveled the session to order as Von Drexler took his place at the other end of the witness table. Like her, he made a show of spreading folders out in front of him.

"General Von Drexler," the chairman began, "thank you for coming so far to help us." Jet lag was written plainly on Von Drexler's face as he responded. Mazie listened as Von Drexler recapped the situation in China and the functions of the Military Assistance Advisory Group.

Between questions, Carroll scribbled a note and shoved it to her. "This is all BS," it said. She agreed. Even in the closed-door session, the senators and representatives were posturing and searching for a way to boost their political reputation. Mazie had never seen so many power-driven egos on parade.

Carroll made another note. "Watch VD perform." She did. His responses to the committee's questions indicated he considered himself a cut above the men and women in front of him. He's lusting for power, Mazie thought.

"Let me speak bluntly," Von Drexler told the committee. "To develop and conduct an effective policy in southern China, all, I repeat all, U.S. resources and forces must be under the control of the Military Assistance Advisory Group."

Another note from Carroll. "Read: under his control. VD's going for the whole enchilada." Mazie wondered if he was going to get it.

"For example," Von Drexler said, "the airborne warning and control aircraft operating out of Hong Kong in support of the British should be under my control." Various murmurs and growlings from the committee answered him.

"Let me draw your attention to another potential problem area," Von Drexler said. "The American Volunteer Group being formed is not suitable for the mission it will be tasked to perform. My request for a composite force of F-

15s for air defense, F-117 Stealth fighter-bombers, and B-1s has been denied. Instead, it is proposed that a wing of obsolete A-10s be made available. Ladies and gentlemen, this is a built-in formula for failure."

Another note from Carroll. "VD wants a big, fancy air force so he gets a bigger hammer." And makes it harder to withdraw without a loss of face, Mazie mentally added.

"As the commander of the A-10s is the grandson of a former president of the United States," Von Drexler concluded, "I am drawn to the inescapable conclusion that political influence has driven the decision to send A-10s. Regardless of that, the AVG must remain under my control as commander of the MAAG." He folded his hands and waited.

Carroll scribbled a note. "VD is afraid that P is a go-getter out after his job." The committee stirred itself and directed a series of questions at Carroll. He leaned forward and justified the administration's policies based on the United States' interests in the area. Finally, he turned to Mazie and asked for her to assess the current situation for the committee.

Mazie shuffled through her papers, thinking. "China is at a crossroads," she began. "Depending on how the current crisis is resolved, China can become a peaceful neighbor or a major threat to peace in the region. At the heart of the problem is General Kang Xun. If he consolidates his power in southern China, he will be strong enough to take over the central government in Beijing. Given his record, he can be expected to destabilize the entire region, much as Saddam Hussein did in the Middle East."

She studied an airline schedule, creating an impression of cautious, considered testimony. The legislators were impressed. "Beijing is playing Kang off against the revolutionaries under Zou Rong in the hope they will annihilate each other. To keep Kang weak, Beijing is limiting the flow of men and arms to southern China, which, in turn, drives the tempo of the fighting. Kang attacks when he has built up a logistics base, hoping to defeat the rebels. When he runs out of fuel and munitions, the fighting stops and both sides regroup."

Various committee members asked pro forma questions

for a few minutes before the chairman gaveled the hearing to a close. "What did all that accomplish?" Mazie asked Carroll.

"You convinced Congress that it is in our best interest to support Zou Rong." He laughed at her perplexed look. "You have to read between the lines. In the next few days, the president will have a friendly chat with the chairman of the committee. They'll exchange confidences about the wisdom of dividing and conquering an enemy. Then the pres will sign the executive order authorizing the AVG."

Mazie turned to leave and bumped into Von Drexler. He shot a hard look at her before murmuring an apology. An aide handed her a note from the committee chairman: He wanted to meet with her in his offices. She handed Carroll the note.

"Offhand," Carroll said, "I'd say you swing a big bat with the senators. How does it feel to make things happen?"

Mazie wasn't sure how to answer his question. She liked the feeling but it frightened her.


## Thursday, May 30
## Near Pingnan, China

Kamigami stalked his makeshift command post like a caged lion. Keep the god's-eye view, he told himself, concentrate on the big picture. He studied the chart his operations officer constantly updated. His First Regiment was operating around Pingnan, cutting off every small PLA outpost, destroying every patrol that ventured out to reconnoiter or pillage the countryside for food. Ultimately, they would starve the PLA out of Pingnan and force them to fall back on Wuzhou, reversing Kang's slow and relentless march up the Pearl River, into the heart of Zou's territory.

Get inside Kang Xun's head like Trimler does, Kamigami thought. It's amazing what's there—like Kang's tactics and strategy. He remembered the heavy, bespectacled general he had seen in Canton and the fear that radiated from him like an insane Chernobyl. The fear was the intangible, invisible part of Kang, but his methods of operation were not.

Kang had turned Wuzhou into a big logistical base. Then

he had leapfrogged up the Pearl River, the main line of communication, and established a forward base for combat operations at Pingnan. He supplied Pingnan from Wuzhou as the PLA established its control over the surrounding countryside. When the area around Pingnan was pacified, he would leapfrog up the Pearl River again.

Kamigami fought the urge to visit one of his companies and get into the thick of the action. Instead, he paced the miserable hovel the Chinese family had gladly cleared so his staff could set up a temporary headquarters.

Kamigami liked the small, well-organized staff Trimler had put together. Command and control was much smoother and logistics was becoming less and less of a problem. But it did bother him that so many of the qualified officers and NCOs now flocking to the banner of the New China Guard were former PLA. Zou had overridden his objections with a cavalier wave of his hand.

Stay focused, he berated himself. Your immediate objective is to starve the PLA out of Pingnan.

The constant talking his staff indulged in fell away and the room was silent. He heard a single whisper, "Miss Li." He turned and she was standing there, her eyes on him. He wasn't sure what he wanted to do, sweep her into his arms and hold her tight or upbraid her for disappearing. He did neither and only nodded. Deep inside, he felt a warmth return. A wisp of a smile played across her face and she sat in a corner.

An incoming mortar round and a burst of machine gun fire ended his mental labors. He ordered Jin Chu and his staff into a sandbagged bunker as he grabbed a submachine gun. Outside, he gathered up five panicked soldiers and led a sweep of the area until they had found the intruders and killed them. He wanted to lead the search for the mortar team but instead promoted a private who had fought well to sergeant and had him lead the search. "I want their weapons," he growled. The sergeant nodded.

Kamigami was calm and composed when he returned to the command post. He was pleased his staff was back at work and all communications had been restored. His intelligence officer bristled with news. "General Kamigami"—

he was barely able to brake his excitement—"we have three reports that a heavily armed convoy is leaving Pingnan by this road." He pointed to the road that connected Pingnan to Wuzhou. "We think it's the division commander and his staff."

Kamigami's mind raced with implications. Were his tactics working and the PLA's defenses crumbling? And why the attack on his headquarters at this particular time? Was it a smokescreen to cover the convoy's movement? Was this a chance to decapitate the command and control of the PLA division holding Pingnan? He had to find out.

"Order Monkey Company," he told his operations officer, surprised that his voice was so calm, "to let the convoy pass and then cut the road." He pointed to a spot farther along the road. "Have Tiger Company move into a flanking position here and destroy the convoy." If it was the PLA divisional commander, he wanted to be sure he was totally sealed off when he died. The radios crackled with commands.

Now he had to wait—the hardest part for a commander. I might have missed this opportunity if I had been out chasing that mortar team, he thought. He dismissed the thought.

The report from Tiger Company was a simple "Convoy destroyed." Kamigami calmly ordered Monkey Company to advance down the road and enter Pingnan. Almost immediately, Monkey Company reported the PLA were surrendering en masse.

A new sensation engulfed Kamigami, a feeling he had never experienced. It was the ego rush that comes when a commander knows a battle is his, that he has defeated the enemy. It was the raw feeling of victory, the lion's roar of a successful kill. He savored the feeling, liking it.

A single report shattered the moment: Three companies he had held in reserve were also entering Pingnan. "Damn!" he swore. What was happening?

"Perhaps," Jin Chu said, "you should see for yourself."

They made a strange sight as they walked down the main street of Pingnan. The huge Japanese-American and the small Chinese woman were followed by a growing crowd of

PLA soldiers who insisted on surrendering to them. At a major intersection, Kamigami came to a halt. His face turned rock hard.

Men wearing the uniform of the New China Guard were looting and pillaging stores. His soldiers were out of control. Jin Chu's voice reached him. "It is only a few, a very few soldiers. Most hold true."

The strange procession stood frozen as Kamigami followed a woman's scream into a nearby store. Inside, he found one of his soldiers raping a teenaged girl. He grabbed the man by his hair and dragged him outside. With a wild gesture, he flung the man against a wall and held him there. "Knife," he rasped.

A soldier handed Kamigami his bayonet as Jin Chu ran to him. She grabbed his hand holding the weapon. Her soft touch seemed to scald him as she stayed his anger. "Do not kill him," she pleaded. "The nine must punish, not you. Remember the riot in Hong Kong. Let him serve as a warning."

Kamigami stared at her. Then he grabbed the man's shirt and lifted, pulling him off his feet and holding him up high against the wall. He snarled a command and the man hesitated. Again, he barked the command. Slowly, the soldier raised his right arm above his head and held it flat against the wall. The bayonet flashed in an upward arc as Kamigami drove it through the man's wrist, pinning it to the wall. He let go and the soldier screamed in pain as he dangled from the bayonet.

Kamigami turned to his operations officer. "Order the regiment to fall in. Here. Now."

The sporadic looting and pillaging slowly halted as Kamigami's nine captains regained control and mustered their companies in front of the pinned soldier. His shrieks of agony filled the street. The drill was meticulous as the regiment formed and reported in. Kamigami ordered his captains front and center. When they were standing in front of him, he said, "I found this man raping a girl. He is one of ours and has brought shame on the spirit of the nine. You decide his punishment." He waited while the captains conferred.

The commanding officer of Rat Company stepped forward. "He is one of my men," the young captain said. "We have decided that he is to die where he is."

"Stay with your men until it is finished," Kamigami barked.

"That was our intention," the captain replied.

Kamigami spun and walked away as rain started to fall. Jin Chu followed him. Behind them, the condemned soldier wailed in agony as the assembled ranks of the First Regiment listened and watched, their officers in front, motionless. The PLA soldiers milled around in confusion as a firing squad was formed.

## Saturday, June 1
## Whiteman AFB, Missouri

The normal number of looks followed Skeeter Ashton as she walked into the Officers' Club casual bar and found a seat at the bar. Maggot pulled at his beer. "She do fill out those jeans," he mumbled.

Another voice said, "Too bad she can't fly worth shit." Maggot said nothing. He had flown with Ashton and knew what she could do. But he let his silence give truth to the lie.

A hulking form wearing a flight suit filled the doorway and paused, taking in the Saturday evening scene. Then he made his way slowly through the crowd, careful not to bump into anyone. "Who made his flight suit?" Maggot asked. "Omar the tentmaker?" The pilots watched as he sat next to Ashton at the bar.

"Hi," the newcomer said. "Moose Penko."

Ashton cocked her head as she looked up at Penko. "Skeeter Ashton," she said, extending her hand. His massive hand engulfed hers as they shook hands. Her eyes darted over his name tag: Moose Penko was a weapons controller, not a pilot. She recognized the patch on his flying suit. "AWACS?" she asked.

He nodded. "Five-fifty-second out of Tinker." They exchanged basics, and Penko told her that John Leonard had requested the 552nd send a weapons controller to brief the 303rd on the AWACS mission in China. As they talked, Ashton found she was drawn to Penko. He listened more than he talked, his words carried a quiet confidence, and he wasn't on the make, looking for an easy conquest. "Dinner?" Penko asked.

"Dutch," Ashton answered.

Maggot watched as they left the bar for the dining room. He ordered another beer. He was attracted to Ashton but in his drunken stupor, he was confused. His irritation at her challenge to the macho world of fighter jocks was all mixed up with feelings of lust. He was still drinking when they returned. "Damn," he muttered, pushing his chair back and spilling his neighbor's drink. He picked up his beer and headed for the bar. His attitude demanded that he sort out the confusion. "Hey," he said to Penko, "I see you've met our crack troop." He thought it was a funny opening salvo but forgot what point he was trying to make.

Ashton read it as a sexist comment from a drunk. She had heard it all before and could hold her own. "Piss off, Maggot," she said.

"Oh, oh," Maggot replied, slurring his words. "That time of the month." He hummed a few bars of ragtime.

"My good Christian friend," Ashton said. "What the hell is bothering you?"

Maggot rocked back on his heels in mock surprise. He was so drunk that he couldn't think. All he could manage was, "Ah, fuckin' broad." He stumbled off in the direction of the men's room. Penko stood and followed him.

"I fight my own battles," Ashton snapped.

"I got that," Penko replied. "But I need to see the man." The man he had in mind was not the men's room but Maggot. Outside, he clamped a hand on Maggot's right shoulder and spun him around, face to face. He grabbed Maggot's left biceps. "You suffer from brain farts?" he asked. Moose Penko had little time for drunks and believed in quick and direct object lessons. Maggot felt himself being lifted off the floor until he was at eye level with Penko. "Do that again and if she doesn't rip your head off, I'll tie you in a pretzel and flush you down the nearest toilet."

Maggot was many things, but he was not a coward. He punched at Penko's chest. The big man didn't even move. Maggot hit him in the face as hard as he could. The only result was an aching hand. "This is gonna hurt," he moaned, realizing Penko was going to crush him. He swung again.

A hand reached out and caught Maggot's fist before it connected. It was John Leonard. "Knock it off," he ordered. "Moose, get this drunken asshole over to the squadron. We just got mobilized."

"Holy shit," Maggot said, thankful for the reprieve.

Waters cleaned out Pontowski's out-basket and told him, "Nothing else—for now." She spun around and hurried out of his office.

Pontowski flipped to the commander's checklist in the appendix of the freshly printed operations plan DARK WING and ran through the list of items to be accomplished by forty-eight hours into the activation of the American Volunteer Group. Thanks to Leonard's plan, the activation was humming along with a minimum of confusion and they were twelve hours ahead of schedule. Leonard had created the 303rd's plan by using a secret operations plan for the activation of a United Nations Peacekeeping contingent that the Junkyard Dogs had "borrowed" from the Marines. No one asked how they got it.

He read the last item on his checklist: Attend to personal affairs. "Good advice," he mumbled to himself and headed out the door. Waters and Leonard were standing in the outer office. He was about to tell Waters where he was going but for some reason, he hesitated. The two were in a quiet conversation, standing close, not touching. She looked at Leonard and raised her right hand, hesitantly touched his cheek and turned away. Tears were in her eyes. Leonard quickly left the office.

Waters watched Leonard leave and felt a pit where her stomach had been a few moments before. The long-dead memories came rushing back. She had been seven months pregnant when her husband had told her he was deploying, taking his wing into combat. What had she felt then? Time had not dimmed the pain of those memories. What had she said that last time? She could only remember that she hadn't let him see her tears. Now she was crying again because she knew that some of these men were going to die.

"I'll be in my quarters," Pontowski said, bringing her

back to the moment. "Call me if anything pressing raises its urgent head." What was that all about? he thought as he left.

"Anything pressing!" Lori Williams snorted from her desk. "We're getting swamped with paperwork from every office in the Pentagon. How much longer you gonna sit on it?"

Waters sat at her desk, bringing her emotions under control. "Until we activate the directed assignment roster. Then as far as the bureaucrats are concerned, we've disappeared."

"What do you mean 'we,' white woman. You and me are still gonna be here."

Waters stared at her hands. "I'm going with them."

"You crazy!" Lori said. "What do you expect me to do when all those frustrated bureau-what'cha-call-its start asking, 'What you doin' about our message telling you to jump through hoops?'"

"Always blame the last person who left," Waters answered.

Lori relented. She had decided long ago that it was time for Waters to quit being a widow. "You like him," she said. "So go get him."

"I like them all," Waters hedged. "Besides, I'm older."

"So?" Lori asked. "It won't hurt you to have a toy boy."

When Pontowski arrived home, he found Shoshana in the kitchen with three other wives. "We're organizing a support group," she told him. The three women made hasty excuses to leave them alone.

Little Matt came out of his room and stood in the kitchen doorway, a sad and confused look on his face. Pontowski picked up his son. "I've got to go away," he told the little boy. "I'll be gone for a while, but I'll be coming back. Can you handle that, good buddy?"

His son nodded gravely, his eyes serious, and threw his arms around Pontowski's neck and held on. "I'll be good, Daddy," he promised. Shoshana stood next to them. She was composed and calm, her eyes dry. "We'll be fine," she told him. She lifted her face to him and they kissed. Little Matt wiggled out of his father's arms and ran off, satisfied that his world was in order.

"I worry about leaving you here all alone," he said.

Shoshana walked over to the refrigerator and started to prepare dinner. "I was thinking of telephoning my aunt Lillian," she said, "and asking her to come over." Pontowski had met Shoshana's aunt in Israel and liked the older woman. "She's been at loose ends since Doron's death." Lillian's husband, Doron, had been killed by a knife-wielding Palestinian teenager in one of the sporadic episodes of violence that swept through Israel.

The phone rang, capturing their attention. He picked it up on the second ring. "Pontowski," he answered. He listened for a few moments without comment. "I'll be right there," he said, and hung up. "That was Waters. The sierra has hit the fan. A congresswoman, Ann Nevers, called a press conference and severely criticized the administration for its policies in China. She's calling it 'Chinagate' and is demanding a full-scale congressional investigation. We've been ordered to launch and get the Warthogs into China ASAP. The president wants a done deal before Congress changes its mind."

Shoshana walked resolutely into the bedroom and helped him pack. Finally, he was ready to go. "I'll drive you to the squadron," she said, collecting Little Matt.

Shoshana pulled up to the squadron building and turned to her husband. There was much they both wanted to say, but they only looked at each other. "How come you're both so brave?" Pontowski asked as he hugged his son.

"In Israel, you learn it as a child," she answered. "But it's not bravery, it's what we must do." Her voice never broke. "A Spartan woman was brave when she told her man to come back with his shield or on it. But I love you too much to be brave. Just come back."

Their lips brushed in a light kiss. Then her arms were around his neck and she held him tightly. "I love you," Pontowski said. "I'll be back."

Shoshana put on a brave smile, remembering another war, her war, when he had made the same promise. "I know," she whispered.

Then he was gone.

# PART 2

## Excerpt: President's Daily Brief, Monday, June 3.

CONSOLIDATION OF MILITARY REGIONS IN SOUTHERN CHINA FINALIZED. The consolidation of the three military regions in southern China into one military region under the command of General Kang Xun will be completed with the relocation of two divisions from their garrison in the city of Wuzhou to small towns in the interior. These moves will increase the visible presence of the central government in Guangxi Province, discourage rebel activity, and decrease armed resistance against the central government.

# CHAPTER 9

**Tuesday, June 4**
**Over Hong Kong**

The flight attendant moved toward the front of the first-class section and glanced at the sleeping Hazelton. "Miss Kamigami," he said, "the captain asked if Mr. Hazelton would like to sit in the jump seat on the flight deck for the approach and landing at Hong Kong International."

"I thought we were landing at the new airport on Lantau Island," Mazie said.

The young man smiled at her. "We were. But when the captain radioed that we had a special assistant to the president of the United States on board, Approach Control diverted us. They want to know if you have any special requirements?"

An uncomfortable smile flickered across Mazie's face as she unfastened her seat belt. She glanced at the sleeping Hazelton to continue the charade that he was the special assistant. "I don't think so."

"Perhaps you'd like to see the approach, then?" the flight attendant ventured. She followed him out of the first-class section and onto the flight deck. The trip to China had been a revelation for her. She had never traveled first class and been pampered by a system that catered to dignitaries. Dignitaries, she snorted to herself. What makes us so special? Still, she did like the ease and comfort that went along with status.

The extra pilot deadheading into Hong Kong gave up the jump seat and stood beside her, explaining what was happening. They had been stacked in a holding pattern over Lantau Island and were now being given priority for landing at Hong Kong International. He also liked the VIP treatment. The lights of Hong Kong and Kowloon cast a fairytale glow as they flew the dogleg approach into Hong Kong, almost touching apartment buildings on final. She was thoroughly excited by the experience.

A harried young man met the airliner and escorted Mazie and Hazelton through Customs. He explained to Hazelton how the airlift into Hong Kong had strained the system to the breaking point and constantly apologized for their missing escort. After a few phone calls, he discovered their escort was waiting at Lantau Island. Hazelton asked in a haughty manner for a car to take them to their hotel. Mazie wanted to countermand his request, but thought better of it. The young man hesitated. He also preferred that they wait for an armed escort but out of politeness, ordered a limousine to take them to the Peninsula Hotel in Tsim Sha Tsui. It wasn't worth his job to say no to a dignitary.

Because of the fuel shortage, the traffic was light as the driver headed for the Peninsula. They had not gone a kilometer before they were stopped by a surging crowd at a blocked intersection. The driver looked about worriedly when a gang of young toughs started rocking and beating on the limousine. He panicked, jumped out of the car, and disappeared into the crowd. Both rear doors were ripped open.

"My God!" Hazelton shouted. "What's happening?" He couldn't credit how fast a normal ride had degenerated into a nightmare. A hard-looking youth with a red bandana tied around his head reached in and dragged him out of the car.

Mazie recoiled in terror before she realized the gang was ignoring her and focusing on Hazelton. She reached into her bag, pulled out her red address book, jumped out of the car screaming at the top of her voice in Cantonese, and waved the little book as if it were an official document. An older man, the leader of the gang, barked an order and Hazelton was released. He flopped against the car. "Swiss?" the leader managed to say in English.

"Speak French," Mazie whispered to Hazelton. "I told them you were Swiss—a representative for the International Red Cross." Hazelton stammered a few words in French. The men spoke in low tones and then disappeared. "Get in," Mazie ordered. She jumped behind the wheel and started the car.

"I'll drive," Hazelton said.

"Special assistants are chauffeured," Mazie snapped.

"International Red Cross? Very good," the British naval captain said after listening to Hazelton tell of their narrow escape. The bloody fool, he thought. Special assistant or not, if it hadn't have been for his quick-thinking interpreter, he would be floating in Victoria Harbor. The captain was resigned to escorting the two Americans from their hotel to the old airfield at Shek Kong Camp that the British had reopened for the emergency. "Ah, here we are," he said. "The American sector." The small convoy of two armored cars with a staff car sandwiched in the middle pulled up in front of the building the AWACS crews were using for their operations.

Inside, Major Marissa LaGrange, the detachment commander, was waiting for them with her Intelligence officer. Like the British captain, she pitched her briefing to Hazelton as she explained the AWACS mission in Hong Kong.

When she had finished, Hazelton tried to look important. "As you know," he said, "we are authorized to task various U.S. government agencies to support the Military Assistance Advisory Group in Nanning." LaGrange hid her irritation at Hazelton's pompous manner. To her, he was just another bureaucrat. "We," Hazelton continued, "are here to liaison and create the control network for your AWACS to provide an early warning function to the American Volunteer Group flying under the command and control of the MAAG."

LaGrange was tired of Hazelton and had more important things to do than listen to him rabbit on. "Cut to the chase, Mr. Hazelton. What exactly do you want us to do?"

Hazelton blushed and stammered. Mazie opened her

briefcase and handed LaGrange a thin folder. "This is what we had in mind." She waited while LaGrange scanned the contents of the folder.

"We can do some of this," LaGrange said. "But you are asking for coverage beyond our capability. You need an E-8." The E-8 was a Boeing 707 with J-STARS, the joint surveillance target attack radar system developed by Grumman for the U.S. Air Force and Army. The J-STARS used a highly sophisticated radar that could operate in either an MTI, moving target indicator, or synthetic aperture mode. The MTI meant the E-8 could track any moving object on the ground and the synthetic aperture gave it the capability to find targets. J-STARS could reach out over one hundred miles and monitor enemy activity while still flying behind friendly lines. Under ideal circumstances, it could reach out farther—much farther.

"The E-8 is arriving tomorrow," Mazie told her.

Neither Hazelton nor the British captain have a clue, LaGrange thought. Kamigami's the expert. Typical. LaGrange decided to do a little more probing. "JTIDS?" The JTIDS, or joint tactical information distribution system, linked the airborne E-8 with ground commanders, other aircraft, and command and control centers to provide real-time intelligence.

Mazie shook her head no. "We're only getting one mobile J-STARS module. It should be operational at Nanning within forty-eight hours after the arrival of the E-8." One J-STARS module meant the airborne system could downlink to one ground station.

"That's better than nothing," LaGrange said. "At least one ground commander will know what's going on. Without JTIDS, everyone else is in the dark."

"Can you set up a communications protocol between the AWACS and E-8 to relay information?" Mazie asked.

LaGrange shrugged. The J-STARS troops were paranoid about protecting the security of their system. She glanced at the folder and allowed a tight smile. "They'll be all cooperation after they get caught in a retrograde." Mazie didn't understand and said so. "A retrograde," LaGrange explained, "is a forced withdrawal when a hostile aircraft

184

comes looking to hose your ass out of the sky. You turn tail, beat feet, and get the hell out of Dodge."

"How will the E-8 know when a hostile fighter is coming after them?" Hazelton asked.

"Only when we tell 'em," LaGrange said. "They'll get real cooperative when they figure that out." The meeting was over.

The British captain ushered Mazie and Hazelton back to the staff car. He made a mental note to tell the governor the Americans were getting very serious about supporting the rebels in Nanning and playing silly buggers at the same time. The woman was the special assistant.

## Thursday, June 6
## Pingnan, China

The peaceful languor of *xiuxi*, the traditional midafternoon Chinese siesta, had settled over the riverfront marketplace in Pingnan. Most of the vendors were asleep behind their stalls, lulled into drowsy stupor by the gently drumming rain on the corrugated fiberglass awning above their heads. Only four black marketeers were eating and doing business at one of the benches in front of the row of noodle stands. They saw Jin Chu the moment she entered the market.

The four women fell silent when Jin Chu paused at one of the stalls to sort through the clothes strung on coat hangers dangling from the pipes that supported the awning. The vendor, now wide awake, was hovering behind his counter, afraid to speak. He couldn't believe his luck when she started to haggle over the price of a western-style denim jacket. He settled on a ridiculously low price for the knock-off imitation. Jin Chu made small talk with the vendor and then moved on.

"Business will now be good for Kwan Zheng," Su Yei, the oldest of the black marketeers, observed, thinking about the price a real Levi's jacket would fetch on the black market.

"We must be careful," another woman said. "Remember what she did to the rice merchants the first day she was here." The women all bemoaned their fate, recalling how the young woman had questioned the *ho wan,* or good luck, of any vendor who charged too much for rice. Within minutes, the rumor had flashed through the marketplace that Miss Li had sent the rice sellers a dire warning of misfortune. Prices fell accordingly.

The four black marketeers gossiped as they marked her progress through the marketplace. Not one mentioned Jin Chu, but each was busy calculating how she could wheedle her way into the young woman's good graces.

Jin Chu spent over an hour talking to vendors and boatmen before joining the four women. She deferred to their age and made customary small talk until the women returned to their stalls when *xiuxi* ended. She spoke quietly to Su Yei about her middle daughter.

After Jin Chu left, every merchant she had spoken to enjoyed a brisk business for the remainder of the afternoon. But Su Yei closed her stall and went home early.

Kamigami was mentally exhausted when he returned to the hotel where the First Regiment of the New China Guard had established its headquarters in Pingnan. The responsibilities of command were bearing down and extracting a heavy price. He longed for the physical activity of leading men in the field to break the drudgery that was dragging him down.

The quiet of their suite enveloped him when he entered the door. Jin Chu was there, helping him out of his rain-soaked clothes. He recognized the subtle change in the way she moved and spoke—she would be leaving him again.

"When?" was all he asked.

"Very soon," she replied.

"You never tell me."

A confused and worried look spread across her face. Jin Chu was far from being inscrutable. "It is hard for me to explain," she said. "A feeling comes over me and grows stronger until I answer it."

He wanted to tell her not to go. But he knew she would not listen to him. She was a flash of light, a warmth of soul, a spirit that was only his to hold for a few moments before she answered that inner voice that drew her from him. "I'll miss you," he said. "As always."

"I was in the marketplace today," she told him, changing the subject. "I spoke to many merchants and boatmen." Her confused look was back. "They said that many PLA soldiers are moving from Wuzhou up the Lijiang River toward Majiang."

It all made sense to Kamigami. The Lijiang was a friendly river that flowed south from the city of Guilin, past the town of Majiang, to Wuzhou where it joined the Pearl. By occupying Majiang, Kang would have a new forward base of operations to the north. "The PLA wants to capture Majiang," Kamigami told her. "They can use Majiang as a base to push upriver to Guilin. Once they capture Guilin, they will control the northern half of the province."

The confused look on Jin Chu's face grew deeper. "The way of the dragon is through here, Pingnan, not Guilin," she said.

Kamigami shook his head. "For now he's going after Guilin." She did not reply and drew a hot bath for him. While he was soaking, he heard a knock at the front door. A few minutes later, the door of the bathroom swung open and a young woman stood there, hesitant to enter. She was older and taller than Jin Chu, but with her lithe body and beautiful, finely drawn features, she could have been Jin Chu's sister.

"I am May May," she said, speaking in English. The steam drifted around her, casting a shimmering veil over her beauty. "Miss Li spoke to my mother, Su Yei. It is arranged for me to . . ." Her hand darted to her face, covering her mouth, while her dark eyes sparkled with amusement at the look on Kamigami's face. "My Chinglish, it is not good?"

"Your English is perfect," he managed to say.

Her hand dropped away and she smiled at him. She quickly undressed, slipped into the tub behind him, and washed his back. Her hand reached around and lathered his groin with soap. She massaged until he responded. "We will have dinner later," she giggled.

"But Jin Chu . . ." he managed to say.

"Miss Li has gone to Nanning. She said you would understand." She felt the muscles in his back tense. "Are you angry? Please do not be angry with me because I must tell you what you do not want to hear."

"I'm not angry with you," he muttered.

# Friday, June 7
# Nanning, China

The ramp at Nanning's airport was jammed with gray Warthogs, trucks and vehicles of all descriptions, crates, conex containers, and tents. The huge C-5 Galaxy taxiing in barely had room to clear its drooping wingtips. Finally, it squatted on its landing gear, the visor nose swung up, and the ramp lowered. General Mark Von Drexler trotted up the ramp and collared one of the loadmasters. "How soon can you have it offloaded?" he asked, pointing at a truck with a big boxlike container bolted to the bed—the J-STARS module.

The loadmaster told him the truck would be off the aircraft as soon as it was unchained. Von Drexler found the U.S. Army major in charge of the module and demanded that it be set up and operating as soon as possible.

"General," the major said, "we'll be in business as soon as we get the power cranked and the antenna erected. If the E-8 is up and looking, we'll have the PLA wired."

Von Drexler paced the concrete ramp, shouting and threatening until the module was driven off the C-5 and the distinct lollipop antenna erected. The major was sweating from all the attention the general was giving him as the equipment came on line. Before he had a chance to run the built-in tests, an image was appearing on one of the monitors. The E-8 was airborne and transmitting.

A civilian specialist tapped at a computer keyboard, ignoring Von Drexler's threats. He pointed to a bright image on the monitor. "This is the city of Wuzhou," the civilian said. "The dark line snaking out of Wuzhou to the west is the Pearl River." He traced a second dark line that ran to the northwest from Wuzhou. "This line is the Lijiang

River," he explained. "What's interesting is that all water-borne traffic is going northwest, up the Lijiang. It's big stuff." He pointed to a bright string paralleling the Lijiang. "This is heavy equipment moving up a road toward the town of Majiang. Judging by its speed and size, we're talking tracked vehicles. Probably tanks."

Von Drexler spun and marched out of the module. "A genuine licensed asshole," the civilian murmured under his breath. The Army major agreed with him but said nothing.

Von Drexler ignored Pontowski and Frank Hester when Colonel Robert Trimler escorted them into the ornate and luxurious conference room where Zou Rong held his combined staff meetings. "Nice way to fight a war," Hester quipped. Unfortunately, Von Drexler overheard the remark and glowered at them.

"He likes to run the show," Trimler told the two fliers.

"Me and Von Drexler go back a long time," Pontowski said. As the junior ranking officers in the room, the three sat at the rear wall, well back from the table. Most of the meeting was concerned with the building of a new MAAG compound, complete with a command post.

"Von Drexler wants his own headquarters," Trimler explained. "We're sinking a helluva lot of resources into the project."

"Recent intelligence," Von Drexler said near the end of the meeting, "indicates Kang will next attack the town of Majiang. By using Majiang as a forward base of operations, the PLA will be in a position to thrust into the northern half of Guangxi Province."

Zou stared at Von Drexler. "A reliable source reports Kang wants to retake Pingnan," he said.

Von Drexler looked at his notes, breaking eye contact with Zou. The "reliable source" Zou mentioned was rumored to be Jin Chu. "President Zou," he finally said, "your source is, of course, correct. But it is a matter of timing. Majiang is Kang's immediate target, to be followed with a thrust at Guilin." A tick of Von Drexler's eyelid betrayed his nervousness. Pontowski listened as the discussion went around the table. Opinion was split. The American staff officers agreed with Von Drexler and the Chinese staff officers with Zou. The meeting ended in a very polite stalemate.

Trimler escorted Pontowski and Hester out of the conference room to his own, very Spartan, offices. Inside the privacy of the office, Pontowski asked, "What happens now?"

The Army colonel sank into his chair. "Nothing. It's difficult to understand the Chinese mind and to tell the truth, I haven't got a clue. One of their main operating principles is to do nothing when in doubt."

"They better do something," Hester said, "even if it's wrong." Pontowski allowed a slight grin. Hester had just voiced a classic fighter pilot attitude.

"Here's my problem," Trimler said. "I'm trying to create the NCG—the New China Guard—out of chaos. Hell, it's a kindness to call what I'm dealing with chaos. Right now, the NCG has only one unit, the First Regiment at Pingnan, that knows what the pointy end of a rifle is for. And it's a regiment in name only—really a battalion. But it's a top-notch outfit. All that's opposing Kang at Majiang is a half-formed, half-trained home militia of farmers and townsmen with light weapons."

"You've got us," Pontowski reminded him.

Trimler nodded, thinking. "Our best intelligence indicates Kang will attack Majiang—soon. Maybe as early as tomorrow morning. It will be a walk-through for the PLA unless—" he paused, thinking, "unless we can surprise the hell out of 'em. How soon can you start flying sorties?"

Pontowski looked to Hester for an answer. "How soon you want?" Hester asked.

The three pilots followed Pontowski across the ramp in the early morning dark. They were all wearing flight gear and carrying their helmets. The unusual weight and bulk of survival vests hindered them as they climbed the narrow ladder into the J-STARS module. It was their last stop before stepping to the waiting aircraft.

Pontowski had insisted on leading the AVG's first mission of four Warthogs and was watching the three pilots as the tension slowly crescendoed. He wasn't worried about Maggot, because he had flown in the Persian Gulf. But he had two virgins in his flight who had never flown in combat. For now, the two pilots were unknown quantities. Combat, and only combat, was the ultimate testing ground. Whatever happened today, Pontowski knew they would never be the same again.

Inside the module, they all clustered around the civilian technician sitting at a monitor. He pointed out the heavy concentration of targets around the town of Majiang. "Colonel, this is real-time," the technician explained. "It's what's going on right now."

"Cosmic," Pontowski said, "a thing of beauty." Maggot Stuart and Skeeter Ashton agreed with him.

"But Majiang is a hundred fifty nautical miles from here," Tango Leonard said. "That's thirty minutes' flying time. It can change."

"It's close enough," Maggot replied. "We can find the fuckheads and shove a few Mavericks up their assholes." Pontowski and Hester had selected Maggot to be the deputy lead for this first mission because of his combat experience. Tango Leonard was his wingman.

Skeeter ignored Maggot and pulled inside herself. It was a mark of their confidence that she had been chosen to fly on Pontowski's wing. But her stomach churned.

The technician concentrated on the display in front of him. "We've got movement, Colonel. I'd say the attack has started and is spearheaded by tanks."

"Let's do it," Pontowski said. He led them out of the module and to the waiting Warthogs. He could feel the adrenaline start to flow as he walked across the ramp and neared the ominous dark shadow of his jet. Colors and sounds were sharper and he could taste his breakfast. He popped a stick of chewing gum in his mouth and felt it crunch between his teeth. He glanced at his three pilots, wondering what they were feeling.

Frank Hester was standing beside the boarding ladder with the crew chief. "Give 'em hell, Boss," he said. "Wish I was going with you."

Pontowski scrambled up the ladder and settled into the cockpit. Automatically, his hands ran through their assigned tasks, strapping in and completing the before engine start checklist. In front of him, the first shafts of morning light etched the eastern horizon as streaks of red painted the few clouds scudding across the sky.

He looked down the line at the three waiting Hogs. A short and wiry pilot, it looked like Snake Bartlett, was in front of Skeeter's jet, giving her a thumbs-up sign. Further down, Sara Waters was standing with the crew chief in front of Tango Leonard's aircraft. Her arms were crossed, folded tightly across her chest. He couldn't see the expression on her face. A pilot was standing in front of Maggot's Warthog, his arm raised in a clenched fist.

Pontowski caught Skeeter's attention and spun his forefinger, giving the start engine sign. She relayed the signal as the building whine of his auxiliary power unit, the APU, split the early morning calm, supplying bleed air to start the engine. He moved the left throttle into idle detent and checked the ITT, interstage turbine temperature, gauge. "Come on, baby," he urged. He fought the impulse to give the throttle a nudge. It had to stay in idle detent or he would loose all bleed air from the APU. He sensed the engine come to life before the RPM gauge confirmed the start. For the first time in years, he was fully alive, doing exactly what he wanted.

The lower branch of the sun had cleared the horizon as the four Warthogs arced to the north of Majiang, heading east. Pontowski planned to attack with the sun at his back. "Go tactical," he ordered. Maggot and Tango peeled off to the right, taking spacing for the attack. Without thinking, he double-checked his armament panel. He touched the master arm switch, insuring it was in the up position. It was a conscious action to guard against switchology errors. A last glance at his HUD and armament control panels. He was going to drop a pair of five-hundred-pound Mark-82 AIRs on his first pass.

Ahead of him, he could see the IP, or initial point, the last checkpoint that pointed the way into the target. "Skeeter," he transmitted on the Have Quick secure radio, "as briefed. Shooter-cover." He would go in first and drop his bombs while Skeeter crossed behind him, ready to use her bombs or cannon on anyone foolish enough to shoot at him as he pulled off target. He firewalled the throttles as he overflew the IP at three hundred feet. The indicated airspeed needle hovered at 340 knots. It was all he was going to get. "Bossman's IP," he transmitted. He was forty-five seconds out.

"Roger that," came Maggot's laconic answer.

Pontowski's radar homing and warning receiver, or RHAW gear, was quiet. The lack of radar activity by the enemy indicated they had not been detected. "A beautiful thing," Pontowski muttered. Surprise was still on their side. He concentrated on the HUD, not looking inside the cockpit.

Skeeter's distinct voice came over the radio. "I've lost a generator and can't get any weapons status lights." The generator failure had caused other problems, but the Warthog was useless if the weapons system wouldn't come up. She held away from the fight as she tried to reset the generator. The flight manual said to try only three times but Skeeter kept at it.

Not good! Pontowski raged to himself. He could see a line of tanks and trucks strung out on the road ahead of him. A perfect target and no one was shooting at him. Yet. "Hold north of the IP for a rejoin," Pontowski ordered. He was fifteen seconds out.

Without his wingman, Pontowski felt naked. But with no reaction from the ground, he committed to the attack and pulled the Warthog's nose up into a pop maneuver. He rolled the Warthog 135 degrees as he apexed at twelve hundred feet and pulled the nose to the ground in a ten-degree dive. The sight picture was perfect. He couldn't believe his luck. The PBIL, the projected bomb impact line that extended from the bomb pipper/reticle, was lying over the column of tanks advancing down the road. His left hand flashed off the throttles and rotated the release mode to bombs-ripple. He was going to walk all twelve of his Mark-82s down the line of tanks on one pass.

"IP now," Maggot transmitted. He and Leonard were one minute behind him.

The pipper dot in Pontowski's HUD tracked over the lead tank. He mashed the pickle button and felt the Warthog shudder as it shed its six-thousand-pound bomb load. The F-15E he used to fly would have leaped into the air but

Warthogs never leaped anywhere. He pulled off to the north to circle back to the IP and pick up Skeeter.

"Hey, Boss," Maggot transmitted, "you didn't leave fuckin' A much for us."

"I'm taking ground fire," Leonard shouted over the radio. His voice was a high-pitch staccato.

"That's your target," Maggot replied. "You lead, I'll cover."

Pontowski could see the two Warthogs maneuver to the south for the attack. Leonard dove while Maggot arced in behind him. Bursts of flame and smoke erupted from the ground as the two Warthog pilots did their thing.

"Someone down here," Maggot radioed, "is having a very bad day. And it ain't us."

"Skeeter," Pontowski transmitted, "say position."

"IP," she answered. "Twelve thou."

"What'cha doing up there?"

"I'm trying to get this damn generator on line," Skeeter replied. Pontowski grunted an answer. She was still trying. "Also, I'm in radio contact with Phoenix," she added. "Negative threat." Phoenix was the call sign for the AWACS orbiting over the South China Sea 150 miles to the south. By climbing to a higher altitude, she was able to establish contact over the Have Quick radio. The Have Quick used rapid frequency hopping to defeat enemy jamming and provide secure communications. But it was limited to line-of-sight range.

Better and better, Pontowski thought. She's using her head. The AWACS would tell them if an airborne threat was coming their way. "Are you in contact with Romeo?" he asked. Romeo was the call sign for the J-STARS aircraft orbiting in the vicinity of the AWACS. By talking to Romeo, they could learn of other targets on the ground.

"Negative," Skeeter replied. "The AWACS is also trying but coming up dry. Hold on. I've got the generator back on line."

Maggot broke into the radio chatter. "Bossman, it looks like the Fuckheads are doing a 'Highway of Death' number down here." During the last day of the Persian Gulf War, Maggot had flown repeated missions over the trapped Iraqis who were trying to escape out of Kuwait on the main highway. That had been a turkey shoot. Here, in the same way, the Warthogs had stalled the PLA advance and bunched them up on the road.

Pontowski called for a fuel check. All but Skeeter reported "tanks dry." She was still feeding on her wing tanks, but they all had lots of fuel. He made his decision. "We work 'em over. Skeeter, you lead, we cover. Fly straight and level at altitude and pickle over the target area. Everyone, guns only, take your Mavericks home." The antitank Maverick rockets they carried were too valuable to waste when they could use their cannons.

Skeeter led the pass and jettisoned her bombs into the area of heaviest smoke and fires. "Generator looks good now," she radioed.

A gremlin in the system, Pontowski thought. "Roger that. Follow me in." He turned inbound and followed Maggot and Leonard as they started their first strafing runs. Skeeter dropped like a bird of prey from her perch high above and was arcing in behind him as he lined up on a tank slogging across a rice paddy. He squeezed and released the trigger. The Warthog gave off a satisfying growl as he sent a short burst of thirty-millimeter depleted uranium and high-explosive rounds into the tank.

"You're taking ground fire," Skeeter transmitted as he pulled off to the west to reposition for another run. Maggot and Leonard were working to the east. He followed her as she strafed a low levy. He didn't see what she was shooting at but there was no answering fire as she pulled off.

The four Warthogs sequenced in for two more runs before Pontowski called them off for a rejoin. The jets fell into a box formation as Pontowski called for an ops check.

Damn! he thought, I feel good.

The low building the wing used as its operations center at Nanning's airport was a madhouse. Every pilot wanted to see the tapes taken from the airborne video recorder in each A-10, which documented everything the pilot saw through the HUD and heard over his headset. The makeshift briefing room was packed with bodies waiting impatiently for Leonard to load the tape from the first aircraft into the VCR. The room hushed as the first images flashed on the TV screen. Then the audience warmed to the subject.

The comments ranged from the totally obscene to a more mild "Fuck me in the heart!" when Pontowski's tape was played. The camera had recorded a perfect bomb run. "The Bossman is one dangerous dude," one Warthog driver announced, summing up the feelings in the room. But it was the tape of Maggot's strafing runs that silenced the crowd. It was a masterful show of airmanship and the employment of the GAU-8 cannon that left the pilots breathless. A lone, whispered, "Shit oh dear" said it all.

Frank Hester appeared at the door and motioned for Pontowski to join him outside. "We've got a problem with Skeeter," he said. "I was on the phone talking to Maintenance." Pontowski listened as Hester related how Maintenance could not duplicate her generator problems. "They can't find any problem with the generators and it didn't show up on the TEMS," Hester explained. The TEMS, or turbine engine monitoring system, recorded the state and condition of the engine on a computer tape whenever a malfunction occurred. It was an invaluable record that pinpointed mechanical problems. "Maintenance thinks she may be the problem," Hester added.

Pontowski took a deep breath. "Let's look at her videotape. I never saw what she was going after on her strafing runs."

The two men walked into the room and watched and listened. Her tape was running when she tried to reset the A-10's generator and restore electrical power. Her loud complaint that the generators were "a piece of shit!" drew approving remarks from the pilots. The level bomb run when she jettisoned her bombs drew a few derisive remarks that any pilot could have expected.

But the replay of her first strafing pass earned her a "Hey babes, what the hell you shooting at?"

Maggot stopped the tape, backed it up, and hit the play button. He froze a frame. A little *w* was in the lower lefthand corner of the screen, signifying the cannon was firing, and the pipper dot was centered over a man pointing a shoulder-held surface-to-air missile directly at her. She had shot the man with a short cannon burst and every one of the rounds was on target. "You blind, asshole?" Maggot asked, letting the tape play out.

Pontowski looked at Hester. He got a shrug in return. Skeeter Ashton might have simply had some bad luck with the A-10's electrical system. Or she might not. But she could certainly shoot.

The aftershocks from the mission arrived seventy-two hours later. Ray Byers and his Junkyard Dogs appeared outside Pontowski's office with a young Chinese man. He was dressed in dirty civilian clothes and his frightened eyes kept darting to Larry Tanaka, the Japanese-American member of the Dogs. "The Bossman needs to hear this guy," Byers told Waters. She hurried to find him and within moments, Pontowski, Hester, and Tango Leonard were in the office.

Byers motioned to Tanaka, who sang a few words in the local dialect and scowled. "My name . . . Wang Peifu," the young man said in broken English. "I drive tank at Majiang. Dragons come out of sun. Bombs bad but Silent Gun kill many men, many tanks. Silent Gun very bad. Very bad. It kills before we hear."

"What's he talking about?" Pontowski asked. Slowly they made sense of the man's fractured English. He had been driving a tank at Majiang and had been told there would-be no resistance. Then four dragons—Pontowski's Warthogs—had flown out of the sun and dropped their bombs. Much damage had been done, but the tanks were ordered to continue the attack. The dragons came back and Wang Peifu saw each one as it rolled in to attack. Smoke belched from their noses and thirty-millimeter slugs ripped into the tanks before he heard gunfire. Wang didn't understand that the velocity of the shells was faster than the speed of sound. But when the survivors of the attack credited the dragons with having a Silent Gun, Wang deserted. He didn't want to face the Silent Gun again.

"Where in hell did you find this guy?" Leonard asked Byers.

"Don't ask, sir," Byers replied. Big John Washington, the

short, stubby African-American anchor of the Dogs, had bought Wang Peifu from a policeman for three cartons of Marlboro cigarettes. "What should we do with him?"

"Turn him over to the New China Guard," Pontowski said.

"He doesn't want to join the NCG," Big John said. "He's afraid they'll shoot him on the spot."

"We can use him at the compound," Waters said. Byers liked the idea and they took the man back to the two tents and four conex containers the Junkyard Dogs called "the compound."

An hour later, Zou Rong walked into the building with an entourage of generals and Jin Chu. Pontowski told Waters to call Von Drexler's office and tell him Zou was in the building on an unannounced visit. It was standard procedure. With a great deal of ceremony, Zou presented the four embarrassed pilots with medals for their first, and very successful, mission. "We must speak in private," he told Pontowski in very good English. Jin Chu followed them into Pontowski's office and sat in a corner, her hands folded in her lap.

"This is most confidential," Zou began. "General Von Drexler does not understand the situation here. He is ordering you to fly missions that are not . . . ah . . . in the interests of the New China Guard." He looked at Pontowski, hoping he would understand.

Zou led a fragile coalition of allies whose only common ground was a hatred of the central government in Beijing. To stay in power, he engaged in a delicate balancing act. But Von Drexler was throwing it out of kilter by insisting on action or forcing Zou to attack. A military victory at the wrong time and place could give the wrong faction in his alliance an advantage that would drive others out. In the Chinese way, Zou had to choose his battles carefully, and in most cases, doing nothing was better than winning. He was desperate enough to be very un-Chinese in approaching Pontowski with his problem.

Pontowski looked embarrassed and wanted to avoid getting caught in a political squabble between Zou and Von Drexler. "You must forgive my ignorance," he said, trying to think of a way to defuse the issue. "But if Kang had won at Majiang, wouldn't that help give him control of the northern half of Guangxi Province?"

"Ah," Zou said, aware of Pontowski's discomfort. "Perhaps you see only the immediate victory at Majiang. The history of southern China is tied to the Pearl. Kang must advance up the Pearl."

Pontowski was even more confused. "If that's true, then you want him concentrating on Majiang and the north."

"Perhaps Miss Li can explain," Zou answered. "We trust our soothsayers."

What is going on here? Pontowski thought. Do we start consulting astrologers next?

Jin Chu spoke quietly from her corner. "We believe all that is important follows the flow of the Pearl. It is the blood of the dragon and gives our people life. When Kang Xun attacked in the north, it diverted him from the true course. In defeat, he learned he was wrong. Now he will move with great cunning to the west, along the Pearl, toward the heart of the dragon."

She is one beautiful weirdo, Pontowski thought, but behind all this nonsense about the blood and heart of the dragon, I'm hearing the way the Chinese think. A knock at the door stopped him from answering. The door swung open and Von Drexler walked in. He shot a hard look at Pontowski and gave a deferential nod to Zou. "Good morning, Mr. President," he said. His ears were red with anger, belying the controlled civility in his words.

Zou smiled and explained how he had dropped by the wing to honor their success at Majiang. It was a spur-of-the-moment decision. He rose to leave as Von Drexler stepped aside, smiled, and followed Zou out of the office. Jin Chu held back. When they were alone, her eyes captured his for a moment. "You have many enemies," she said. "Kang will send men to kill you."

"They'll probably go after General Von Drexler first," Pontowski replied. She only shook her head no and left.

When Zou and his entourage pulled away in their convoy of staff cars, Von Drexler marched back into Pontowski's office. "You should have called me the moment Zou showed up," he said, his voice sharp and commanding. Pontowski buzzed Waters on his intercom and asked if she had passed word of Zou's arrival to Von Drexler's office.

Von Drexler heard her reply with the name of the man and the time she had passed the message. But Von Drexler wouldn't let it go. His face was flushed and he was shouting. "I command all U.S. forces in China. Not Zou, not you. Do you understand me? You will follow my orders and my orders only. Cross me again, Pontowski, and I'll . . ." He let the threat dangle.

"The mission against Majiang," Pontowski reminded him, "was laid on by the MAAG, not me." He told Von Drexler all that Zou had said. "I'm not the guy you have to worry about. Worry about Kang. The Chinese think he will move up the Pearl River now."

Von Drexler's anger slowly cooled. "He won't. Kang will continue to focus on the Lijiang River and try to take Majiang. Then he'll take Guilin. I'm right about this." He studied the chart hanging on the wall. His eyes narrowed. "Yes," he said, a decision made. "I must present Kang with a threat on his northern flank to keep him looking northward—not westward up the Pearl. I will deploy ten or twelve A-10s to Guilin."

Well, Pontowski thought, that makes sense. Von Drexler is giving Kang a reason to concentrate on the north, which is exactly what Zou wants. So why all the hassle?

## Wednesday, June 12
## Washington, D.C.

The national security advisor scanned the thin, slickly packaged and printed PDB, the President's Daily Brief. The PDB was prepared by a committee at the CIA's headquarters in Langley, Virginia, and supposedly summarized the most important and best intelligence the agency had for the president. Fewer than a dozen people were on the distribution list, and Bill Carroll was number three on the list.

As usual, the PDB concentrated on the Middle East and did not mention China. Carroll had spent years working in intelligence and had learned the one simple, extremely hard lesson that escaped the bureaucrats at Langley: Never overlook the obvious. "We did it with Saddam in Iraq and now we're doing it in China," he mumbled to himself. He had to keep the president looking at China before events overtook them and blew the United States out of the saddle in Asia.

He briefly considered talking to the DCI, the director of central intelligence, who was in charge of all U.S. intelligence agencies and functions. He discarded the idea. The DCI was ferociously territorial and was fond of saying that he determined what intelligence was important. He drove what was in the PDB. No help there, Carroll decided. The DCI would resent any intrusion on his home turf.

Carroll buzzed his new chief of staff. "Margaret, get a message to Mazie. I want her to go to Nanning and start sending daily reports on the situation over there. Tell her we're suffering a severe case of tunnel vision at this end. She'll understand." He crumpled the PDB into a ball and threw it at the door. His frustration was building and he needed a release. He called his secretary. "Tell Chuck and Wayne I'm going for a run in ten minutes." He hoped the two Secret Service agents were up to it.

They weren't.

# CHAPTER 10

**Tuesday, June 18**
**South China Sea**

The E-3 Sentry, the AWACS, rolled into a gentle turn when it reached the southern end of its orbit over the South China Sea. On the flight deck, the navigator cross-checked their position, insuring they were fifty miles off the China coast and well within international waters. The radome mounted above the fuselage continued its relentless, reassuring rotation as its beam reached out over 250 miles to sweep the skies above the Pearl River.

"I hate boring holes in the sky," Moose Penko complained to the other two weapons controllers and the senior director. He stood up and stretched. They were in the eighth hour of the mission and he was bored. Inside China, all was quiet and only the heavy, but routine, traffic flying into Hong Kong had been detected by the highly sophisticated Westinghouse surveillance radar array.

A sudden spike of activity between the three ASTs, the air surveillance technicians, at the rear bank of consoles caught his attention. When they motioned for their boss, the ASO, air surveillance officer, to get on headset, Moose jumped back into his seat in the weapons pit and jammed on his own headset. One of the ASTs had a track. Within seconds it was tagged up and a red, upside-down V flashed on the screen. It was a hostile track and Moose was no longer bored. He grinned at the two other weapons controllers and the senior director.

"Get Major Mom on headset," the senior director ordered. The airborne radar technician hurried back to the bunks at the rear and woke the mission crew commander. Within seconds, LaGrange was fully awake and on headset, standing in the aisle between the senior director in the weapons pit and the ASO.

"Nothing coming our way," the ASO told her. As the mission crew commander, LaGrange's first priority was to protect the E-3. The lives of the twenty-six people on board hung on her ability to maintain situational awareness and never lose sight of the big picture. More hostile tracks were tagged up. "It's all in a corridor between Wuzhou and Pingnan," the ASO said.

LaGrange looked over his shoulder and studied the multicolored display. "They're in a CAP," she muttered. The hostile tracks were tracing the distinct pattern of a combat air patrol, or CAP, between Wuzhou and Pingnan. "What's Romeo reporting on the ground?" she asked. Romeo was the call sign for the J-STARS-equipped E-8 aircraft. It was orbiting two thousand feet above their altitude of thirty-one thousand feet and closer to the coast.

"We're talking to them on the tactical net," the senior director said. The tactical net was used to warn aircraft of airborne threats. "Otherwise, they don't want to talk to us."

"Time to wake them up," LaGrange said. "I'll talk to them on secure." Her fingers danced over the switches on her intercom panel as she contacted the mission director on the E-8 to correlate what the AWACS was detecting in the air with any hostile movement the E-8 might be monitoring on the ground. The mission director on board the E-8 was less than helpful. "Look, dickhead," LaGrange snapped, "there's a shitpot full of bandits in a CAP between Wuzhou and Pingnan. We've never seen this much activity before and we don't think they're up and flying because they feel good this early in the morning. We don't know how that correlates with what you're seeing on the ground and we ain't talking to anybody in Nanning. You are. Give 'em a heads up." She broke the transmission.

On board the E-8, the mission director conferred with his ground surveillance monitors, downlinked with the J-STARS module at Nanning, and relayed a warning.

## Tuesday, June 18
## Nanning, China

The Army major burst out of the J-STARS module, sprinted across the ramp, dodged a taxiing A-10, and ran into wing operations. "The shit has hit the fan!" he yelled. "And nobody is answering the phone at MAAG headquarters."

Waters glanced at her watch. It was 5:52 in the morning. "I'm not surprised," she said. "No one comes to work there before nine-thirty. But Colonel Trimler is here." She paged Trimler and within moments, the Army major was talking to both Trimler and Pontowski. In graphic terms, he made the obvious connection between the combat air patrol and heavy ground traffic moving toward Pingnan.

"I'll be damned," Pontowski muttered, recalling Jin Chu's warning about Kang moving with great cunning to the west, toward the heart of the dragon. "She was right," he said to himself. Kang was moving up the Pearl River and Pingnan was his next objective. He was aiming for the heart of the dragon and Kamigami's First Regiment was at Pingnan, directly in his path.

Trimler picked up the phone and spun the old-fashioned rotary dial to call Von Drexler's quarters. Whoever answered refused to put him through to the general. Trimler slammed the receiver down. "I'll have to go over there and break his damn door down. You load out the A-10s."

"Should we warn the New China Guard?" Waters asked.

"We need Von Drexler's okay to do that," Trimler growled. He ran to his car.

Within minutes, the wing was alive with activity and the first weapons trailers with their deadly cargo were leaving the bomb dump to be uploaded on the waiting A-10s. An hour later, the first four pilots were on their way to their aircraft to sit cockpit alert when a phone call summoned Pontowski to the command post. It was Von Drexler.

"I did not order an alert," the general shouted. "Stand down immediately."

"Sir," Pontowski replied, "we need your presence here." But he was speaking to a dead line.

"My God," Hester said. "I could hear him over here. He was pissed. Stand down?"

Pontowski pulled into himself, recalling what his grandfather had told him about politicians. The spur that drove politicians and the key to understanding them was power. Zou and Von Drexler were politicians fighting over power—and control of the AVG was one of the prizes. But the job of the AVG was to fly and fight. "The man did say stand down. I assume he meant from alert. Bring the pilots into the squadron for training but have Maintenance continue the loadout."

Hester shook his head. "That's splitting some fine hairs. VD won't buy it."

"Probably," Pontowski replied. "But I want the jets ready."

## Tuesday, June 18
## Pingnan, China

Kamigami came awake, not sure what had disturbed him. May May was curled up against him, her gentle breathing slow and measured. He heard the door creak and reached for the nine-millimeter automatic on the floor beside the bed. The door swung open and a familiar shadow stepped through the doorway. He relaxed. Jin Chu had returned. He watched as she padded to the bed and touched his cheek to wake him.

"Please," she said. "You must come. Kang will attack today."

"Where?" he asked.

"Here. At Pingnan."

He rolled out of bed and quickly dressed while Jin Chu roused the sleeping May May. The three left the hotel and hurried to his command bunker. Jin Chu ran beside him, her slender shoulders shaking and her eyes wide with fear. "What do you see?" he asked.

"Fires," she answered. "There are many fires."

The short and wizened colonel who served as the First Regiment's intelligence officer hesitated before telling Kamigami the bad news. He searched the crowded command bunker for his captain but couldn't find him. The colonel screwed up his courage, remembering what his American advisor had repeatedly told him: Never delay telling your commander the bad news. But it was not the Chinese way. He approached Kamigami hesitantly. "General," he blurted, "twenty-four more tanks, supported by infantry, are reported ten kilometers to the east and advancing in our direction." Kamigami nodded and thanked him. The colonel exhaled and scampered away.

Kamigami conferred with his operations officer. There was no doubt that a full-scale attack was imminent and that it was coming from the east. He studied the large situation map on the wall and circled an area in front of the advancing tanks. "Reinforce the eastern approaches with Ox and Ram companies," he directed. He asked his logistics officer if Ox Company had received the first of the Dragon antitank missiles the MAAG had delivered. The Chinese colonel assured him that Ox Company had received the missiles.

His intelligence officer, encouraged by his recent experience in telling Kamigami bad news, pulled him aside and whispered that Ox Company had not drawn the missiles from supply because the logistics officer's brother-in-law had not received an appointment as an officer in the New China Guard. Again, Kamigami thanked him and ordered Ox Company to meet him at the supply dump to draw the weapons. He grabbed the logistics officer and dragged him out the door, leaving his executive officer in charge.

Two American advisors and their interpreters were with Ox Company at the supply dump when Kamigami arrived. "Sir," the senior of the two sergeants said, "we haven't seen a single Dragon, much less trained with one."

Kamigami gritted his teeth. "Use the RPG-7s we captured from the PLA," he said. The Soviet-designed RPG-7 was an old, simple-to-use, shoulder-held antitank rocket. It was effective against light armor but only a lucky shot could take out a main battle tank.

"The RPGs were never issued," the same advisor told him.

"There were crates of them," Kamigami rasped. He turned to his logistics officer. The Chinese colonel started to shake and babble about how the RPG-7s had gone missing. Graft and corruption, the time-honored way of doing business in China, was flourishing in the New China Guard and the colonel had sold the RPGs back to the People's Liberation Army.

The scream of incoming artillery ranging overhead drove the men to the ground. Only Kamigami and the two American advisors remained standing. "Take the Dragons," he told the advisors, "and do what you can." He dragged the colonel to his feet and ripped off his rank. "Give him one and let him say hello to a tank at close range." He shoved the colonel toward Ox Company. There was no doubt his orders would be carried out. He jumped into his staff car and told the driver to return to the command bunker.

Advanced elements of the PLA had penetrated into Pingnan and forced Kamigami to abandon his car a kilometer short of his destination. Twice, he and his driver were pinned down by gunfire. He desperately wanted to take charge of the men around him and lead them in a counterattack. But the responsibility of command demanded that he lead his regiment from the relative safety of the command bunker. He berated himself for giving in to the anger that had driven him to the supply dump and made a mental promise not to make that mistake again.

It took two hours for Kamigami to reach the command bunker. The news that he was back shredded the tension like a sharp knife and within moments, relative calm was restored. For the first time, he saw the difference his presence made. The relief on his executive officer's face was almost comical as he recapped the situation: Four tanks had broken through the outer defenses and were in the town.

The PLA was slowly advancing in brutal, house-to-house fighting. More tanks were reported approaching from the east.

"Have you called for close air support?" Kamigami asked. The executive officer did not answer. Calling for close air support was too important a decision for a subordinate to make. Damn! Kamigami raged to himself. When are you going to learn? The Chinese don't do business the way we do. "Please do it now," he said.

## Tuesday, June 18
## Nanning, China

"Twelve minutes," Frank Hester said. "Not bad at all." The booming thunder of the first flight of Warthogs taking off filled the building near the runway. A sergeant grease-penciled the launch time on the big status board as four more jets taxied out onto the active runway. "If that doesn't impress old VD," Hester grinned, "nothing will. Our first birds should be over target in twenty-four minutes."

The tasking order to fly CAS, close air support, for the NCG had come in from the MAAG on the hour and Pontowski had sent his pilots racing for their waiting Warthogs. The "numbers," or specific details of mission, were relayed by radio to the pilots once they had cranked engines. Tango Leonard had led the first flight of four onto the runway and started his takeoff roll exactly twelve minutes past the hour while Maggot followed with four more. It was fast and it was effective.

Pontowski stood to leave. "You got the stick here. I'll lead the next go."

"Thanks a bunch, Boss," Hester grumbled. "When do I get a turn?"

"If I read this right," Pontowski told Hester, "the NCG is going to need beaucoup help. Plan for a max effort. You'll get your chance before the day's over."

When Pontowski finished briefing the three other pilots in his flight, they headed for personal equipment to collect their flying gear. All honored the ritual of a final stop at the only latrine in the building. The last thing a pilot needed was the distraction of a full bladder in the heat of combat. Because Skeeter Ashton was flying on his wing, she had to wait for the latrine to empty. "Squatting is a pain in the ass," Snake Bartlett called to her when she entered one of the open stalls.

"Not if you do it right," Skeeter shot back. "Put a door on one of the stalls and it won't be a problem."

A good idea, Pontowski thought. But it bothered him that Skeeter was losing her privacy. He made a mental note to talk to Waters about it.

The takeoff and climb out was routine and they flew a box formation to maintain good visual lookout. Damn, Pontowski thought, where are those bandits? We need to be talking to the AWACS. Another mental note. They met Maggot's flight returning to base. All were still carrying their Mavericks. "Maggot, what happened?" Pontowski radioed.

"The place is a fuckin' madhouse," Maggot answered. "Tango was still working the area when we got on station. We were late getting in and only had time to drop our Mark-82s before hitting bingo fuel. We need a FAC for control."

Pontowski made another note about using forward air controllers. Then he remembered. "Didn't Hester use to be a FAC?"

"So the man says," Snake Bartlett answered. "Hester the Molester, they called him."

"Maggot," Pontowski transmitted. "When you land, tell Hester to scramble as a FAC."

"Rog," Maggot answered. "We didn't see any bandits in the area. If you run in from the south, you'll get sun advantage on the Squints."

The four Warthogs arced around Pingnan to the south. They could see columns of smoke belching above the city and numerous fires along the road to the east. "Folks, this is going to be sporting without a FAC to tell us where the Gomers are."

"Our side doesn't have tanks," Skeeter said.

"Roger that," he answered. "Skeeter, cover-shooter on the first pass. I'll keep their heads down. Take your time sorting out the bad guys." The two Warthogs turned inbound as Snake and his wingman orbited to take spacing.

For the next twenty or so minutes, a Warthog would be constantly overhead the target.

A fresh wind knocked the smoke down and rolled it across the ground in heavy waves. As the Warthogs descended through fifteen hundred feet, they were forced to look more obliquely through the smoke, and the tanks they had seen at altitude disappeared. Pontowski leveled off at seven hundred feet. But he was in the smoke and couldn't find a target. He pulled off dry and broke out on top in time to see Skeeter pull up. No bombs separated from her Warthog either. "Off with a malfunction," she transmitted.

"Say problem," Pontowski replied.

"LASTE," came the answer. "The HUD was flickering."

Damn, Pontowski thought, that was what got Tango Leonard on the range. "Jettison your bombs on the road," he ordered. "Hold to the west and contact the AWACS." The troops are going to give her hell for jettisoning her bombs again, he thought.

"Snake," Pontowski transmitted, "dogshit vis down low. Forty-five-degree dive bomb." His grammar was terrible, but the message was very clear to Snake Bartlett and Jake Trisher, Snake's wingman. The smoke was too heavy to see targets on low-level passes but by dropping from a high-angle dive of forty-five degrees, they could look down through the smoke. The Warthogs climbed to twelve thousand feet.

Pontowski watched as Snake led the attack. From his position to the south, the forty-five-degree pass didn't look too steep. But from the cockpit, it looked almost straight down. The view from the ground was even more disconcerting. "Jink!" Jake Trisher yelled over the radio. "They're hosing the shit out'a you!" Pontowski watched as Snake disregarded the warning and pressed the attack. He couldn't see the ground fire but knew it was there. Six bombs separated cleanly from under Snake's Warthog and dropped into the smoke.

"SAM!" Pontowski yelled. But it was too late. A small rocket riding a stick of flame reached up out of the smoke and exploded, engulfing Snake's A-10 as it bottomed out of its dive.

A rush of anger and guilt swept over Pontowski and raked him with iron claws. Then Snake's Warthog pushed its ugly snout out of the fiery cloud and staggered southward for safety, rapidly losing altitude. As quickly as it came, the raging emotion released its grasp.

"Oooh shit!" Snake shouted over the radio. "She's comin' apart."

Pontowski headed for the stricken Warthog to fly cover. Flames enveloped the rear half of the aircraft as it descended through a thousand feet. "Snake," he radioed, *"eject!"* But it was too late. The Warthog broke in half and tumbled forward onto its back. The canopy flew off and the seat came out of the cockpit—headed straight down, less than three hundred feet above the ground. A gut-wrenching pain cut through Pontowski as he watched the rocket on the ACES II ejection seat ignite.

But he hadn't counted on the magic the engineers at McDonnell Douglas had built into the ACES II. The parachute streamed out and jerked Snake free of the seat. The parachute snapped open as Snake's feet hit the water. The chute partially collapsed into the river. But a puff of wind caught the canopy and dragged him onto the southern shore, on the opposite side of the river from the main PLA forces. Pontowski made another mental note, about Snake being one lucky SOB. Within moments, Snake was clear of the parachute and talking on the PRC-90, his survival radio. "Head for the road about a mile south," Pontowski told him. "Try to cross the road and reach the hills on the other side."

"Moving," Snake answered. "But some Fuckheads are shootin' at me."

"I've got them in sight," Pontowski replied. He rolled in and lined up on the soldiers he could see running toward Snake's position. "Jake, fall in behind me. Make 'em keep their heads down." This time there was no smoke hiding his target and the sight picture was perfect. He walked a long cannon burst through the men. Jake was right behind him. The two Warthogs established a tight orbit over the area, their slow speed allowing them to work close in and maintain visual contact. Any movement on the ground other than Snake's gained their instant attention. When the downed pilot was well clear of the area, they started dropping bombs.

Skeeter was in radio contact with the wing at Nanning and arranging for more Warthogs to fly cover for Snake before they ran low on fuel and had to return to base. The frustration building in Pontowski turned to despair as he worked the problem. Snake was in a losing situation. They had no search and rescue helicopters to extract him and they couldn't fly cover during the night. Once free of the Warthogs, the PLA would have no trouble sweeping the area before sunrise and capturing the downed pilot.

Skeeter Ashton checked in. "I've got a visual on Snake," she told them.

"Say position," Pontowski answered.

"Holding over the road. No Gomers in sight. I'm going to land on the road and pick him up."

"Negative," Pontowski transmitted. "Maintain a low CAP." Where are those bandits? he thought. So far, he had only lost one A-10 and he didn't want to risk losing another pilot and aircraft in a foolish attempt to save the downed pilot.

"Jettisoning my Mavericks now," Skeeter radioed as if she hadn't heard Pontowski's last order. She rapid-fired her six Mavericks over the river, striking the north shore. Again, Pontowski ordered her to stay in a CAP above Snake. "Bossman, your transmissions are coming through garbled," she said. "Turning final." She lowered her flaps and gear and circled to land on the narrow road. "Say, boys, I would appreciate a little cover."

Pontowski cursed under his breath as he and Jake headed for the makeshift landing strip. He saw Skeeter touch down on the only straight and clear stretch of road within miles. She rode her brakes and dragged the big jet to a stop. Pontowski wondered if she had enough room to take off straight ahead, because there was no way she could turn around. The canopy raised and he could see her waiting patiently as Snake Bartlett ran for the Warthog. Time slowed and the seconds dragged.

"Bossman," Jake transmitted, "we got company coming down the road. I'm in." Jake lined up on two trucks that were speeding down the road, approaching Skeeter's A-10 from the rear. Jake fired when he was directly overhead her bird. Pontowski was in close trail and fired a burst into the trucks. But soldiers were fanning out from the trucks, still moving toward the waiting Warthog.

He orbited back over Skeeter as Jake made another strafing pass. Bartlett scrambled up the crew boarding ladder and sat on Skeeter's lap. The canopy came down as the Warthog started to move. Not enough room, not enough airspeed, Pontowski thought, as the A-10 staggered into the air at 110 knots. Then its gear came up as it leveled off at treetop level and accelerated. Suddenly, he realized he hadn't been breathing and inhaled with a deep feeling of relief. His stomach untwisted as the three Warthogs climbed into the sky and headed back to Nanning.

Jake's voice came over the radio. "You two look real cozy in there." Snake's head was jammed up against the canopy and the top of Skeeter's helmet was barely visible above the canopy rails as he pressed her back into the seat. The cockpit of the Warthog was definitely not built for two.

"It would be," Skeeter grunted, "if he wasn't such a lard ass and hadn't wet his pants."

Tango Leonard sank into the big overstuffed chair in the corner of Waters' office and took a long pull at his cold beer. He had developed a taste for the local brew and it tasted good after flying combat. A feeling of contentment warmed him as he listened to Waters talk to her daughter over the phone. He checked his watch: Eight in the evening in Nanning meant six in the morning in Missouri. At least twenty other pilots had also wakened their families, calling on the new satellite communications system that had been installed that afternoon. "I love you, too," Waters said as she hung up. The look on her face touched him deeply.

"Where did all this come from?" he asked, gesturing at the new phone.

"The Junkyard Dogs," Waters answered.

"Where did they get it?"

Waters frowned. "I never ask." There was no doubt in her mind that the Junkyard Dogs were engaged in serious criminal activity as they created their own supply system.

Trucks and aircraft arrived at all hours with everything from dental floss to VCRs to high-output electrical generators. The wing was better-supplied than the MAAG and staff cars from the NCG were constantly parked in front of the Dogs' compound.

"What's the Bossman want to see me about?" Leonard asked. He didn't expect an answer but enjoyed the chance to be around Waters and share her company.

"He didn't say." Her smile sent a shiver of hope through the lower regions of his body. Her intercom buzzed and she sent Leonard inside before he could pursue the thought.

Pontowski waved him to a seat near Hester. "We've been talking about Skeeter," he began. "Do we have a problem?"

"Is this about the problem she had with LASTE today?" Leonard asked. Pontowski told him that was part of it. "A few of the hard asses are on her case about it. But hell, how many of the swingin' dicks around here would have landed like that to snatch Snake out of there? It worked because they're both squatty bodies. And she's as good as Maggot with the gun."

"Maintenance can't confirm the generator problems she had the other day or duplicate the HUD malfunction today," Hester grumbled. "Personally, I don't believe she had radio problems today either. She heard every word the Bossman said."

"Are you saying she disobeyed a direct order?" Leonard asked. There was no answer.

Pontowski buzzed for Waters to come in and leaned back in his chair. His face was haggard and his eyes bloodshot. The strain from the mission and the long hours were taking a ferocious toll. "Let's tie up the loose ends so we can get out of here and get some rest." He ran his list of mental notes. "First, when LASTE works, it is super. But the system needs constant care and attention to keep it peaked and tweaked. Any ideas?"

"Charlie Marchioni," Leonard replied. He explained how the civilian who worked for the Air Force Material Command at McClellan Air Force Base in Sacramento, California, was considered the expert on LASTE. "He's an absolute wild man," Leonard explained. "But he knows LASTE."

"Ripper, see if we can get him here," Pontowski said. Waters made a note.

"Second," Pontowski continued, "General Von Drexler wants to station ten of our A-10s at Guilin. I'm proposing we send sixteen pilots and a group from Maintenance. Two hundred people all together. That's a good-sized detachment." He considered the two men in front of him. "Frank, by all rights, you're in line to be the detachment commander. If you want it, you got it. But I do need your body here. We're growing like gangbusters and you're the right man to train our forward air controllers. Your decision."

"I'd like a shot at training the FACs," Hester said. "Just call me Hester the Molester." He grinned. "Besides, I'm getting real good at unscrewing you from the ceiling after a visit by VD."

"Recommendations for the detachment commander?" Pontowski asked.

Hester didn't hesitate. "Give the job to Tango here."

Leonard's mouth fell open and Waters shot a worried glance at Pontowski. She took notes while the men worked out which pilots would make the move to Guilin. "Third item," Pontowski said. "The Gomers were up and flying today but never came out of their CAP. We won't be so lucky next time. We need to be in direct radio contact with the AWACS for early warning." Hester said he would work the problem.

"Fourth," Pontowski continued, "without Search and Rescue and Sandies"—Sandy was the call sign for the aircraft dedicated to suppressing enemy ground fire for search and rescue operations—"we're hanging our jocks out to dry if they're shot down. Snake was lucky because Skeeter had a mile and a half of straight road for a runway. I don't want the jocks thinking that's the standard way to do business."

Leonard laughed. "We do phone box training in the cockpit and find out who we can stuff in with who. My guess is that we'll be lucky to find two other jocks who can sit two in a cockpit."

"Colonel," Waters said, "we're flying over friendly territory and might be able to do what the original Flying Tigers did. They paid a reward to anyone who helped a downed pilot get safely back to base. Let me work the problem with the MAAG. If that fails, I can get the Junkyard Dogs involved."

"See what you can do," Pontowski said. "And last but not least, we don't want to underestimate the PLA. They are one tough bunch and calling them Fuckheads or Squints is an easy way to get caught in a mindset and get blown away. Besides, Squints is too easily applied to a lot of people I like. Encourage the troops to call them Gomers or something like that. But don't underestimate them. Okay, that's it. Get some rest."

When Hester and Leonard left, Waters held back. "Colonel, the sat com system is up and working. You can be talking to your wife in two minutes."

"In a moment," he said. He sank into his chair. "God, I'm tried . . ." Waters sat down and waited. She knew when her boss wanted to talk. "I froze out there today," he said. "For a split second, when I thought Snake had bought it, I couldn't move." He looked at her. Did she understand?

The memories were painful as Waters recalled a distant conversation with her husband. "Was it guilt or anger?" she asked.

Pontowski closed his eyes. She did understand. "Both," he answered.

"Muddy talked about it once," Waters said. Her voice was warm and soothing, the calm after a storm. "Responsibility goes with the job and it hurts when your people are killed. It's worse when you see it. The anger is natural and the guilt is the price paid to your humanity."

"For a moment," Pontowski said, his voice low, almost inaudible, "it consumed me."

"Colonel, have you seen the sign on Frank Hester's desk?" She didn't wait for an answer. Waters had lived with a fighter pilot and knew when to force the truth into the open. "It says it all: 'Do something—even if it is wrong.' Hesitation can kill you out there."

Pontowski stared at the wall. He knew the truth when he heard it. If it happened again, he would have to stop flying combat. His relentless mind pursued the truth. What kind of leader would he be then? He knew the answer to that as well. He wouldn't be a leader. "Thanks, Sara. You help."

Waters wanted to touch and hold him, to share the burden as she had with Muddy. But that was different and this man was not her husband or lover. It was something she couldn't give him. "Sir, I have a request." She looked at him expectantly. He nodded. "I would like to go on the deployment to Guilin."

## Wednesday, June 19
## Pingnan, China

Heavily armed soldiers cleared a path in front of the small procession as it made its way down Pingnan's main street. Kamigami's bulk loomed above the protective shield of staff officers that clustered around Zou Rong as he inspected the battle's aftermath. Jin Chu followed a few steps behind with Zou's bodyguards. Fires were still burning themselves out and the stench of burning tires, oil, and animals drifted down every street. A baby girl, maybe a year old, sat in the gutter crying. Kamigami picked the child up and handed her to Jin Chu. "Please take her to the hospital," he said. Jin Chu cuddled the child and hurried away.

"This was a costly victory," Zou said. "The town is destroyed."

"There is no victory here," Kamigami rasped. His voice carried a savage, guttural quality. "We were saved because Jin Chu warned me of the attack minutes before it started. Even then, if close air support had been immediately available, we could have stopped them outside town."

Zou's eyes narrowed as he reacted to the death and destruction around him. His spies had reported how the AVG had responded to the warning the American reconnaissance plane had sent. But Von Drexler had delayed in warning the NCG and had held the A-10s on the ground until the First Regiment was fighting for its life.

Zou held up Von Drexler in his mind's eye for inspection. What is it you desire? he thought. With a logic born of his culture and the Orient, he circled in on a decision: Von Drexler had to be controlled and then destroyed. As the two men made their way through the wreckage and debris that had been Pingnan, he considered the weapons available to the task. No emotion betrayed his choice. He would control Von Drexler the Chinese way and let him destroy himself. "I want to see the hospital," Zou said. Now he was thinking of Jin Chu.

The hospital was a violation of Kamigami's being. He had lived with the horrors of combat and the shock of first-aid stations and field hospitals. But this was beyond his experience and was a hospital in name only. The halls were littered with bodies near death. Many beds held two people, their bloody bandages soaking the mattress. Sanitation was not a concern and the doors of the operating room stood open. The exhausted surgeons did not change their gloves before the next patient was wheeled in. "It is much better in the military hospital," one of Zou's aides said, loud enough for him to hear.

Kamigami walked out the front door. "We need to fix this," he told Zou.

Zou was unconcerned. "It is the Chinese way," he said. Another aide scurried up and spoke in a low, very rapid voice. "He wants to show us a body," Zou said, following the aide to a truck in the courtyard.

The corpse was lying in the back of the truck wrapped in a blanket. It made Kamigami think of a loose bundle of rags. A soldier peeled back the blanket with his bayonet. Kamigami could feel the sour taste of bile rise in his throat. "The death by a thousand cuts," the aide said, visibly shaken by the sight. The body had been skillfully dismembered and even the fingers had been sectioned at the knuckles.

"My God," Kamigami whispered. "What happened?"

"He was executed," Zou explained.

"Was he alive when they cut him up?"

"When they started," Zou replied.

"Who did this?" A fierce rage was building in Kamigami.

"Kang ordered it carried out in his presence," Zou said. "This is why we call him the King of Hell." He turned away from the grisly sight. "We are a civilized people," he told Kamigami. "This has not been done in a hundred years."

"But why?" Kamigami asked. There was no answer.

Zou spoke to the aide and was handed a small package. "I am told he was an American captured by the PLA." He handed Kamigami the package. Slowly, Kamigami unwrapped the brown paper. Inside were a set of dog tags: WANG PEIFU, JUNKYARD DOGS, USAF. The name meant nothing to him but he had heard of the Junkyard Dogs. This man wasn't an American, he thought.

He stared at the two pieces of gray metal and the chain. But so much like my own, he thought. So much like my own. A gentle touch on his arm broke the spell that bound him. It was Jin Chu, standing close to him, still holding the baby girl. "Please," she said, loud enough for everyone to hear, "may I return to our home?" Kamigami jerked his head yes and led her out of the hospital compound.

Shocked looks followed them. Jin Chu had spoken in a very personal way, much as a wife would when talking to her husband. Zou had also heard. He spun around and walked toward a waiting staff car. His aides exchanged nervous looks as they sought excuses to avoid riding with him. One of them would bear the burden of his anger.

## Friday, June 28
## Nanning, China

The black limousine pulled into the covered portal at the side of the combined headquarters building and glided to a stop in front of the steps at exactly 9:30 A.M. The twelve members of the honor guard formed a corridor leading up the steps and into the building and presented arms as Mark Von Drexler stepped out of the backseat. He was wearing the three shiny new stars of a lieutenant general on each shoulder. One of his aides, an American Army colonel, matched his stride as he walked briskly up the steps and into the building.

"Are you telling me they have ambassadorial rank?" he snapped at the colonel.

"Well, yes and no," the colonel stammered. "The message came from the White House . . . they are here at the request of the president . . ."

"But they are not ambassadors," Von Drexler growled. He barely controlled his anger. "Let me make this perfectly clear," he said. "I am the senior United States official in the

Republic of Southern China. I will not tolerate being second-guessed or overruled by two bureaucrats from the National Security Council."

The colonel struggled to find a way out of his dilemma. "Sir," he finally stammered, "I think their position is adequately manifested by the fact they are waiting for you in your office." He was sweating. He opened the door to Von Drexler's office suite and stepped back, eager to escape the general.

"Mr. Hazelton, Miss Kamigami," Von Drexler said as he entered his offices, "so good to see you again." He shook their hands and escorted them into his reception room. They sat down and a steward appeared pushing a tea cart. "May I offer you some tea or coffee?" he asked.

Mazie sipped her coffee and let the caffeine do its work while Hazelton did the talking. She needed the jolt to offset the effects of jet lag, which physically drained her and had killed her normally healthy appetite. Fortunately, Hazelton had no trouble sleeping on airplanes and seemed to be unaffected by it all. He was eating like a horse and thriving.

"I want to assure you, General," Hazelton said, "we are not here to set policy. Our sole function is to create an interface between the Republic of Southern China and those nations that want to lend support but cannot openly do so."

"Yes," Von Drexler replied, "I understand that. Nations like Japan, South Korea, Taiwan, and the Philippines must maintain the facade of good diplomatic relations with the People's Republic of China while at the same time searching for ways to control its aggressive tendencies."

My, Mazie thought, we do sound like pompous idiots. Come on, Went, cut to the chase.

Hazelton took the mental equivalent of a deep breath and did exactly that. "We are going to implement a supply pipeline into Nanning through Hanoi," he explained.

The look on Von Drexler's face warned them that he did not like that idea. But his voice betrayed no emotion. "That will present certain problems," he said. "However, I am certain they can be overcome if the MAAG controls the distribution of those supplies to the Republic of Southern China and the New China Guard."

And that way, Mazie thought, he has Zou by the short and curlies.

"I'm certain that can be arranged," Hazelton said.

Mazie gave a mental sigh. Hazelton had overstepped his marching orders and she had to intervene. "We have to be very careful," she said, "and cover our tracks. The People's Republic of China must never be able to trace the source of the supplies and money reaching Zou."

"Miss Kamigami," Von Drexler said, infusing a stiffer tone into his words, "the duties of the MAAG are very clear. I cannot let you encroach on my area of responsibility."

Mazie fought to control her anger. She had seen the Concept of Operations, the thin document that guided the MAAG, and knew what his responsibilities were. Come on, she mentally added, you know all about credible denial. Why do you want the MAAG visibly involved? It was a question she wanted answered.

The vague suspicion tugging at the edges of her thinking demanded her full attention. She had an answer to her question. The Military Assistance Advisory Group had been given a free hand in its relations with Zou's new government and Von Drexler was carving out an empire. Mazie reluctantly gave him full marks for the way he moved into any power vacuum and expanded his influence. He was successful because there was no one to tell him no.

"General," Mazie said, "we are here to help you so let's take it one step at a time. We set up the pipeline and the MAAG furnishes us a shopping list. Once we've got the supplies flowing, then we worry about covering our tracks." She decided to churn the waters a little further and see if the general was truly on a power binge or if she had misread the situation. "It is my understanding," she ventured, "that all policy decisions in theater are coordinated through your office." She studied his reaction. Bingo! she thought. That was exactly the ego stroke he needed.

The meeting spun down to polite formalities, and Von Drexler escorted them to their waiting limousine and held the door for Mazie to enter. "I realize you must catch a flight, Miss Kamigami," Von Drexler said. "Perhaps we will have an opportunity to arrange a visit with your father the next time you are in Nanning." He allowed a tight smile when he saw Mazie stiffen. He pursued his advantage. "It will be an easy matter to arrange as General Kamigami reports to me."

That's another lie, Mazie thought as the limousine pulled away for the short drive to the airport. The First Regiment falls under the New China Guard, not Von Drexler. Mazie sank back into the plush upholstery. Von Drexler had sent her a message that he would use her father as a club to control her.

"I screwed up in there," Hazelton said. "Thanks for covering for me. The man's an absolute egomaniac." Mazie gave him a hard look and then shot a glance at the Chinese chauffeur. Hazelton got the message and shut up. They would discuss it later.

The chauffeur split his concentration as he drove to the airport. Whom should he tell what he had overheard? the man who worked for Zou or the woman who spied for Kang? Then it came to him: Both would pay well for what he had overheard about General Kamigami. The other information was worthless—even the whores were talking about Von Drexler.

It was past midnight when Von Drexler returned to his quarters. The large house quieted the moment he entered and the staff hurried to their assigned locations should he require their services. His new majordomo was waiting in the entrance hall. "Good evening, General Von Drexler," he said in his excellent English. "Miss Sun is not feeling well and retired early."

Von Drexler's face registered his disappointment at the news that his current mistress was ill. Few men in this day and age, he raged to himself, have the power and influence I do. Why should I be denied this? "That is very unfortunate," he said.

The majordomo caught the harsh tone in Von Drexler's voice. He nodded, his bland expression not betraying his disdain of the American. He was not afraid of the man, but he did fear power. It was the true aphrodisiac that could destroy or reward when it lured men like Von Drexler. "I have made other arrangements," he said. He caught the signs of interest and allowed a slight smile. "They will explain."

The three girls were waiting for Von Drexler in his bedroom. They rushed to surround him, their naked bodies shimmering with the glow of youth. They chattered in broken English as they undressed him, teasing him with soft, quick touches against his bare skin. A thigh brushed against his erection. Von Drexler tried to act indifferent to their ministrations, as if he had done it all before. I must thank Zou for recommending the majordomo, he thought. The man is invaluable.

The girls led him into the bathroom. The big tub was filled with hot water that overflowed when they climbed in. He relaxed as a hand held his penis and warm lips brushed his cheek and then his mouth. A tongue played across his lips. The girls giggled as they helped him out of the tub and dried him off. He walked into his bedroom and sat on the bed. Now, according to the girls, he had to choose which one of the three would perform. He studied them, deciding which one he no longer wanted. His choice made, he pointed to the oldest. Tears welled up in her eyes and she turned to the corner and waited. A naked boy emerged from the shadows and took her hand. The two lay on the floor and started to make love.

Von Drexler lay back in the bed as one of the girls mounted him, kneeling over his head. He felt a tongue lick at the inside of his thigh as it worked its way upward. He twisted his head so he could watch the couple on the floor.

No one, he promised himself, will ever take this away from me. I've earned it and I'll keep it. He shuddered as he gave in to the moment.

# CHAPTER 11

**Monday, July 1**
**Tokyo, Japan**

Mazie's body ached with fatigue when she followed Hazelton into the large conference room. She hadn't seen a bed in two days and wanted to collapse into the nearest chair. But like everyone else in the room, she remained standing. It was highly unusual for a woman to attend so important a meeting in Japan and the men kept throwing disdainful looks in her direction. An elderly Japanese man entered and studied her face longer than the others. "Miss Kamigami is my personal translator and aide," Hazelton explained.

The old man only said, "We all speak English." He walked to the head of the table and stood looking out the window. Far below, a panoramic view of Tokyo came to life as the glow of neon signs and street lights emerged from the settling twilight.

"That's Hiro Toragawa," Mazie whispered. "We were introduced at a reception in the Japanese Embassy in Washington. He was the guest of honor. If there is a Japan, Inc., he's the CEO."

"Do you think he remembers you?"

"I doubt it. That was four years ago. I was one of the nobodies invited because I speak Japanese."

"Should you leave?" Hazelton asked.

"I'm not sure. But if I stay, it will keep them honest and

224

they'll speak English. There won't be any sidebars in Japanese."

Hazelton was in over his head. "You best stay. I don't know if I can do this. You may have to pick up the pieces afterward."

The meeting started when Toragawa sat down. In unison, the Japanese gave a short bow before sitting. Mazie hoped Hazelton keyed on what was happening. The men sitting at the table were among the most powerful and influential in Japan and they were all deferring to Toragawa. She listened carefully as Toragawa's aide explained why they were here. As the meeting progressed, she paid more attention to the nuances—who was speaking the longest, who was speaking after whom, who was not asking questions—than to what was actually being said. Hazelton deftly fielded many polite questions but Mazie could sense the meeting was not going well. The financial, business, and political leaders of Japan were not going to support Zou Rong and the fledgling Republic of Southern China.

Toragawa spoke in a low voice to his aide, who then announced a short break. Everyone rose and gave a bow when Toragawa stood. Toragawa's aide approached and asked if Hazelton would follow him. When Mazie held back, the aide turned to her, "Mr. Toragawa would be pleased if you would also join him, Miss Kamigami." Everyone in the room heard him.

The two were escorted to a large office suite. The same magnificent view of Tokyo spread out below the huge picture windows. "Look at that," Hazelton whispered when he saw the painting on the wall. "That's a genuine Van Gogh." His head was on a swivel. "That's a Matisse . . . a Monet." He almost lost his composure when he saw the small painting above the seated Toragawa. "That can't be the . . ."

"I would guess," Mazie said, "the original is not in the Louvre." She would not tell Hazelton that Toragawa was part buccaneer, part samurai, and more powerful than a shogun. He had had enough shocks for one day. She smiled at the man seated next to Toragawa—Bill Carroll.

"Please," Toragawa's aide said, motioning them to deep,

overstuffed chairs next to Toragawa and Carroll. Hazelton sank into the chair, his face a study in confusion.

"I just arrived," Carroll explained.

"I asked him to come," Toragawa said. His words were grammatically perfect but heavily accented. "We are not convinced that it is in the best interests of Japan to become involved in the politics of China."

Carroll leaned forward and spoke in a low voice. "A very understandable decision. But my government believes China is going after the four Little Dragons. First, they'll secure Hong Kong. Then they'll press their historic claim for Taiwan. After Taiwan, China will look south to Singapore, which is 80 percent Chinese. Once Singapore is in the fold, they'll either neutralize Korea or tie it to China with trade agreements. By taking over the four Little Dragons, they will have a ready-made industrial base. By adding in its large population on the mainland, China will be in a position to dominate every labor-intensive industry within ten years."

"We have discussed all of this in the past," Toragawa said.

"With China in control of Taiwan and Singapore," Carroll replied, "she can block, or threaten to block, the main shipping lanes leading to Japan."

"China is not a maritime power," Toragawa said.

Carroll looked at Toragawa. "Sir, China has excellent antiship missiles and with launch sites in Singapore, Taiwan, and Korea, can control all sea lanes leading to Japan. Further, China has successfully tested Ocean Wind." Toragawa looked at his aide, an unmistakable sign that he had never heard of Ocean Wind. "Ocean Wind," Carroll explained, "is a satellite guidance system for targeting ships far out to sea. It is part of the Silken Web satellite system."

A sharp hiss escaped from Toragawa. It was so totally uncharacteristic of the man that Carroll was shocked into silence. Toragawa's aide had heard it only once before and then a government had fallen. "Japan," Toragawa said, his voice not betraying his anger, "helped the People's Republic of China launch the Silken Web satellites." His mind raced with new implications. Economic strength gave China the ability to become a military power and the only reason for China to use its antiship missile system would be to protect or further its economic interests. So obvious, Toragawa thought.

Carroll pressed his advantage. "We keep asking the question, What are the targets for those missiles?"

Toragawa knew the answer—shipping, Japan's lifeblood. He looked into the future and concluded that the ultimate target was Japan itself. He stood and paced the floor. His aide almost fainted. Toragawa's anger when he was aroused was deadly. "Now I understand your concern. We will provide the assistance you have asked for. I presume Miss Kamigami is our point of contact?" Carroll nodded, and Toragawa marched back into the conference room.

He stood at the head of the long table and gave a short speech in Japanese, recapping what Carroll had said and what it meant for them. Mazie translated for Hazelton. Toragawa asked the men to sit down and he rattled off "suggestions." There was no discussion and only an occasional *"hai"* to signify agreement. Hazelton's hands shook when he wrote down the numbers and the sums of money Toragawa kept repeating.

Toragawa pressed a button and a wall panel raised revealing a map of China. "Our main problem," he said in English, "is transportation. It would be best if we used the harbor at Haiphong in Vietnam and transshipped by rail." He used an electronic pointer to outline the railroad from Hanoi to Nanning. He nodded and the meeting was ended.

Toragawa remained standing while the men filed out. "Miss Kamigami," he said, his voice hard and cutting, "Japan's contribution must remain a secret. We will do our part in Japan. But security outside Japan is your responsibility." Then his face softened. He could see she was exhausted from traveling. "You will be very busy during the next few days arranging details. My family would be honored for you to stay with my granddaughter. It would be much more convenient and comfortable." It was quickly arranged and Mazie left with Toragawa.

"I can't believe that," Hazelton told Carroll.

Carroll gave a short laugh. "Believe what? That the Japanese can make decisions so quickly when their interests are threatened?"

"I mean how did he know about Mazie?"

"I told him," Carroll answered.

"Is that why he invited her to stay with his grand-daughter?"

Carroll closed his briefcase. "His granddaughter is the last of the Toragawa line. He knows Mazie can be a role model and show her what a woman can do in the modern world. The old gentleman doesn't miss a trick when it comes to preserving his family."

Pieces started to fit together for Hazelton. "Is that why you picked Mazie to head the China Action Team?" Carroll allowed a slight smile but didn't answer. "Did you suggest using Haiphong and the Hanoi railroad?"

Carroll snorted. "No. I didn't have to. Toragawa is heavily invested in rebuilding Haiphong and Vietnam's transportation network."

"Toragawa's going to make a profit out of this?" Panic edged Hazelton's words.

"Megabucks," Carroll replied. "Make that megayen. It was just one more reason for him to buy in. If you will, the frosting on the cake."

Hazelton was incredulous. "That's illegal! We can go to jail."

"Only if we personally make money. So don't take kickbacks and don't get caught."


Miho Toragawa, Hiro Toragawa's only grandchild and the last of his family, was waiting for Mazie when she emerged from her bedroom the next morning. "I hope you slept well," Miho said. She was a slender, very pretty twenty-nine-year-old woman with beautiful doe eyes.

"Very well," Mazie replied as they sat down at the small table that had been set for a western-style breakfast. "And thank you for the use of the kimono. It's beautiful." They exchanged pleasantries as Mazie picked at her food. She still hadn't found her appetite. Miho's English was perfect and Mazie learned she had studied at Mills College in Oakland, California, before earning a graduate degree at Harvard in business and finance. Mazie found herself drawn to the young woman and they were soon good friends.

"My grandfather," Miho confided in Mazie, "hopes that I can make a good marriage to continue the family heritage."

Mazie had read the dossier on Hiro Toragawa. "Your grandfather is a most unusual man," she said. "He may have other plans for you. Did he explain why I'm in Japan?" Miho nodded. "Perhaps," Mazie ventured, "we can work together?"

"Yes," Miho said, "I would like that." She became very businesslike. "We will have to work behind the scenes through male surrogates—shadows within shadows." She sipped her tea. "It is the Japanese way. My grandfather says you have such a man and he has arranged certain connections." She smiled. "We must be very discreet."

The two women spent the next hour plotting their strategy. Mazie soon realized that Miho had an insider's knowledge of how the system worked and would be invaluable in creating what they started calling "The Japanese Connection."

Mazie stood and tugged her borrowed kimono into place. It was four sizes smaller than anything she had worn in years. The constant traveling and crossing time zones had played havoc with her appetite and metabolism and she was losing weight. "Miho, I know that appearances are very important, and none of my clothes seem to fit. Can you help me select the right clothes to wear? I don't wear makeup and perhaps I can do something with my eyes, like yours."

Miho's hand came to her mouth to hide her smile. "My eyes were like yours," she said. Miho explained how a plastic surgeon cut the eyelid muscles that created the epicanthic fold of the eyelid. "It is a simple operation and only takes a few minutes. Your eyes are black and blue for a few days. But it's better than being poked in the eye with a sharp stick." They giggled at Miho's use of American slang. "It can be done while you're here," Miho said. "I can arrange it."

Mazie found the idea intriguing. "I could never fit it into my schedule," she said. Miho only smiled.

Wentworth Hazelton paced the ramp in front of the twin-engined Gulfstream IV business jet as he waited for Mazie.

He glanced at his watch—ten minutes before they lost their takeoff slot. "Come on," he grumbled, "where are you?" He was tired and irritable after spending a week in Tokyo and had staked his claim to the bunk on board Toragawa's personal jet. He intended to sleep for the entire flight to Hanoi. When he saw the black limousine speeding across the ramp, he climbed on board and told the pilots to start engines.

"Miss Kamigami is on her way," he told the two Air Force sergeants who were going with them. "When I told her you were going with us," he said, making conversation, "she called you the Junkyard Dogs. That's a very unusual name."

Ray Byers shrugged. "That's Colonel Pontowski's name for us," he said.

"We're procurement specialists," Little Juan Alvarez added.

"Well, then," Hazelton said, "you can help us in Hanoi."

"That's the idea," Byers replied.

Four suitcases preceded Mazie into the airplane and Hazelton barely recognized her. Her hair had been cut and styled and she was wearing new, and very expensive, clothes. "Why the sunglasses?" he asked.

"My eyes are tired," she replied. She dropped the bags she was carrying and hurried back down the boarding steps to say goodbye to Miho.

Little Juan Alvarez looked out the window and said, "Nice."

## Sunday, July 7
## Nanning, China

"This is a shoot and scoot exercise," Trimler said as he escorted Zou Rong onto the observation platform that had been constructed for Zou's visit to the training range. He was the only American on the range and stood beside Zou as an eleven-man crew towed an M-119 105-mm howitzer into position. "It's a race against time," Trimler explained. "They must set up, fire three rounds, and be moving within minutes. Otherwise, they can come under counterbattery fire. The weapon weighs four thousand pounds and can hurl a shell over thirteen kilometers."

Zou waved him to silence. "I'm pleased," Zou said, "that the New China Guard now has artillery. But when will we receive the tanks General Von Drexler has promised?" He did not wait for an answer and descended the stairs.

Most of Zou's staff were clustered under a canvas canopy behind the observation platform sipping orange juice. Like Zou, they were bored. To a man, they flinched when the howitzer fired. "Bring the staff cars," a freshly minted general ordered when he saw Zou move down the stairs. He checked his watch. They were ahead of schedule. "Call the restaurant," the general ordered. "President Zou will be arriving early for lunch." He turned to his aide. "Was Miss Li invited to join the president?" The aide assured him that both Kamigami and Jin Chu had arrived from Pingnan that morning and would be present.

The "lunch" was a twelve-course meal. Zou sat at the head table and listened as his staff discussed the status of the New China Guard. He automatically discounted 90 percent of what his staff said as posturing and lies. He turned to Trimler. "Eighteen days ago the First Regiment won a major victory at Pingnan. I saw for myself the cost of that victory. They suffered many casualties. Yet now"—he made a graceful gesture toward Kamigami's end of the table—"they are combat ready while my main divisions remain in training. Why?"

The staff officers around Zou fell silent and waited for Trimler's answer. "I can think of many reasons," the American said. "Among them are leadership, training, and logistics. For some reason, the First does not have a supply problem." Zou looked at the three generals who coordinated the flow of supplies to his army. They steal, he thought, but not from the First Regiment. "And the First," Trimler concluded, "has high morale. The men trust their leaders and believe in what they are fighting for."

"Is it ever that simple?" Zou asked. The Americans will never understand, he thought. The twentieth century and fifty years of communism had not changed China.

For Zou, it was Jin Chu who breathed life into the First Regiment. Her powers as a fortune teller were reaching mythical proportions and her visions of the future were never wrong. Because Kamigami's officers trusted her and his men held her in awe, she gave a legitimacy to Kamigami only the Chinese could understand. In the past, it was a mark of "the mandate of heaven," which gave an emperor the right to rule.

Zou was acutely aware that she was sitting near him, next to Kamigami.

It was late afternoon when Kamigami returned to their home in Nanning. He was tired after spending the afternoon in an endless round of meetings at the Combined Headquarters with Zou's staff and Von Drexler's advisors. The only break in the frustrating routine had come at midday when he and Jin Chu had attended the luncheon for Zou. For a brief time, he had relaxed in her calming shadow and touched reality.

For a moment, he stood in the doorway to the family room and watched as she and May May played with the baby girl he had rescued from the gutter in Pingnan. The women were cooing in a language he did not understand. They could be sisters, he thought. Slowly, the tension of the day slipped away. I'm in over my head playing staff politics, he concluded. I belong here and in the field, with my men.

Jin Chu sensed his presence and looked up. May May smiled and carried the baby from the room. "A gift arrived this afternoon," Jin Chu said. She showed him an exquisite jade carving of a dragon and a tiger. It was about ten inches long and mounted on a black lacquer base.

"It looks very old," he said.

"It was carved during the Ming Dynasty over four hundred years ago," she told him. "It is priceless."

"From Zou?" he asked. She didn't answer.

That night he dreamed of Jin Chu recounting the legend of the four beauties.

Von Drexler's majordomo stood quietly, waiting to be of instant service while the general ate breakfast. "James, where did you learn to speak English?" Von Drexler asked.

The majordomo told him that he had been born and educated in Hong Kong. "Yes, I see," Von Drexler said. He rose to leave. "Bring my car."

"It's here, sir," James said. He was offended that Von Drexler would think he could overlook such a basic duty.

"Get rid of the girls," Von Drexler said.

"Do you require others?" There was no answer. "Perhaps you desire some other type of diversion?"

Von Drexler paused, considering the offer, teased by its implications. "Surprise me," he replied.

James escorted the general to his waiting staff car and bowed when it pulled away. He walked sedately to his office, a study in composure. However, he did allow a slight smile when he made the necessary phone call.

"I need to see the bossman," Trimler said when he walked into Sara Waters' office. "All hell is breaking loose over at Combined Headquarters. You got any sanity pills here?"

"We used them all up last week," Waters replied as she paged Pontowski.

"Call the Junkyard Dogs," Trimler said. "We need to talk to them." He set a small zinc-lined tin box on her desk and dropped a set of dog tags beside it.

"What's that?" she asked.

"The worldly remains of Wang what's-his-name, the deserter the Junkyard Dogs adopted."

"Wang Peifu," Waters said. She telephoned the Dogs' compound. "Washington and Tanaka will be right over," she explained. "Byers and Alvarez are in Hanoi."

Within minutes, Pontowski and the two Junkyard Dogs were staring at the box as Trimler related what Kamigami had told him. "The PLA executed Wang . . . they call it the death by a thousand cuts. I think the bastards sent the body back as a warning. Kamigami had the body cremated and brought the ashes with him yesterday. What in hell was Wang doing that got him captured in the first place?"

"We wondered what had happened to him," Big John Washington replied, avoiding the question. What Pontowski doesn't know won't hurt the Dogs, he decided. When Byers had heard the rumor about ten Warthogs going to Guilin, he had called in some markers owed him at the

MAAG. It was better than being a stockbroker with insider information and he had sent Wang to Guilin to do some advance trading. But he had never returned.

Washington touched the box and then, his decision made, picked it up. "He was a good dude. There's a temple in Nanning with a house of the dead. We'll buy space for him on the wall. He'll like looking down."

Trimler sank into a chair when the Junkyard Dogs left. "Brace yourself," he grumbled, "Von Drexler is turning into a megalomaniac. I think he fancies himself a reincarnation of Douglas MacArthur and a grand strategist. The war's slowed down and we're not seeing any fighting. I think the PLA and New China Guard are feeling each other out, looking for soft spots, places to attack. VD claims the PLA is going to make a major push into northern Guangxi Province and take Guilin. But Zou isn't buying it."

"So," Pontowski said, "one of them ends up with egg on his face if the other one is right."

"That's not all," Trimler said. "VD has turned this into a pissing contest with Zou. Remember those ten Warthogs you're sending to Guilin? Scratch that. He's ordered the entire wing to go."

"So our supply line gets a little longer," Pontowski said. "It could be worse."

"It is worse. You stay here."

Anger shot across Pontowski's face. "What the hell's going on?"

"He's assigned you to a staff job at Combined Headquarters to 'liaison'—whatever that means."

"There is no way," Pontowski gritted, "that he's going to take my command away." He jammed his hat on and headed out the door.

"Matt," Trimler called after him, "change your uniform. He doesn't allow flight suits or BDUs."

"I'm not a REMF," Pontowski shot back.

"I've never seen the colonel so angry," Waters said. "What's a REMF?"

"A REMF is a rear echelon motherfucker," Trimler explained. "And it's time I quit being one."

General Von Drexler never saw the flight suit or the anger. What he did see was a well-turned-out lieutenant colonel in a class A uniform with every ribbon properly displayed. The general was painfully aware that Pontowski's decorations had been earned in combat, not from staff duty like his own.

"I take it," Von Drexler said, "that you do not agree with my decisions."

"I didn't at first," Pontowski replied. "Then I thought about the possible benefits of a headquarters assignment. After all, I did work for you in the Pentagon and learned a great deal." The last was true, but not in the positive way he made it sound. His tour in the Pentagon had been a depressing experience. "Liaison duties will allow me a chance to . . . ah . . . reestablish my former contacts and . . . ah . . . look to the future." The hint of using political influence was obvious. He looked expectantly at Von Drexler, whose face suddenly resembled a frozen halibut. That put a little tension in the old sphincter muscle, Pontowski thought.

Von Drexler considered his next move. Originally, he had intended to capitalize, as he had at the Pentagon, on having the grandson of a former president of the United States work for him. Since Pontowski had never played politics at the Pentagon, he considered it a safe move. Apparently, Pontowski had changed. The last thing he wanted on his staff was an ambitious subordinate officer who had the inclination, and the connections, to play politics.

So much for the stick, Pontowski thought. Now it's carrot time. "As you know, sir, Captain Leonard was recently promoted to major. I've selected him to be the detachment commander at Guilin and he's there now doing a site survey. He reports that base defense is nonexistent. I don't see how we can provide proper security for ten Warthogs, much less thirty-six." He didn't complete the thought. Someone would have to take the heat if an infiltrator destroyed any parked A-10s.

Von Drexler had a nominee for that someone. "I need you on the combined staff," he said. His voice was smooth and reasonable. "But I also have an obligation to protect my resources at Guilin. Given your experience, it would be best if you bedded down the wing at Guilin. We can reconsider your assignment to my staff later, once the operation at Guilin is up and running."

Pontowski made sure his voice carried the right amount of disappointment when he acknowledged his new orders. Twenty minutes later, he walked into the squadron, twirling his flight cap on a finger. "We're moving to Guilin," he told Hester and Waters.

"We?" Waters asked.

"All of us," he replied. "I just had to explain it to the general in terms he understood."

## Friday, July 12
## Guilin, China

The two Warthogs approached from the south, flying a relaxed route formation above a carpet of white puffy clouds that reached to the far horizon. Patches of vibrant green broke through an occasional gap in the clouds below them and set a contrast to the brilliant blue of the sky.

Inside the cockpit of the lead jet, Pontowski relaxed into the seat and scanned the sky, taking in the panorama. The grinding burden of command slipped away and a rare feeling of contentment claimed him. I haven't smelled the roses in a long time, he thought. His mind roamed and a memory of Shoshana running down a golden beach on their honeymoon teased him for a moment, only to be replaced by an aching feeling. He missed his wife.

"Guilin on the nose," Maggot radioed. "Twenty miles." The forty-minute flight from Nanning was coming to an end and reality with all its harsh demands was back. He and Maggot were the first of the Warthogs flying in from Nanning and he had to get the wing bedded down and operational as soon as possible. Pontowski rocked his wings and Maggot collapsed into a tight formation as they descended through a break in the clouds. "Storybook time," Maggot said.

It was true. Below them, green rice paddies and five-hundred-foot-high, steep-sided karst mountains wove a spectacular mosaic with the Lijiang River. It was a landscape that existed only in fantasies and Guilin. Pontowski led Maggot up the Lijiang and circled the town, prolonging the flight. Finally, he contacted the tower and the two

Warthogs circled to land at the only airport, located six kilometers south of town.

A crowd of Chinese waved at the two Warthogs as they taxied past the passenger terminal to the ramp where a large collection of green tents and vehicles indicated the Americans had set up base. The area was alive with activity as they taxied into the chocks. Two crew chiefs unfurled a large, freshly painted banner: WELCOME TO NEVER NEVER LAND. "Oh, I hope so," Maggot radioed just before he shut engines down.

Tango Leonard was waiting with a staff car and a broad smile. "Welcome to Guilin," he said. "When do the rest of the Hogs get here?"

"They'll be coming in later today," Pontowski told him. "Has the main convoy arrived?" He was worried about the trucks and buses that had taken the overland route.

"They pulled in an hour ago. No problems."

Pontowski decided to let him off the hook. "Sara is flying in tomorrow on a C-130 with the stragglers."

Leonard beamed. "Boss, this may be the fastest and best unit move in the history of the Air Force. Wait till you see our quarters. We've got the Holiday Inn downtown. It's fantastic."

"How did you manage that?"

"The Junkyard Dogs bought it." Leonard managed not to laugh at the shocked look on Pontowski's face. "They said it was a fire sale," Leonard told him.

The wing had been at Guilin two weeks when Sara Waters decided it was time to do something. She had sent out all the right signals, said the right words, and certainly let John Leonard know she was available. Now she had to get him out of neutral and moving in the right direction. There was no doubt that he was attracted to her and equally, she was sure of her feelings about him. Maybe, she thought, it's because I'm older than him. Maybe seven years does make a difference. "What the hell," she mumbled, "do something, even if it's wrong."

Working and living with fighter pilots had given her a new approach to problem solving. She plotted her tactics, chose her weapons, and went on the attack. First, Pontowski. She cornered him in his office and fired her opening salvo. "Sir, the men are getting bored. We're not flying that much and the war seems to have died down. They're calling it a 'phony war' and need something to occupy their attention."

Pontowski had heard the same grumblings. "We're not flying as much as I'd like because of a fuel shortage," he explained. "We need to hold a reserve for combat. And this isn't a phony war, it's just the way it's being fought. It will heat up again." He grinned at her. "You have 'something' in mind about the boredom?"

"Yes, sir. I'd like to scout around the countryside and find a school or orphanage we can adopt. I'd be gone a day or two." She smiled sweetly when he said it sounded like a good idea. "I can't go alone"—she hoped she wasn't blushing—"and we'll need a project officer." He asked if she had a name. "Tango Leonard," she answered. "Well," she hastened to add, "we've worked together before and he was a schoolteacher."

"See if he'll volunteer," Pontowski said, certain that he would.

Now it was Leonard's turn. Waters drove back to the hotel and checked the pool. Leonard was stretched out on a sun lounge reading. You are looking better, she thought. He had lost his pudgy, potato shape and looked lean and hungry. She went to her room and changed into a swimsuit, a conservative one-piece. She appraised herself in the mirror. Not bad, she thought. Then she stripped it off and changed into plan B. My God! she thought, I feel naked. The flimsy string bikini was shocking. "Perfect," she announced to the image in the mirror. She picked up a towel, suntan lotion, and a book and went down to the pool. Twenty minutes later, she had her volunteer.

A morning mist drifted over the river, shrouding the bases of the mountains and the far shore. Leonard opened the window of the room he had found at the best hotel in Yangshuo, a small town thirty-five miles south of Guilin. He sat on the sill and took the morning in. A fisherman poled his long raft of five bamboo logs out of the mist. Below him, the first of the farmers bringing their produce to market made their way down the narrow street.

Sara Waters padded across the room and sat on his lap. She was wearing his shirt and leaned back into his arms. "I love this place," she said. He held her and said nothing. "Do we have to go back?" For the first time in years, she felt content. Too often in the past, she had found herself looking for a substitute for Muddy, and she knew that was wrong. Now that was behind her. They sat in the window, saying nothing as the town came to life.

"We do have to go back," Leonard finally said. "But we had better find a school or orphanage first."

"I've already found a school," she said. "Orphanages are harder to come by."

"Sara!" he was shocked. "Did you plan this?" Now it was time to play coy and she didn't answer. "One thing," he said. "Please don't ever wear that bikini in public again."

He kissed her neck, sending shivers down her back. She felt like a schoolgirl again. "I did have to get your attention." She understood fighter pilots only too well. They liked to chase wild, flashy women. But once caught, they wanted respectability. Only Leonard would see that swimsuit again, in or outside the bedroom. She laughed to herself at how easy it was.

The squadron building was quiet when Pontowski arrived. He checked his watch: 0715. He wandered through the offices. Only Frank Hester was at work. We're too kicked back, too relaxed, he thought. We need some tension, an edge, or it won't be long before boredom will cause problems. It's this place, he decided.

"Ripper called in," Hester told him. "She'll be back later this afternoon. She says they found a school." A crooked grin crossed his face. "I'll bet that's not all they found."

Pontowski walked outside, thinking. He was responsible for fifty pilots, counting himself and Hester, thirty-six Warthogs, 625 maintenance troops, 174 support personnel, and four Junkyard Dogs. They were isolated in a beautiful resort town in southern China on the end of a tenuous supply line, living a pampered life in a luxury hotel, and all bored silly because the war they had come to fight had suddenly evaporated. Or had it?

Time to start doing walkabouts, he decided. It was a trick

he had learned from his grandfather. Nothing, the late president had often claimed, shakes the tree more than the boss dropping in for a friendly chat from time to time. Strictly unannounced, of course.

He headed for the flight line two kilometers away. Rather than drive, he decided to walk, since he felt the need for exercise. The road looped around a fruit orchard and did not run directly to the flight line. He followed the road until it reached a well-worn path that cut through the trees. Without thinking, he turned down the shortcut. It was a mistake.

At first, he didn't see the two men and only a darting movement at his deep left caught his attention. A warning sensation rocked him with an intensity that sent his adrenaline racing. He keyed the hand-held radio that had become a permanent part of his existence and tied him to the squadron. "Groundhog," he transmitted. "How read?" No answer. The schedulers and SOF hadn't reported for work yet.

He chanced a quick look, checking his back. Now he could see two men coming toward him, moving from tree to tree. With a force he could not credit, Jin Chu's words came back. "You have many enemies and Kang will send men to kill you," she had said. He cursed himself for not believing her. He started to run. Again, he keyed his radio. "Mayday! Mayday! Bossman transmitting in the blind. I'm being chased by two men through the orchard west of the flight line." Again, no answer.

Another backward glance. The men were running, silently and with purpose. A bitter taste flooded his mouth and he ran harder. Ahead of him he could see the hangars and safety. His body responded as he put on a burst of speed and jinked to his left.

A third man was angling in from that side, carrying an automatic pistol with a distinctive silencer. Pontowski cut back to the right, away from the hangars. He heard a soft pop—the man was firing—and bark flew off a tree to his immediate left. Three more pops. He was outdistancing the two men behind him but the lone man on his left was forcing him to cut back farther and farther to the right.

Pontowski was no hero and had no self-delusions. He was bigger than the Chinese pursuing him and for the moment, faster. But he had experienced enough combat to know the odds. He had to escape or be killed. Then he realized the two men behind him were deliberately lagging as his pursuer on the left herded him away from safety and back into the trees.

It was a well-executed, fast-developing cutoff tactic. His internal clock, the sense of elapsed time that is the key to situational awareness, clicked to ten. He had been running approximately ten seconds. It was going down fast and he would be dead within seconds. More pops.

There was only one choice open to him and he didn't like it. Pontowski buttonhooked to his left and ran straight at the single man who had been running the cutoff. Less than twenty feet separated them. Pontowski snarled as the man skidded to a halt and leveled his pistol straight at Pontowski's chest. Pontowski faked a move to his right and cut back to his left. Two rapid pops. He was still moving.

Pontowski yelled as he hurled his small radio at his assailant. Just before they collided, his right hand swept across and knocked the pistol out of his opponent's hand. It flew into the trees as he threw a massive body block into the smaller man. He never lost his balance and kept on running.

And he knew he was dead.

Ahead of him, a boy was aiming an automatic at him. An ugly sneer split his face as he fired. "Colonel!" the boy yelled. "Drop!" The boy was aiming behind him and he was in the way. He rolled to the ground as the boy fired again. Silence. The boy darted past him and examined the bodies of the three men lying on the ground.

Pontowski pushed himself to his knees and took deep breaths. Slowly, his breathing returned to normal. The boy came back, a disappointed look on his face. "I'm very sorry," he said, "they are dead. We can't question them now. You are very lucky, Colonel Pontowski."

"I owe you," Pontowski said. Then he placed the boy. He was one of the numerous Chinese civilians the wing hired to do odd jobs and build revetments for sheltering the A-10s. "Who do you work for?" Pontowski asked. Coherent thought was starting to return. There were many questions he wanted to ask.

"General Kamigami sent us because Miss Li said you

were in danger." The boy looked around, now nervous and wanting to leave.

"How did you know I was in trouble?"

The boy reached behind his back and unsnapped a radio from his belt. It was a duplicate of Pontowski's. "I heard you call for help."

"Who sent them?" Pontowski gestured at the three bodies.

The boy shrugged. "Kang, perhaps." Then he was gone, running through the trees.

Pontowski looked around. He was very much alone. Slowly, he retraced his steps and examined the bodies. The boy was an excellent shot. He found his radio, knocked the dirt off and hit the transmit button. This time Hester answered. "Where are you, Boss?"

"In the orchard," he answered. "I was bushwhacked. Send security." Supposedly, the base was guarded by a unit from the New China Guard. A lot of good they did, he thought. But he was grateful for his unknown protectors. He made a mental promise to thank Kamigami and return the favor.

He headed back for the squadron, reconstructing the incident in his mind. He calculated less than three minutes had elapsed since he entered the orchard. "You die quick in China," he muttered to himself.

# CHAPTER 12

Saturday, July 27
Hanoi, Vietnam

It escaped the maitre d' of Hanoi's newest tourist hotel why four of his country's most influential government bureaucrats wanted to discuss business in the lounge. It was hurting business but, until they left, he had to give them the privacy they demanded. He glanced at the growing line—no one of importance. He would keep the lounge closed until the bureaucrats finished their business. But his curiosity was piqued. Who were the two Americans they were talking to?

He breathed a sigh of relief when the four officials stood and the men shook hands. He dropped the rope when the four marched out, obviously uncomfortable in their new western-style suits and doing business in an informal setting. After years of stagnation, Vietnam was rapidly changing.

Ray Byers sank back into the low overstuffed chair and signaled a waiter for two more beers. Little Juan Alvarez eyed the crowd that was now flooding into the lounge. He was hoping to see the pretty staff assistant who was part of the U.S. congressional delegation that was also in Hanoi. She had been a welcome distraction during the boring evenings. "Whatcha think?" he asked.

"We got a deal," Byers said. It had been easier than he had expected and the Junkyard Dogs had reserved the tonnage needed to move freight on the Hanoi to Nanning railroad.

The lounge was full when Hazelton appeared at the rope. Byers waved at him and the maitre d' allowed him to enter. "Damn," Hazelton swore as he settled into a chair, "we're getting nowhere with the Vietnamese. Are you doing any better?"

"No problem," Byers replied. "Drink?"

"A Dubonnet would be fine," Hazelton said. Byers made a face and ordered the drink.

"What's the hangup?" Alvarez asked, still scanning the crowd. If the staffer didn't show, he would find another target of opportunity.

"They want truck parts," Hazelton explained. "Now where is the U.S. government going to find parts for Russian trucks?"

Byers shot Alvarez a quick look. "Zils or Urals?" he asked. Both Soviet-designed trucks were outstanding workhorses and did yeoman duty in Vietnam.

"Zil 157s," Hazelton replied.

"We can do that," Byers told him. "But we'll need TVs to trade."

"Nice," Alvarez said, looking at the crowd. Hazelton looked up, wondering what female had caught his attention. Alvarez did have a way of attracting beautiful and interesting women. Hazelton only saw Mazie, the Frump, who was his boss, walking toward their table. Well, he thought, she has lost weight. Then he noticed the approving looks from two men at a nearby table. It's her eyes, he decided. Having them fixed like Miho Toragawa's gave her an exotic, innocent look.

"Any progress on the truck parts?" Mazie asked as she sat down.

"Not until now," Hazelton replied.

"Two years ago," Byers explained, "the Chinese bought truck factories lock, stock, and barrel from the Russians. We can tap them for parts—for the right price." Mazie raised an eyebrow, her way of asking what the price was. "TV sets," Byers answered.

"No doubt tuned to Chinese frequencies," Mazie added.

"That's the way we do business," Byers said.

Alvarez stood and smiled when he saw the congressional staffer walk in. She was petite, pretty, and had tears in her eyes. "Juan," she said, not sitting down, "she's on a warpath." They all understood the "she" was Congresswoman Ann Nevers. Nevers was the most aggressive member of the congressional delegation that was visiting Hanoi. Unlike Mazie and her China Action Team, the delegation was primarily concerned with media coverage for the upcoming election in November.

"She found out you and I have been seeing each other," the young woman said. "I've been fired and sent home." She slipped a note into Alvarez's hand. "I've got to go."

Alvarez watched her leave before reading the note. His forehead furrowed as he read. "Nevers knows what we're doing here and is going to break the story on TV," he said.

"That's a problem we don't need," Mazie said. "I'd better call Mr. Carroll. He's good at damage control." She hurried out of the lounge.

Hazelton shook his head. "This is classic Nevers. She'll ride any issue to make the seven o'clock news and doesn't care who she hurts."

"Shee-it," Byers grumbled. "We got a sweet deal going here and that bitch is going to screw it up. I need a drink. Waiter!" The maitre d' and a waiter scurried up to the table at the sound of the sudden disturbance. Byers ordered another round of drinks and asked for Tabasco sauce and two raw eggs to go with his beer. "It makes a great appetizer," he told Hazelton. The maitre d' asked if a Vietnamese pepper sauce would be satisfactory, since they didn't have Tabasco sauce. Byers nodded and the waiter left with a very perplexed look on his face.

"I can see it now," Hazelton said. He read from imaginary headlines: "Congresswoman Nevers discovers Hanoigate." He looked sick.

"Can Carroll fix this one?" Alvarez asked.

"I doubt it," Hazelton replied. He looked even sicker when Congresswoman Ann Nevers barged past the maitre d' and headed straight for their table with four members of her staff in tow. Nevers was a tall and willowy woman in her mid-forties. She was slightly hunch-shouldered and had clear blue eyes. She would have been pretty except for the permanent inner scowl that marred her outer looks. Byers whispered a few words to Alvarez, who stood and left. Byers and Hazelton stood as she approached.

Nevers hovered in front of Hazelton like a vengeful banshee. "I want to meet Kamigami," she demanded. "Now."

"I just sent for her," Byers lied. "She should be here in a few minutes." He motioned to a seat. Nevers sat while her staff retreated to the bar. "Can we help you?" Byers asked as he sat down.

Nevers disregarded Byers as a nobody and fixed Hazelton with a piercing stare. "What the hell do you people think you're doing?" she said. Her tone of voice was calm and controlled, but her words rang with danger. She ignored the waiter when he set down the drinks Byers had ordered. The two eggs and little dish of pepper sauce confirmed her opinion of Byers.

"Miss Nevers," Hazelton began, "we are here at the express order of the president—"

"Who is going to be impeached for what's going on here," she snapped.

Hazelton soldiered on, trying to make her listen to reason. "Perhaps you could talk to the national security advisor before you—"

"Why?" she interrupted. "So he can tell me what you're doing in Hanoi is in the best interests of the United States? I would have thought you people would have learned from the Watergate and Iran-Contra scandals."

There it is again, Byers thought. "Excuse me, Ma'am," he said in his most respectful voice. "Who is this 'you people' you keep talkin' about?" He hoped she would react to his southern accent.

She did and her eyes drew into narrow slits. "Who," she said, seeing him for the first time, "are you?"

"Ray Byers," he answered. "Just a good old boy from Alabama."

"I've heard about you," Nevers said, stressing the last word.

"That's nice, Ma'am." Over her shoulder, Byers saw Alvarez return with a TV reporter and a cameraman. He was pointing to the table.

"Care for a drink?" Byers offered, taking off his right shoe and sock. His bizarre behavior captured her attention and she watched in fascination as he dropped the two eggs into the sock. With deliberation he peered down the sock and shook the eggs into the toe. Satisfied, he poured some of the hot sauce on top. He twisted the neck of the sock closed and bashed it once on the table. He leaned back, opened his mouth, sucked at the toe of the sock and followed it with a beer chaser. He smiled and offered the sock to Nevers.

The TV cameraman had his video camera on in time to catch Ann Nevers retching on the floor.

Byers contented himself with, "Damn, this is good stuff." Then he gulped his beer to quench the flame burning in his mouth from the pepper sauce.

## Sunday, July 28
## Guilin, China

Waters held the door open as Big John Washington and Larry Tanaka filed into Pontowski's office. She didn't move, wanting to see what would happen next. The two Junkyard Dogs stood in front of Pontowski's desk, braced for what was coming.

"Where is he?" Pontowski asked, fixing the two with a hard look.

"Ah . . . well . . . sir," Washington answered, "we don't know."

"You don't know?" His voice was menacing. "Do you know where Byers and Alvarez are?"

Tanaka brightened. "Yes sir. They're still in Hanoi."

Pontowski grunted a response. "That still leaves Marchioni. We're having problems with LASTE and it turns out that one Mister Charles Marchioni is the only person with any talent when it comes to fixing the system. I had to do some serious arm twisting to get him here. He shows up, the only civilian we've got, by the way, and the next day he's gone missing." Pontowski stood and leaned across his desk. "I need him—bad—and he was last seen with you two. What did you do with him?"

The two exchanged worried glances. They had never seen

their boss so angry. Washington drew himself up to his full five feet two inches and squared his shoulders. He was going to tell the truth. "Sir, we gave him a Junkyard Dog's checkout."

"And what is that?" Pontowski asked.

Tanaka answered. "It's the way we welcome new bachelors to the wing. We do it the first night they're here. But Charlie is sorta special so we . . . sorta overdid it." He lost his nerve and couldn't finish.

"What did you do?" Pontowski was getting worried.

"It's like a welcoming party," Washington explained. "We took him downtown to the New Bar and got him elbow-walking, knee-crawlin' drunk. I gotta tell you, that takes some doing with Marchioni. Anyway, we turned him over to a pro."

"Pro?" Pontowski interrupted.

"Hooker, sir. A call girl."

"Have you two ever heard of AIDS?"

"No problem, sir," Tanaka answered. "We've got our reserve stock all checked out and certified by a doctor."

"I can't believe this. Okay, so what happened next?"

Washington steeled himself. "She took Marchioni off to a hotel someplace. She doesn't speak English."

Pontowski had to force a straight face and stifle a laugh. As a lieutenant, he would have loved pulling off a practical joke like that. But as a commander, he couldn't allow it. He caught Waters giving him a hard look. There was the matter of the girls. "I see," he said. "So your victim wakes up, hung over, and in bed with a woman. He's lucky if he remembers her name."

"She's a real princess," Washington added. He couldn't see Waters, who was steaming mad.

"And he has no idea where he is," Pontowski said, "doesn't speak the language, and probably has no money. A stranger in a strange land under very strange circumstances."

"That's the idea," Tanaka admitted.

Time to play the hard ass, Pontowski thought. "Come with me," he ordered as he stomped out of the building. He walked next door to the security shack manned by the New China Guard and asked to speak to the captain in charge.

"Show them the photos and what you took off the bodies," he told the captain.

The captain handed them a set of photos of three very dead young Chinese. "They almost nailed me yesterday," Pontowski explained.

"We heard the rumors," Tanaka said.

The captain set a box in front of them. It contained two submachine guns, a pistol with a silencer, six hand grenades, six knives, rolls of adhesive tape, thin wire, a block of C4 explosive, detonators, and a packet of syringes. "These are lethal," the captain said, pointing to the needles. "They were well-equipped and well-trained assassins. Very dangerous."

"The question is," Pontowski gritted, "who's next?" He stared at the two men. "Find Marchioni. Now." The two men saluted and hurried out of the room, glad to escape the wrath of their commander.

"The Bossman is really pissed," Tanaka said. "Where do you think Charlie is?"

"Beats the shit outa me," Washington replied. "Marchioni's a fuckin' wild man. I think he took off with the lady."

Pontowski walked back to the squadron. Maybe, he thought, the hard-nosed routine is what we need to break the spell of this place. Time to do some ass kicking before someone does it for me.

"Tango!" he bellowed as he stomped down the hall. A surprised Leonard stuck his head out of the mission planning room. "Get Hester the Molester and be in my office in two minutes." Leonard ducked back into the room. Hell of a way to run a railroad, Pontowski thought. But it does get results.

## Monday, July 29
## Nanning, China

James, Von Drexler's majordomo, entered the bedroom and drew the curtains back. A misty sunlight streamed into the room. "Good morning, sir," he said, waking the three inhabitants in the bed. He surveyed the room. It was a disaster and offended his sense of propriety. A silken cord with six small wooden balls strung along its length lay on the floor beside the bed. Rather than pick it up, he nudged it under the bed with his foot. He saw traces of dried blood on the balls. He hoped it was Von Drexler's.

The older woman stirred and sat up. "Good morning, Mrs. Soong," James said in Cantonese. "Breakfast is ready." Soong Yu Ke nodded, not concerned that she was naked. James clapped his hands and a maid wheeled in a breakfast cart set for three.

"Mark," Yu Ke said, speaking English to Von Drexler, "it is time to get up. People will get the wrong idea." Her accent and diction were perfect. She stood and appraised herself in a full-length mirror, pleased that her body did not betray her fifty years. Von Drexler sat on the edge of the bed and stroked the bare back of Yu Ke's daughter. "Ailing," she said. It was enough. The younger woman came awake and smiled at Von Drexler.

"You are wonderful," Ailing said, smiling at him. She got out of bed, went to the breakfast tray, poured a cup of coffee, and handed it to Von Drexler. She tossed her hair over her bare shoulder and struck a sultry pose in front of him. She watched his reaction and knew what he wanted. She knelt in front of him and licked his penis.

Yu Ke sat in a chair, crossed her legs, and studied Von Drexler's face as Ailing sucked at him. "You are right, you know," she said, making casual conversation. "You, even more than Zou, understand the importance of rivers in China." She dropped the subject. She had planted the seed a week ago that the city of Wuzhou, which lay at the confluence of the Pearl and Lijiang rivers, was the key to Guangxi Province.

"May I select your uniform?" she asked. He groaned a reply. Ailing's head was bobbing furiously between his legs. She padded to his huge closet and chose a set of khakis patterned after the uniform of General Douglas MacArthur. A loud sigh escaped from Von Drexler as he climaxed. He pulled Ailing up to him and kissed her full on the mouth. "Please," Yu Ke said, "your staff meeting is in thirty minutes." Ailing led him into the bathroom for a bath and shave while the woman pinned five stars onto each collar of the shirt.

Von Drexler preened in front of a mirror after the two women had dressed him. He touched the circle of stars on each collar and smiled. "No," he said, "not yet." Reluctantly, he let the woman replace them with his three stars. Finally, he was ready. One last glance in the mirror. His face looked slightly bloated but not enough to worry about. He turned to the woman. "I can't believe we've known each other for only three weeks," he said. "You are a treasure." Soong Yu Ke bestowed a gracious smile on him and walked with him to the door.

She closed the door and glared at her daughter. "You talked too much last night," she snapped in Cantonese. "Get dressed." A few minutes later, James, the majordomo, entered unannounced. "Tell Zou we have him," Yu Ke said as she carefully examined her face in a mirror for any signs of aging.

The twelve Americans who formed Von Drexler's personal staff waited nervously for the general to arrive for his Monday morning staff meeting. It was part of the week's ritual they dreaded. "What the hell," Colonel Robert Trimler mumbled when he saw Von Drexler's latest uniform. "He's designing his own uniforms now."

The American officers exchanged worried looks. Von Drexler's growing megalomania was the number-one topic of discussion among his staff. They had all seen perfectly rational officers change as they moved up in rank. Some became more humane and considerate while others became tyrants. For a very rare few, becoming a general was the chance to use all their talents and become true leaders. Every man in the room admitted that Von Drexler was an organizational genius and an expert at moving supplies and materiel. But increased rank had brought out the dark side of his personality, for he savored power for its own sake. He wanted to control and dominate people. Most of the officers on his staff accepted the good with the bad and hoped to get through the assignment with their careers unscathed.

"Seats," Von Drexler said. He stood in front of his staff

and stared over their heads. "Two items. First, I want action on the new MAAG compound. We are growing and need to move into our own headquarters. Second, gentlemen, it is time we bring the war to the PLA," he announced. He paced the floor and outlined his plan to attack Wuzhou. "It is imperative," he concluded, "that we winkle Kang out of Wuzhou before he makes further advances into Guangxi Province. We are going to push him back to Canton." He marched out of the room.

"Winkle?" an Army lieutenant colonel asked.

"My God," Colonel Charles Parker, the vice commander, grumbled to Trimler, "he fancies himself a MacArthur. I've never seen anyone come unglued so fast in my life. You're lucky to be reassigned."

Trimler agreed with him. He had convinced Von Drexler to reassign him to the First Regiment to create an ASOC, air support operations center, for Kamigami. The ASOC's job was to have the Warthogs in the right place with the right ordnance when the First Regiment needed them. It was called close air support, or CAS for short. "Someone," Trimler said, "had better tell the heavies back home we've got a first-class wacko running the show. I'm out of here."

Trimler found the sanity he was looking for with Kamigami's First Regiment in Pingnan. He relaxed when he discovered it was at its full strength of four battalions, almost three thousand men. The more he saw, the more he was convinced the First Regiment could handle anything up to a division that Kang could throw at it. But the real difference was Kamigami. He was distant from his men, yet one of them. Thanks to Jin Chu, a mystical quality surrounded his orders and his soldiers were willing to live and die following his lead.

"Von Drexler is talking about an offensive against Wuzhou," Trimler told Kamigami. "He wants to push Kang back to Canton."

Kamigami stiffened. "Does he have any idea what he's talking about?" He leaned over a map spread out on a table. "It looks simple on a chart, but Wuzhou is a major PLA stronghold. I wish he had to deal with real bullets, real tanks, and real bodies."

"What do you need to do it?" Trimler asked.

"Dedicated close air support," Kamigami replied. "Pontowski's A-10s have got to be totally committed to us from the get-go. They have to be there when we call for them."

"That's a problem," Trimler said. "VD uses the A-10s as a bargaining chip to control Zou. Zou does what VD wants or Zou doesn't get the A-10s. We've got to change that." He wished he knew how.

Kamigami sat down, recalling the work detail when he and Jin Chu had been pressed into burying bodies in Wuzhou. He wanted to talk to her. But she had disappeared the day before without a word and he wasn't sure when she would return.

## Tuesday, July 30
## Southwest of Guilin, China

The two Warthogs descended to five hundred feet and flew southward along the Luoqing River. The Luoqing was a fierce river, flowing swiftly to the south, where it joined the Pearl. Ahead of them, the Luoqing was forced into a narrow river valley by a well-developed mountain range to the west and a single jagged ridge line of karst peaks, the sharp-sided limestone buttes that jutted out of the land, to the east. It looked as if the river were flowing into the mouth of the mountains, with a set of huge teeth on the bottom.

Maggot's voice filled the headset in Pontowski's helmet. "I call this 'the Gullet' and the ridge of karsts to the east 'the Dragon's Teeth.'" It was a good description of what Maggot had found. Pontowski had told him to find an area where they could conduct intensive training. Now Maggot was showing Pontowski the results of that search.

Pontowski zoomed to two thousand feet, rolled inverted, and took in the scenery. Below him he could see Maggot's Warthog snaking a flight path along the river. He continued the roll and descended onto the broad plain on the eastern side of the Dragon's Teeth. He flew at one hundred feet over the rice paddies and firewalled the throttles. To the west, the jagged peaks of the Dragon's Teeth hid Maggot and the

Luoqing. To the east, rice paddies and an occasional karst formation extended into the summer haze.

He descended even lower and laughed to himself as he raked the throttles aft to slow his Hog. He knew what was coming. Ahead of him, Maggot's jet popped over the ridge line and rolled 135 degrees. He was poised to slice down into Pontowski's six o'clock position—if he could find him. Pontowski popped in the opposite direction and disappeared over the Dragon's Teeth and into the Gullet. They were still hidden from each other.

Enough playing, he thought. He climbed out of the Gullet and rejoined Maggot. "Let's go home," he radioed. "This looks like the perfect area for training. You did good." Two clicks of Maggot's mike button answered him.

But Pontowski still wanted to play and they cut lazy eights over the landscape, dodging an occasional karst and skirting villages. They split to avoid flying over a small collection of mud hovels. They knew what jet blast at low level could do to flimsy structures. Maggot went to the right and Pontowski left. "I'll be damned," Maggot transmitted as they bracketed the village. "One of our trucks is down there."

They slowed and flew a lazy wheel around the village. Below them they saw what looked like a fiesta in progress. The villagers waved at them and they rocked their wings. A tall, bearded figure climbed onto the truck bed and waved. They had found the missing civilian, Charlie Marchioni.

Does everybody go crazy in this place? Pontowski asked himself. He gave himself a mental kick.

The ramp was alive with activity when they landed. Maintenance was in the last stages of a practice load out and Pontowski counted twelve Warthogs ready to launch with full bomb loads. Hester and Leonard were waiting for him in the squadron with the results. "How long did it take?" Pontowski asked.

"It took four hours to load out twelve jets," Leonard answered.

Pontowski shook his head. "Too long. Download the birds and we'll do a repeat tomorrow morning. I want twelve jets loaded out in two hours and twenty-four in four."

"That's a max effort, Boss," Hester said. "Maintenance will bitch like crazy."

"Tough tortillas," Pontowski snapped. "I want four Hogs launched to the Dragon's Teeth." Hester looked confused. "Maggot will explain it. Also, I want some severe training to start tomorrow with the pilots you're training as forward air controllers. From now on, we're flying twenty training sorties a day and we're keeping four jets on a quick reaction alert, twenty-four hours a day."

Hester knew better than to argue. "Ordnance on the alert birds?"

"Load 'em out wall-to-wall for air to mud."

"Sir," Leonard said, "we've got two big problems getting in the way. First, we are not getting enough fuel shipped in to fly that heavy a training schedule and keep a combat reserve. Second, we've got LASTE problems. For some reason, LASTE doesn't like Guilin. Maintenance is having a hell of a time keeping the system peaked and tweaked."

"Is Byers back from Hanoi?" Pontowski asked. He got a nod in answer. "I want to see him. Now."

The meeting with Byers was short and sweet. Two hours later, he and Larry Tanaka were on their way to Nanning and Charlie Marchioni was standing in front of Pontowski. "What in hell were you doing in that village?" he asked.

Marchioni was a throwback to the sixties, a hippy grown old. His clothes hung on his tall and slender frame, he needed a haircut, and his sandals were falling apart. His eyes smiled as his mouth spread into a big smile, proving there was life behind his bushy beard. He had sparkling white teeth and a friendly voice. "That's where I live now. I threw a party."

"I needed you here," Pontowski said. "We've got problems with LASTE."

"I've been around. I like to work at night."

"I wish somebody had told me," Pontowski growled.

Marchioni's smile was still in place. "You've got one laid-back outfit here."

"Not anymore," he promised. "Do you have any idea why we can't keep LASTE aligned?"

The transformation in Marchioni was instantaneous. He became all business. "It's the inertial navigation unit. It doesn't like high humidity. I told Byers to scrounge up all the Honeywell units he can find. Until we get them, I'll see what I can do about creating moisture barriers around the black boxes."

"Get to it." Pontowski stomped out of the room to set a few more fires.

"What got under his saddle?" Marchioni asked.

Sara Waters looked at him. "A war," she answered. Marchioni didn't believe her.

Charlie Marchioni was trudging toward the end hangar when he saw the KC-10. He stopped and watched the Air Force version of the McDonnell Douglas DC-10 as it turned final. "No way," he mumbled to himself. The tanker was too big to land at Guilin. Still, it came down final at 150 knots, its huge size making it appear to be flying much slower. The pilot set it down on the main gear at 140 knots and threw the reverse thrusters into the jet exhaust, dragging it to a halt.

The big tanker paused at the turnoff to the taxiway and let two wing walkers off to guide the pilot. Marchioni was fascinated by the big jet and followed it to the fuel pits, the only place it could park. It was a tight fit and one of the wings blocked the taxipath to the main runway. The engines were still spinning down when the main cargo door popped open and Ray Byers stuck his head out. "Hey, Ray!" Marchioni shouted. "Is this all you could find in a week?"

"Blow it out your ass," Byers shot back. He was smiling as the KC-10's crew chiefs started to defuel the tanker, pumping 135,000 pounds of JP-4 into Guilin's fuel storage tanks. "We got ourselves one gen-you-ine flyin' fuel truck," Byers yelled. The KC-10 was Byers's solution to the fuel shortage problem. He had convinced Mazie that if an airborne tanker could off-load into fighters, it could off-load into fuel bladders on the ground at Guilin. She had forwarded the idea in her daily report to Carroll and he had made it happen. Besides the fuel, there was another benefit—inside the KC-10 were twenty-three pallets of cargo for the wing.

Marchioni walked under the jet, examining its main gear, thinking. He talked to one of the crew chiefs and learned they were the California Free Style, the seventy-ninth AFRES out of Travis Air Force Base in California. When he asked what base they were staging out of, the reply was a startling "Cam Ranh Bay." The old air base in southern Vietnam had been opened up for the Americans by the Vietnamese government.

Byers joined Marchioni. "Fuel delivery problem solved," Byers said. "We're scheduled for two, maybe three a day."

"These babies take up a lot of room," Marchioni said. "Nobody moves while one is on the ground. We better get some ground support equipment in case one breaks and can't take off."

"I can't think of everything," Byers grumped. He promised to take care of it. "I got four of the Honeywell units you asked for," he said. "They're on the last pallet."

The fuel and supply problem for the wing had been solved and a modern version of "flying the Hump" from World War II was underway. But this time, there was no hump, only a short hop from Vietnam.

As Marchioni had predicted, the KC-10 stopped all movement on the ramp and Frank Hester had to delay his takeoff until the tanker was airborne. He chafed at the delay, anxious to go play as a forward air controller. He loved flying as a FAC, controlling A-10s on close air support missions. It gave him a rare feeling of independence and freedom.

The close air support procedures that Trimler had worked out with the First Regiment were classic NATO and Hester calculated he would have four pilots checked out as forward air controllers within a week. But today, he had to train ALOs, the air liaison officers the FACs talked to on the ground. A big smile crossed his face as he lifted off and headed for the training area east of the Dragon's Teeth.

He never saw the Chinese J-6 fighter that blew him out of the sky with a PL-2 air-to-air missile. The PL-2 was a clone of the Soviet-designed Atoll missile, which in turn was based on the first-generation Sidewinder—a U.S. missile.

This time, there was no SIB to investigate the crash, only a small ground party made up of Leonard, Maggot, and Skeeter Ashton. They examined the wreckage, thankful the Chinese had removed the charred remains of the pilot before they got there. But they did have to transport what was left of the body back to Guilin. It was three in the morning when they arrived and Pontowski was waiting for them.

"What happened?" he asked.

"Without a full-blown SIB," Maggot answered, "we'll never know for sure."

"We got some clues," Leonard added, drawing on his experience as a safety officer. "Normally, the engines are pretty much in one piece in a crash like this one. The left one was blown all to hell."

"I talked to some villagers," Skeeter said. The time she had spent learning Cantonese was paying dividends. "They saw two other aircraft in the area about the same time. What they described sounded like a Farmer." The J-6 was a Chinese copy of the Soviet MiG-19, which carried the NATO code name Farmer.

The men said nothing but Skeeter wouldn't let it go. "Sir, I'm positive Major Hester was jumped by two Farmers. They got him with an Atoll." She had her missiles mixed up but not the sequence of events. "If we had an AWACS . . ." She didn't need to finish the thought. They all understood that without early warning, even an old fighter like the J-6 could eat the Warthog alive.

"I'll see what I can do," Pontowski promised. He looked at Leonard. "Tango, you're the new ops officer. Maggot, you step into Tango's old job in training. Starting tomorrow, we train in air-to-air. Hit the sack and get some rest." He studied their faces. Which one would be next? "This little war is going to get very hot," he warned them. "Very soon."

After they had left for the hotel, Pontowski sat at his desk and tasted a bitterness he had never experienced. Hester was his first loss. He reached for a piece of paper to write the obligatory letter to the dead pilot's wife. Please, he thought, let me say the right thing. He didn't know it, but he was praying.

Dear Lorraine,
    Frank was a good man, one of the best we had, and I know there is little I can say to help with the pain of losing him. Perhaps it helps to know that he believed

in what we are doing here, even though some people
say it is senseless to be fighting in a foreign country for
a people we don't really know or understand.

But they are wrong. There is the same basic good-
ness in these people you find in your neighbors. They
hurt and cry the same as we do when their children
die, they long for peace as we do, and they have the
same hopes for the future. Perhaps that is the best gift
we can give them—a future.

Frank was willing to risk his life for that.

Sincerely yours,
Matthew Z. Pontowski

He fell asleep on the couch in his office.

Sara Waters walked into the office just after sunrise and
saw the dark shape stretched out on the couch. She picked
up the letter and read it in the harsh light of day. "Matthew
Zachary Pontowski," she said, "you got it right."

# CHAPTER 13

**Wednesday, August 14**
**Pingnan, China**

With an iron will, Kamigami forced himself to remain calm as more situation reports filtered into the command bunker of the First Regiment. He listened to the reports and his misgivings eased. Operation Dragon Looks East was underway and progressing smoothly. As Trimler had warned, the New China Guard was moving on Wuzhou and his First Regiment was the spearhead.

Fifty miles, he thought, fifty long miles to Wuzhou. On the map, it looked simple: The New China Guard controlled Pingnan and blocked the PLA from advancing up the Pearl River into the regions controlled by Zou Rong. On the other hand, the PLA controlled Wuzhou and blocked Zou's forces from threatening Canton and Guangdong Province. It was a classic standoff and for Kamigami, the distance was a no-man's-land.

He glanced at the master clock—six hours into the operation. More reports came in and his operations staff updated the situation map. The arrows and small rectangular boxes that identified the units kept advancing on the map with precision toward Wuzhou. They were ahead of schedule.

A major handed him a note from Trimler in the ASOC, air support operations center. "No enemy activity reported in the vicinity of Teng Xian. Recommend holding A-10s on ground alert and scramble when troops in contact." Teng Xian, Kamigami thought, the small town that marked the halfway point. He considered Trimler's recommendation. The AVG had four attack aircraft and two FACs airborne at all times to fly cover for the First Regiment. As of now, the attack birds were just burning fuel. He gave the order to make it happen.

A deep worry settled over Kamigami. It was too easy.

He couldn't stand it any longer. He had to move. He had to see for himself. "Send the headquarters advance party to Teng Xian," he ordered. He wanted his command post nearer the action.

"Once they've got a new command post established, move the main headquarters unit there. I'm going to the visit the battalions."

Kamigami called for the old Huey helicopter that Trimler had found for the headquarters unit and headed for the field. Now he was doing what he wanted.

The plan called for three of his battalions to advance on a front toward Wuzhou, one south of the Pearl, one along the Pearl, and one to the north. The fourth was held in reserve. He found the headquarters of the First Battalion on the road and landed in a field. The only problem the CO reported was with cheering villagers and PLA soldiers surrendering.

"Where are their weapons?" Kamigami asked. The embarrassed officer told him the soldiers were part of construction crews and didn't have any. He climbed back into the helicopter and told his pilot to find the two other battalions.

The story was the same with the other two battalions, and he flew to Teng Xian in time to meet the headquarters advance party. Trimler was with them and motioned Kamigami aside. "Damn it, Victor," he complained, "you can't go off and leave your headquarters every time you get a bug up your ass. Especially when you're relocating your command post. That's a sure way to shoot off your own foot."

"I know," he admitted. "But I've got to be with my men, in front."

Trimler understood only too well. It was the age-old question of where. Does a commander lead from the front or from the rear? Kamigami knew modern warfare required a commander to be at the hub of command and control at the rear. But his heart was with his men.

A captain hovered just out of earshot for them to finish talking. Kamigami recognized the symptoms and motioned for him to come forward. "Miss Li is here," the young man said in Cantonese. Kamigami thanked the man as he headed for his new command post. He felt better and the intense worry he felt whenever Jin Chu disappeared on one of her expeditions into the countryside subsided.

Early the next morning, advance elements of the First Regiment entered Wuzhou unopposed. The general commanding the PLA surrendered the city and immediately pledged his allegiance to Zou Rong and the Republic of Southern China.

That evening, Kamigami ate a quiet meal with Jin Chu. "I don't understand it," he told her. "It was a walk in the sun, nothing. We only experienced token resistance from a few units."

"Why are you so worried?" she asked.

"Because we captured very few weapons," he answered. "We didn't get a single tank and only a few crew-served weapons. The soldiers who did surrender were mostly from production or construction crews, not combat units."

"Perhaps," she said, "that is because Kang is going to attack another place."

"I know. But where?"

"I dreamed of many fires around our house at Nanning."


## Friday, August 16
## Nanning, China

General Kang Xun provided the answer to Kamigami's question at four o'clock the next morning when a rocket and mortar attack pounded the airfield at Nanning. The empty building the wing had occupied and the J-STARS communication module were leveled in the first barrage. A large commando force swept across the field, killing everyone they encountered.

Within minutes, the field was secured as a smaller force

hit the combined headquarters building in downtown Nanning. The commandos slaughtered the security guards and the four Americans on duty in the communications section. They searched through the offices, blowing open safes, before torching the building and withdrawing. Von Drexler's new headquarters compound was not touched.

Another commando team attacked the compound where Zou Rong lived. But they encountered stiff resistance from his bodyguards and were not able to penetrate beyond the outer wall. They retreated after sending four mortar rounds into the big house.

Von Drexler learned of the attack when his majordomo woke him with the news.

## Friday, August 16
## Over the South China Sea

"We have multiple unidentified tracks over the mainland," the ASO announced over net one of the intercom. The announcement sent a shock wave through the AWACS. Major Marissa LaGrange stood behind his scope and watched as two more bogies were tagged up, bringing the total to nine. "None are hostile," the ASO said. "All appear to be transports. No fighters." The red, upside-down Vs that tracked each aircraft changed to green.

Three more bogies were tagged up. "More of the same," the ASO announced. They now had twelve tracks. "Definitely not routine traffic," he said. "But not hostile."

"As I recall," LaGrange muttered, "you said that last time." The ASO cringed at the prospect of another tongue lashing and changed the green inverted Vs back to red.

The week before, he had tagged up two Farmers as a routine training mission and then watched as they closed on Frank Hester's A-10. He had told LaGrange and she had tried to warn the A-10 over Guard, the frequency reserved for emergencies. But the A-10 was out of radio range. The J-STARS aircraft had passed the warning to Nanning for relay to the wing. Even that hadn't worked. LaGrange had watched helplessly as the Farmers gunned Hester out of the sky. Her profanity had reached epic proportions that day.

"I want to know where they're going," she snapped, pointing at the twelve tracks. She called the orbiting J-STARS on the secure radio to learn if they detected any unusual activity on the ground. J-STARS claimed that all was quiet on their monitors but they could not establish contact with their ground module at Nanning.

LaGrange's voice was hard. "The shit is hitting the fan and we haven't got a fuckin' clue what's going on."

## Friday, August 16
## Guilin, China

Shoshana was sitting on the edge of his bed, smiling at him. Her hand reached out and her fingers extended to touch his lips. A warm feeling surged through Pontowski. Shoshana twisted around at the sound of three sharp raps at the door and pulled her hand back. Then she was gone.

Three more quick knocks at the door dragged Pontowski out of his dream. "Boss," Waters said from the other side, "wake up. We've got problems."

He jerked his body into a sitting position on the edge of the bed. The dream had been unbelievably real. "Coming," he said as he pulled on his flight suit. He opened the door.

"We got a phone call from combined headquarters," she told him. "They said they were under heavy attack. Then the phone went dead. We've lost all contact with Nanning."

"Are you in contact with the First Regiment?" he asked.

"Affirmative," she answered. "Wuzhou is quiet."

"Damn," he muttered. "It doesn't make sense." He looked at his watch. Four-thirty in the morning. "Where's Leonard?"

"On his way to the base."

Pontowski pulled on his boots, thinking. How could he make a decision based on this? Frank Hester's words came back. "Do something—even if it's wrong."

He made his decision. "I'm declaring Condition Red," he told her. Condition Red meant an attack was expected within one hour. "You initiate a recall here. I'm headed for the base."

"Sir," Waters said, "you need an armed escort. Don't go alone."

He agreed and ran down the hall. His escort turned out to be the first of the pilots and maintenance troops to answer the recall. They all piled into a truck and raced out of the roundabout in front of the hotel. Eleven minutes later, they reached the airfield. Leonard was already inside and had ordered the base security detachment to full alert.

"We've lost all communications with Nanning," Leonard told Pontowski. "We're in contact with the National Military Command Center in the Pentagon. They know less than we do. Damn! I wish we could talk to the AWACS directly." Von Drexler had insisted all communications from the AWACS come through the J-STARS system to his staff at Nanning for dissemination. It was one way he controlled the flow of information.

"Call their base on the sat com telephone," Pontowski ordered. "I think they're at Shek Kong in Hong Kong. They've got to be in contact with the AWACS."

Leonard picked up the phone and jabbed at the buttons, calling Hong Kong information for the phone number to the old British base. "I hope this works," he said.

"Hester was right," Pontowski mumbled. "Okay, here we go. Generate all aircraft with standard conventional loads to cockpit alert. I want two FACs airborne and over Nanning at first light and a flight of four Hogs ten minutes behind them. Get all personnel on base and hunker down for an attack."

Thirty minutes later Leonard was off the phone with their first hard information. But the AWACS duty officer had insisted on encoding the information, figuring if the phone call was a clever ruse, the caller would not be able to decode the message. It took Leonard another five minutes to decode it.

"The AWACS," Leonard said, "reports twelve hostile tracks launched from airfields near Canton. Two have landed at Nanning and the others are headed that way. All appear to be transports. The J-STARS reports no unusual activity."

"The war just got hot," Pontowski said. "And we're swinging at shadows."

The combat reports radioed in by the FACs gave Pontowski the key to what was happening. A large force of lightly armed soldiers had launched a surprise attack and overrun the airport at Nanning. Once the runway was secure, cargo aircraft started to land, bringing in reinforcements and heavy weapons. Judging from the numerous fires in Nanning and the loss of communications, the combined headquarters building and the large army base on the outskirts of town had also been hit.

I underestimated the opposition, Pontowski told himself. We call them Squints, Fuckheads, and Gomers and they kick the hell out of us. Every preconception he had about the enemy died in the early morning hours as he ordered launch after launch. There was no doubt he was up against a formidable enemy.

Pontowski turned his fierce intellect away from their failure and worked the problem in front of him. He needed to talk to one of his FACs. When Snake Bartlett radioed in that he was ten minutes out and was landing for a gas and go, Pontowski headed for the fuel pits and was waiting when the Warthog taxied in.

Snake summarized the situation for him in a few short phrases. "It's all fucked up," he said. "We're not talking to anyone on the ground and can't tell the good guys from the bad. I find targets by trolling low and slow and call in a strike on anybody who shoots at me. Hell of a way to do business."

"What's happening at the airport?" Pontowski asked.

"Can't get close to it. Too fuckin' many SA-7s." The SA-7 was a shoulder-held surface-to-air missile with a very limited range. "A strange thing," Snake added, "there's no Triple A."

A pattern was finally emerging. "All they've got is what they carried in on their backs," Pontowski said, more to himself than to Snake.

"And what's coming in on those transports," Snake added.

"Damn," Pontowski muttered. "Surprise was their best

weapon." A nasty grin split his face. "Now we're going to surprise them. Snake, we're going after those transports." He beckoned for a maintenance line chief and told him to download the bombs off eight Warthogs and upload two external fuel tanks and four AIM-9 air-to-air Sidewinder missiles.

He raced back to the squadron to brief the pilots. When he finished telling them they were to fly a CAP in the vicinity of the airport and engage any PLA aircraft, especially transports, shouts drowned out all coherent conversation. The pilots from Missouri were still fighter jocks who firmly believed that a "kill is a kill." Two squared off in a violent argument about who was to fly the first go and Leonard had to separate them.

"You'll all get your chance," Leonard promised. "And you can damn well bet some of you are going to be seeing MiG-19s. Chew on that, assholes!" He was thinking of Frank Hester.

"Ripper," Pontowski shouted over the noise, "Get me in contact with the First Regiment."

Waters hurried from the room, eager to do her part. She used the STU-III secure phone and the satellite communications phone system the Junkyard Dogs had scrounged up for the wing to make the connection. Four minutes later, Pontowski was recapping the situation to Kamigami.

"I'll get two battalions moving toward Nanning," Kamigami promised. "That's all I can spare. I doubt the PLA was able to sneak too much past us." A long pause. "I'll be leading them."

"Any idea how long before you get there?" Pontowski asked.

"It's over three hundred miles by road," Kamigami answered. "Three days, max." He hoped it wasn't an idle boast.

"Take your ASOC and ALOs," Pontowski told him. They would need an air support operations center and the air liaison officers for coordination between the FACs and the troops on the ground. "We've hardly trained together and friendly fire can be a problem," Pontowski explained. "We need some visual recognition signals so we won't hit you."

Kamigami agreed and turned his end over to Trimler while Pontowski called for a FAC to work out the details.

Pontowski waited until they were finished before he told Waters to connect him with the National Military Command Center in the Pentagon. He dreaded that conversation. He spent the next two hours explaining the situation to a series of colonels and generals. Finally, he faked lost communications so he could get back to work. He passed Waters in the hall and called, "Are we having fun yet?" I can't believe I said that, he thought.

The big room the wing used for an operations center and command post was packed with pilots when he entered. Leonard was hunched over a radio by the mission status boards talking to a recovering Warthog. Maggot's distinctive voice came over the squawk box. "Splash one Crate." Crate was the NATO code name for the Ilyushin 14, an old, Soviet-built two-engine transport that resembled the slightly smaller C-47 Gooney Bird. Disparaging comments about Maggot gunning his own mother out of the sky to get a kill filled the room. Then, "Oh, I almost forgot," Maggot transmitted. "And splash one J-5." The room was absolutely silent. The J-5 was a Chinese copy of the MiG-17 Fresco, a formidable adversary for a Warthog. Pandemonium broke out as the pilots rushed Leonard to get a jet.

Pontowski shared the feeling with his pilots. Maggot had done what every one of them wanted to do—to down an enemy fighter in combat. It was the ultimate macho mountain to climb and Pontowski had been there before. But he had to get the message to his pilots—the Chinese air force had finally shown up and it was going to get very dangerous out there. Can we do this? he asked himself. Then he corrected himself. Can I do this?

## Saturday, August 17
## Guilin, China

The roar of two Warthogs taking off on the first mission woke Pontowski. He glanced at his watch. He had been asleep four hours on the couch in his office. He shook his head, trying to clear the fuzz, and headed for the latrine. He stuck his head under a tap and turned the water on full cold. The previous day had worn him out and he hadn't flown a single mission. It wasn't physical exhaustion, but mental, and he was certain this day would be a repeat.

He came out of the latrine and the aroma of coffee and bacon and eggs drew him back to his office. Waters had a hot breakfast waiting for him. "Eat," she said. Pontowski wolfed down the meal, surprised by his hunger. "I've got a fresh flight suit, your shaving kit, and a clean towel," she told him. "The Dogs rigged a shower out back. Use it." He nodded. "One of my jobs is to keep you healthy and going," she told him.

"What happened last night?" he asked. When he had stretched out for a catnap it was past midnight and the wing was in the midst of a regeneration, fueling and loading healthy jets and fixing the ones that were broken. Three of the Warthogs had taken battle damage, one seriously.

"Maintenance got thirty-two turned. Jake Trisher's bird won't fly again."

Pontowski wasn't surprised. "Jake was lucky to recover," he said. "He took some heavy hits." Two numbers, 49 and 32, flashed in his mind. He had 49 pilots and 32 aircraft available for combat. "Estimated time in commission for the other two Hogs?"

"Later today," Waters told him.

The number 32 in his mind flashed to a 34. His wing was still healthy. He headed for the operations center. Leonard was collapsed behind the scheduling desk, exhausted. He had been up all night driving the regeneration and was in no shape to fly.

Leonard dragged himself to his feet. "It went pretty good last night," he said. "We kept two birds in a CAP near Nanning and as far as we can tell, no aircraft landed. So we still got 'em isolated." A tired grin crossed his face. "Maggot's videotape when he stuffed the Fresco is in the VCR." He turned the TV on.

A picture of the horizon as seen through the HUD flashed on the screen and he could hear Maggot make a radio call. "Maggot's got a bandit at eight o'clock. Engaged." The horizon tilted crazily into the vertical as Maggot honked his Warthog around, into the threat. His breathing was heavy and rapid. Two aircraft appeared in the HUD, one a transport, the other much smaller, and both were coming head-on. At the same time, a loud growling noise drowned out Maggot's breathing. The sound was generated by one of his AIM-9 missiles, telling Maggot the infrared seeker head was tracking a target.

The picture jerked as Maggot lined up on the fighter. "Fox Two," Maggot called over the radio. The distinctive smoke trail of the missile appeared as it flew at the fighter. The Fresco pitched over and disappeared off the lower part of TV screen as Maggot pulled up to reposition. There was no bright explosion. The tape had played for exactly twenty-eight seconds when Leonard hit the stop button.

"Maggot's missile was the golden BB," Leonard said. "He was inside minimum range when he fired and the missile never armed. There was no detonation. It flew up the intake. He is one lucky son of a bitch, spearing the bastard like that." Pontowski agreed with him. They played the rest of the tape.

The video documented how Maggot had repositioned on the slow-moving transport. Again, Maggot's voice could be heard as he identified the aircraft as a Crate and closed for a cannon shot. The transport came inside the two lines on the HUD that resembled a funnel—the low-aspect gunsight funnel. "That's all she wrote, motherfucker," Maggot growled. The Crate came apart as he walked a short burst of 30-millimeter rounds across the fuselage.

In the hands of Maggot Stuart, the ugly, ungainly, and slow A-10 became a deadly aerial killer.

"Get some rest," Pontowski told Leonard. "I'll need you tonight."

Waters moved through the operations center with her journal, making notes. She noted the time—1200 hours local—and the number of sorties flown that day—fifty-two. She had decided to keep a war diary and document the squadron's combat record. This is turning into a bean count, she decided. She walked out onto the flight line and listened to Skid Malone, one of the FACs, debrief intelligence as his Warthog was refueled and rearmed for the next mission.

Malone told of confusion on the ground and a lack of targets but claimed the defenses around the airfield were weakening. He confirmed the CAPs had stopped all airborne resupply of the attackers. She followed the intelligence debriefer from revetment to revetment as he talked to more pilots. All told the same story. She walked into the maintenance hangars and noted the number of aircraft the wrench benders were repairing.

Then she found Charlie Marchioni and rode with him in his pickup truck. He was waiting for every A-10 when it landed to quiz the pilot on the status of LASTE. Occasionally, he would rip open a panel, jerk out a black box, and slap a new one in. "Humidity," he kept mumbling to himself. Then he would race for the shop, where two technicians would work on the box. "Drying out and realignment works most of the time," he told her.

All the grumbling and complaining she had heard the last few weeks had died away and everywhere she went, men and women were hustling and yelling at each other. But it was all for a purpose. Then she saw it. Many of them were wearing their old 303rd caps. True, they all had AVG patches sewn on their uniforms, but she was seeing the old 303rd from Whiteman Air Force Base. They hadn't forgotten who they were and where they came from.

Marchioni dropped her off at the squadron and she went inside with a different perspective. It's Pontowski, she concluded. He's the glue. He keeps us on track. Now she studied her commander and made more notes.

She was with Pontowski when Skid Malone was returning from his last mission and radioed in his combat report while still airborne. His voice was strained. "Groundhog," he transmitted, "Skid. Battle damage." The room went silent. "Right engine out, no hydraulics and in manual reversion." A long pause. "We were jumped by Farmers in the target area. Buns took a missile and ejected. I saw a chute and heard his beacon. I saw another Hog fireball. I think it was Willie. Aircraft now landing at Nanning."

Pontowski's face went granite hard. Rod "Buns" Cox was the youngest pilot in the AVG, and "Willie" Sutton was among the most experienced. He had lost two more pilots and the 49 he carried in his head flashed to 47. "Tell the pilots to monitor Guard," he ordered. "Buns may come up talking on his PRC-90."

He concentrated on his more immediate problem. Skid's Warthog had taken major damage and was flying without hydraulic controls. He had little rudder authority. He was in a backup mode designed to get the pilot to a safe area where he could eject. Pontowski keyed his radio. "Skid, Bossman. I got lots of Hogs, only one you. Recommend you overfly the base and eject." He didn't want to make the number a 46.

"I'll do this one gear up," Skid replied.

Waters saw the anguish on Pontowski's face as he answered. "Roger that." His voice didn't betray what was written on his face. He turned to Waters. "Let's go see him do it." She followed him out to his waiting pickup.

They parked on the taxiway well back from the runway and watched Skid come down final. The lower half of the tires of the main gear on the Warthog do not fully retract into the wheel well pods under the wings and hang out in the breeze. They watched as Skid settled the Warthog onto the runway and puffs of smoke belched from the main gear. He held the nose up as the A-10 slowed. Finally, the nose came down in a shower of sparks, smoke, and dust. At the last moment, Skid gunned his one good engine and skidded the big jet off the runway onto the grass, clearing the runway.

"A thing of beauty," Pontowski muttered under his breath.

Waters sensed the tension drain away and studied his face. Then she saw his eyes. For a moment it was all there—his doubts, his anguish, and his humanity. Did Muddy suffer like this? she thought. Why do they do this to themselves?

## Sunday, August 18
## Guilin, China

The ramp was alive with activity as the early morning sun cut the mist that drifted across the runway. The first Warthog taxied out of its revetment and headed for the runway. Soon, it was joined by three others, all loaded with external fuel tanks, four air-to-air missiles, and CBU-58s— cluster bomb units.

Pontowski's face was haggard and drawn as he stood at the end of the runway and watched the four jets go through a last quick check and arming. Crew chiefs darted under the A-10s and ran out in front, holding up bundles of safety pins with red streamers for the pilots to see. The four birds taxied onto the Active and took off single-ship at twenty-second intervals. They lifted through the haze and headed south. How many today? he thought.

He made his decision and headed for his operations center. He found Waters and pointed to his office. Inside, he closed the door and paced the floor. "Ripper, we got problems." Waters did not respond. "This is day three, we don't know shit-all what's happening, and we're hung out here all alone. The situation improves today or we're getting the hell out of China."

Waters nodded. "When?"

"Starting tonight." He collapsed into a chair. The strain was taking its toll. "You've got the stick. See what airlift you can get in here. Get the Junkyard Dogs on it. We got lots of trucks and buses. Check out an overland route."

"Demolition?" she asked.

"I hadn't thought of that. We'll blow up what we can't take with us."

"Where are we heading?" she asked.

He stared at her. Hard. "Remember Tucker the Fucker?" She nodded. "He once said that if anything went wrong, our government would hang us out to dry. I don't want that to happen, so start talking to the NMCC in the Pentagon."

"I'll get back to you in an hour," she told him as she left. Thanks a bunch, Colonel, she thought. She made her first call to Bill Carroll.

Leonard burst into his office twenty minutes later. "The First Regiment is at Nanning!" he yelled. "Kamigami is kicking ass and taking names." The First Regiment had covered the three hundred miles from Wuzhou in less than forty-eight hours. "Their ALOs are talking to our FACs," Leonard continued, "and are giving us good targets. The FACs are calling for everything we got."

A shot of adrenaline drove Pontowski out of his office. "And we got visitors," Leonard called at his back. The adrenaline rush crashed, stopping Pontowski dead in his tracks. Von Drexler was standing in the operations center.

"Now do you understand why I sent you here, Colonel," Von Drexler said.

Sara Waters scanned the list of items Von Drexler had demanded and permitted herself a rare outburst of profanity. "He's a fucking maniac," she announced. But no one heard her. Feeling better, she continued to make entries in her war diary.

18 Aug 1700

Von Drexler established headquarters in hotel with remnants of MAAG staff. About half of MAAG are MIA in Nanning. Two Chinese nationals are with Von Drexler, mother and daughter, most beautiful women I have seen in China. Intelligence reports all resistance crumbling in Nanning. Only airport still held by PLA. Contact with headquarters New China Guard established at 1635.

Sortie count: 105. Bossman pleased.

CAP: Tango Leonard, Skeeter Ashton, Goat Gross, and Jake Trisher.

FACs: Snake Bartlett and Skid Malone.

Plans for evacuation on hold.

She snapped the book closed and stood by the scheduling board, waiting for Leonard to land.

Snake Bartlett's voice came over the Have Quick. "Tango, move your CAP to the east. I've got a flight of two inbound and we'll be working targets under your present position. My ALO reports the PLA has abandoned the airport and moving in your direction."

Leonard acknowledged Bartlett and entered one last orbit. To the west, he saw fires still burning in Nanning. He called for an ops check. All four Warthogs were still feeding on their wing tanks and he calculated they could maintain the CAP until sunset. Then low fuel would force them to return to base. By then it wouldn't matter, since they couldn't do much at night.

"You heard the man," he told his flight. "Let's move ten miles to the east." He gave them new coordinates for their CAP points. "Heads up," he said as they entered their new CAP. "Check six." It was a routine warning. Missiles and radar combined with high-speed aircraft had changed air combat. But one fact had not changed since World War I when air combat was in its infancy. The majority of air-to-air kills were still made from the rear, or six o'clock position, and most pilots never saw the fighter that gunned them out of the sky. What they did was not the work of the chivalrous knight but of an aerial assassin.

"Tango," Bartlett radioed, "I've got three trucks making a break down the main road, coming your way. My Hogs are busy, can you handle it?"

Leonard considered the request. Their thirty-millimeter cannon could easily do the job and the Chinese Air Force had stayed on the ground. They had enough fuel but only a few minutes of usable light remaining. Enough for one pass, he figured. He'd do it. "We got it, Snake." He called his flight. "Skeeter, we'll do a low-level visual recce along the road. First one with a tallyho on the trucks is the shooter. One pass, haul ass. The free fighter will fly cover. Goat, you and Jake CAP overhead. We don't need an Atoll shoved up our ass."

He led Skeeter down to the road and they flew a figure eight pattern at 240 knots with Skeeter always passing behind him on the crossover. She saw the trucks first. "Tallyho," she called. "I'm in." Leonard pulled his nose up and rolled to take spacing. He would engage anyone foolish enough to shoot at her when she made her strafing pass.

Bright flashes winked at them from the trucks. "Ground fire from the trucks," Leonard transmitted. "Small arms only. Nail the lead truck and stop 'em." He watched Skeeter jink the Warthog as she lined up on the lead truck. But the pass didn't look right and she pulled off dry. At the same time, the distinctive plume of a shoulder-held surface-to-air missile arced toward him from a clump of trees fifty meters back from the road. He turned into the missile and hit his flare dispenser button. Six flares popped out behind his tail and captured the seeker head of the Grail missile.

Leonard turned hard and walked a long burst of thirty-millimeter through the stand of trees. He circled back to the road. But it was too dark to find the trucks. He climbed, looking for Skeeter in the fading light. He found her orbiting at six thousand feet. "Join up for RTB," he radioed. "What the hell happened on your pass?" he asked. It should have been a piece of cake.

"The tail-end truck looked like an ambulance," she replied.

What the hell, he raged to himself. I didn't see any red cross on any truck. Besides, those fuckers were shooting at us. So aim for the lead truck and let the ambulance take its chances for traveling in bad company—if it was an ambulance.

He would talk to her about it on the ground.

## Monday, August 19
## Tokyo, Japan

Miho Toragawa was waiting for the Gulfstream IV jet when it arrived from Hanoi. She guided Mazie and Wentworth into the limousine and directed the driver to take them to the Akasaka Prince Hotel in downtown Tokyo. "It is fortunate you came so quickly," she told the two. Miho chose her words with care, tiptoeing along the fine line of discretion and indirection the Japanese followed when dealing with a problem. Mazie understood perfectly what she was saying—because of the attack on Nanning, the Japanese were losing their nerve.

"We need to speak to Mr. Carroll," Mazie said. "I think it would be best if he explained the situation. He will know if the worst is over." She knew every word she said would be repeated verbatim to Toragawa. She smiled at Miho. "But I think Kang shot his toe off." Miho's hand came to her mouth and her eyes sparkled at the American slang.

"Kang," Mazie explained, "needs most of his forces for internal security because Zou is very popular in Guangdong

Province and Canton. To stay in power, Kang had to show he could hurt Zou. He did it by attacking where Zou is the strongest—Nanning. He threw all he had at Nanning, knowing he couldn't win. But he will claim it was a close thing, a moral victory."

"But to attack Zou at Nanning . . ." Miho let her words trail off.

"I think," Mazie ventured, "the attack was much like the 1968 Tet offensive in the Vietnam War. It was for political purposes, not military. Much can be won from a defeat— but I could be wrong. Your grandfather understands such things better than I do." She knew that also would get back to Toragawa.

Miho gave a slight nod and cast a sideways glance at Mazie. She understood exactly what Mazie was doing. "You look very tired," Miho said, deliberately changing the subject. "You need to rest." She smiled beautifully. "I hope we have a chance to go shopping. You need new clothes. That suit fit perfectly when you bought it."

"I keep losing weight," Mazie said. "I don't know why."

"Ah, but that is good." Her hand was back to her mouth as she looked at Hazelton.

The limousine pulled into the hotel and they were escorted to their suites on the top floor. "What was that all about in the car?" Hazelton asked when they were alone.

"We're explaining to the Japanese what happened in Nanning," Mazie explained. "But it's better if they figure it out for themselves." She paused. "With a little help from their friends." She sighed and kicked off her shoes. "I'm bushed." She walked into her suite.

Hazelton shot a quick glance her way as she closed the door. She has lost weight, he thought. I hope she's not sick.

Jet lag was weighing heavily on Bill Carroll when he arrived in Tokyo. He slumped into the rich leather seat of the limousine. "I wish I could sleep on a plane," he complained. Mazie sympathized with him. "Are the Japanese still pinging?"

"Not as bad as when I got here," she replied. "The situation has stabilized and Toragawa has calmed them down. But they can't understand how Kang could get kicked out of Wuzhou and then attack at Nanning, deep inside Zou's territory."

"It was classic Mao doctrine," Carroll said. "Kang diverted our attention at Wuzhou while he slipped a large commando force into Guangxi Province. They came upriver in small groups, carrying their weapons with them. It took some time to do."

"That explains the lull in the fighting," Mazie added. "That may have been Kang's hardest punch."

"I don't think so," Carroll replied. He fell silent, thinking. "Kang is unorthodox, dangerous, and much stronger than we suspected. He's going to keep the pressure on. Now he can go to the central government in Beijing and demand more men and supplies. He's going to attack again. Soon. We've got to keep the supplies flowing to Zou or his supporters will think we've deserted him."

"The Japanese have two ships at anchor in Haiphong with supplies for the New China Guard," she told him. "But they won't let the Vietnamese unload it."

"I'll convince the Japanese to release it," Carroll said. He paused, still working through the fog of jet lag. "Mazie, my gut feeling tells me that Kang hurt Zou and the New China Guard much worse than Von Drexler reported. I want you to go to Nanning and find out."

# CHAPTER 14

**Thursday, August 22**
**Over the South China Sea**

"Rio One, Rio Two," Moose Penko transmitted over the UHF. "Snap one-eight-zero at forty-five. ID only." La-Grange hovered behind him as he ran a routine training intercept of two F-15s against a single F-15. It was the last mission for the F-15s before they returned to their base in Okinawa.

She was worried because the crew was bored silly and going through the mission like robots. Even Moose's voice sounded flat and uninterested. The J-STARS aircraft had been unexpectedly recalled two days before and her instincts warned her it was time for them to leave. She decided to call Tinker Air Force Base when they landed and talk to her commander, Colonel Tucker, about it.

The intercept went smoothly and the three F-15s headed for Hong Kong, low on fuel. Moose turned and looked at her, boredom written on his face. "We're as useless as hemorrhoids in an elephant's ass."

She wanted to agree with him, but that would only make the situation worse. "It's what we get paid for," she snapped, walking away.

Moose turned back to his scope. "Cut some slack, Major," he grumbled under his breath.

Twenty minutes later the ASO tagged up two hostile tracks. "Major," he was almost shouting over the intercom.

"Two bandits on us! Three-four-five at sixty." The boredom was shattered.

LaGrange took one glance at his scope. Two inverted red Vs on a bearing of 345 degrees at sixty miles were tracking directly toward the AWACS. She wanted to ask how they had gotten so close without the air surveillance techs detecting them. She knew the answer—boredom, slop, and routine. But for now, she had another, much more serious problem.

"Flight deck, MCC," she said over the intercom. "Retrograde *now*. Heading one-six-five. Gate." The AWACS banked sharply to the right as the pilot turned and firewalled the throttles. They were going to give ground and run away from the threat coming at them. The pilot rolled out on the new heading and nosed the aircraft over into a shallow descent as the engines spun up to max power. They were trading altitude for airspeed.

"Point nine-six Mach," the pilot told her. "That's all we're going to get."

LaGrange punched at her communications panel and called the military air controller at Hong Kong for help. "Hong Kong Mil. Request immediate scramble of Zulu Alert. Bandits on us." Zulu Alert was the two F-15s that sat quick reaction alert at Hong Kong.

A crisp British accent replied, "Roger. Scrambling Zulu at this time."

"Major," Moose called. "I got the numbers."

"Go," LaGrange said. Moose explained the two hostiles chasing them had an overtake airspeed of 190 knots, and it would take fifteen minutes to close the fifty miles that still separated them. "Say type aircraft," LaGrange asked.

"Finbacks," Moose answered. "J-8s."

J-8s, LaGrange thought. She recalled everything she had memorized about the Chinese delta-winged fighter, which was an enlarged version of the Soviet MiG-21. Her lips compressed into a tight grin. "They can't do it," she announced. "They're in afterburner to get that much overtake airspeed and are sucking gas at one hell of a rate. They ain't got that much gas to spare and they got to fly all the way back to land. Expect them to break off shortly."

Four minutes later, the ASO announced the two bandits

had slowed and were turning back to China. The mission deck tensed as LaGrange sorted out the confusion and canceled the F-15 scramble. They knew what was coming next. She pointed at the ASO and motioned toward the galley in the rear. She wanted to know why the two bandits had gotten that close before they were tagged up as hostile. The ASO was about to have a moving experience he would never forget.

"Rats," Moose muttered. "We'll never get home now." All hopes that LaGrange would request a return to Tinker were gone.

"Why not?" the weapons controller sitting next to him asked.

"Because she'll want to return the favor," Penko explained.

"Lighten up, Moose," the controller said. "Why are you always on Major Mom's case, anyway?"

Moose thought about it. It was true, he did have an attitude when it came to LaGrange, and he never called her Major Mom. "Because she's a ballbuster when she doesn't have to be," he replied.


## Thursday, August 22
## Nanning, China

Von Drexler's pace through the debris and destruction that had been Nanning's airport was slow and deliberate. His voice matched his cadence and he spoke in slow rolling tones. He was the expert explaining the situation to an appreciative audience. "This was the A-10 operations building," he told Mazie and Hazelton. "It was the prime target, not the runway. Fortunately, I had deployed the wing to Guilin to counter the danger of an attack."

Hazelton panned the area with his camcorder, documenting the destruction. Von Drexler waited patiently and continued the tour. He was dressed in BDUs and carried a walking stick he used as a pointer. "The J-STARS module took a direct mortar hit," he said, "killing the civilian and the Army major on duty. Once they came across the fence, they slaughtered every man, woman, and child they found."

He paused for effect. "It is an indication of the enemy we are fighting."

"How did the PLA manage such a complete surprise?" Mazie asked. She sensed Von Drexler bristle at the question.

"According to the prisoners we interrogated," Von Drexler explained, "they were ordered to travel in small groups and trained to avoid detection. Many of them came upriver in small boats, traveling at night. It took them two months to move approximately ten thousand men into place."

Now it was her turn to bristle. She had seen the CIA estimates that fewer than two thousand men had been involved. "I'm surprised they could move so many men into place without being detected," she said.

Von Drexler seethed at the implied criticism. "Miss Kamigami, I hope you're not suggesting it was a breakdown in my intelligence. You cannot believe how corrupt the system is here. With the right bribes, you can do anything in China."

She changed the subject. "I understand the First Regiment relieved Nanning."

"They played a small part in defeating the PLA," Von Drexler huffed. "Please remember, only two battalions from the First Regiment were engaged. It was the A-10s under my personal command that stabilized the situation."

"I see," Mazie replied. What game is Von Drexler playing? she thought. Why did he lie about the number of attackers? To make himself look good?

The CIA's preliminary analysis claimed the main objective of the attack was to secure the airfield to open an airbridge into Nanning. The plan called for commando units to create confusion by killing Zou Rong and destroying the combined headquarters building while reinforcements were flown in. Kang's goal was simple—decapitate the rebels' leadership by leapfrogging into Nanning.

It was a bold plan that was spoiled by the quick reaction of the A-10s in sealing off the airport until Kamigami's First Regiment could recapture it. But from all the reports she had seen, Von Drexler had been missing until the third day of the battle.

An idea started to form: Pontowski and the First Regiment had reacted independently of Von Drexler. He had contributed nothing to the victory. She needed to verify her hunch. "We understand you were almost captured."

"It was touch and go," he replied. "Fortunately, I'm an expert at escape and evasion."

"How long were you forced to evade?" Hazelton asked.

It was an innocent enough question but Von Drexler gave him a hard look. "For approximately fifty hours," Von Drexler replied. "That was the time it took to reach Guilin. Once there, I took charge. Under my leadership, the situation was soon under control and the A-10s were properly employed."

My, we are taking all the credit today, Mazie thought.

"For the record," Von Drexler continued, warming to the subject, "you can tell Mr. Carroll that Colonel Pontowski's response to the crisis was totally inappropriate. He directed his staff to prepare for an evacuation and did not employ my A-10s in accordance with Air Force doctrine. He wasted valuable resources by flying combat air patrols. I will have to replace him."

"General," Mazie ventured, wanting to change the subject, "can I visit the First Regiment?"

"Out of the question," he answered. "I have ordered it back to Wuzhou and the situation is still unstable, too dangerous for civilians. Especially foreigners."

"Perhaps," Mazie said, "we could visit the Tenth Division." She decided to apply some pressure. "Mr. Carroll would like a firsthand report on the status of the New China Guard."

"I have trained observers for that," Von Drexler replied. "They will answer any questions you might have." He marched rigidly back to his car.

"What do you make of that?" Hazelton asked.

"The good general is covering up," Mazie answered. "The question is what?"

"Why don't you keep the general occupied," Hazelton said, "while I talk to an old friend."

The old friend was Ray Byers. While Mazie worked with the MAAG and coordinated the flow of much-needed supplies and relief through Vietnam, Byers gave Hazelton a quick education by taking him to an open-air market in Nanning. Four teenagers Byers used as interpreters and runners went with them.

"The key to what is going on in Nanning," Byers said, "is right here. The Chinese love to talk and gossip but they clam up when a foreigner comes around. My four buddies here are along to eavesdrop. You'd be surprised what they hear." The two men sat on a bench and waited. Soon, the teenagers reported back with overheard tidbits. Slowly, Byers pieced the situation together. Most of Nanning had escaped undamaged, and the brunt of the fighting had taken place around the airport. But the people were very upset by the number of civilians the PLA commandos had butchered and many were in mourning for lost relatives.

"Are the people still behind Zou?" Hazelton asked.

Byers shrugged. "It's hard to say. For the most part, they want to get on with their lives. I guess that's why I like them." Suddenly, he motioned Hazelton to be quiet as he peered intently into the crowd. He looked away. "There's a woman coming our way."

What woman? Hazelton thought. The majority of the people in the marketplace were women. Then he saw her. It took all his powers of concentration not to stare as she walked past. She paused, looked briefly at them, and moved on. Hazelton whispered a soft, "Wow." He was breathless. "Who is she?"

"That," Byers explained, "is Jin Chu." They rose and followed at a discreet distance. "She shows up from time to time in the damndest places." One of the teenagers ran up with the rumor that Jin Chu was in the marketplace. When Byers pointed to her, the boy's mouth fell open and he stared. "She's the most famous fortune teller in China," Byers said. "But she won't take money and she picks the person. The Chinese consider it . . . well," he was at a loss for words to describe the faith the Chinese put in her powers.

"It is very good luck," the teenager said, "for Miss Li to tell your fortune." His eyes widened as she turned and walked toward them.

She stopped in front of Hazelton. "May I tell your fortune?" she asked. Hazelton nodded dumbly as she led him back to the bench where they had been sitting. The crowd fell back, giving them space but staying well within hearing distance. Jin Chu held his right hand and studied his palm. Then she closed it into a fist and held it with both of her hands while she studied his face. Her touch was warm and reassuring.

"You," she said, "are in love with someone you do not see. Open your eyes and you will live long and have many children." She pulled her hands away and Hazelton felt a fleeting touch of sadness. She touched Byers' arm. "You will prosper in China and must not leave." She rose and walked back into the marketplace.

"What is she doing here?" Byers wondered.

"She talks to people and listens to gossip," the teenager said. "The same as us."

Hazelton felt an urge to move on. "Can we visit the army camp? I'd like to see how the New China Guard is doing."

Byers said, "Good buddy, right now we can go anywhere we want." The teenager agreed with him.

Mazie was sitting at a table pecking at her notebook computer when Hazelton returned to the guest house where they were staying. She was wearing a dark green silk kimono and one of her slippers had fallen to the floor while the other dangled from her toes. Hazelton smiled. She has changed, he mused, and looks much younger. Her head was bent over the keyboard and her hair, styled in a short pageboy, hung forward, hiding her face. "The daily report to Carroll?" he asked.

She nodded, not looking up. "Problems?" he asked. A short shake of her head. He knew the signs. There was a problem.

"Do you have anything for the report?" she asked.

"Based on what I saw today," he said, "the Tenth Division of the New China Guard is a farce. I've seen turtles with more get up and go."

"Can you be more specific?" she asked, still not looking at him.

"All Zou did was replace the leaders of an old PLA division with his officers. Everything else is the same. Personally, I think if they switched sides once, they'll do it again. They are poorly led, poorly trained, and poorly supplied."

"What's happening to all the supplies we're pumping in here?" Mazie asked.

"According to Ray Byers, most end up on the black market. This place is unbelievably corrupt."

Mazie pecked at the keys. "Von Drexler is a puzzle," she said. "One minute, he's talking good sense and the next he's off on some grandiose plan talking about 'forces in being' and how he's going to 'sacrifice pawns to save the king.' I don't understand him at all."

She finally turned to look at him. Her eyes were red from crying. "What happened?" he asked.

"I talked to my father on the phone." She pounded on the keys. "We had nothing to talk about. We were strangers."

"Maybe you need to see him . . . in person. Von Drexler should be able to arrange it if you press him."

"Maybe," Mazie whispered.

## Sunday, August 25
## Guilin, China

"Sir," Waters said, catching Pontowski's attention. He looked up from his desk and saw her smiling at him. She stepped aside and First Lieutenant Rod "Buns" Cox walked into his office.

Pontowski shot to his feet and extended his right hand to shake the lieutenant's. "We wondered what had happened to you." The number he carried in his head flashed to 48 and he felt good. He had only lost one pilot. "Skid reported seeing a good chute," he said. "But we never heard your emergency beacon and you never came up talking on your PRC-90." Each pilot carried an emergency radio, the PRC-90, in his survival vest.

"It was the damndest thing, Colonel," Cox said. "I was picked up by some villagers. They held me captive until they heard the PLA had gotten its ass kicked out of Nanning and Zou Rong was alive and well. Then they brought me here. I'd have called in but they wouldn't let me near a phone. They keep repeating something about a reward."

"That's news to me," Pontowski told him.

"I'm the guilty party," Waters announced. "I had the Junkyard Dogs pass the word that we pay ten thousand dollars in gold for any downed pilot returned alive and well."

"I ought to dock your pay," Pontowski grinned.

"Where did we get that much gold?" Cox blurted.

"Don't ask," Waters answered. The Junkyard Dogs had turned the Japanese Connection to their advantage.

It was too good a day to stay in his office and Pontowski headed for the flight line. He drove slowly down the line of freshly completed revetments. Parked inside each was a gray Warthog. The jets were showing the wear of combat and were no longer the spotless aircraft they had flown in from the States. The leading edges of the wings were chipped and dented, many sported temporary aluminum patches that covered bullet holes, and they all needed to be washed. But only two were reported as nonoperational. The numbers were still good: 48 pilots and 30 Warthogs.

He recognized the teenager who had saved him in the orchard and wanted to stop and talk to him. But the way the boy looked away warned him not to do it. Better his bodyguards remain unknown. This is still a dangerous place, he told himself.

A KC-10 entered the pattern and turned final. He saw Charlie Marchioni and two of the Junkyard Dogs head for the only spot on the ramp where the huge aircraft could park. He followed them.

Ray Byers was the first man off the KC-10. "Got it all," he told them. He ticked off the items on board. "We got one engine, one nose gear assembly, one complete tail and empennage, two canopies"—he grinned at Marchioni—"and twenty-six Honeywell nav units. Your LASTE problems are fixed."

Marchioni couldn't believe it. "Twenty-six? How'd you do that?"

"Don't ask," Byers replied.

That seems to be the operational phrase when the Dogs get involved, Pontowski thought. Sooner or later, those con men are going to get my ass in one big crack. Later, I hope, because I can't do this without them.

The chief of Maintenance examined the cargo as it came off the KC-10. He was amazed the engine could be loaded through the cargo hatch. "We'll have those two hangar queens flying in forty-eight hours," he told Pontowski.

A rare feeling of contentment swept over Pontowski as he drove back to the operations building. For us, he thought, this is the bottom line. It's not a profit and loss statement at the end of a quarter, but accomplishment. The two numbers, 48 and 32, flashed in front of him. Surrounding the numbers, he could see the faces that made them possible. This is what I'm all about, he told himself.

Matthew Zachary Pontowski was having a good day. "Watch some SOB screw it all up," he muttered to himself.

The SOB was Sara Waters. She was waiting for him with Leonard and Maggot. "We need to talk," she said.

He settled into his chair and leaned back. "What's the problem?"

"Skeeter and Buns are lovers," Waters said.

"I'm not surprised," Pontowski replied. "They're both young, healthy, and single. I suppose it was only a matter of time until sparks were struck. Since they're both first lieutenants, it's all legal."

He listened while Waters related the emotional trauma Skeeter had gone through when Buns had been reported missing. "I was with her most of the night," Waters said. "Fortunately, she wasn't scheduled to fly on the first go. She was totally strung out."

"We all take losses hard," Pontowski told them. It surprised him that Leonard and Maggot were letting her do the talking.

"It's one thing when it's a friend," she argued. "It's another when it's your lover. Love and sex are much stronger emotions."

"She's a good pilot," Pontowski countered. "I haven't seen anything get in the way of that."

Now it was Leonard's turn. "I'm not so sure about that, sir." He recounted the strafing pass incident. "There might have been an ambulance there. But I didn't see it and it wasn't clearly marked. She should have pressed the attack. You can't wait until you're on familiar ground or in the heart of the envelope to take a shot or drop a bomb. An opportunity only exists for a fraction of a second and then it's gone. You shoot because it looks right at the time. There's no time to worry about missing or making a mistake. Most likely, one shot is all you're going to get."

Maggot joined in. "I saw the same thing in the Persian Gulf. It's the opposite of buck fever, when a jock gets trigger happy."

Pontowski ran what they were saying through his own set of mental filters. Maggot's dislike of women flying fighters was well-known, which explained his point of view. Still, Maggot had more combat experience in A-10s than anyone else in the wing and he had defended Skeeter in front of the other pilots. As for Waters and Leonard, he suspected they were sharing the same bed and felt a strong emotional bond. Would that affect their judgment about Skeeter and Buns? "So what are you recommending?" he asked.

"I think you should send her home," Waters answered.

"I don't think it has anything to do with being a woman," Leonard added. "I'd make the same recommendation for any of the other pilots under the same circumstances. Whoever said timing is the most important thing got it wrong—it's the only thing. She's going to hesitate at the wrong time and get someone killed."

Maggot interrupted. "Most likely herself."

"I need to think about it," Pontowski told them. Leonard and Maggot left while Waters held back. "I noticed you did most of the talking."

"This was my idea," Waters said. "Getting those two in here was like dragging a bull to a vet for castration." Pontowski didn't smile and she knew an explanation was in order. "Skeeter's a good pilot. But I don't think she's got the killer instinct I see in the others."

"You see that in us?"

She nodded. "When the challenge is there, I see it. Everyone, you included, has it. It's part of your personality."

Pontowski mulled it over. It was the truth. He had no reservations about dropping bombs on people or shooting a hostile aircraft out of the sky. Are we that primeval? he wondered. "And you don't see it in Skeeter?"

Waters shook her head. "I know male pilots who don't

have it. Maybe she's like them. Maybe it's the mother instinct in her. Who knows? I don't have it."

"But you're here," he reminded her.

"We all have an obligation for service," she said.

"I'll think about it," he said, dismissing her. Why bring this up now? he thought after she had left. Killer instinct, obligation for service . . . we've got more important things to worry about. He shoved the problem to the back of his mind.

## Sunday, August 25
## Washington, D.C.

Bill Carroll slumped into his chair and rubbed his eyes. He surveyed the clutter on his desk, stood, and stretched, forcing his fatigue to yield. He wanted to go for a run and blow the mental cobwebs away. But it was nearing midnight. Too late. Besides, he had to be ready for the morning meeting with the president. The Middle East crisis was not yielding and the Islamic fundamentalists were consolidating their strength. Only in Saudi Arabia was there a glimmer of hope. It was just possible the CIA might be able to destabilize the fundamentalists and return the Saud family to the throne. How many times can we save their bacon, he thought. He snorted. What a bad joke, Muslims don't eat bacon.

He read the memo on his desk. The Honorable Ann Nevers, the congresswoman from California, was demanding a full-scale congressional investigation into what she was calling "Chinagate." Damn! Carroll raged to himself. Doesn't she understand how limited our options are in that part of the world? He made a note to personally call on Nevers. Maybe he could talk her into backing off.

Mazie's report was next. Not good. Zou's government had been seriously shaken by the attack on Nanning, the New China Guard was mostly show, and Von Drexler was coming unhinged. At least the supply channel from Hanoi to Nanning was open and flowing. Thanks to Toragawa, the Japanese were pumping in much-needed relief and money to Zou. That will help stabilize the situation, he calculated, if the corruption doesn't get too bad. Carroll shook his head. If Nevers ever found out about that. . . . He didn't pursue the thought. It was too painful.

He scratched a note on Mazie's report—"Find replacement for VD"—and headed out the door for his health club. He hoped Chuck and Wayne were awake.

## Saturday, August 31
## Nanning, China

The force of the dream forced Jin Chu to sit up in bed. She was awake and fought to control the rapid breathing that pounded at her body. Slowly, she regained control. She had never experienced so vivid a dream. Kamigami reached out and gently rubbed her back. "Are you okay?" There was no answer. "Was it a dream?"

She shuddered. "It was very real. It frightened me." Kamigami didn't answer and waited for her to tell him about it. He had seen it before. Jin Chu never consciously reacted to the gossip and news she picked up when she wandered through marketplaces telling people's fortunes and practicing *feng shui*.

Her sensitive nature was attuned to the emotions of people around her and by touching them, she felt what they felt. She chose with care the people whose fortunes she told, and because she never accepted money, they paid by talking. But she did not consciously evaluate what they told her. It was absorbed into her subconscious where it came out in dreams.

"You must return to Wuzhou," she told him.

Kamigami smiled in the dark. She had responded to his emotions. He had been at Nanning for two days, arguing with Zou's staff for more TOW antitank weapons and Stinger surface-to-air missiles. It had been a losing argument and he wanted to return to his First Regiment in Wuzhou, even though it meant Jin Chu would probably not accompany him. He looked at his watch: one-thirty in the morning. "I had planned to," he told her. "Later today, when it's light." But she knows that, he thought.

"We must go now," she said.

He heard an urgency in her words that surprised him. Before, she had always been sad when she spoke of her dreams. Then the "we" cut through the sleepy haze he had been drifting in. "You're coming with me?" He saw fear in her eyes when she nodded. He rolled out of bed and hurriedly dressed. "What happened in your dream."

"We were in Wuzhou," she said, "like the first time." He recalled when the PLA had forced them to dig graves and bury bodies. "But you were wearing a uniform and fighting. There were many people killed and many fires. May May was running with the baby and I was following her." She took a deep breath. "It was this morning and I could see the sun rising."

Kamigami didn't hesitate. He made three quick phone calls. The first was to alert his helicopter crew for an immediate takeoff. The second was to his First Regiment's command bunker in Wuzhou. "Order a full alert," he told the duty officer. "Expect an attack before dawn." The third was to the New China Guard. "Thank God I don't have to go through Von Drexler," he muttered. He told them of the attack warning and asked if they would relay the information to Von Drexler's new command post and have the A-10s placed on alert.

Jin Chu was ready and they ran for the helicopter.

The First Regiment's command bunker on the western side of Wuzhou was humming with activity when Kamigami arrived. Most of the American advisors were huddled in a small group in the rear with nothing to do and his staff kept giving him confident looks. A good sign. The big situation board was current and all of his sixteen companies were moving into their forward positions. He checked the master clock—0410. Two and one half hours into the alert. A better sign.

He looked around for Jin Chu. She was gone. She's probably with May May and the baby, he decided. He wandered through the bunker. Everything was in order. Now he had to wait. A lieutenant updated the situation board. Horse Company was in position.

One of the original nine, he thought. A mental image of the young captain who commanded the company flashed in front of him. That's where I should be, he told himself. Not in here. He fought down the old urge to go to the front. Now three more companies reported in position. Again, all were part of the original nine.

Trimler caught his attention. "I'm in contact with the MAAG's new command post in Nanning," he said. "They don't take this seriously and won't alert Von Drexler." He frowned. "I backdoored them and called Guilin on the secure line. Pontowski is loading his birds out but he takes his tasking from Von Drexler, not us. At least he'll be ready to launch—if he ever gets the order."

"We need to cut Von Drexler out as the middleman," Kamigami said, "and talk directly to Pontowski."

The American colonel shook his head. "Nothing has changed. The A-10s are still Von Drexler's trump card for controlling Zou."

"Politics will kill us," Kamigami muttered.

A major caught his attention. "Miss Li is here," he said in Cantonese. Kamigami followed the major to the bunker entrance. Jin Chu was standing there with May May and the baby.

"May we stay here?" she asked. The major beamed when Kamigami nodded his agreement. Jin Chu's presence was a morale boost for the Chinese.

The shrill whine of an incoming artillery shell passed overhead. But there was no explosion. Kamigami listened as four more shells ranged overhead. Still no explosions. He ran onto the main floor of the bunker and shouted, *"Gas!"*

The alarm went out, the bunker was sealed, and reports flooded in. Kang was laying a mustard gas artillery barrage over Wuzhou. Trimler appeared beside him, his face granite hard. "The First Regiment is okay," he said. "They're trained and equipped to handle chemical warfare. But this—" he paused to gain control of the deep anger that was engulfing him, "is criminal. They're hitting innocent civilians. They have no protection at all."

Kamigami said nothing and stared at the situation board as more reports came in. The gas barrage had stopped and conventional artillery was pounding the city. All four battalions reported they were in position and two were in contact, the military euphemism for locked in combat, with numerous tanks. "Kang tried to catch us by surprise, like at Nanning," Kamigami said. "This time we were ready for them."

"A sitrep might get some attention," Trimler said, thinking who would react to a situation report that detailed a major attack in progress. He drafted the short message and handed it to Kamigami.

SITREP

AS OF 31 AUG: 0450L (30 AUG: 2050Z)

PLA INITIATED MAJOR ATTACK ON WUZHOU AT 0430 LOCAL TIME WITH MUSTARD GAS ARTILLERY BARRAGE FOLLOWED BY CONVENTIONAL ARTILLERY. MANY CIVILIAN CASUALTIES, TANKS ADVANCING FROM EAST IN FORCE. SITUATION FLUID, REQUEST CLOSE AIR SUPPORT.

A wicked look crossed Trimler's face. "Let me send it. Since I fall under the MAAG, I can send an information copy to the MAAG's higher headquarters—which happens to be the National Military Command Center in Washington, D.C. Let VD ignore this one."

The artillery barrage stopped as jets roared overhead. Horse Company radioed that tanks were advancing from the east. "For what we are about to receive," Trimler muttered, "may the Lord make us truly thankful."

# CHAPTER 15

**Saturday, August 31**
**Nanning, China**

Hazelton was in the communications section of Von Drexler's new headquarters compound dispatching Mazie's daily report to Bill Carroll when the first sitrep detailing the fighting at Wuzhou came in. He listened for a few moments and then called Mazie. "You best get right over here," he told her. "I'll meet you in the command post."

He wandered into the deserted command post, impressed with the new facility. The first officers to arrive were angry because their weekend plans had been disturbed. "What's all this for?" he asked an American Army colonel while he waved at the large room.

"Beats the hell out of me," the colonel answered. "Von Drexler started building this place the day he arrived. It's patterned after the NMCC in the Pentagon. It doesn't make sense. All this to command thirty-two A-10s. Hell, you could run a major war from here."

Von Drexler walked onto the command balcony dressed in his MacArthur uniform. He picked up the microphone. "Gentlemen," he began, "this appears to be a probing action on the part of the PLA. We've seen it before. Don't overreact and let's wait for the dust to settle."

A small figure dressed in a dark warmup suit appeared at Von Drexler's side. At first, Hazelton didn't recognize

Mazie. He watched, fascinated, as the two talked. She turned and walked away, disappearing from his view. What was that all about? Hazelton thought. A few moments later she appeared on the main floor. The graceful and lissome way she walked captivated him. He was seeing a different person, and he would never think of her as the Frump again.

"The general," she said, "refuses to take this seriously. He says Kang shot his bolt when he hit Nanning and this is just to keep us off balance. He won't even bring the AVG onto alert status." She glanced at the big situation boards on the front wall. No change from normal readiness. "Went, can you go to Wuzhou and see for yourself what is going on? Call or get back to me as soon as you can. I'll be right here."

"Ray Byers has a helicopter he flies around in," Hazelton said. "I'll see if I can borrow it."

"Hurry," Mazie urged. He ran from the room.


## Saturday, August 31
## Guilin, China

Pontowski drove down the flight line in his pickup with the chief of Maintenance. A Warthog stood ready and loaded in each revetment. "Every jet ready to go," he said. "Maintenance did good." It was a classic understatement.

The radio in his pickup squawked. "Colonel," the controller in the operations center said, "the tower reports an inbound chopper from Wuzhou."

"Rog. I'll meet it." Pontowski gunned the engine and headed for the helipad. The helicopter had barely touched down when Trimler jumped out.

"The balloon has gone up big time," the American colonel shouted as he climbed into the truck. "We're getting stomped bad and Von Drexler has his fucking thumb up his fucking ass." He looked at Pontowski. "He claims this is a probing action and says using the AVG is an overreaction. Overreaction my ass!" He made a visible effort to control his breathing. "We need close air support. Now."

It must be bad if Kamigami had to send Trimler to plead for support, Pontowski reasoned. He made his decision.

"You've got it." He sped toward the operations center. "We haven't a clue what's going on. Can you brief the pilots?"

"Can do. But I haven't much time. I've got to fly to Nanning and try to change Von Drexler's mind."

Waters stood in the rear of the operations center as Trimler outlined the situation at Wuzhou. She opened her war diary to make an entry. She paused, thinking about Von Drexler. Stick to the facts, she reasoned. VD may use this against us. She wrote:

31 Aug: 1035

   Colonel Robert Trimler arrived by helicopter from First Regiment. Situation on ground at Wuzhou desperate. Orders from AVG confused. P trying to clarify.

She closed the diary as Pontowski joined her.

"Get with the Dogs, Ripper," he told her. "Get ready for an evacuation. We're in deep trouble here."

## Saturday, August 31
## Wuzhou, China

Ray Byers was screaming at the top of his voice so Hazelton could hear him over the noise of the helicopter. "You're on your own, Good Buddy. I've got to book for Guilin."

Hazelton nodded, finally understanding, and jumped out of the helicopter, carrying the new video camcorder he had purchased in Japan. He planned on documenting the conditions at Wuzhou to convince Von Drexler but immediately regretted the move when the old Huey lifted off. He was alone in the middle of a war zone. He ran over to a young soldier and shouted, "Kamigami!" The soldier pointed at a big pile of sandbags—the command bunker for the First Regiment. Hazelton panned the area with his camcorder before he ran for cover.

He found the purposeful activity inside Kamigami's

bunker a reassuring contrast to what he had seen in Von Drexler's command post. A major who spoke excellent English was assigned to escort him. "I will introduce you to General Kamigami as soon as he's free," Major Sun said. "Do you speak Cantonese?" Hazelton shook his head no. "I see," Sun replied. "I think the general is free now." He led Hazelton over to Kamigami.

Hazelton found it hard to believe the huge man standing in front of him was Mazie's father. He introduced himself, feeling like a clumsy teenager meeting his girlfriend's father for the first time. He managed to stammer the reason he was there.

Kamigami stuck out a huge hand. "Welcome aboard, Mr. Hazelton. We can give you what you want but it would be better if you saw for yourself and drew your own conclusions. Are you up for a quick tour?" Hazelton felt himself drawn to Kamigami, and he nodded. "Good," Kamigami continued. "Major Sun here will be your interpreter and guide." He issued orders in Cantonese and Hazelton was amazed at the authority his soft voice carried. He was beginning to understand Mazie better. "We'll get you a helmet, gas mask, and flak vest," Kamigami said. "I want you back here in two hours and we'll fly you to Nanning in my helicopter."

Major Sun led Hazelton out of the bunker and found him the necessary equipment. Within minutes, they were on a motor scooter, darting through the town. Twice, Sun stopped while Hazelton recorded the hundreds of civilian casualties from the gas attack. Hazelton shouted through his mask, describing what he saw as he filmed. On the eastern side of town, Hazelton filmed the carnage from a direct hit by an artillery shell. It was the first time he had seen dismembered bodies. Sun waited patiently while Hazelton ripped off his mask and vomited.

"Do we have to keep wearing these?" Hazelton gasped. Sun shrugged and removed his own mask. "Can you get me closer to the fighting?" Sun nodded and they sped out of town. Ahead of them, to the east, the thunder of artillery grew stronger.

"This is Dragon Company," Sun shouted, pointing at a

small village. "Dragon Company is one of the nine." The "nine" meant nothing to Hazelton and he made a mental note to ask about it later.

Hazelton was talking to the company commander when tanks were reported advancing on the village. The men ran for cover and Hazelton found himself in a ditch next to Sun. "You must look," Sun told him, pointing to the edge of the ditch.

Hazelton lifted his head and froze. Nothing had prepared him for the sight of a charging thirty-six-ton tank coming directly at him at over thirty miles an hour. Sun snatched the camcorder out of Hazelton's hand to record the action. Hazelton felt his knees go weak as the turret traversed toward them. Behind the tank he could see three more tanks and was vaguely aware of a missile being fired from his far right. The camcorder recorded the TOW missile as it destroyed the tank.

"There," Sun said, pointing to the sky. "Warhogs. We call them the Silent Gun." He recorded the two Warthogs as they rolled in on the advancing tanks. Hazelton had never seen a more beautiful sight. Within minutes, the Warthogs had destroyed the tanks.

"We must go," Sun said, pulling Hazelton back to the village.

"My God," Hazelton gasped. "I didn't know tanks were so huge."

"Those were Type 59 main battle tanks," Sun explained. "They are an improved version of the Soviet T-54 tank and have a one-hundred-millimeter gun." He smiled. "We are very good at killing them with your TOW missiles. But the Silent Gun is better." He kick-started the motor scooter to life as Hazelton relieved himself on the ground.

Trucks and vehicles were streaming out of Wuzhou when they reached the command bunker. It was deserted and Hazelton felt the knife-edge of fear scrape his skin. Sun spoke to a lieutenant and then translated for Hazelton. "We are too late," he said. "The headquarters has moved. Many tanks have broken through and we must go to Teng Xian." Hazelton's fear turned to panic. He was caught in the middle of a retreat, a rout.

\* \* \*

Richard Herman, Jr.

Two days later, Hazelton and Sun walked into Teng Xian, the small town thirty-five miles to the west where Kamigami had regrouped the First Regiment. Kamigami found Hazelton collapsed against a wall outside his bunker, sucking at a canteen. Hazelton's clothes were ripped and dirty, his hair was matted to his scalp, and he was shaking with fatigue. His camcorder was lying in his lap, firmly clutched in one hand. Hazelton pulled himself up, determined to make a good impression, and would have saluted had he known how. "I have seen enough, sir," he said. Why am I acting like this, he thought.

Kamigami's face was inscrutable. "Major Sun says you destroyed a tank with a Molotov cocktail."

"It's not like I had a choice," Hazelton replied.

Kamigami stifled a grin. It was the right answer. "My helicopter will take you to Nanning." Then he unbent a little. "Please give this to Mazie." He handed Hazelton a letter.

Wentworth Hazelton pulled himself up straight. "I hope we meet again, sir. I am very fond of your daughter." He felt like a fool for saying that. Suddenly, he didn't care. It was the truth.

## Monday, September 2
## Nanning, China

Mazie gasped when she saw Hazelton climb out of the helicopter. She ran across the open area outside the headquarters compound to the helipad. "I was so worried," she said.

"Cheated death again," he grinned. Mazie cocked her head to one side and took him in as he recounted what he had seen. He was a mess and needed a bath. Two days before, he would have never said "cheated death again" and he no longer was speaking in the pompous tones of a good bureaucrat. He had changed and she liked what she saw. "Your father asked me to give you this," he said, handing her the letter.

She stopped and opened the envelope. Her face glowed as she read the short note. She carefully folded it and put it into a pocket. "We're still a family," was all she said. She would never show him the note.

"I'm worried about Von Drexler," she continued. "He has three different teams drawing up separate plans for a counteroffensive and he keeps saying Zou must be overthrown and replaced by a competent general. He's turned this place into a madhouse."

"Does he know Pontowski is flying close air support for the First Regiment?"

"Yes, but he insists on personally approving each mission. I think you should talk to Colonel Trimler," she told him. "He's still here. Von Drexler won't let him leave."

"We need a VCR," Hazelton said, tapping his camcorder. "But what I've got isn't Loony Tunes."

Trimler watched the unedited tapes without comment. He replayed the segment that showed Hazelton charging a T-59 tank from the rear. He was holding a gasoline-filled bottle with a flaming rag stuck in the neck. He hurled the glass bottle onto the engine's air intake and flames engulfed the rear of the tank. "They never saw me," was all Hazelton said in the way of explanation.

Trimler grunted something about "titanium testicles" and ran the rest of the tapes. Mazie rewound the tapes while Trimler stared at his hands, thinking. "You've documented an absolutely brilliant tactical withdrawal," he finally said. His voice was hard and bitter. "And I'm missing it." He made a decision. "Mazie, Von Drexler is cracking up under the strain. I'm no shrink, but I think his ego is totally out of control. He's acting like his rank gives him absolute power. He's got to control people and events or it's a personal attack on himself. He's lost contact with reality.

"He's got to be relieved—quick. We'll have to double-bang him to make that happen. I'll send a message to my bosses in the Pentagon recommending Von Drexler be relieved while you take these tapes to Carroll. Tell him what you've seen here the last few days."

"Went," Mazie said, "I think you should stay here." Hazelton nodded, agreeing with her. "Colonel," she asked, "where can I find you?"

"Where I can do some good," Trimler answered, "with the First Regiment."

## Tuesday, September 3
## The Executive Office Building, Washington, D.C.

The dark-suited aide escorted Mazie through the deserted Executive Office Building. She checked the time—almost midnight. Jet lag was still playing havoc with her internal clocks. They reached the luxurious office suite in the southeast corner on the top floor that overlooked the White House. Next to having an office in the White House, insiders considered it the most prestigious office location in the capital. Why was Carroll working here so late at night? The aide motioned her to a chair in Carroll's outer office. "The national security advisor is in a meeting," he told her.

Mazie dozed, her mind a blank. She jerked awake when Carroll came out of the office, ushering four uncomfortable-looking Asians. The mental haze that had bound her in a cobweb of lethargy blew away in a gust of recognition. She knew these four men! They were the same Vietnamese they had negotiated with in Hanoi, that Byers had cut deals with on the side. What was going on?

Carroll shook hands with the men and the same aide escorted them out. She followed Carroll into the office and sank into a comfortable chair. She wanted to ask why the Vietnamese were in Washington, D.C. But it was an improper question. He pulled a chair up next to hers. "Is it as bad as it looks?" Carroll asked.

"Worse," she replied. "Chaos is the best word for what's going on." Carroll listened without comment while she described the situation in Nanning. Then she played Hazelton's videotapes and summarized what Trimler had said.

"Colonel Trimler's message registered a nine on the Pentagon's Richter scale," he told her. "Even the Joint Chiefs are involved. I think we've got a solution worked out. What's your impression of Trimler?"

"Intelligent," Mazie answered, "competent, and steady as a rock."

"We're going to split the AVG off from the MAAG. It was a bad idea to have Von Drexler in command of both. Trimler is going to take over the MAAG."

"I think that's a good choice," Mazie said. Jet lag was

reclaiming her and she was too tired to think of the next, obvious question.

"The Honorable Ann Nevers is turning her opposition into a personal crusade. I want you to take a copy of these tapes over to her. Answer any questions." He stressed the word "any."

"Even about the Japanese Connection?" she asked.

"If she asks, yes." He trusted Mazie not to volunteer information and not to get caught in a fishing expedition by Nevers. "Get some rest," he told her. "You look beat."

"I am," she replied. She pulled herself out of the chair and left. Carroll reached for the phone and started making phone calls.

## Wednesday, September 4
## Guilin, China

Sara Waters parked Pontowski's pickup beside the empty revetment and waited. Jake Trisher, the pilot sitting beside her, counted out loud as the Warthogs circled to land. All had recovered safely and for a moment, the anxiety and stress that had become a part of her existence eased. Then it was back. Within minutes, the aircraft would be serviced, armed, and launched on another mission.

The sergeant from intelligence who debriefed the pilots during combat turns stuck his head inside the window. "It's not good," he told them. "The last flight reported numerous tanks advancing on Guigang." He showed them the map he had taped to the back of his clipboard. Guigang was seventy-five miles to the east of Nanning. "The First Regiment is pulling back." The noise of four Warthogs taxiing in drowned out any further conversation.

A crew chief marshaled Pontowski's Warthog to a stop in front of the revetment. Before the engines could spin down, a tug with a tow bar was pushing the A-10 into the bunker while a fuel truck drove up. Four weapons trailers were already parked inside the revetment with a waiting load of Mark-82 AIRs and Mavericks. The crew chief dropped the boarding ladder and Pontowski climbed out of the cockpit.

The crew chief pointed to four holes punctured in the

fuselage aft of the engines. "Damn," Pontowski said, "I didn't even know I'd been hit."

The crew chief dropped an inspection panel and stuck his head inside the fuselage. "You were lucky," he said. "Only minor damage." He grabbed a roll of repair tape and slapped makeshift patches on both sides of the holes. "Load her up," he said. "She's still OR."

Pontowski grunted an answer. OR—operationally ready—was what he needed to hear. "It's getting tough out there," he told the sergeant from intelligence. "What's our status?"

The sergeant answered, "Counting your jet, we have twenty-seven Hogs operational. Three are down for battle damage and two for hydraulics. No wounded or killed."

The tension in Pontowski's face eased. He hadn't lost another pilot. But he knew it couldn't last. He finished debriefing the sergeant as the ground crew hurried to refuel and rearm the Warthog. Waters and Jake got out of the pickup and walked up. "Whatcha got, Ripper?" Pontowski asked.

"Jake will have to take the next mission," she said, handing him a telefax message.

Pontowski scanned the message. "I'll be . . ." he whispered. The message stated he was promoted to full colonel and was to immediately assume command of the American Volunteer Group at Nanning. He was to appoint an interim commander for the wing, subject to confirmation by higher headquarters.

He looked at her. "You've read this?" She nodded. "Anyone else?" She shook her head. "Okay, here we go. I need to see Tango ASAP." Waters' face paled. "I know how you feel, Ripper. But he's the best man to take over for me."

"Congratulations on your promotion, sir." Her voice was controlled and formal. She walked to the pickup and held the door open for him.

"Lighten up," Pontowski said.

"General Trimler is waiting for you in operations," she replied. He cocked an eyebrow at her. "He's been promoted to brigadier general," she explained, "and is assuming command of the MAAG mission." She allowed a tight smile. "They got that one right—finally."

"We'll have to go to Nanning," he told her. "I want you to come with me."

Her body went rigid and she wanted to argue that her place was here, with the wing. That was a lie—she wanted to stay because of Leonard. But she was Pontowski's executive officer. The words came hard. "Yes, sir."

The helicopter circled Nanning, overflying the roads clogged with refugees streaming out of the city to the south and west. Trimler yelled at the pilot and they landed outside the headquarters compound. Pontowski jumped out and led the way to the security shack at the main entrance with Trimler and Waters close behind.

"Please call the chief of security," he told the American sergeant on duty. A few moments later a worried-looking captain entered.

"Thank God you're finally here, sir," the captain said. The relief he felt was caught in every word. "The general received a message hours ago directing him to relinquish command to you and General Trimler. He's gone crazy and won't come out of the command post. When you didn't show up, he claimed you had been wounded or killed." He straightened up. "I'll escort you."

Von Drexler was standing over a map table when Pontowski entered. He shot Pontowski a disdainful look. "You are out of uniform," he snapped. "You are only a lieutenant colonel. Remove the eagles and wear your correct rank." Then he saw the single star on Trimler's collar. "Captain," he said to the chief of security, "place both of these men under arrest. I have a war to fight." His voice was calm and matter of fact, a total contrast to his haggard and drawn face. Even his normally crisp and fresh uniform was rumpled and disheveled. His egomania was still driving him, destroying what was left of his rationality.

"I'm sorry, sir," the captain replied. "I can't do that."

Pontowski handed Von Drexler the message directing him to assume command of the AVG. The general slapped it away. "This is mutiny," he rasped. "Captain, place them under arrest."

"General," Pontowski said, "let's go to your office."

Von Drexler turned, walked to the front of the room, and

picked up a microphone. "Gentlemen," he announced to the command post, "let me have your attention. We have two officers in the command post who have assumed a rank they are not legally entitled to. I can only assume a mutiny is in progress, therefore—" The loudspeakers went dead.

The captain had disconnected the cord and approached Von Drexler. "Sir," he said, "I must ask you to return to your quarters." Von Drexler ignored him. The captain leaned forward and spoke in a low voice. "Unless you leave now, I will forcibly escort you. Under restraint, if necessary."

Von Drexler glared at the captain for a brief moment, his face full of hate, before he marched out of the command post. "Call my car," he commanded, "I'm returning to my quarters."

"Ripper," Pontowski ordered, "go with the captain and make sure Von Drexler stays there." He turned to Trimler. "Let's see if we can salvage this."

Von Drexler marched into the main hall of his mansion and called for James, his majordomo. There was no answer. He ignored Waters and the captain and climbed the main stairs, calling for the two women. "Yu Ke." Silence. "Ailing!" Again, no answer. He disappeared into his bedroom.

"I've got to get back," the captain told Waters. "I'll leave a sergeant here with you." He hurried out the door as Waters scouted the main floor. The house was a wreck and had been ransacked. She found a telephone and dialed the command post. "Please tell Colonel Pontowski the general is in his quarters." She dropped the phone when she heard a single shot.

Waters followed the sergeant as he pounded up the stairs, his weapon drawn. "Holy shit!" he blurted when he entered the bedroom. Waters halted, afraid to look inside. Then she forced herself. Von Drexler was lying on the floor, his head in a pool of blood. A nine-millimeter Beretta semiautomatic was beside his body. "He took it in the mouth," the sergeant said.

He checked the adjoining sitting room. "Captain," he called. "There's two more in here." Again, Waters had to force herself to look. Yu Ke and Ailing were lying naked on the floor, their throats cut. "They've been dead at least a day," he said. "He couldn't have done it. He hasn't left the command post since Saturday."

Waters shuddered and threw open a window. She needed a breath of fresh air. In the distance, she heard the heavy thunder of artillery. "How far away?" she asked.

"I don't know," the sergeant answered. "But it's getting closer." He covered the bodies and called the security shack. "We need to get the general to the morgue and get the hell out of here," he told her. "I'll check his personal effects."

The ambulance had left with Von Drexler's body when the sergeant handed her a box and a list of the items he had found. "The house was ransacked," he said. "Everything of value is long gone." She looked inside the box. "If I were you," he said, "I'd trash those videotapes. They were deliberately left behind so we'd find them."

She carried the box out of the house, leaving the door open.


Pontowski leaned forward over Von Drexler's map table and bowed his head. Panic, he thought, is coming out of the woodwork. It was a deadly cancer he had to cut out before it killed them. But he was on the edge of an unfamiliar situation and dealing with too many unknowns. He studied the chart under his hands. Was it current? Was it all there for him to see?

How long did he have? The answer was clear—not long. In one respect, it was the same as flying combat. He was relying on his skills, his abilities, all that was in him, to survive and win. He was only going to get one shot. And if he missed? What was the price for failure? It was a burden few men willingly shouldered, yet he wanted it. Frank Hester's words came back, strong and clear: "Do something, even if it's wrong."

"Here we go," he said to no one. He started by talking to Charles Parker, the vice commander he had inherited from Von Drexler. "Where do I start?" he asked.

Charlie Parker was a senior colonel, heavy with time in

grade and experience. The heavyset, slightly balding, middle-aged man was on his last assignment before retiring. He had no illusions about his future, had suffered under Von Drexler, but was still a consummate professional. As long as he was Pontowski's vice commander, he would do his best. "We need to streamline the way we control the A-10s," he told Pontowski. "Von Drexler personally approved every single mission you flew. He got in the way."

Pontowski was encouraged. Parker's thinking paralleled his own. "What else?" he asked.

"We need an AWACS bad." He responded to the look on Pontowski's face. "We need centralized control of the airlift operating out of Cam Ranh Bay in Vietnam, fighter escort"—he was on a roll—"and for God's sake, cut the number of people here in half."

Pontowski had a vice commander he could rely on. He issued his first orders to the American Volunteer Group and within minutes, the headquarters was alive with purpose. It was one of the quickest reorganizations in Air Force history.

He found Trimler huddled with Hazelton and the remnants of the MAAG mission in the back of the compound. "Von Drexler was right in one respect," he told Trimler. "The MAAG and the AVG must work together. This is twice the building the AVG needs, so why don't you set up a logistics center in the command post? Talk to my vice commander, Charlie Parker."

Hazelton joined in. "We can help. The railroad is still open and we've got tons of material stockpiled at Hanoi. But we don't know what to do with it."

"Getting it to the right people, at the right place, at the right time is always the nut cruncher," Trimler told him. A wicked look crossed his face. "I can make that happen. Besides, I'm tired of getting kicked around by Kang."

"Don't underestimate him," Pontowski said. Outside, the sound of artillery punctuated his warning.

Then it came to him, clear and complete. The key had been on the map for him to see all along. It was so obvious, so basic. "Kang is running out of gas," he said. He walked out of the room, his strides long and quick. Then he ran for the command post. The A-10s had to go after different targets.

Wednesday, September 4
Washington, D.C.

Congresswoman Ann Nevers split her attention between the videotape playing on the TV screen and the young woman sitting in her office. Although they had been in Hanoi at the same time, they had never met, and Mazie wasn't what she had expected. Her staff had described Mazie as short and dumpy. This woman was petite, stylishly dressed, and very pretty. Nevers caught her reaction to the segment where Hazelton destroyed the tank.

"You are very fond of him," Nevers observed when the screen went blank. She smiled at the astonished look on Mazie's face. "The young man who made these tapes," she explained.

The smile disappeared and she turned to the heart of the matter. "I know how your Mr. Carroll works and understand his message: If I continue to oppose the administration's current policies in China, he will give the media the scenes showing the carnage from the chemical and artillery attacks. The public will be outraged, and the fact that I opposed the policies that caused those attacks in the first place will be lost in the allegations that I support the very regime that committed the atrocities—which I do not."

"Mr. Carroll never said that," Mazie declared. She sensed it would be useless to remind Nevers that Kang Xun had been committing atrocities against the southern Chinese long before the United States had gotten involved or had a policy.

Nevers ignored her. "I'm not stupid, Miss Kamigami. These tapes are excellent trump cards." Nevers liked the analogy she was drawing and ran with it, since they both knew she had a weak hand. "But I need to win a trick or two to stay in the game."

"If Mr. Carroll knew what you had in mind . . ." Mazie ventured. Both women knew they were cutting a deal.

"I will drop my demands for an investigation into Chinagate if these tapes are never made public." She paused and smiled, calculating how to even the score. The news clip of her vomiting in the hotel lounge in Hanoi had made the national evening TV news on a slow news day. The damage was compounded when TV talk show hosts had replayed the tape for the amusement of their audiences. She was a methodical and patient woman and could wait to take her revenge. It was one of the reasons she had entered politics.

# PART 3

## Excerpt: President's Daily Brief,
### Tuesday, September 3.

FIGHTING IN SOUTHERN CHINA SUBSIDES. Zou Rong's New China Guard has withdrawn to the west, consolidated its position, and stopped the PLA advance on the Republic of Southern China's capital at Nanning. The PLA and the New China Guard have exhausted their respective logistical bases and stopped fighting. Knowledgeable observers predict the two sides will try to negotiate a cease-fire.

# CHAPTER 16

**Thursday, September 5**
**Guilin, China**

Skeeter Ashton stood in front of Leonard's desk and glared at him. "I volunteered for this," she shot at him, "while most of your pilots still had their thumbs up their fat asses. I'll match my record against anyone in the wing."

"Skeeter," Leonard said, trying to explain his concern, "I know what you've done here."

"You're still pissed because I didn't nail those trucks."

"Skeeter, a kill is a kill," Leonard replied. He was blowing it and not getting his point across. There was more to running a wing than he had thought. "Look, what I'm trying to say is, take the shot at the first opportunity. It may not look perfect but don't worry about making mistakes. The first shot may be the only chance you'll get. Okay?"

"Is that all, Colonel," Skeeter asked.

Leonard was acutely aware that this was his second day wearing the silver leaves of a lieutenant colonel. "That's all," he answered. She threw him a smart salute and stomped out of the office. He breathed a sigh of relief, wondering what had happened to his well-intentioned counseling session. It was one more dent in a hectic morning.

Morale in the wing had skyrocketed as the word spread that Pontowski was taking over command of the AVG, and within hours, they received an air tasking order that made sense. Leonard had cheered when he read that most of the wing's aircraft were tasked to provide close air support and the wing was to coordinate directly with the First Regiment's ASOC. Then he read the next paragraph: Six of his Warthogs were tasked for BAI, battlefield interdiction. It was a new type of mission for his pilots and he was worried.

As ordered, the six Warthogs had launched at first light on the new mission and were due back. Leonard tried to hide his concern and told himself yet again that BAI was very similar to close air support. His Warthogs were not supporting troops in contact but going after the supply lines feeding the enemy troops at the front.

Like Pontowski, he hated being on the ground and waiting for his aircraft to recover. Now they're my aircraft, he thought, not ours. He tried to act unconcerned when he entered the operations center. But his relief was obvious when Goat Gross told him the Warthogs were five minutes out. Leonard fought the urge to hop in "his" pickup, drive out to the runway, and watch them land. "Bring them in for the debrief," he told Gross.

The six pilots burst into operations and told a story of success. They had flown down the Pearl River and along the roads at first light looking for barges and trucks that had been moving during the night. "They're camouflaged," one pilot said, "and pulled over to hide during the day. But the IR seeker head on the Maverick picks up the heat signature from their engines. Like shootin' fish in a barrel." The other pilots agreed with him.

"How can you be sure they're not friendlies?" Skeeter asked.

"How come they're camouflaged and moving at night?" Maggot replied. Skeeter didn't answer.

Leonard made his next decision. "Let's keep 'em from moving. Skeeter, take a flight of four and work this area." He drew a long rectangular box that ran north and south and centered on the Pearl River. The box cut the Pearl, the railroad, and every main road that led toward Nanning, eighty miles to the west. "We've got ourselves an interdiction box," he said. "Don't let anything through."

This time, Leonard could not stay in the operations center and followed the four pilots out to the flight line to watch them launch. How long will this work before we have to change our tactics? he thought. The first mission had been too easy.

The flight to the interdiction box was uneventful, and Skeeter broke her flight into two elements. She sent two Hogs to recce the Pearl River while she and Mako Luce patrolled to the north. On their first sweep, they saw the distinctive smoke of a steam-driven locomotive. "Mako," she radioed, "cover-shooter. I'll lead." She planned to approach the target first and suppress any hostile fire while Mako attacked the train. "I'll ID the train," she continued. "If it's civilian, I'll call you off." Before Mako could protest, she added, "We'll stop it by taking out a bridge."

"We oughta do both," Mako answered. Thanks to Charlie Marchioni, their LASTE systems were peaked and tweaked and they could easily take out a bridge. While that would stop any rail traffic, it wouldn't destroy any material headed for the front.

Skeeter answered by two clicks of her transmit button. She dropped down to the deck, firewalled the throttles, and headed for the smoke. At a mile from the target, she pulled into a pop maneuver, rolled 135 degrees, and apexed at twelve hundred feet as she pulled her Hog's nose onto the train. It was clearly a passenger train, with only a single flatbed car attached to the rear. Canvas covered what looked like two trucks.

She banked away instead of flying directly at it. "It's civilian," she radioed. Her radar warning system exploded with sound. She glanced at the radar warning azimuth indicator in the cockpit. The symbol for a monopulse targeting radar flashed at her. A hostile radar had locked on and was tracking. *"Break Left!"* Mako shouted over the radio at the same instant.

Mako swore as Skeeter turned into the threat. The canvas had dropped away from the trucks on the flatbed car and two missiles were streaking toward her. The nose of her Warthog came up as chaff and flares streamed out behind. The first missile committed to an upward vector, matching her maneuver. Then she wrenched the big fighter into a tight turn, pulling six gs. The missile couldn't follow her and went ballistic.

The nose of Skeeter's jet turned into the second missile as she tried to defeat it. But her airspeed had bled off in the hard turn and she had lost maneuverability. The missile struck her aircraft forward of the right engine and she disappeared in a fireball. Only the nose of the A-10 was visible as a large burning flare shot out of the fireball. It was the ejection seat. The human flare arced skyward and then curved downward, still burning.

Deep inside Mako, a white-hot emotion erupted, as bright and consuming as the fireball that had killed Skeeter Ashton. It was primal, born in a distant past when instinct governed survival. But the basic urge to protect had not changed over the centuries. Civilization had only masked it, turning it down acceptable paths and now, a cold, driven fury captured the pilot. He wanted to kill.

Unbidden, Mako's left hand twisted the wafer switch on the HUD control panel to WD-1. The symbols in his HUD flashed, giving him a gunsight for his cannon as he dropped his Warthog down to the deck and circled out in front of the train. He jammed the throttles forward, not worrying about airspeed as he turned into the train. Bitching Betty, the computer-activated woman's voice in the ground collision avoidance system, filled his headset with *"Pull up! Pull up!"* when he went below ninety feet. He ignored it and dropped even lower, barely twenty-five feet off the ground. Ahead of him, he could only see the nose of the train coming at him. The engine shielded him from the surface-to-air missile battery and radar at the rear of the train.

Again, his left hand flicked forward as he selected high rate of fire, forty-two hundred rounds per minute, for the GAU-8 "Avenger" cannon. The snout of the steam engine surged into the gun pipper reticle. He mashed the trigger and held it. The Avenger growled as he flew down the length of the train.

Mako pulled off to the left and positioned for a second run. This time he drove the crosshairs on his TV monitor over the flatbed car. When he had a lock on, he pickled off a Maverick antitank missile. The screen went blank as the Maverick launched. The system stepped to the second missile and the screen came alive. He locked on a second time and sent another Maverick at the train. Satisfied that both missiles were tracking, he pulled away.

His left hand moved the wafer switch on the HUD control panel to WD-2. Bombs. Then he selected bombs ripple on the armament control panel. His radar warning gear was quiet and the train was stopped.

He dived on the train. It was a perfect low-angle bomb pass, exactly like he had practiced many times on Cannon Range in Missouri. The pipper dot was on target as his altimeter touched seven hundred feet. He mashed the pickle button and walked a stick of six five-hundred-pound bombs down the length of the train.

Mako circled the train, the dark shadow of his Warthog a gray cross of death in the sky. A lone survivor was running from the wreckage of the train. He called up the gunsight on the HUD and rolled in. It took him two passes.

Four times he circled the area at low level. But he couldn't find the ejection seat.

He climbed into the sky and headed for Guilin.

The pilots were all standing in front of the VCR in the operations center watching the replay of Mako's videotape from the mission. The room was silent and only the regular, rhythmic beat of Mako's breathing could be heard coming over the TV's loudspeaker. The screen went blank and Leonard knew he had to say something. But he couldn't find the words.

"That was overkill," Maggot finally said, breaking the silence.

"You weren't there," Mako said.

## Thursday, September 5
## Nanning, China

Pontowski was oblivious to the activity swirling around him in the command post. He stood at the map table and for the first time appreciated what Von Drexler had accomplished. The general had built a textbook example of a command and control structure and assembled a well-trained staff. That was the tragedy of Von Drexler. He was an organizational and logistical genius destroyed by his uncontrolled ego and lust for power. Are we all like that? Pontowski wondered. Fatally flawed?

Trimler joined him and leaned against the table. "We're getting this sorted out," he said. "We've got the beginnings of a logistics center up and running and we're in contact with Zou Rong."

"Where is he?" Pontowski asked.

"He's with the NCG's Tenth Division," Trimler replied. "I talked to him on the phone. He wants to reestablish a combined headquarters. He sounds shaky."

"You're going to have to hold his hand," Pontowski said, "and prop him up."

Trimler considered the idea. "I'll do what I can, but he's got to be able to take the heat. I'll go see him tomorrow, but I don't want the MAAG combined with his headquarters."

Charlie Parker, Pontowski's vice commander, agreed with Trimler. "Have you seen the results from today's missions?" he asked. He handed him a summary of the mission reports taken from the A-10 pilots. "They reported one loss."

Pontowski's head snapped around and he drilled Parker with a hard look. It was nearing midnight, he was tired, and he had to control his temper. "Next time," he said, "please tell me immediately."

Parker pointed at the lower left corner of the big status boards on the front wall. "It was posted there, Boss. I thought you saw it."

The name Ashton was written clearly on the board with the time of the loss. He bent over the map table and leaned on his arms. His head was bent. They told me, he thought, and I didn't listen. The searing brand of guilt burned and pulled away, leaving a scar he would carry for the rest of his life.

The AVG's intelligence officer approached the small group and misread the silence surrounding his new commander. "Sir," he blurted, "the latest sitreps." He laid the situation reports on the map table and, reacting to the scowl from Parker, retreated.

Pontowski scanned the reports. "The First Regiment reports the PLA has broken off contact."

"Probably regrouping," Trimler said. "This may give us a chance to stabilize the front. And if Zou can get the Tenth Division to move into a flanking position to the north . . ." He stopped in midsentence. "I'm doing a Von Drexler," he grumbled, "trying to control the Chinese when my job is to help them."

"Still," Pontowski said, "it's a good idea."

"I'll talk to Zou," Trimler said. He made a mental promise that he would act like an advisor as he left the room.

Pontowski watched him go, deciding that Trimler was all that a general should be. He turned to Colonel Parker. "I need to speak to my exec."

"Which one?" Parker asked. "You've got two."

"Captain Waters," Pontowski answered. She joined him within seconds. "How's it going?" he asked her.

"You inherited one great exec from Von Drexler," she told him. "There's nothing for me to do here."

"You heard about Skeeter?"

"I heard." There was pain in her voice.

"Maybe," he ventured, "it would be best if you returned to the wing."

She nodded in agreement. "Tango is going to need some help."

Parker said, "You can catch a hop on the helicopter taking tomorrow's air tasking order to Guilin. It takes off in an hour."

Pontowski studied her for a moment. "Be on it," he said. "Tell Tango we need a current operational status report. I'm worried about fuel and munitions . . ." He hesitated. He was still thinking like a wing commander. "We need to know what he's got and what he needs."

Waters rushed from the command post.

"You should have kept her here, Boss," Parker muttered. Pontowski agreed with him but said nothing.

Pontowski paced the floor. "Charlie, the AVG consists of this command post and a wing of A-10s that is little more than a glorified squadron. Our job is to give the Republic of Southern China the core of an air force and keep the PLA's air force off their backs. How can we best do that?"

Parker had the answer. "Simple, Boss. We need to consolidate what is in theater under your command. The AWACS is still flying out of Hong Kong, the squadron of F-15s never rotated out after the PLA tried to jump the AWACS, and we got two KC-10s flying in supplies out of Cam Ranh Bay."

"All of those are high-value assets," Pontowski said. "No way the U.S. Air Force will ever release those to the AVG."

"We don't give a damn who owns them," Parker grumped. "We just want to task them." He stressed the word "we."

"But that's the same thing," Pontowski protested.

A sly grin split Parker's face. "True. But never tell the politicians that."

"Can we make that happen?"

"Not we, Boss, you. You need to talk to the right people."

Pontowski recalled Shoshana's advice about using political influence. How long ago was that? he thought. A heavy fatigue weighed down and he closed his eyes for a moment. Unbidden, a strong memory of Shoshana flashed in his mind. She had been cuddled in his arms and her words were still crystal clear: "Political influence comes with your name and you can't change that."

He drove the sharp ache of longing away and forced himself back to the moment. He needed rest. "Charlie," he said, "you are one hell of a guy."


## Thursday, September 5
## The Executive Office Building, Washington, D.C.

The packed elevator stopped at the third floor of the Executive Office Building and Mazie braced herself as the doors opened onto the black and white marble-floored corridor. Instead of the usual pushing and shoving the bureaucrats indulged in as they rushed to work, two men held back and smiled at her, letting her get off first.

She stepped into the wide corridor and ran into Ashley Sinclair, the blonde goddess who ran the South American Division of the NSC. "Mazie," she chimed, her voice full of charm and friendliness. "I hardly recognized you. You look wonderful. Whatever did you do to your eyes? We must have lunch so you can tell me all about it." Ashley flashed her magnificent teeth without breaking her makeup and disappeared into the crowd.

Mazie was surprised. Ashley had barely spoken to her in the past. The two fashionable secretaries everyone called Heckle and Jeckle commented on her new outfit and wouldn't let her escape until they had all the details. Men smiled at her, wishing her a good morning. One tripped over himself to open a door for her.

What's going on? Mazie thought. She had no illusions about who or what she was. Her own secretary, a matronly African-American woman in her fifties, supplied the clue. "Enjoy it while it lasts," she said. She smiled at the confused look on Mazie's face. "The attention."

"Don't be silly," Mazie said, walking into her office. But it was true. Because she had lost some weight, had her eyes fixed, and bought new clothes, she had become one of the beautiful people. She bridled at the injustice of it. She was still the same person.

Her secretary buzzed. "Ms. Sinclair's secretary is on the line to arrange lunch."

"I've got too much to do," she snapped. "Send my apologies."

Moments later, her secretary appeared in the doorway. "Mazie, we have to talk. Take a good look at yourself."

"I'm still the same person," she protested.

"Child, you are not listening. What people see has changed. Thank the Lord you are smart enough to not let it go to your head. Use it while you got it."

"That's . . . that's—" Mazie searched for the right words, "that's a form of sexism!"

"Damn right," the secretary said. "In your case, it's also justice." She turned to leave. "By the way, you're having lunch at twelve-thirty with La Belle Sinclair and others at La Maison."

"I can't afford La Maison," Mazie protested. The menus were printed without prices and it was said that if you needed to ask, you couldn't afford to eat there.

"You will never see the check," her secretary assured her.

Mazie ignored her and went to work. She fell back into her old routine and within minutes was engrossed in sorting through the wealth of reports and intelligence summaries that had piled up in her absence. The first flicker of a new pattern came at 9:15. By 10:00, the flicker had turned into a flame and she hurried down to the CIA liaison office in the basement. She was back at 10:45. She sat down at her computer and called up the National Security Agency. By 11:22 the National Security Agency had searched its bank of intercepted messages and phone calls and confirmed her suspicions. She was now dealing with a raging bonfire. At 11:35 she canceled her luncheon engagement and made an appointment to see the national security advisor as soon as he came back from his morning run.

"Margaret tells me you're onto something hot," Carroll said as he entered his office. His hair was still wet from the shower and his skin glowed with health. But his eyes were tired.

Fortunately, the short break waiting for Carroll had given her time to compose her thoughts. "The situation in southern China will go critical in two or three weeks and it looks bad for our side."

"Have you seen Hazelton's latest report?" Carroll asked. Mazie shook her head and he handed it to her. "It came in about two hours ago," he explained. She scanned the report. Hazelton claimed the situation had stabilized. The PLA had broken off contact and the A-10s had cut the flow of supplies and reinforcements to the front lines. Kang's troops were reported to be withdrawing. She paused and reread the last line: First Lieutenant Denise Ashton had been killed in action. She recalled the woman who went with the name.

Mazie handed the report back to Carroll. "It fits the pattern," she told him. "Kang builds up his supply base and attacks. When the supplies run out, he stops fighting and regroups."

"That explains the long quiet spells," Carroll added. "Why do you see a major change in the pattern?"

"Kang and the central government in Beijing are locked in a power struggle. Beijing has maintained the upper hand by withholding supplies and money." She paused and then plunged ahead. "But Beijing has a much stronger counter. They are relying on Zou Rong and the New China Guard to keep Kang preoccupied."

Carroll frowned. "Are you saying—"

"Yes, sir," she interrupted. "Beijing has been secretly encouraging Zou to play him off against Kang."

"This is getting Byzantine," Carroll mumbled.

"Actually, the Chinese are acting like Chinese," Mazie corrected.

"You said the situation will go critical in a few weeks."

"Yes, sir. Kang is winning the power struggle. He's getting tanks, fuel, and ammunition. The CIA calculates he'll have what he needs to open a new offensive in two to three weeks."

"Any good news?" Carroll muttered.

"Kang is acting more and more like a warlord. That gives Zou the moral high ground."

"Mazie, the moral high ground doesn't count in this game." She arched an eyebrow at him. "Come on," he grumbled. "Don't do that to me." His fingers drummed a tattoo on his desk as he thought out loud. "We've got some time . . . let's use it . . . we need a conference . . . with all the players . . . maybe Hong Kong . . . it's quiet now . . . that would send a signal of our intentions . . ."

"Not Hong Kong," Mazie said, thinking of her narrow escape from the mob. "It's too unstable and Kang has sent hundreds of agents there to engage in wet operations. Did you know he tried to assassinate Pontowski?"

Carroll shook his head no. His fingers stopped their drumming. The decision was made. "Tokyo," he announced. "It's safe and the Japanese will see it as Mohammed coming to the mountain."

"It will certainly get their attention," Mazie said. "But I'm not sure if Toragawa will buy into an increase in aid."

"He will," Carroll predicted. "The old bastard's an imperialist at heart." Mazie agreed with him.


## Friday, September 6
## Near Nanning, China

The crying baby woke Kamigami. He lay on the pallet for a few moments listening for the thunder of artillery. It was quiet and only the fussing baby broke the ghostly silence of the village. He heard May May crooning to the baby in the next room. He rolled to his feet and picked up his boots, careful not to disturb Jin Chu, and walked outside.

A moon had risen over the Pearl River and laid a path of light across its smooth surface. He walked to the riverbank and sat on a low levee.

A rare feeling of accomplishment claimed him. He had fought a tactical retreat, forced Kang to a standstill, and made the PLA disengage. Kamigami was not an introspective man and preferred action to thinking. Yet, lately, he did little else but think. He knew he was changing. He had a makeshift family of sorts, with Jin Chu, May May, and the baby. Two women, he mused to himself. What would his old buddies think? *And my family travels with me, sharing the danger, always there to comfort me. What a strange way to fight a war,* he thought.

A soldier appeared out of the shadows and saluted when he recognized him. "What is your company?" he asked the man.

"Horse Company," the soldier replied.

Kamigami recognized his voice. "Sergeant Wan Yan Fu," he said, recalling the man's name, "what are you doing at this hour?"

"I was checking on my sentries," Wan replied. "They have fought well and are very tired." There was pride in his voice. He would tell his officer of the chance meeting and that the general had remembered his name. It was one more piece of the legend that was building around Kamigami.

"What are your men talking about?" Kamigami asked.

"They know we must fight again. Miss Li has said we will win when the dragons are at peace. Miss Li is good luck. But they worry when she is near the fighting."

"Thank you, Sergeant Wan. I will tell your captain that you were looking after your men." Wan saluted and disappeared into the night.

He tensed at a soft rustling sound behind him. Jin Chu appeared out of the dark and sat down beside him. "I was dreaming," she said.

"Did you dream of fires?" he asked.

"No." Her voice was drowsy. "It was a good dream. You

were sleeping with May May and I was watching, holding Mai Ling."

"Mai Ling?" Kamigami asked.

"The baby. It is time we named her. Mai Ling means Beautiful Bell. It is a very popular name."

"Are you going away again?"

"Not for a while," she answered, half asleep. "I'll go when you tell me."

Kamigami relaxed. Her sensitive emotional antenna was still working. There would be another lull in the fighting and they would have some time together. When would he send her away? Probably when the fighting started again. It had been touch and go during the retreat from Wuzhou and like his soldiers, he had worried about her. It was a distraction he didn't need.

"Let's go to bed," he said.

"You go," she replied. "May May is waiting for you. I will take care of Mai Ling."

# CHAPTER 17

**Monday, September 9**
**Over Osaka, Japan**

The Japanese copilot squeezed out of his seat on Hiro Toragawa's Gulfstream business jet to make the announcement in person to the five passengers. "General Trimler," he said, addressing the highest-ranking person, "we have been diverted into Gifu Airport. We will be landing in ten minutes. I am sorry for the change and hope it doesn't inconvenience you. No reason was given." Then, in the way of the Japanese, he put the best face on the change. "The scenery is most beautiful in this part of Japan."

Pontowski looked out the window and agreed. The air was unusually clear and they could see for sixty miles as a beautiful sunset played out over the mountains to the northwest. "I wonder why the change?"

"Who knows?" Hazelton answered. "Actually, I don't like Tokyo. Any place would be better to hold a conference. Not so many distractions." Ray Byers grunted his displeasure. He had planned on doing some wheeling and dealing in Tokyo. It was his kind of town. Little Juan Alvarez was still asleep.

The pilot treated them to a spectacular view as they descended over Kyoto and passed Lake Biwa. The landing at Gifu was routine and as they taxied in, Pontowski counted numerous guards and security vans. Trimler was also aware of the increased security and shot Pontowski a meaningful look. The meeting was more than it seemed. Behind them, a Boeing 727 taxied in. The crimson and gold flag of the Republic of Southern China was painted on the fuselage. "Zou Rong is here," Trimler said. "That's why the change."

Three dark sedans were waiting for them as they stopped in front of a large industrial hangar, well out of sight of the main terminal. A large smile spread across Hazelton's face when he saw Mazie and Miho. The two Junkyard Dogs, Ray Byers and Little Juan Alvarez, were the last to exit the Gulfstream. "Nice," Alvarez allowed when he saw Mazie and Miho.

"Lay off," Byers muttered. "I don't need you screwin' deals up by screwin' around."

Mazie explained why they had landed at Gifu. "We received a report the Yakuza are very interested in this meeting."

Byers stiffened at the mention of the Yakuza but it meant nothing to Pontowski. "The Yakuza," Miho explained, "is the largest criminal organization in my country. They can be very dangerous. My grandfather offered his country home and Mr. Carroll accepted." Neither woman would reveal the source of their information—the PUSIO.

The Public Security Investigation Office, or PUSIO, was the Japanese equivalent of the FBI and produced excellent intelligence. A highly placed informant in the Yakuza hierarchy had passed a tip to the PUSIO that Chinese agents had approached the Yakuza with a hit contract on someone attending the meeting. The informant did not know the name of the target but after checking with Toragawa, the PUSIO assumed it was Zou Rong.

The samurai in Toragawa welcomed the challenge and the old man responded with a vigor and will that his subordinates had not seen in years. He came alive, issuing orders and laying plans. Toragawa's face was frozen in its normal steely reserve, but he could not hide the joy in his voice at the chance for doing battle with the Yakuza, a formidable enemy. At the last minute, he selected the battlefield—his country estate on the Kiso River above Inuyama. Only the Imperial Palace in Tokyo matched his estate's security systems.

Mazie took charge and organized the small group. "Colonel Pontowski," she said, "under the circumstances, it would be best if you rode in the last car." Miho's hand darted to her mouth to hide her smile as Pontowski climbed into the rear seat.

Shoshana was waiting for him. Without a word, she was in his arms. "How?" he whispered.

"I pulled strings," was all she said. Her lips were trembling as they touched his. The driver raised the privacy window between the seats and followed the first two cars out of the airport. A minivan fell in behind.

The young motorcyclist saw the small caravan the moment it turned onto the main highway leading to the southwest. He was puzzled because Toragawa's estate was in the opposite direction. He briefly considered breaking radio silence to report the change but decided against it. His instructions had been very clear—remain undetected. He did not relish chopping off a finger, the normal penance demanded by the Yakuza for a mistake. He waited until the security van had passed and then followed at a discreet distance.

Suddenly, a large truck pulled out in front of him, blocking his view. It was a minor irritation common in heavy Japanese traffic. He twisted the throttle to accelerate around the truck but a car flashed up on his right and cut him off, forcing him to stay behind the truck just as it braked to a halt. The motorcyclist hit his brakes, skidded his bike around, facing in the opposite direction, and reached for a handful of throttle. But he was facing yet another truck. He was boxed in with nowhere to go.

Toragawa's men had trapped him. He pressed the radio transmit button that was built into his motorcycle's dimmer switch and told his control he had been made. He killed the engine and sprang off the bike, ready to go down fighting.

A technician in the minivan behind Pontowski's car monitored the radio transmission and immediately broadcast orders to the vehicles blocking the motorcyclist. They had no further use for him. Doors sprang open and two men approached the motorcyclist. They offered their apologies for the near accident. The driver from the lead truck came around to the back and joined in the conversation. Everyone was most polite and within minutes, it was over. The men returned to their vehicles and the motorcyclist roared off into traffic, looking for the three cars he had been trailing. He had lost them and a finger.

Toragawa was told of the incident three minutes later. The intercepted radio call confirmed the Yakuza knew the meeting had been changed and were still very much interested in his business. He actually smiled.

Zou Rong sat at the conference table and forced himself to concentrate. He was still on an ego rush and savoring the deference being paid him. He had come to expect it in China, but this was different. He was the guest of honor at the estate of the most powerful man in Japan, the national security advisor to the president of the United States was courting his opinion, and representatives from Singapore, Taiwan, South Korea, and Great Britain were seated below him.

He decided to speak. "My goal is a simple one," he said in Cantonese. He could have as easily spoken English as Toragawa, but his position demanded they listen to him in his native tongue and his words be translated. "I will give my people their voices and lead them into the twenty-first century."

He considered his next words. "But I am opposed by an evil man, General Kang Xun. It is easy to forget in this day how thin the veneer of civilization is and how readily men can slip into barbarism." He motioned to an aide and the room darkened. A large TV flickered on and the screen filled with scenes of violence and carnage. "This is the city of Pingnan after Kang's army reoccupied it. He butchered half of its population—man, woman, and child. There was no mercy." The even tone of his voice set a harsh contrast to the brutality on the screen. "This is what I oppose," he said in English. The screen went blank.

During a break in the conference, Carroll cornered Pontowski, Trimler, and Mazie. "I can't believe the size of the military aid package Zou is demanding," he said. "What does he really need?"

"I've got a shopping list of essentials," Trimler answered. "Antitank missiles are at the top."

"The AVG is down to seven Mavericks and we need support aircraft," Pontowski said. He listed the other aircraft he wanted.

"We'll be lucky to get you some more A-10s," Carroll said. "I don't think the Pentagon will release the AWACS and KC-10s to you."

"How about I touch base with some old family friends in the D.C. area?" Pontowski asked.

Carroll thought about it for a moment. Private arm twisting often solved a problem and Pontowski had the connections to apply the torque. "Be my guest," he said. "Mazie, how's the supply pipeline on your side doing?"

"Thanks to Toragawa and the Japanese, it's stuffed. The problem is corruption on the Chinese end. Half of it ends up on the black market."

"Maybe it's time for some economic advisors from Singapore and Taiwan?" Carroll ventured. He liked the idea and decided to work it when the conference reconvened.

"This is so beautiful," Shoshana said to her husband. "I never realized Japanese gardens were so—" she searched for the right word, "exquisite." The conference had recessed and they were walking in Toragawa's gardens. She led Pontowski down a narrow path and into an area landscaped with small boulders and bonsai trees. She pointed to a gnarled dwarf. "The gardener said that one is over three hundred years old and the most famous bonsai in Japan. It is priceless."

"I don't think Toragawa worries what things cost," Pontowski said. "Look at this place."

They walked in silence for a few moments as the garden worked its magic. "You seem pleased with yourself," Shoshana said.

Pontowski allowed a tight smile. "The conference is going well and I did something today I never thought I'd do. I called Cyrus Piccard and told him we needed AWACS, J-STARS, F-15s, KC-10s, and C-130s to support the AVG." Cyrus Piccard had been his grandfather's secretary of state and was still considered one of the most influential power brokers in Washington, D.C. "We'll get what we need."

Shoshana changed the subject. "I love this place," she

told him. "It is so peaceful and serene." The path ended in a grove of willows on a small hill that overlooked the Kiso River Valley. Ahead of them, Toragawa and two old women were sitting in the grove watching the sunset. They were dressed in traditional kimonos and mute as statues at the spectacular panorama before them.

With a sureness he seldom experienced, Pontowski knew why Toragawa had chosen this place for his country estate. Shoshana pointed at the two other figures sitting to Toragawa's right. Mazie and Miho were also dressed in kimonos. He was struck by the doll-like beauty of the two younger women. A sense of tranquility swept over him as they stood there, Shoshana holding his arm, equally at peace.

They ambled down a path toward the river. "They call this river Nihon Rhine, the Rhine of Japan," Shoshana said. "It's a favorite spot for honeymooners."

"It's much more scenic than the Rhine," he allowed. "Where are we going?"

She smiled and led him into a bathhouse. "There's a hot springs here." Inside, a middle-aged woman attendant bowed them into a dressing room and pointed at the wooden pegs on the wall. They undressed and the attendant sat them on small stools while she scrubbed them down with hot soapy water and a sponge. When she reached Pontowski's groin, she handed him the sponge and said, *"Hai, dozo."* Yes, please.

"You've got to be squeaky clean before you get in the water," Shoshana said. He complied and the attendant gestured gracefully to a door. They entered a steam-filled rock grotto and stepped down into greenish-tinted water.

"Wooo," he gasped, "this is hot!"

"Don't be a baby," she chided as she slipped into the water. Shoshana was a big woman, yet her breasts were surprisingly buoyant and floated just below the surface. She glided into his arms, threw her arms around his neck, and locked her legs around him. She held him tight before breaking free. "Rub my back," she said. He sat on a ledge and she leaned forward as he massaged her back and shoulders. He stroked her waist. "That feels good," she whispered, her voice deep and throaty.

She twisted around and pressed against him as her mouth sought his. He felt her hand squeeze between their bodies, reaching for him. *"Hai, dozo,"* she whispered.

After they had dressed, the attendant held the door open. She smiled gently as she bid them *"Sayonara."*

"I think she knows," Pontowski said.

"Well, you did make enough noise," Shoshana said.

"I almost drowned in there," he protested.

"I am proud of you." Laughter caught at the edge of her words. "All that and you still managed to keep your end up."

The six men swam up the Kiso River and came ashore slightly after three in the morning. It had been a difficult swim against the current and they lay motionless for a full six minutes regaining their strength. Only when their breathing was under full control did they spring into action.

They were little more than moving shadows as they stripped off their wet suits and pulled waterproof equipment bags open. Quickly, they donned dull-black clothing and equipment belts. The Uzi submachine guns were already loaded and charged. The men froze when a safety clicked off. The noise was not audible twenty feet away, but to them, it was as loud as a clap of thunder. Night vision goggles were donned and hand signals flashed before the men moved up the path, past the bathhouse, and into Toragawa's gardens.

When they reached the willow grove, a bright light flashed and their night vision goggles flared, blinding them. In the same instant, figures emerged from hiding places and the six men died as silently as they had come.

Toragawa was furious when his chief of security woke him with the news that six assassins had managed to penetrate as far as his gardens before being stopped. The chief of security explained how the men had penetrated their detection net by swimming upstream, through the rapids.

"How far did they swim against the current?" Toragawa asked.

"A kilometer."

Toragawa was impressed by the feat of strength and

honored them by having their bodies and equipment returned. "Tell Morihama," he growled, "that I have no quarrel with the Yakuza but it is a matter of honor that my guests be safe."

The conference ended late that afternoon and the seven Americans gathered in the large guest suite Toragawa had provided for Carroll. The national security advisor paced the floor as they recapped what had been accomplished. Pontowski found it easy to split his attention and follow his own thoughts as Carroll talked. What a strange group, he thought. And a stranger situation.

Then it came to him—this small group was involved in world-shaking events. But they were normal people who could be his neighbors. As the national security advisor to the president of the United States, Bill Carroll was one of the most influential men in the world. Yet he reminded Pontowski of a high-school teacher in his mid-thirties. Mazie Kamigami looked and acted more like a young college coed starting out in the business world. And Wentworth Hazelton was the classic East Coast establishment preppie moving down a gilded road smoothed by family connections and driven by an ambitious mother. What had Shoshana said about Hazelton? He's in love with Mazie but hasn't screwed up the courage to admit it to himself—yet.

None of them had sought power and influence, but it had come to them by virtue of their jobs. He and Bob Trimler had found homes in the military, although for very different reasons. Trimler was the perfect example of a southern boy from an impoverished background who had found a career and promotion in the U.S. Army.

What about Ray Byers and the Junkyard Dogs? How did they get here? Because of me, Pontowski admitted. I wanted some hustlers who knew how to short-circuit the system and get a job done. What a bizarre set of circumstances that brought us all together.

Pontowski filed that thought away when Carroll turned to a new subject. "I wish I could figure Toragawa out," the national security advisor said.

"He's enjoying himself," Mazie replied.

"How can you tell?" Hazelton asked.

"Miho told me," Mazie replied.

"I got the distinct impression he didn't like Zou," Pontowski said.

"He doesn't trust him," Mazie said, "and neither do I."

"Still," Trimler added, "we got most of what we needed."

"We're still hurting for Mavericks and TOW missiles," Pontowski reminded them.

Ray Byers dropped the remnants of the greasy cheeseburger he was eating. "I know an arms dealer," he said. "His name is—"

"I don't want to know about this," Carroll interrupted. He walked out of the room and motioned for Mazie to follow.

"What the hell," Byers muttered. He went back to eating his cheeseburger.

Mazie came back in with a strange look on her face. "Ray, fill me in on the details," she said.

"Well," Byers began, "the Saudis bought a bundle of Mavericks and TOW missiles after the Gulf War. We're talking a whole shitpot full. I met the guy in charge of the program in a poker game in Tokyo."

"Is he a Saudi?" she asked. Byers nodded. "But Islamic fundamentalists have taken over Saudi Arabia. What makes you think we can buy the missiles from them?"

"Saudi Arabia," Byers explained, "is so screwed up right now that you can't tell the players from one day to the next without a program. The fundamentalists and the royal family are going for each other's balls, the radicals run euthanasia drills on both of them, and during time-outs, the moderates are scurrying around to pick up the pieces. My poker-playing buddy has the keys to more ships, airplanes, warehouses, and weapons storage igloos than he can count. All he wants to do is make a fast buck while he can. Like any good Arab, he's good for anything as long as he doesn't have to work."

Hazelton was incredulous. "Look here, Byers, Saudi Arabia is my area of expertise"—he realized he was sounding like a pompous bureaucrat again—"and the fundamentalists will not sell us those missiles."

"We pony up the money," Byers said, "and use a front man."

"Who?" Hazelton asked.

Mazie knew the answer. "Toragawa," she whispered. Miho had told her the old man was having the time of his life and had even given up the poker games he loved so he could devote all his time to what everyone was now calling "the Japanese Connection."

"Sounds good to me," Byers said. "Maybe we can borrow one of his planes. A big one."

The Gulfstream business jet was waiting at Gifu Airport when the dark sedan approached. Trimler hopped out to give Pontowski a few moments alone with Shoshana. "Hug Little Matt for me," Pontowski said, "and tell him I'll be home as soon as I can."

Shoshana touched his cheek. Her hand was warm and soft. "He doesn't understand but acts very brave," she said.

"Just like his mother."

She didn't pull her hand away. "I'll miss you," she whispered. "As always."

"I'll be back," he promised. How many times have I said that? he thought.

She answered in the same old way. "I know." Her lips brushed his and then he was gone.

Trimler made light conversation as the Gulfstream taxied out. "I heard you mention R and R in the car," he said.

"That was Shoshana's idea," Pontowski explained. "She's going to stay here for a few days to arrange a rest and recuperation program for the AVG where the families or significant others can come over from the States."

"R and R is great for morale," Trimler allowed.


## Sunday, September 15
## Narita Airport, Japan

Shoshana Pontowski would never grace a fashion magazine because she was too big. Yet she captured attention as she moved down the main concourse of Tokyo's Narita Airport. Her lustrous black hair was pulled back off her face and accentuated her high cheekbones, doe eyes, and full mouth. She was a tall woman and stood six feet in high-heeled shoes. Childbearing had given her figure a mature, sensual look and she would never be thin. But constant exercise had toned her body and she moved with the feline grace of a lioness.

A blue-uniformed maintenance worker motioned to his assistant when he saw Shoshana and the two disappeared into a service gallery. "Is the Toragawa bitch with her?" the leader of the two asked. A sharp jerk of the head answered him. The leader keyed his radio and ordered the other two members of his team to join him as they ran down the narrow corridor.

They skidded to a stop outside a service closet and unlocked the door. The leader knelt beside the inside wall and felt for a seam. His hand blurred in a rapid chopping motion as he cut the wall away. Inside were four Uzi submachine guns and eight fragmentation grenades that had been hidden years before. He pulled the weapons out as the other two members of his team joined them.

"I'm sorry you can't stay longer," Miho Toragawa said. They were sitting in a VIP lounge near the gate for Shoshana's flight.

"I love Japan," Shoshana said, "and I'll be back. But many of the wives suggested Hawaii as a possible spot for R and R. I need to see what can be arranged there."

Miho blushed. "My friends tell me Hawaii is very romantic." The hostess interrupted and told Shoshana she could board her flight any time. The two women stood and the hostess held the door open for them.

A vague, uneasy feeling tickled at Shoshana as they walked toward the gate. At first, it was merely an annoyance and she disregarded it. An old warning from her distant past came back—believe your senses, even when everything appears normal. The warning opened a floodgate and all the memories from the time she served as an agent of the Mossad, the Israeli version of the CIA, burst free of the dam that held them hidden in darkness. But were the skills still there? And what was wrong?

She looked around with a new awareness, searching for telltale signs. You are so stupid! she raged. Miho's ever-present bodyguard was gone and she should have caught it immediately. She drew Miho behind a pillar. "Wait," she commanded. Every sense came alive as she slipped out of her shoes. Behind, she saw a blue-uniformed maintenance worker walking toward them. A little too fast. She stepped clear of the pillar and did a quick visual sweep of the concourse. Three more maintenance workers were converging on them but were much further away. The man coming from behind was almost to the pillar. She saw his face. It was frozen.

Shoshana pushed Miho behind her as he raised a small tube of aerosol spray. It should have been an easy kill. But Shoshana knew. With a speed the man could not credit, her left hand grabbed his wrist while her right hand knocked the deadly aerosol tube out of his grasp. Automatically, he kicked, aiming for her knee. It wasn't there. She stepped into him and drove her knee into his groin as her right hand jabbed into his throat, just above his Adam's apple.

He was going down. She grabbed his hair and twisted, forcing his body around as a shield. But she couldn't see the other three. They had disappeared into the crowd, which was scattering in confusion. A hand grenade rolled along the floor toward her. She kicked at the back of the man's knee and he collapsed to the floor. She forced him to lie flat on the grenade and threw herself onto his back, pinning him to the floor. The grenade was trapped under his belly. For a moment, nothing happened. She banged his head against the floor, feeling the gun that was hidden under his shirt, tucked into the back of his waistband.

The explosion knocked her back.

"Run!" Shoshana yelled at Miho as she jerked the Uzi out of the dead man's clothes. Shock masked the pain, but she knew some of the grenade fragments had cut into her legs. Could she move? Her legs responded and she darted for the safety of the pillar, leaving a trail of blood. Thank God, an Uzi, she thought. She charged the weapon as another blue-uniformed figure ran at her. She cut him down with a short burst. The Uzi was an old friend.

A grenade rolled across the floor. She kicked it back and pressed against the pillar. Another explosion was followed by more screams. Her head bobbed around the pillar and pulled back. It was enough. She had seen the body of the third man. Was Miho safe?

She turned to look in the direction Miho had run. Her last conscious thought was of a blue-uniformed man firing at her with an Uzi. Pain exploded over her. Automatically, she fired back.

Her training had held.

## Sunday, September 15
## Over Siberia

The silver Boeing 747 arced steadily across the vast Siberian taiga, toward Japan. The Toragawa logo on the tall tail glowed in the fading light as the huge airplane crossed the Ob River. The cargo deck was full of TOW and Maverick missiles Toragawa had purchased from the Saudis. Hazelton excused himself from the poker game with Toragawa and Byers and walked across the upper deck of the huge cargo airplane that had been converted to a VIP suite.

"I had no idea Russia was so big," Hazelton told Mazie as he settled into the captain's chair beside her. In unison, they pivoted and gazed out the window. Below, the forest was dark and the lights of Novosibirsk could be seen far to the south. "Toragawa made dealing with the Saudis seem easy," he said.

"The Saudis are very anxious to do business, any business, with him," Mazie said. She looked across the cabin toward Toragawa and Byers, who were still playing poker. "How's the game going?" she asked.

"Toragawa's a tough teacher, and I've learned not to draw to an inside straight." He swiveled so he could see the card players. "Look at Byers. He looks like he should be playing in a bar in Las Vegas." Mazie agreed with him. A cigarette dangled from Byers's mouth, his sleeves were rolled up, and a half-consumed glass of bourbon sat beside his poker chips. "I can't understand why Toragawa likes him."

Mazie didn't have an answer. Instead, "Byers is a stereotype. What you see is what you get."

"Mazie, remember when this all started? Why did Mr.

Carroll leave the room when Byers started talking about buying missiles from the Arabs?"

She looked out the window. How should she answer if he didn't understand? Didn't he remember the Iran-Contra affair from the mid-1980s? They were wheeling and dealing for missiles in the shadowy world of the international arms market and could not afford to get caught. She dropped the thought, not wanting to think about the consequences. Bill Carroll had insulated himself by not knowing and letting her run with the ball. He could always fall back on credible denial and claim he knew nothing about it.

Mazie glanced at her watch. "Five hours to go. I wish I could sleep on planes." A pilot came off the flight deck and handed Mazie a long message. She paled as she read it. She walked over to the card table and spoke to Toragawa. "I am so sorry to tell you of bad news," she said in Japanese. She chose her words carefully as she told him what had happened at Narita Airport. Toragawa's eyes were almost closed and he said nothing. "Miho was unharmed," she said.

Toragawa bowed his head to Mazie and spoke in Japanese. "I am most grateful for what Mrs. Pontowski did. I will be forever in her debt."

Toragawa's words were spoken quietly and without passion. His facial muscles never betrayed the raging emotion coursing through his body. Yet Byers and Mazie moved back from the anger radiating from the old man. He stood and walked to a window where he remained standing, his back a rigid spike, until they landed at Gifu Airport in Japan.

## Monday, September 16
## Near Guilin, China

A golden-red sunset framed the row of peaks the pilots called the Dragon's Teeth and cast a diffused light across the expanse of rice paddies and the Luoqing River. A beautiful world at rest, Pontowski thought as he waited for the last flight of A-10s to check in. He was with Trimler on the ground, observing the New China Guard's Tenth Division on its first full-scale training maneuvers with his Warthogs. "So far," he said, "the Tenth is doing okay."

"Barely," Trimler corrected, thinking about Kamigami's First Regiment.

Pontowski heard a low rumble coming from the gorge formed by the river cutting through the Dragon's Teeth. "Sounds like they're flying up the Gullet," he said. "They'll pop out in a minute." Two A-10s flew out of the river gorge and established radio contact with the Tenth's ASOC. The Chinese officer skillfully handed them off to an air liaison officer on the ground who was in contact with the make-believe enemy.

"There is hope," Trimler allowed.

A low-flying helicopter approached from the north, the direction of Guilin. "Looks like the Junkyard Dogs' Huey," Pontowski said. The two men watched as it came in for a smooth landing. Pontowski cracked a smile when he saw Sara Waters climb out and duck her head to miss the whirling rotor. A natural but unnecessary reflex.

She walked briskly up to them and saluted. "Colonel Pontowski, may we speak in private?"

"Lighten up, Ripper," he said, waving a salute in return. He immediately regretted saying it. She was very upset. Oh, my God! he thought. Someone's bought it. Another casualty. He followed her as she walked to a quiet spot.

She turned to face him, the tears now streaking her cheeks. "I'm so sorry," she whispered, handing him a message. "I'm so sorry."

He scanned the message. Then, to be sure, he reread it. For some reason, he had to reread it a third time. He carefully folded the paper and buttoned it into his chest pocket. He turned and faced the sunset. Waters waited, not moving. The two Warthogs were joining up to return to base and they could hear the crackle of the UHF radio as they checked out. Then it was quiet. The sky streaked with red and gold as the sun disappeared below the horizon.

"I've lost her."

The pain in his voice touched a deep memory in Waters. She had been there. "You haven't lost her. You just won't see her again."

# CHAPTER 18

Tuesday, September 17
Inuyama, Japan

Pontowski walked slowly, matching his pace to Miho's as they made their way through Toragawa's garden. Both were silent, not disturbing the early morning peace. Ahead of them, he could see the grove of willows that overlooked the river below. A lone figure sat on the bench. Toragawa. "He has been here all night," Miho said. "Please wait."

She kneeled in front of her grandfather, bowed her head, and spoke quietly. Toragawa stood and Miho motioned Pontowski to come. She rose and left, no longer able to mask her worry. The two men faced each other, one tall and lanky, the other short and stocky. The warmth of the rising sun beat on Toragawa's back, warming him as it framed Pontowski's face.

A generation and different cultures separated the two men, yet they were bound by a shared code of conduct. Duty and honor hold little value in the modern world, but for these men, duty was the touchstone of their existence and honor the moral gyroscope that guided their actions. Both had engaged in combat, one in business and the other in the profession of arms, and had ruined and killed other men. They had not done so out of a killing lust or insatiable greed, but because the choice between duty and honor or submission to a lesser ethic was forced on them. No matter the twisting and turning of their paths, they had held constant and both had reaped the rewards of success. Now, they were paying the price.

Toragawa spoke first, his grammatically perfect English heavily accented. "May I be of service?"

"You already have. Everything is arranged and I wanted to thank you. I'm taking Shoshana home to Israel." Pontowski paused, gazing out over the valley below him, recalling another hill in Israel, outside Haifa. "Her father wants to bury her next to her mother. It's on a hill . . ." He took a deep breath. "May we talk about it?" They had come to the reason for Pontowski's visit. Toragawa nodded. "Do you know who is responsible?"

"Not yet," Toragawa answered. "I know the assassins were Yakuza. I don't know who hired them to do this. Or why. Even if they were still alive, the four assassins would not know the answer." Silence. "Your wife was very brave and saved Miho."

Pontowski shook his head. "I think Shoshana was the target, not Miho." He told Toragawa of the attempt to assassinate him at Guilin. "I'm a very visible target and Kang Xun may be getting at me through my family. But there's another possibility." He told Toragawa of Shoshana's past as a Mossad agent. "The Islamic Jihad or the Mana family from Iraq may have taken out the contract."

"I will discover the truth," Toragawa promised. "May I offer you an airplane to fly your wife to Israel?" Pontowski was stunned by the offer. "It is a small thing," Toragawa added. "It is the least I can do."

Pontowski accepted the offer and thanked him again. Miho escorted him to a waiting car and hurried back to the old man. "Please, Grandfather, I beg you, don't do this." She was kneeling in front of him, her eyes full of tears, worried that he would commit suicide because of the blow to his honor. "I will do my best, Grandfather, but who will guide me? Who will chose my husband?"

Toragawa stifled a sigh. The new generation! he thought. He was in contemplation, his way of honoring Shoshana Pontowski. True, his honor had been deeply wounded because she was his guest. But he could live with that.

Suicide in this day and age? In modern Japan? It was unthinkable.

Besides, he believed in vengeance.

## Friday, September 20
## Cam Ranh Bay, Vietnam

Major Marissa LaGrange stood between the pilots on the flight deck as the AWACS entered the landing pattern. "One busy harbor," the copilot said. "I had no idea it was so big."

"Supposedly, this is the best natural harbor in Asia," the pilot explained.

Below her, LaGrange counted two tankers and at least eight cargo ships. An oceangoing tug was towing a floating dry dock into the harbor. They turned final to land on the north runway and she could see a KC-10, four C-130s, two J-STARS E-8 aircraft, and a line of F-15 fighters parked on the ramp. We're getting serious, she thought. At least it would be a change after Hong Kong. Riots and muggings in the crown colony had kept them confined to their base at Shek Kong Camp for the last few weeks and the morale of her crew was in the dirt. We need to get home, she decided.

A crew bus was waiting and drove them to their new operations building. The old U.S. base was alive with activity and hundreds of Vietnamese workers at work cleaning up and renovating buildings. "Hey, Major Mom!" a voice called from the back of the bus. "How long we going to be here?"

"The message said two weeks," LaGrange answered. "Then we rotate back to the States."

Everyone but Moose Penko took the announcement positively. He hunched his big shoulders and stared out the window, feeling mutinous. He made a mental promise to request a transfer off LaGrange's crew when they got back to Tinker. Hell, he thought, make that a transfer out of the Air Force.

Their commander, Colonel Charles Tucker, was waiting for them in operations. He gave a short speech, more of a warning than a welcome, to the crew and pulled LaGrange inside an office. "What's going on here?" LaGrange asked.

"I thought it was obvious," he answered. "We're getting involved."

"History repeating itself," LaGrange muttered.

"Think big," Tucker said. "We've been kicked out of the Philippines and lost the naval base at Subic Bay. China is causing all sorts of problems and scaring its neighbors silly. We still need a presence in the Far East, this is the best harbor in the area, and it's got an air base. Vietnam and China have never gotten along and the Vietnamese want us as an ally to discourage any aggressive moves by the Chinese in their direction. They've offered us a ten-year lease on Cam Ranh Bay and are putting it back in shape. Good deal for them, good deal for us."

"This is all above my pay grade," LaGrange said. "My crew is tired and needs to get home."

"Two weeks, tops," Tucker assured her, "and you'll be out of here."

"And the check's in the mail," she retorted.

The beach party was going well and LaGrange lay back on the sand to watch the volleyball game. Morale had definitely improved. Even Moose had gotten over his sulks and was playing lifeguard for the swimmers in the unbelievably blue and clear water. She needed the break after sorting out the communications protocols between the J-STARS and her AWACS to provide the New China Guard with state-of-the-art warning and control. It had been easy once U.S. liaison officers were on the ground in China. She let the sun soak into her body. Cam Ranh Bay could be a great resort, she decided, falling asleep.

Loud and angry voices woke her. She squinted in the direction of the commotion. A large group of young men were moving in on the volleyball game and eyeing the female members of her crew. The fighter pilots had arrived. She stood up and tugged her bikini top into place. Better get a handle on this before it gets out of hand. She had been through it before.

"Sorry, fellas," she said, "private game. Maybe next time."

"Hey, another player," one of the newcomers said. He leered at her, appreciating how she looked in a swimsuit.

LaGrange sighed. Fighter pilots were like dogs, some were brighter than others. "You're not listening," she said.

"You the den mother?"

"In a manner of speaking, yes."

It worked and the pilots started to wander away. Most were good-natured and only looking for fun. But one wouldn't let it go. His ego demanded he have the last word. "AWACS?" he asked. She could smell his beery breath.

"Congratulations," LaGrange replied, not giving an inch of ground. "You broke the code."

"Unh," he muttered. "A flying whorehouse."

Before she could respond, Moose Penko was there. He clamped a hand on the pilot's shoulder and spun him around. The pilot tried to resist, but he didn't have a choice. "Moose!" LaGrange barked. "Bug out." Penko stared at the pilot for a moment and walked away.

LaGrange turned on the pilot. "You are," she snarled, "one oversexed, walking, talking, turbocharged hormone." He started to protest. "Get off my turf and stay off unless you got your pecker in your pants and under control. "Or—" she leaned into him, her hands on her hips, "do you want heel marks all over your body? Am I speaking in a foreign language? Have I said anything you don't understand?" The pilot retreated without saying a word.

She walked over to Penko. "Moose, I fight my own battles. Got it?"

"I got it."


## Thursday, October 3
## Near Nanning, China

The new M998 Humvee pounded down the dirt road, its aerials whipping in the wind. Inside, Kamigami rode in the passenger's seat, checking his chart. Occasionally, one of the radios would squawk and the radio/telephone operator in the back would acknowledge the call. "No change, General," the R/T operator said in Cantonese. Kamigami half-translated the words and half-thought in Cantonese.

"Resolute Company is ahead," the driver announced. Resolute Company was his newest company and had picked its own name, since the twelve animals of the Chinese calender had been claimed by other companies. Kamigami checked the personnel roster of the company, putting faces with most of the names. The Humvee slammed to a stop and he got out, not waiting for the two other Humvees in his small convoy.

He was determined to visit each one of his companies before the attack started and was in a hurry. But he walked slowly, giving his full attention to the young captain in command of Resolute Company. The company was well-positioned and dug in, and morale seemed high. A group of officers and ranking NCOs surrounded him as he spread out his chart. "The latest intelligence reports no change," he told them.

Two Warthogs screamed overhead, looking for targets. The men paused and watched as one popped and dove for the ground. They didn't see a bomb come off but an explosion was followed by a big secondary. "It seems," he said, "intelligence was wrong." They all laughed.

It was time to leave, but he knew what they were waiting for. "Miss Li says the road is very dangerous. But the brave will know victory."

He pulled the captain aside. "Expect a short artillery barrage around four o'clock this morning. An attack should start soon after that." The captain stepped back and saluted, confidence in every gesture.

Kamigami lay in bed wide awake. The luminous glow of his watch told him it was one in the morning. Three hours to go, he thought. Relax, there's nothing else you can do now. He hated the waiting, but that was war. He itched to check on activity in the J-STARS module that had arrived at his headquarters two days before with an American liaison officer. The ability of the E-8 J-STARS aircraft to paint the current ground situation on its radar and downlink it to the module gave him real-time intelligence. It was so good that Jin's marketplace sources of information only confirmed what he already knew.

Trimler had done wonders in reorganizing the MAAG and they had received much needed TOW antitank missiles and Stinger surface-to-air missiles. At the same time, Trimler had told him the AVG was "flush with Mavericks." Some nasty surprises were in store for the PLA.

One of those surprises is the AVG, he decided. Leonard knows how to use A-10s and is hurting the PLA. The interdiction box campaign had worked beyond their wildest expectations, although it puzzled him why the Chinese air force was staying on the ground. They probably know about those Stingers, he decided.

Somehow, more aircraft had shown up. Four C-130s were helping the two KC-10s they were using as airborne fuel trucks. The AWACS and J-STARS were flying regular missions in the Gulf of Tonkin and along the Sino-Vietnamese border and had the PLA wired for sound. No wonder their intelligence was so good.

But he wished Pontowski would return.

Kamigami propped himself up in bed. Had he done all he could? Was the First Regiment ready? Again, he ran through all his training and planning. It was as good as it was going to get. Now the ultimate test of battle would pass final judgment.

Jin Chu stirred beside him, her gentle breathing reassuring. He wanted to hold her and make love. Will this be the last time? he thought. She stirred and came to him, half-asleep. Suddenly, her urgency matched his and she whispered, "Now, now, now."

She held him tight afterward, not wanting to let him go. Finally, he rolled out of bed and dressed. "It's time," was all he said. Jin Chu looked at him, waiting. "I want you to go to Bose." Bose was the city 150 miles to the northwest where he had sent May May and the baby for safety. She did not answer. "I'll have my helicopter fly you there this morning."

"Do you remember the time on Cheung Chau Island?" she asked.

How long ago was that? he thought. An age. He nodded.

"You are still my love and you are here, where my life is. I want to stay with you."

"You must go," he told her. He looked at his watch. Two more hours. "It will be very dangerous here when the fighting starts."

"Please," she replied, "let me stay."

Against his better judgment, he gave in.

The first warning the attack was underway came from the J-STARS module. The operator interpreted the bright returns on the monitor's display for Kamigami. "We're here," he explained, pointing to a spot north of the Pearl River. "It looks like two tank divisions are coming our way. The length and intensity of the columns indicate mechanized infantry and artillery regiments are with them."

Kamigami turned to his intelligence officer. The man's face had paled and he was shaking. He knew the numbers. "If both are at full strength—that's a total of 582 tanks, forty one-hundred-millimeter field guns, and over twenty thousand men." Kamigami focused on the monitor. The battle was developing north of the river and only his First Regiment and the New China Guard's Tenth Division, which was on his left flank, to the north, stood between Kang's army and Nanning.

"More movement," the J-STARS operator announced. "South of the river." The screen flickered as more activity was detected by the orbiting E-8 aircraft.

What do we have south of the Pearl? he thought. A quick glance at the situation map. Three regiments, much like his. They were supposed to be the core of the New China Guard's Fifth Division. How good are they?

The communications monitor beeped. A message was coming through: The AWACS was detecting numerous aircraft launching out of two bases near Canton. Again, Kamigami's intelligence officer provided the details. "The Twenty-sixth and Thirtieth Bomber divisions are stationed at those airfields. Each has thirty-six H-5 light bombers." The H-5 was a Chinese copy of the Ilyushin Il-28 bomber NATO called the Beagle. More information scrolled up on the communications monitor. Fighter aircraft were launching and heading for Nanning. The numbers kept increasing, but at least forty-six bombers were headed for Nanning escorted by over one hundred fighters.

"Sir," the J-STARS liaison officer said, "more information." He enlarged the scale on his ground monitor, showing more detail. "The attack appears to be focused on this point."

Kamigami's eyes narrowed into tight slits. Resolute Company was going to take the brunt of the attack. The sound of distant thunder echoed over them. Artillery. Kamigami checked the time—exactly 0400 hours. At least his intelligence was good. But he knew what the numbers meant. Can we do this? he thought. Are we good enough? Am I good enough?

At the same time, all water and electricity into Hong Kong was shut off and widespread looting and rioting broke out in Kowloon.

The battle for southern China had begun.

## Friday, October 4
## Guilin, China

"Twenty plus bandits coming your way," the high-frequency, long-range radio squawked. John "Tango" Leonard waited for the AWACS to complete its warning message. "Bearing one-three-five degrees at 120 nautical miles. Heading three-one-zero, speed 435 knots."

Leonard didn't hesitate. He picked up the microphone for the UHF radio and mashed the transmit button. "All aircraft scramble. Repeat scramble. No change." He took a deep breath. Outside the bunker, he could hear the first engines spin up. With a little luck, he would have all his aircraft airborne in eight minutes. The Warthogs wouldn't be caught like sitting ducks on the ground. He ran the mental arithmetic. At a speed of 435 knots the bandits were traveling a tad over seven miles a minute. Seven goes into 120 seventeen times. Subtract a little. The bandits should be overhead in sixteen minutes. He checked his watch. Time to hunker down.

"Sound red alert," he ordered. The Klaxons scattered around the base blared with a nerve-jangling warbling and everyone in the bunker reached for flak jackets and helmets. "Get the crew chiefs to cover ASAP," he said. He knew it was a stupid order. They could hear the Klaxon. What now? He didn't like the answer. Wait.

He listened to the radio traffic as the first jets taxied out. Thank God we were ready, he thought. The wing had received its first warning order twenty-four hours earlier, and he had methodically brought the base up to full alert. The A-10s had been armed and cocked for a scramble and the pilots had been sitting cockpit alert since two that morning. The first eight Warthogs to launch were carrying Sidewinder air-to-air missiles and would have gear in the well within five minutes. He held little hope for their intercepting the bandits in the dark, but he wasn't going to roll over and play dead. Perhaps some of the Stingers we got for base defense will nail a few of 'em, he thought. He didn't have much faith in the antiquated antiaircraft artillery the New China Guard had scattered around the base.

Sara Waters rushed into the bunker, and he breathed easier. She had insisted on running the base defense team and had been out on a last-minute check, making sure everyone was taking cover. The last Warthog taking the active checked in on the UHF. "Uncas doing his thing," Buns Clark radioed.

"Uncas?" Waters asked.

"The Last of the Mohicans," Leonard told her. He managed a grin. "Buns would rather die than sound bad on the radio." Now they had to wait. "Didn't the Bossman have you working on base evacuation?" he asked.

She nodded. "He was always concerned about getting out of here. We went through the motions twice and are pretty good at it."

Leonard thought for a moment. "Good. Get ready again."

He checked the master clock on the wall. The attacking aircraft were seven minutes out.


## Friday, October 4
## Over the Gulf of Tonkin

LaGrange punched at the control panel of her intercom, making sure she was on net one. She fought down the perverse urge to cut the pilots off and let them stew in ignorance. But that would be petty and a reaction to the incident on the beach. Even the drivers in the pointy end deserved to know what was going down. She pressed the talk button on her extension cord. "It's rock and roll time, folks," she announced. "J-STARS is reporting massive ground movement and we've got beaucoup hostile tracks tagged up. Most are headed for Nanning with a minor sideshow inbound for Guilin. So far, they're ignoring us."

Moose Penko muttered, "Let's keep it that way."

"They know we're here," LaGrange said, "so heads up. I want to stay on top of this and get as close to the action as possible."

Penko was not happy. Although the AWACS Westinghouse radar could reach out 250 miles, the capability of the radar improved at shorter ranges. The range of the J-STARS radar was even less. How close does she plan on getting? he wondered. An orbit over the Gulf of Tonkin in international waters was fine with him.

LaGrange saw him staring at her. She couldn't resist the opportunity. "Relax, Moose. We're not going into China." A long pause. "Yet."

"We can't do that!" he protested.

"Wanna bet?"


"Major," Moose Penko said over the intercom, "we can do something here." LaGrange caught the hard, cold, detached tone in his voice. Experience had taught her not to ignore it. She moved behind him to look over his shoulder. "We got eight Warthogs in a CAP near Guilin," he said. She knew that, but Guilin was beyond the range of their radar. "We can't paint the Warthogs or Guilin, but we can give them range and bearing calls to the bandits off a bull's-eye."

It made sense to LaGrange. But the bull's-eye had to be inside the range of their radar. "We need a common point," she said.

Moose's thick fingers danced over the keyboard like a concert pianist and an overlay appeared on his monitor. "This is a schematic of their training area. They call it the Dragon's Teeth. This point is called the Gullet. We can use it as a bull's-eye. It's in radar range and they know the area like the back of their hand." Moose had done his homework.

"But how do we talk to them?" she added, mulling Moose's suggestion over. "The Hogs are still out of UHF range." The range of the Warthog's UHF radio was limited to line of sight—approximately 180 miles. The solution came to her. "But we're close enough to use a radio relay."

A message was sent over the high-frequency radio to the wing's bunker at Guilin and Leonard ordered Mako Luce to shoot the moon and fly southward until he was in UHF radio contact with the AWACS. It worked and Moose transmitted his first range and bearing call. "Mako, four bandits bearing one-two-zero at forty from the Gullet. Heading three-two-five, speed four-three-five." Mako relayed the range and bearing call to the Warthogs and they headed for the bandits. Moose kept feeding updates to the fighters, but they never found the bandits in the dark.

Moose stared at his monitor as the red inverted Vs, the bandits, reached the maximum range of the radar and disappeared in the direction of Guilin. He wanted to nail them, keep them from dropping their bombs. But he had failed. His frustration increased when the red inverted Vs reappeared, headed south and for safety after dropping their bombs. For Moose, the dots on his monitor were reality.

LaGrange saw the corded muscles in his neck bulge and his shoulders flex. Please, Moose, she thought, don't hit anything. She wanted to touch him but knew it would be all wrong. For reasons she didn't understand, Moose hated her guts. Tough tortillas, she told herself, he's here for the same reason I'm here. "Next time," she told him.

## Friday, October 4
## Nanning, China

For the first time in his life, Colonel Charles Parker experienced true rage. It seared him with a torchlike heat, burning away all his doubts, all the misgivings that had come with his assignment to the MAAG.

He had worked hard and as a reward, Von Drexler had made him the vice commander of the AVG. As second in command, he had experienced the depths of Von Drexler's ego-driven mania. A brief period of sanity had been restored to his life when Trimler had taken over command of the MAAG and Pontowski the AVG. But Pontowski was on emergency leave, burying his wife, and Trimler had gone missing in the chaos of the attack on Nanning.

Bombers had appeared overhead at exactly 0415 in the morning. They had not aimed for any specific target and had dropped their bombs at random on the city, killing and maiming innocent Chinese. But the AVG's headquarters compound was untouched and only two of his security police had been cut by flying glass. Parker had sent one of them to a nearby hospital to have a glass splinter removed from his left eye. But he had returned untreated because the hospital had been bombed.

The security policeman's eyewitness account of the carnage at the hospital was only the first spark. More reports came in of nerve and mustard gas casualties—Kang was using chemical weapons on his own people. When communications with the New China Guard were reestablished, he learned of special forces units operating in the city with orders to kill everyone they saw.

His smoldering anger grew into a raging inferno. This was not the way to fight a war! Parker forced himself to think rationally. Slowly, he banked the fires burning inside him and in the ashes, a cold fury remained and he found hate.

A PLA special forces unit lobbed the first mortar round into the AVG compound at first light. The mortar attack lasted four minutes before they stormed the command post. Their orders remained the same as before.

Kamigami knew he was in the midst of a miracle. He had reinforced Resolute Company with Ox and Rat companies and the three had held. Five hundred men had stopped a division. They had used the narrow roads, flooded rice paddies, and detailed knowledge of the terrain to their advantage. But it had been a narrow thing and only the arrival of the Warthogs at first light had made the difference.

His communications were still good and the information coming through the J-STARS module was giving him the edge he needed to understand the situation around him. The three regiments south of the Pearl had also held and were proving their worth. But the Tenth Division on his left flank was crumbling.

An air liaison officer was begging for his attention. He wished the Chinese would be more direct and butt in when they had something important to tell him. But he understood. "General Kamigami," the ALO said, "Guilin has been attacked and the runway is severely damaged. Their aircraft are recovering at Bose and the Americans are abandoning Guilin."

Kamigami had lost close air support.

"Are we still in contact with the AVG at Nanning?" he asked. He needed to know when the A-10s would be able to launch.

The ALO dropped his eyes and studied the floor. "We've lost all contact with the AVG."

Kamigami considered his next move. There was a lull in the fighting as Kang regrouped, and now was the time to disengage and start a tactical withdrawal. How long did they have before the Tenth Division on his left flank crumbled and he was faced with a total rout? He needed to force a decision from his own headquarters at the New China Guard. But unless Zou Rong was there to make the decision, nothing would happen.

He told his communications officer to place him in contact with the New China Guard command bunker at Nanning. It took thirty minutes to reach his immediate superior—an excellent general who had defected from the PLA to support Zou.

"President Zou has given strict orders," the general said. "You must stand firm at all costs. The New China Guard will not retreat another inch."

"If we do that," Kamigami told him, "Kang will roll right over us and be in Nanning in an hour. By withdrawing now, I can slow him down."

The general understood perfectly and he leveled with Kamigami. "It is chaos here. No one knows what to do. Zou is frozen with fear and can't make a decision. If he cracks and leaves, many officers will desert our cause, steal what they can, and join Kang."

Kamigami heard the desperation in the man's voice. "Is Zou still in the bunker?"

"Yes, but he has ordered his pilots and bodyguards to be ready to leave on a moment's notice."

"Can you hold things together until I get there?"

"Maybe," the general answered. "But you must hurry. When Zou leaves, we are lost."

Kamigami cut the connection and looked at the situation map on the wall. Damn! he thought, I can't leave now. He owed his men leadership and he had to do it from his own headquarters. To leave now would be the same as desertion. He had learned his lessons well.

"General Kamigami," a familiar voice said. It was Trimler. The American was dressed in BDUs and still wearing a flak vest and helmet. He had gathered a small group of Americans and Chinese together and fought his way out of Nanning to reach the First Regiment. "It's all coming unglued," the general growled.

Kamigami reviewed the situation with Trimler and realized what he had to do.

The helicopter came in low over the outskirts of Nanning, flying at rooftop level to avoid hostile fire. It settled onto the helipad of a heavily fortified compound next to Zou's helicopter. Trimler jumped out, spoke to the waiting general, and motioned at the helicopter for the other passenger to join them. The three hurried into the bunker.

Zou Rong was pacing back and forth like a caged animal. He stopped and jerked his arm at the situation map on the wall. "Reinforce General Kamigami with thirty tanks from the Tenth Division and order him to immediately counterattack." He dropped his arm. No one told him the Tenth Division did not have thirty tanks. "Issue a new general directive!" he shouted. "Anyone retreating will be shot on the spot." Again, no one answered, and he resumed his pacing.

Trimler paused in the doorway—he could sense defeat in the men around him. It crackled in the air with its own kinetic energy, waiting to release its destructive power. "President Zou," he said, announcing himself.

Zou turned at the sound of his name. "You!" he shouted, pointing an accusing finger at Trimler. "This has been a plot by the Americans to destroy me from the very first." He pointed to one of his colonels standing against a wall. "Arrest the American bastard and execute him. Now!" The colonel didn't move.

Trimler scanned the room, gauging the situation. He had never seen so many men on the edge of panic. Zou had lost his nerve and was crumbling, and with him, the Republic of Southern China. Trimler drew himself to attention and stalked to the situation map, every step confident and sure. He gestured at the big map. "You are far from being lost, Mr. President."

"Do you know what will happen to me if I am captured?" Zou shouted. The graphic picture of the corpse of Wang Peifu, the PLA deserter who had joined the Junkyard Dogs only to be recaptured and executed by the death of a thousand cuts, was etched in his consciousness.

"You are not going to be captured, Mr. President, because General Kamigami is going to stop Kang here." He jabbed at the map and circled the area west of Bose. "But you"— he stressed the "you"—"must make certain things happen. You must order a tactical withdrawal and make Kang bleed with every step."

Zou stopped his pacing and cocked his head, staring at the map while Trimler rattled off what Kamigami wanted to do. For a fraction of a moment, Zou's face calmed. Then his fear was back, riding him hard. "No," he rasped, "it is not enough. How can Kamigami guarantee my safety?"

Trimler pointed to the door. Every head looked in the direction he was pointing—at Jin Chu. She was standing in the doorway, frail and trembling, dressed in the same clothes she had worn when Zou and Kamigami rescued her from the PLA. The tension in the room shattered as Zou nodded, his face again calm.

In his desperation, Kamigami had given Jin Chu to Zou.

# CHAPTER 19

**Monday, October 7**
**Washington, D.C.**

The woman's name carried a "Hazardous to Your Career" warning and Bill Carroll's secretary was all smiles and attention when she entered the office. "Good morning," she chimed. "Mr. Carroll is with the president and will be with you at any moment." She gestured gracefully to a wing chair. "May I get you some coffee? Tea?"

Elizabeth Martha, better known as EM to her friends and confidants, sat down and crossed her legs. "Tea would be fine," she said. Reluctantly, EM mentally conceded a meeting with the president of the United States was a valid excuse for keeping her waiting. But she didn't like it. Elizabeth Martha had political clout and believed in using it.

Bill Carroll came through the door, smiled, and ushered her into his office. The woman was not what he expected. She was elegantly dressed, slender, and young-looking, and not a single strand of gray was visible in her dark hair.

EM came right to the point. There was no hint of politeness or civility in her voice. "Where is my son?"

Carroll sat down. "Please have a seat, Mrs. Hazelton." She ignored him and remained standing. "Wentworth is at Cam Ranh Bay in Vietnam," he told her.

"Then why haven't I heard from him?" she demanded.

"I can't answer that. Perhaps you would like to speak to his immediate superior. She arrived from Cam Ranh this morning." He hit the intercom. "Please ask Mazie to come in," he said.

EM sat down. "I've been wanting to meet your Miss Kamigami. It escapes me why someone like her would be placed in a position of such responsibility."

Carroll briefly considered two replies, both of which would have destroyed whatever chance he had of appeasing the woman. Astute operators on the Washington scene did not, at least knowingly, cross EM Hazelton. She had worked hard to earn the name "Bitch Queen of Capitol Hill" and considered it an accolade. A fleeting regret at involving Wentworth Hazelton crossed his mind. Originally, he had hoped Went's participation would mute, perhaps even channel, his mother's political influence into supporting the administration's efforts to contain the trouble in China.

The expression on the secretary's face warned Mazie that danger lurked in Carroll's office. She went inside anyway. Mazie estimated the wind chill coming from EM Hazelton to be around minus fifty degrees but she gave her a beautiful smile as Carroll asked about Went. Mazie explained she had left Hazelton in Cam Rann Bay less than twenty-four hours before and he was fine. "Why don't you telephone him?" Mazie suggested. She scribbled a number down and handed it to her. "We can call him right now, if you wish," she said.

EM studied Mazie. Her eyes were cold and hostile. "Thank you." She rose to leave, her mission accomplished. Wentworth had been deliberately avoiding her since he had become involved with this woman and now that she had met the "poor, unfortunate child," one of her codes for "a piece of trash," she could end his infatuation. Carroll escorted EM out, turned her over to a young military aide, and returned.

"What was that all about?" Mazie asked.

"China's gone critical and Washington is choosing sides," he answered. "La Belle Hazelton is deciding which one to join. Mazie, we may have lost our window of opportunity in China. All along, my goal was to contain China's expansionist tendencies by helping Zou Rong and his rebels. I thought we had a chance to create a buffer state between China and Southeast Asia."

"And losing southern China and Hong Kong to Zou," Mazie added, "would sufficiently weaken the central government in Beijing to curb other moves against Taiwan, Singapore, Korea, and Japan—in that order." Nothing new was being said and they were only rehashing the "Soviet Option" as applied in Asia.

Carroll paced the floor, needing to talk. "Beijing has been playing off Zou against Kang to keep them both weak, counting on picking up the pieces later. But everybody, us included, misjudged Kang's strength. He's consolidating his position and emerging as the new Mao Zedong of China."

Mazie shook her head, disagreeing with Carroll. "Kang is nothing but a vicious warlord and Beijing has already shut off the supply tap. Kang is rapidly running out of options. He must defeat Zou quickly or Beijing will turn on him."

"According to the latest reports," Carroll said, "he's doing it." He looked out his window. "We've got to get the AVG out. Now."

Mazie studied her hands, thinking. Was Carroll losing his nerve? "Sir, there's a rhythm to the fighting in China. Kang has to pause and regroup. Zou may still be able to put together a defense and hold on. But if we pull the AVG out now, he's certainly lost. We've still got some cards to play here. Congress hasn't passed legislation cutting off aid to Zou."

"They will," Carroll said, "they will." He played a videotape for her. "Recorded off C-Span yesterday," he said.

The Honorable Ann Nevers was giving a speech to a large crowd gathered in front of the Washington Monument. "We must not," she shouted into the microphone, "allow the misguided policies of our government to draw us into another quagmire in Asia. Did we learn nothing from Vietnam? Must we sacrifice more of our men and women in the name of political expediency? How many more like Mark Von Drexler, one of our finest young generals, will be sent to their deaths? How many more!" A roar of protest swept over the crowd.

"I can't believe she's making a martyr out of VD," Mazie muttered.

Nevers waited for the shouting to subside. "We must force Congress to act"—her face was flushed with success—"and force the administration to respond to the will of the people!" Carroll switched the TV set off.

"I can't believe that woman," Mazie said. Anger boiled in every word. "A month ago . . . we reached an agreement . . . she knows Kang is a butcher. He'll slaughter half a million Chinese. It's his way of sending them a message about dreaming of a better future." She stopped, considering the future. "It scares me to think what will happen if he succeeds. What is Nevers thinking of?"

"There may be all of two Chinese-American voters in her district," Carroll replied, "and she's concerned with one thing—getting reelected. She plans on doing that by running us over with a congressional steamroller. How do we stop her?"

"Pontowski," Mazie said. "He inherited a political base from his grandfather. If he goes back to China, that will slow Congress down." Her eyes widened and her mouth opened in surprise. She understood. "You . . . us . . ." She took a deep breath. "You picked us all for a reason. You wanted Went involved to control his mother and Pontowski because of his political connections."

"You're looking at a future president of the United States," Carroll said.

"Why did you pick me?"

A sad look crossed Carroll's face. "The Japanese Connection. I needed Toragawa to get the Japanese involved and Miho was the key. She's the last of the Toragawa line and he's grooming her to take his place. You are a role model for Miho. That, and a chance to make an obscene amount of money, brought him on board."

"But you chose Von Drexler."

"I thought he was the perfect political general for the job. He did have his strong points. I was wrong." He saw confusion on her face. "Mazie, it's people who make things happen." Did she understand?

"You use people." Her words were flat and toneless, without emotion.

Silence ruled the room. She's almost there, he thought. Come on, Mazie, don't quit now. Make the right decision.

She did. "We can't stop now. Failure has too high a price." Slowly, she gained momentum, more sure of herself. "The last I heard, Pontowski had taken Shoshana to Israel."

"He's still there with his son."

"I think I can convince him to go back," she said, hating what she had to do. Another revelation came to her. Carroll wasn't even close to losing his nerve. He had been leading her, helping her reach the decision he wanted, still using her.

## Wednesday, October 9
## Near Bose, China

The ragtag convoy inched its way toward the bridge, caught in the mass of refugees fleeing westward. The people were strangely quiet and the sounds of crying babies, animals, and laboring truck engines gave an eerie punctuation to the silence. Behind them, to the east, the familiar rumble of artillery started again and the crowd surged forward, anxious to cross the bridge.

The two Junkyard Dogs, Big John Washington and Larry Tanaka, had gone ahead to scout the bridge and were forcing their way back to the convoy, pushing against the throng that was shuffling forward. "Where's Captain Waters?" Tanaka asked when they reached the lead truck of the convoy. The driver said she was in the communications van, four vehicles back. They elbowed their way through more refugees surging past the convoy. Waters saw them coming and opened the door for them. "The bridge is about two miles ahead," Tanaka told her. "It's one lane across a deep gorge and some soldiers from the New China Guard have set up a barricade on our end. That's what's causing the holdup. The refugees have to bribe them to get across."

Two Warthogs circled overhead and the UHF radio in the van squawked. "Ripper, how copy?" It was Maggot.

Waters grabbed the mike and looked up, relief in her face. They had been without air cover for most of the day and the strain of commanding the convoy was taking its toll. "Copy you five by," she said. In the distance, the sound of artillery grew louder. The battle was coming their way.

"The bridge ahead of you is blocked," Maggot radioed.

"I know," she replied. "Is there any way around it?"

"Negative," Maggot answered.

Waters fingered the mike as she considered her next move. She hadn't brought sixty vehicles and over five hundred people three hundred miles in five days to let it go now. She made her decision. "Maggot," she radioed, "can you convince that roadblock to go away?"

"Can do" came the answer. The two Warthogs peeled off and disappeared toward the bridge.

Waters keyed the hand-held radio that kept her in contact with the various sections of the convoy. "All section commanders report to the communications van ASAP." She turned to the two Dogs. "Get Marchioni here. He's either with his precious black boxes or with his village." The eccentric, bearded civilian had saved all the spare black boxes and equipment he needed to keep the LASTE systems in the Warthogs working and was guarding them like precious diamonds. But before he left Guilin, he had collected every man, woman, and child from the village where he lived and was moving them right along behind the convoy.

Within moments, the section commanders and Marchioni were gathered around her. She explained the situation. "Once we start moving, we are going to push right across the bridge. If we have to, we'll bulldoze our way through. Charlie, load your villagers on our trucks and buses. We're not going to leave anyone behind."

"Thanks, Bosslady," Marchioni said. "We owe you one." He hurried back to the rear of the convoy.

Maggot's voice came over the UHF radio. "The bridge is open, start movin'." She gave the order and the convoy moved slowly forward, parting the mass of humanity in front of her like a snowplow. Then the refugees were moving with the trucks as an avalanche of people surged across the bridge.

They reached the bridge an hour later. Two destroyed trucks were off to the side, riddled with cannon fire from Maggot's Warthog. Angry soldiers wearing New China

Guard uniforms glared at them as they passed. Charlie Marchioni's voice came over the radio when he reached the burning hulks. "Remember, friends, they are on our side."

Behind them, the sound of artillery grew louder.

"You did good," Leonard told Waters. He was slumped in a chair in the wing's operations tent. Around them, the airfield at Bose was alive with noise and activity. "How bad was it?"

"Piece of cake," she lied. Getting the convoy through had been the hardest thing she had ever done in her life. It surprised her that she didn't need anyone's praise. She knew what she had done.

The phone rang—another problem he had to solve to keep his jets flying. Leonard's face was drawn with worry and dark shadows under his eyes were mute testimony to lack of sleep. He hunched over the telephone, his voice strained and tense. "Marchioni came in on the convoy," he said. "Get him on it." He hung up. "We got LASTE problems again. You got Marchioni here in the nick of time."

There's no escape for him, she thought. He's carrying a burden that won't go away and there's no one for him to share it with. The Klaxon blared with a red alert, jolting them into action. He dropped the phone and they ran for a slit trench outside the tent. She huddled beside him as he yelled into his radio. Aircraft were less than three minutes out, headed straight for the field.

"They've got a nasty surprise," he said. "We got a Hawk missile battery in last night. It's up and operational." A plane roared overhead as a smoke trail reached up, homing on the attacker. The attacker fireballed as the Hawk missile found its mark. Debris fell to earth on the far side of the field but no bombs fell.

The moments passed as they waited for an all-clear signal. She touched him and felt the tension that knotted his muscles and drove his breathing. How long can he take this? she thought. Did Muddy have to live through this hell? Did it wear him down the same way, with a steady, grinding pressure until death ended it? Am I strong enough to watch it happen to the man I love?

A steady tone on the Klaxon announced the all clear. Leonard stood up, stretched, and looked around. He pulled her to her feet beside him. "Scratch one Gomer," he muttered.

They stood there for a moment, close, touching, but saying nothing.

He climbed out of the trench. "Why don't you crash in my tent and get some rest?" He spoke into his walkie-talkie and a Chinese guard escorted her to the far side of the field, into a tranquil village of tents where the Americans were bivouacked.

It was dark when Waters woke. A maid was waiting and led her to a common shower. "Here, Miss Waters," she said, her English surprisingly good. She waited patiently while Waters showered, savoring the hot water. The luxury of it all grew as the maid handed Waters a fresh towel, clean underwear, and a freshly laundered BDU. Even her boots had been polished. The maid took a few minutes to blow dry and comb her hair. "Colonel Leonard," the maid explained, "said to take good care of you and make sure your clothes were clean."

Waters' morale soared. Tango knows, she thought. The simple things make the difference. Five minutes later, she walked into the operations tent and found herself back in the caldron. But she was ready for it.

General Trimler was there with a few of his staff, laying out the resupply operation that was under way. "We've got four C-130s flying resupply out of Cam Ranh Bay," he explained. "The Pentagon won't allow the KC-10s inside China now. Too dangerous, and the KC-10s are too high value to risk."

"They were our main source of JP-4," Leonard told him. "Without the Tens, we're going to run out of fuel real fast."

"I know," Trimler conceded. "We've got a possible work-around. The rail line from Hanoi to Nanning has been cut, but the Vietnamese are opening the track from Hanoi to Kunming. We might be able to solve your fuel problem that way." He shook his head. "It's getting dicey and Zou is barely holding on."

"Maybe it's time to get the hell out of Dodge," Leonard replied. "My troops are ready to cut and run."

"You may be right," Trimler conceded. "Right now, the girl, Jin Chu, seems to be the only thing holding Zou together. For some reason, the Chinese consider her good luck."

"If Zou loses," Waters said, "Kang will butcher people by the thousands."

"It will be a bloodbath," Trimler predicted.

"We all know that," Leonard said. "It's the main topic of conversation around here." He walked to the side of the tent that had been rolled up for ventilation and looked across the airfield. "Three pilots asked to be sent home. I granted their requests and they left. The funny thing is, two came back." He turned back to Trimler. "But if we don't solve the fuel problem, we are all out of here. One KC-10 sortie bringing fuel in means twelve combat sorties for my Hogs."

"I'll see if I can get the KC-10s back in here." Trimler jammed on his helmet, motioned to his staff, and disappeared into the night.

"There goes the world's only combat-ready, armed-to-the-teeth logistics officer," Waters said.

"We can't do this without him," Leonard replied. "Sara, I want you back working on base preparedness. We've been lucky so far and have only been attacked once. It's not going to last." He sat down in his chair and leaned back. His face was etched with fatigue and he hadn't slept since she arrived. "Do you remember the mockup airfield at Cannon Range in Missouri?"

How long ago was that? she thought. It seemed like years before when the 303rd had launched sorties to practice dropping bombs on Cannon Range. But even that had been a dangerous place, and Leonard had crashed there. "The one the Junkyard Dogs built," she said.

He nodded. "Get with Byers and build another one here. The Junkyard Dogs know how to make it look realistic from the air. I want a fake airfield to draw the attention, and the bombs, of any attacking aircraft."

"We can camouflage and tone down the main base at the same time," she told him. "I even know where we can get the labor we need."

"Get to it," he told her.

Two hours later, Charlie Marchioni introduced Waters and the Junkyard Dogs to his village. The village elders thanked her for saving them from Kang's troops and promised they would help in any way they could. She had a work force of almost five hundred people. "You guys got it," Marchioni told them. "I got work to do on the Warthogs." A big grin split his scraggly beard. "Smart jets beat smart bombs any day of the week."

"Too bad you have to keep retraining them," Byers deadpanned, knocking Marchioni's beloved LASTE. Marchioni ignored the remark and left. "Okay, Captain," Byers continued, "you are looking at the finest construction team in Asia and we are going to build you one eye-watering, awe-thin-teek-looking airfield." The sound of distant artillery punctuated his words.

## Wednesday, October 9
## Haifa, Israel

The dark gray sedan dropped Mazie off in front of the apartment in the Hadar, the old residential district halfway up the hill above the city of Haifa. She knocked on the door and a bearded, hunch-shouldered bear of a man answered. She instantly recognized Avi Tamir, the most famous living scientist in Israel, the father of Shoshana Pontowski. "Doctor Tamir, I'm Mazie Kamigami and I'm trying to contact Matt."

The bear held the door open and pointed toward open French doors that led onto a balcony. A spectacular view of the broad bay spread out before her and she heard a little boy's laughter as she walked through the open doors. Pontowski looked up. "Matt," he told the little boy, "go inside and harass your grandfather. He needs cheering up."

The miniature image of Pontowski was very serious as he studied Mazie. "You're pretty," he said, scampering past her.

"Kids," Pontowski allowed.

"There is no doubt he's your son," Mazie replied. Silence. "How's he doing?"

"Kids are amazing," he answered. "They get on with life.

He still cries occasionally, mostly when he goes to bed. He loved the bedtime ritual . . . that's when he really misses his mother . . ." His voice trailed off into his own, private memories. He was still coming to terms with his grief. He offered her a seat and stood at the railing, his back to the sea, waiting for her to speak.

A slender, dark-complected woman in her mid-fifties appeared in the doorway. "Lillian," Pontowski said, "this is Mazie Kamigami." The two women exchanged greetings.

"We'll take Little Matt to the beach," Lillian said. "We'll be back in a few hours." Pontowski nodded and again, a difficult silence came down. It held until Lillian and Tamir had corraled Little Matt and hustled him out of the apartment.

"Lillian," he explained to Mazie, "is Shoshana's aunt and has been taking care of Little Matt. She wants to take him to their kibbutz in the Huleh Valley. It's a great place to raise kids."

"He still needs a father," Mazie said. They were still skirting the reason for Mazie's sudden appearance and it hung between them, dark and foreboding.

Let's get to it, Pontowski decided. "Why?" was all he said. Mazie stood, joined him at the railing, and gazed out to sea. Little Matt was right, he thought, she is beautiful.

She didn't look at him. "We need you," she said. Mazie's voice matched her image, beautifully crafted and composed. "The situation in China is very bad."

"So I've heard, but I don't think I can help. Not now."

"We can still stabilize the situation if—"

He interrupted her. "Mazie, our side is getting its ass kicked." Now he had to talk. "We're in over our heads, trying to play policeman to the world. Of all the places to get involved, to take sides, China is the worst. What were we thinking of? Hell, what was I thinking of?"

She let him talk, not interrupting. He had to come to terms with his grief and doubts, he had to tame the demon of responsibility that tore at his soul. She listened until the hurt was yielding. Finally, he looked at her. "How many times has China died before?" he asked. He didn't want an answer. "Yet it has always been reborn after the old rubbish has been cut or burned away."

"You've been reading a history of China," she said.

He nodded. "I should have done that before I got involved." Bitterness surrounded every word.

"China was your karma," she told him.

"Because of my involvement, Shoshana was killed. That's not fate, that's responsibility."

"What about your responsibility to the wing?" she asked.

"I know why Carroll wants me back," he said, ignoring her question. "Congress is going to pass legislation tying the administration's hands and forcing us out of China. My name, my connections, still carry enough weight to stall Congress for a while. Carroll hopes that will give him enough time to get his irons out of the fire." Now she could hear a new anger in his voice. "It's politics, pure politics. Damn him to hell. That's why he wanted me over there in the first place."

"Carroll uses everybody," she said. "It's the way he makes things happen."

"I don't like being used."

"He's used me, Went, everybody."

"Mazie, I'm not going back."

"Someone has to bring the wing out," she told him.

It was the second time she had linked the wing to him. This time it registered. "Where does responsibility end?" he asked himself. He knew the answer. "My grandfather showed me many times. But I wasn't listening until the very last." He made his decision. "I got them in there—I'll get them out. I hope I can make my son understand why I'm going away again. He's been hurt a lot."

"His aunt and grandfather will help," Mazie said. "The Israelis understand duty."

Now she could tell him the rest. "Matt, we know what happened at the airport and why Shoshana was killed." He tensed at her words and she waited, fearing the anger she saw in him. "It was Kang. He took a contract out with the Yakuza to kill you or any member of your family."

"Who found out?"

"Toragawa," she told him. "He went through the Yakuza like the grim reaper until they told him the truth."

"They probably lied to get him off their backs," Pontowski said.

Mazie shook her head. "I don't think so. The two men who arranged the contract committed suicide. Toragawa demanded it be done properly."

"But why my family? I was the enemy—not Shoshana."

"Not to Kang's way of thinking."

"Why did you wait until after I had decided to go back to China before telling me?"

She considered her answer. "Revenge is the worst possible reason to go back."

His eyes were cold blue steel. "It's the best."

# CHAPTER 20

**Friday, October 11**
**The Philippine Sea**

Weathermen call it an "equatorial wave," as it resembles an
eddy in the tropical easterlies, the winds that blow constantly out of the east over the low latitudes of the great
oceans. Normally, an equatorial wave brings a spell of rain,
a band of showers as it moves westward. Occasionally,
about ten times a year, a wave will deepen into a tropical
depression and moist tropical winds will flow into it,
gaining speed, building into a storm.

A weather satellite in orbit twenty-two thousand miles
above the equator imaged the formation of one of these
storms in the eastern reaches of the Philippine Sea and
transmitted its discovery to a station in Australia. Within
hours, weathermen were plotting its course as it moved to
the west and bent northward. When its wind speed passed
seventy-four miles per hour, they named it Typhoon Kewa,
the eleventh of the season.

**Saturday, October 12**
**Bose Airfield, China**

Maggot was the first to see the approaching C-130.
"There it is," he said, pointing to the west. The rumor that
Pontowski was on the inbound Hercules had swept over the

base hours before and most of the wing was waiting on the ramp. For reasons known best to themselves, most had polished their boots and changed into clean uniforms. Even a few fresh haircuts were seen in the crowd. A sergeant had washed and polished Pontowski's old pickup truck and parked it nearby.

Leonard stood patiently with Waters and for the first time in weeks, the strained look on his face was gone. Now he was only tired, and the thought of a good night's sleep figured big in his immediate plans. The C-130 touched down and its props slammed into reverse, dragging it to a halt before the first turnoff. "Nice landing," Leonard observed. The Hercules taxied into the blocks and its engines spun down. The crew entry hatch opened and Pontowski climbed down the steps. Mazie and Hazelton were right behind him.

The crowd was uncommonly silent as Leonard stepped forward and saluted. Before he could say "Welcome back, sir," they erupted in loud shouting, clapping, and whistling. A big smile spread over Leonard's face. "I couldn't say it better myself," he said, happy to be an ops officer again.

Pontowski waved a salute back. "I couldn't stay away when I heard you were having so much fun kicking ass around here." More shouting and cheering followed him as he walked to his pickup.

Waters held back. There was a new sound in Pontowski's voice, and it worried her. He was not the same man. "Miss Kamigami, Mr. Hazelton," she called. "Why don't you come with me?" They had been totally forgotten in the hubbub.

"How's it going?" Mazie asked.

"Tight, very tight," Waters answered. "Listen." The rumble of artillery in the far distance rolled over the horizon. "What can we do for you?" she asked.

"Hopefully," Mazie answered, "it's exactly the other way around. Mr. Carroll wants to stay on top of the situation and we're his eyes and ears on this end."

"It's an understatement to call the 'situation' here fluid," Waters told her. "Beijing keeps starting and stopping the logistical pipeline to Kang and that drives the tempo of the fighting. But it allows us to hang on."

"I'd like to visit the front," Mazie said.

"You'll have to talk to Colonel Pontowski and General Trimler about that," Waters replied.

Jin Chu sat up in bed with a jerk, waking Zou Rong. "What is it?" he asked.

"A dream," she answered. He was fully alert, hanging on every word. "You were at a bridge, talking to soldiers," she told him. "Then we traveled west and came to a city. It was very hilly and peaceful. You were surrounded by smiling children."

"Did you know the city?"

"No. I have never been there, but in my dream, you said you had been there once before."

"Kunming. It has to be Kunming." He got out of bed and paced back and forth. "Your dream is a sign. Kunming is the headquarters for the Yunnan Military District. The commander there wants to join us but I don't trust him. He is too eager. Perhaps I was wrong. I must talk to him again. Did you know the bridge?"

"When I left my village, my grandfather took me to the bridge, where I caught a bus. It is near here." She told him of her first glimpse of the Pearl River. "The dragons there are angry because of the bridge."

"I must see this bridge," he said.

"Perhaps you can also visit the Americans on your way."

"Yes, that is a good idea," he replied, "now that Colonel Pontowski is back."

Zou Rong's helicopter approached from the west at low level, barely clearing the trees and power lines. Kamigami was waiting outside his command bunker and called his sixteen-man honor guard to attention as it touched down.

The honor guard, made up of one man from each of the First Regiment's sixteen companies, stood at attention, eager to see the drama play out. Like their commander, they were motionless, and not a flicker of emotion betrayed their thoughts. To the man, they knew of his gift to Zou and considered it the privilege of a lifetime to see the two meet. Not one saw Kamigami stiffen when Zou, Jin Chu, and two other passengers emerged from the helicopter. Kamigami recognized Hazelton immediately, but the identity of the last, a petite and very pretty woman, escaped him. The stoic composure that was part of his growing legend was nearly destroyed when he recognized his daughter.

Kamigami called for his men to present arms and saluted his commander. Zou returned the salute and reviewed the honor guard. "Your men have fought well," he said so they all could hear when he had finished. "I believe you know Mr. Hazelton, and of course, your daughter." The last was for the benefit of the sixteen pair of eyes that focused on Mazie. The stories surrounding Kamigami took on a new dimension.

"I am told," Zou continued, "that the bridge near here is very important to our defense. I want to see it."

"The bridge is the key," Kamigami said. "If Kang takes the bridge, he can move artillery across and shell Bose. Once past Bose, he can move into Yunnan Province."

A muscle twitched in Zou's face at the mention of Yunnan. "Can Kang outflank us to the north?" he asked.

"He would have to divert men and supplies from here," Kamigami replied. "That would weaken his position and you could launch an offensive to retake Nanning. That would mean a major setback for him. Kang needs the bridge."

"Miss Li said *feng shui* at the bridge is very bad and that the dragons are angry. Perhaps she can discover a way to appease them."

That settled the issue, and Kamigami called for two Humvees and an escort to take them all forward. Jin Chu spoke quietly to Zou and he relayed her instructions to the driver. Instead of going directly to the bridge, the small convoy turned off to the south and stopped on a small promontory. Below them, the bridge was clearly visible.

"This is where I first saw the Pearl River," Jin Chu told Zou. She gestured gracefully, sweeping the view with her right hand. "But the bridge is built in the wrong place and jars the harmony of the land. There are many angry dragons here." Zou shot her a worried look. Two of the drivers were listening and her words would spread like wildfire among his soldiers. "The dragons," she said, "are not angry at us but we must destroy the bridge." The two drivers relaxed and Zou raised his binoculars to study the scene below him.

Mazie joined Kamigami and they walked away from the others. Both wanted to talk, but neither was sure what to say. "We are a mismatched pair," she ventured.

"You've changed," he told her.

"And you." It was the truth. Mazie had become more American while he had become more Chinese. The two cultures had pulled them apart, the one drawing her in while the other was absorbing him as it had so many others in its long history. The difference was not superficial and went deep—Mazie thought in English while he thought more and more in Chinese. Both wanted their family to survive, but they were losing what little they had in common. They walked back to the vehicles in silence.

"You must destroy the bridge," Zou told Kamigami.

Kamigami didn't answer. He fully intended to blow the bridge—at the right time. But for now, he needed it to keep his men fighting in the east and hold Kang at bay. Taking his silence for consent, Zou said, "I've seen enough."

"It's getting tough out there," Leonard said when he entered Pontowski's operations tent. He had to wait while a KC-10 took the runway and ran up its three General Electric turbofan engines for takeoff. Each engine developed over fifty-two thousand pounds of static thrust and the blast blew over three shacks a quarter of a mile away. With the burden of command off his back, he didn't worry about it.

The KC-10 rolled down the runway and the huge jet leaped into the air. "Washington has reopened the air bridge out of Cam Ranh," Pontowski told him. "That Ten offloaded 135,000 pounds of fuel and twenty-two pallets of cargo. We're scheduled for two a day."

"The modern version of the Hump from World War II," Leonard said. "I don't think it's gonna last."

"What's the problem?" Pontowski asked.

"I sat in on the debrief for Maggot's last mission. They got four bandit calls from the AWACS. But the bad guys can't find us because their warning and control system sucks. But they're up there and a KC-10 or a C-130 is a sitting duck."

"It won't happen," Pontowski told him. He walked over to the map table and spread out a chart. "We're only seventy nautical miles from the Vietnamese border—less than ten minutes' flying time for the KC-10. And we got F-15s flying CAP with the AWACS here"—he pointed to the AWACS orbit point inside Vietnam but close to the border—"and a pair of F-15s will be on any bandit who heads for a Ten or C-130 like a pit bull on a French poodle in heat."

"The politicians in D.C. are getting serious about this," Leonard allowed. "It's nice to know we're not out here all alone." He paused, considering what he had to say next. "Maggot had more bad news. He got mucho, and I mean mucho, SA-2 hits on his RHAW gear."

Pontowski sat down. "We didn't need that." Leonard had just given him a new problem to deal with. The A-10's RHAW, or radar homing and warning system, detected hostile radar threats. The SA-2 was an old, obsolete, radar-guided surface-to-air missile that still presented a very real threat to his Warthogs and any cargo plane.

"We need to find 'em and take 'em out," Leonard said.

"We need to get in bed with the AWACS troops and have an intimate conversation," Pontowski said.

Leonard faked a shocked look, "Not me, Boss. According to the F-15 drivers, the mission commander is a good-looking, ball-busting femme they call Major Mom."

"Figuratively, meathead, figuratively," Pontowski replied.

"I'll get right on it," Leonard said.

Moose Penko arrived on a C-130 that evening and was immediately driven to operations where Pontowski, Leonard, and Maggot were waiting for him. Moose listened while the Warthog drivers laid out the problem. "Our jets have been modified with ESM, electronic support measures," Moose told them, "and we can locate a radar transmitter the moment it comes up."

"How accurate is it?" Maggot asked. Moose mentioned a figure none of them believed. "Shit-oh-dear," Maggot muttered. "If it's half that good, we can find those puppies in a heartbeat."

"We have to counter their 'shoot and scoot' tactics,"

Moose said, "and sucker them in." The tone of his voice was light and bantering but his face was deadly serious. "I've got some ideas we can play with."

"I can't believe this," Pontowski deadpanned. "Warthogs doing air defense suppression."

## Tuesday, October 15
## Near Bose, China

Lieutenant Colonel Sung Fu, Second Company, Fourth Battalion of the Twentieth Air Defense Regiment, People's Liberation Army, trudged up the wide path leading from the village to his missile site. He surveyed the area, his practiced eye measuring every detail. The power line leading from the village's lone generator was installed. It had best be working, he promised himself, calculating what punishment would best suit that particular failure.

Sung had learned much from Sun Tzu's *The Art of War* and took great pains to insure that his orders were clear, simple, workable, and most important, understood. When his commands were not properly carried out, he would investigate and discover which of his officers had failed. He always started with the fool who held the rank of senior captain before working his way down to the two captains, the four first lieutenants, and finally, the eight second lieutenants.

Occasionally, harsh, and very visible, discipline was called for. He was not averse to calling the entire company out to witness an execution by firing squad and had once, very briefly, considered a beheading to instill proper motivation. But after due consideration, he had decided that would be counterproductive and encourage more defections to the New China Guard. Desertions were a problem in other units, especially those with a high percentage of personnel from southern China. But not his.

Sung ran through the personnel roster he carried in his head. Who in his company was from the southern provinces? Only that fool of a senior captain. And he wasn't likely to desert as long as his family was in northern China.

In addition to Sun Tzu, Sung had learned much from his commander, General Kang Xun.

The six missile launchers of Sung's first missile battery were laid out in the star pattern that characterized an SA-2 Guideline surface-to-air missile battery. At the heart of the complex was a van-mounted acquisition and guidance radar NATO called the Fan Song. It was an old system with a maximum range of twenty-five miles and effective at altitudes from two thousand to sixty thousand feet.

Sung had never fired a Guideline and longed to give the fire order so one of his cherished missiles with its three-hundred-pound high-explosive warhead could destroy an enemy aircraft. As he looked around his missile site, he was certain today would be the day.

"Phoenix, how copy?" Leonard transmitted over his secure radio. No answer. Since he and Maggot were talking to each other, the problem had to be with the AWACS. He called Maggot over to the UHF radio and tried again, this time in the clear. They made contact and Moose's voice came through loud and distinct.

Moose checked with his ASO, who controlled the AWACS' passive detection system, and told the two Warthog pilots that all was quiet. "Time to go trolling," Leonard radioed. "We got to get 'em interested."

"Roger that," Maggot replied. The two Warthogs climbed out of their low orbit to three thousand feet, well inside the engagement envelope of an SA-2. Their radar warning gear exploded with a harsh chirping sound and the symbol for an SA-2 flashed on their RHAW azimuth indicator. A Fan Song radar was locked on.

"We got 'em," Moose transmitted. The two Warthogs dove for the deck and leveled off at three hundred feet, breaking the Fan Song's radar lock.

The AWACS was over one hundred miles away, established in an orbit over Vietnam, but within milliseconds, its electronic support measures program had detected the signal, measured its electrical parameters, identified the transmitter, and determined its location. A red target symbol flashed on Moose's screen—the missile site. "Tango, Maggot," Moose radioed, "your target is bearing one-three-five at thirty. Stand by for coordinates." Moose's thick fingers danced on the keyboard and the target's coordinates appeared by the red triangle. He gave the Warthog pilots the numbers and waited.

"Maggot, go tactical," Leonard transmitted. Two clicks answered him as the two Warthogs moved apart and headed for Lieutenant Colonel Sung Fu's missile battery. They were six minutes out.

"Shooter-cover," Leonard ordered.

"Give me a break," Maggot answered. He wanted to drop some bombs.

Leonard almost laughed. "Okay, I'll cover your worthless ass." Another two clicks answered him.

Maggot took the lead, angled fifteen degrees away from the missile site, and at one mile, pulled back on his stick to pop onto the target. He couldn't see the missile site but he knew where to look. He rolled inverted at twelve hundred feet and pulled his nose to the coordinates the AWACS had given him. "Tallyho the fox," Maggot called when he saw the camouflaged missile launchers. He was well below the minimum altitude of the SA-2s but inside the envelope for ground fire. He looked for the telltale flashes of AAA. Nothing. He pickled off a string of Mark-82 AIR, five-hundred-pound bombs, and pulled off.

Maggot's LASTE system worked its magic and his bombs walked across the missile site with uncanny accuracy. "Shack," Leonard called, as he rolled in behind Maggot. "I'm in," he called, strafing the target at a right angle while Maggot positioned to engage anyone foolish enough to shoot at him. Then Maggot strafed the site and the two Warthogs headed north.

"Scratch one missile site," Leonard told Moose. They deliberately climbed into the envelope for the SA-2, still trolling for radar activity. Nothing.

"Say," Maggot radioed, "I like this business."

Lieutenant Colonel Sung Fu lurched through the debris that had been his first missile battery. He was not prepared for the destruction and carnage around him. He stepped over a three-foot-deep trench Leonard's cannon had plowed when he had marched a burst of thirty-millimeter cannon fire through the Fan Song radar van. The bullets had riddled the van and it had collapsed on itself like so much Swiss cheese.

An officer from Kang's headquarters stood back, not wanting to go any closer in case Sung's misfortune touched him. The officer functioned as an intelligence and liaison officer out of Kang's headquarters, explaining the correct meaning of events and orders to field commanders. In reality, he was a spy insuring complete loyalty to Kang.

Sung straightened his shoulders and joined the liaison officer. "I will avenge this," he promised. "My second battery has six missiles and I will destroy six Americans."

"We monitored the radio transmissions of the Silent Guns," the liaison officer told him. "Normally, we only hear a rasping chatter from their radios. But this time, we heard everything. It was the aircraft they call the AWACS that directed the Americans to you."

Sung stared at the man. Kang's treatment of commanders who had failed had been graphically implanted and he had to redeem himself. His life depended on it. Yet he also feared the Warthogs and did not want to engage them again. He found a solution to his dilemma. "I will destroy this AWACS," he announced.

"That's not possible," the liaison officer replied. "The AWACS only orbits in Vietnamese airspace."

"How close to the border does it come?" Sung asked.

"Maybe within twenty miles," came the answer.

"Then I will take my company to the border."

"Impossible," the officer snorted. "It's too mountainous. You can never get your missiles into position."

Sung's face turned into a death mask. "I will take my company to the border," he repeated, "and destroy this AWACS."

## Tuesday, October 15
## Washington, D.C.

A stabbing pain in the left side of his face woke Bill Carroll. He glanced at the clock beside his bed—3:30 in the morning. "Call the dentist," Mary, his wife, told him. "Quit trying to ignore it." She wasn't big on dispensing sympathy in the early morning hours. His jaw sent him a fresh message of agony and he gave in to the inevitable.

When the national security advisor to the president of the United States calls for a dental appointment, his dentist is instantly available. So when Carroll arrived at the dental office forty minutes later, the dentist, his technician, and the receptionist were waiting for him. That was as good as the day was going to get.

Carroll was in his office before six, his face still numb from the Novocaine. As usual, his secretary was already at work, laying out his desk. The day's schedule and the PDB, the President's Daily Brief, were on top. He scanned the PDB, not expecting to find any significant intelligence in the highly classified summary produced by the CIA. He wasn't disappointed. "You need to see this," his secretary said, turning on the VCR. "It was recorded off the Buddy Prince show last night." Ann Nevers flickered to life on the screen.

The congresswoman was the last person he wanted to watch but he trusted his secretary's judgment. Nevers was pounding the same old stake of reckless foreign involvement into the administration's heart. And sitting next to her was James Finlay, his former chief of staff.

"Technically," Finlay said at one point, "the United States has sent mercenaries to China to support one side of a civil war."

Damn! Carroll raged to himself. Finlay knows that everyone is on the DASR and that our support of Zou Rong qualifies as a covert operation. Even Congress has bought into it. But he had witnessed how quickly congressional support could wither and blow away in the cave of the winds called the Capitol. Carroll inadvertently chewed his numb tongue, tasting blood. Even the existence of the DASR was classified and couldn't be revealed. Thanks to Finlay, Nevers had him over the proverbial barrel.

"Didn't you have a part in that decision?" Prince asked.

Go get him, Buddy, Carroll thought. Prince had done his research and was keeping Finlay honest.

"I resigned in protest over that decision," Finlay replied. Prince gave Finlay a look that implied he was speaking less than the truth. "But aren't the Chinese being massacred by the general Beijing placed in charge of southern China?"

Nevers jumped in. "Many of those reports are gross fabrications by the administration."

"Is our government lying to us?" Prince asked.

"Really, Buddy," Nevers answered, "are you surprised? Our government has progressively involved us in the domestic affairs of China when we should be concentrating on problems here, at home. A fine young Air Force general, Mark Von Drexler, was in China, reporting the situation for what it was. Unfortunately, he was killed and our only voice of reason was lost."

"Was he one of the so-called mercenaries?" Prince asked.

"No," Nevers answered, "most assuredly not. He was a true patriot and I intend to hold the administration responsible for his death."

Prince took a phone call from a viewer who asked if it was illegal for U.S. citizens to be mercenaries. "That's correct, and they can lose their citizenship," Nevers answered. "Under the circumstances, I intend to see that they do."

Prince leaned forward, his voice intense. "But isn't the grandson of the late President Pontowski in command of the Americans in China?"

"He's in command of the American mercenaries in China," Finlay corrected. "And he will be held responsible for his actions. No man, regardless of his political connections, is above the law."

Carroll jabbed at the VCR and turned it off. "Sumbitch," he mumbled, barely able to wrap his frozen tongue around the word. Finlay had thrown in with Nevers and was feeding her inside information, and with the reverse spin he gave it, Nevers had all the ammunition she needed.

That afternoon, a large troop of key congressional leaders marched into the Oval Office and met with the president for over an hour. Immediately afterward, the president called in his advisors and told them to start working the China problem—hard. "I want two things to happen," he ordered. "Start getting our people out of China and find a way to muzzle Nevers."

Carroll returned to his office and drafted a message for

Mazie, explaining the situation. He stared at the message with its devastating implications: The administration was losing political backing in Congress and its support of Zou Rong was approaching meltdown. Hundreds of thousands of Chinese were going to be sacrificed to Kang, Hong Kong was going down the tubes, and the chance to prevent a major war in Asia was all but lost. What was the answer? He needed time to think. Rather than send the message, he went for a run.

The two Secret Service agents, Chuck Stanford and Wayne Adams, were hard pressed to keep up with Carroll, until he slipped and fell, straining his Achilles tendon and spraining an ankle. He was taken to the hospital in pain. The message was still lying on his desk.

## Wednesday, October 16
## Bose Airfield, China

Mazie stood at the wooden-framed door of the tent where Trimler and the MAAG had set up a temporary office and listened. The intensity of the artillery barrage to the east left little doubt that a major attack was underway. She walked back inside and joined Hazelton, who was trying to coordinate a shipment of much-needed supplies up the Hanoi-Kunming rail line. "It isn't going to happen," he told her.

Trimler overheard the comment. "This is no probing action," he said. "We're looking at a major offensive. Resupply may be a moot point. We need to talk to Pontowski."

Mazie followed the two men out the door and into the early morning dark. A faint glow etched the eastern horizon. Two figures emerged out of the shadows of Pontowski's operations tent. "Miss Kamigami," Jin Chu called, stopping Mazie cold.

"Went," Mazie called. "Go on in. I'll catch up in a moment." She turned to Jin Chu and waited. Up close, she could see that the other person with Jin Chu was a woman carrying a small child.

"This is May May," Jin Chu said. She paused, searching her limited English vocabulary for the right words.

Mazie solved the problem for her and spoke in Cantonese. "I speak a little Cantonese," she said.

"May May is your father's temporary wife," Jin Chu explained. "She is pregnant with his child." Mazie stiffened. Parents were not always what their children wanted—or thought they should be. "Can you fly her to safety on one of your airplanes?" Jin Chu asked. "I had a dream with many fires. All were here."

Well, Mazie thought, I do have a family—of sorts. But it is all mixed up.

May May shifted the child on her hip. "Her dreams always come true," she explained. "The fires mean there will be much destruction and fighting here."

"There is more," Jin Chu said. "Zou is leaving for Yunnan Province in a few hours. The general there is his ally and Kunming is his new capital."

"Stay here," Mazie said. "I'll see what I can do." She hurried inside the operations tent. Jin Chu spoke in a whisper to May May before disappearing into the early morning mist. May May sat on the ground and waited.

The tent was crowded with Pontowski's staff and they made room for her so she could sit at the front and see the briefing map. "This is the offensive we've been expecting," Pontowski said. He pointed to the map and circled the bridge she had seen three days before. "This is Kang's next objective. If he captures it, we will be within artillery range. So we're going to launch at first light and try to change their minds." He looked at Mazie. "Any words from your sources?"

"By all reports," Mazie said, "this is a do or die situation for Kang. He's got to win on this one or his masters in Beijing will cut him off at the knees and try to work out an accommodation with Zou Rong. Zou has cut some sort of deal with the military district commander in Yunnan Province and they've declared Kunming the capital. Zou's moving there today."

Trimler grunted. "This is news to me. But it could be the break we need. I'll have to take the MAAG with him. I'll leave a liaison officer here with you."

The high-pitched scream of an incoming rocket arced over them. *"Hit the deck!"* Ray Byers shouted. Hazelton knocked Mazie to the ground and threw his body over her. She buried her face in his chest and threw her arms around him as six explosions rocked the far side of the airfield. She didn't move.

"Great," Byers growled. "Fuckin' great. Unguided rockets."

"You two can get up now," Trimler said. Hazelton rolled to the side and Mazie looked up into a circle of standing men. She stood and brushed off her clothes, blushing brightly.

The phones started ringing and the radios came alive with damage reports for Waters' base defense section. "Those were 140-millimeter rockets," she told them.

"Max range about six and a half miles," Trimler added. "That means they snuck some across the river. We can probably expect a few more."

Waters was busy plotting the impact points on her base chart. "One hit the airfield," she reported, "and started a major fire." She listened on the phone as more reports came in. "Colonel, the fire is in the cargo area. All our cargo-loading equipment is lost."

"Not good," Pontowski grumbled. Without a constant flow of fuel, munitions, spare parts, and hundreds of other small items, flying operations would dry up in a few days. The survival of his wing depended on at least two KC-10s bringing in fuel along with twenty tons of supplies each day. He turned to his transportation officer. "See what you can do to get it replaced."

"Roger that," the young major replied. He hurried back to his logistics command post, his work cut out for him.

"The other rockets," Waters said, "overshot and missed the airfield. They landed here." Marchioni stared at the chart for a moment and uttered an obscenity. He bolted from the room.

"That's where his village is camping," Byers explained.

Pontowski's face was rock hard. "We need to send Kang a message he won't forget." Anger burned in his words. "Don't kill the innocent."

Waters' right hand clenched tight, her knuckles white. The sound in his voice frightened her.

* * *

Ray Byers walked with Mazie and Hazelton as they headed back for their makeshift office. Outside, they found May May still waiting, the child asleep in her arms. "She's pretty," Byers said. "Who is she?"

Mazie didn't know how to answer his question. "I guess she's part of my family now. Ray, can you take care of her?"

"No problem," Byers answered. "She can stay with us." He and May May disappeared into the dark.

Mazie watched them go before turning to Hazelton. There were tears in her eyes. "This is so stupid. She's one of my father's mistresses. I don't understand him at all."

Hazelton stopped and put both his hands on her shoulders. For the second time that morning, she found his closeness reassuring. "I don't understand my mother," he said. "She drives me crazy and wants to control everything I do. I still love her, though." Then he took the plunge. "But not as much as I love you."

The "Oh" that came from Mazie was more of a squeak than a word. Then she was in his arms, holding on to him, her cheek against his chest. He bent over to kiss her, but the difference in their heights made that ridiculous. He scooped her up in his arms and she threw her arms around his neck. Their lips brushed, tentatively, hesitantly. She pulled back and looked at him, their faces inches apart. "Oh," she murmured, much stronger. Then they kissed again.

## Wednesday, October 16
## The bridge near Bose, China

Kamigami stood in the middle of his battle staff as a babble of voices engulfed him. But he had learned how to listen and there was no panic or confusion in the swirling sounds competing for his attention. The reports streaming in confirmed what he had sensed form the very first: This attack was different. The artillery fire they were receiving carried a different tempo and intensity. That bothered him.

He motioned for his operations and intelligence officers to follow him to the J-STARS module next to the command bunker. Inside, the American liaison officer was equally perplexed. "We should be detecting heavy targets, like tanks, moving into postion," the American said. "But there's nothing. As best as we can tell, all the heavy stuff is still fifty miles to the rear."

The two Chinese officers put their heads together and spoke quietly. "Does the J-STARS," the intelligence officer asked, "detect people? Many people."

"Not yet," the American replied.

The two Chinese looked at Kamigami. They had asked the right question and as their general, it was Kamigami's job to put the pieces together. He did. "So where are the tanks?" He didn't wait for an answer. "Kang is holding them back because he knows we can detect them with our J-STARS and destroy them with the Warthogs. He has changed his tactics and is using the Chinese version of stealth—people." The Chinese officers nodded in agreement. "The incoming is mostly rockets," Kamigami said, "because rockets can be carried by people one at a time and not detected."

"So what does it all mean?" the American asked. High-tech warfare he understood. But this was different.

"Human wave attacks," Kamigami answered. "Probably at first light. Move your module to the airfield at Bose. Now."

"Yes, sir," the American replied. "We're gone."

Kamigami strode back into the command bunker calling for the officer in charge of the ASOC. "Tell Colonel Pontowski to load his A-10s with antipersonnel ordnance," he ordered. "We will need them at first light." He spent the next ten minutes on the radio talking to his four battalion commanders, warning them what to expect. Then he ordered the command bunker to relocate to the airfield at Bose. He intended to use his Humvees as a mobile command post and would lead from the front.

# CHAPTER 21

**Wednesday, October 16**
**Mindoro, The Philippines**

Nothing, short of evacuation, could have saved the islanders of Mindoro from Typhoon Kewa. The entire island was turned into a wasteland as Kewa moved over Mindoro, flattening homes, twisting and rolling cars over like a child at mad play, and literally blowing people away. Sustained winds of over 170 miles per hour and huge waves pounded at the island until it was populated more by the dead than the living. A supertanker plying northward to Japan ran ashore, splitting its hull and spilling more than twenty-five million gallons of crude oil.

The fury of the typhoon grew as it moved over warm water and continued on its relentless course. Over a thousand miles to the northwest, the first of the clouds pushed by Kewa came ashore off the Gulf of Tonkin and penetrated into southern China.

**Wednesday, October 16**
**Bose Airfield, China**

"Tango calls this the Gopher Hole," Waters said as she led the way down the wooden steps and into the sandbagged underground bunker. The smell of freshly dug earth was strong, almost overpowering.

"He got it right," Pontowski said, looking around the operations center. The bunker reminded him of a World War II movie, but it was surprisingly roomy and well organized. All the telephones and radios were working, the big boards that tracked the status of the base were nailed up against the wall, and fans hummed in the background, circulating fresh air.

The sound of the first Warthogs launching reached into the bunker and he checked the operations status board—two A-10s led by Maggot. Two more were taxiing out, led by Mako Luce. Tango Leonard and his wingman, Jake Trisher, were scheduled to take off in thirty minutes. All were loaded out with CBU-58s, cluster bomb units. The CBU canisters split open when they were dropped and spread 650 baseball-sized bomblets over a wide area. Each bomblet exploded into 260 fragments that could chew up soft targets like people, houses, and vehicles. For an added kick, each bomblet had two five-grain titanium incendiary pellets to heat things up. The CBU-58 was one of the ironies of modern warfare. It was developed to replace the older, much-reviled napalm, and in terms of lethality, was a quantum leap beyond napalm. But it was a politically correct weapon.

Pontowski settled into his chair in front of a communications panel. Damn, he thought, I'd rather be out there, launching. He glanced at the board and the numbers were back to haunt him—46 pilots, 30 operational Warthogs. The monkey of command was back on his back, firmly in the saddle.

The AWACS broadcast an air-raid warning twenty-five minutes later as Tango Leonard and Jake Trisher were taxiing out for takeoff. Pontowski grabbed the radio mike, "Tango, bandits five minutes out. Hustle."

"Rog," Leonard answered laconically, as if he hadn't a care in the world. "Hustling now." A warning siren echoed over the base, and the minutes dragged as he took the active. Finally, "Rolling." Pontowski turned to Waters. She was standing, looking up at the beams in the ceiling, launching with Leonard. The radio crackled. "Gopher Hole, Tango. We can jettison our load and discourage those bandits."

Pontowski checked the status boards. Tango and Jake were on a close air support mission carrying CBUs. But each had a cannon and two Sidewinder missiles. It took him three seconds to make a decision. "Cleared to jettison, contact Phoenix on secure." Phoenix was the call sign for the AWACS orbiting one hundred miles to the south over Vietnam. He hit the switch that allowed him to monitor the secure radio.

"Tango, Jake," Moose Penko's distinctive voice called, "snap zero-seven-zero. Bandits on your nose at eighteen, angels three. Kill, repeat, kill."

Pontowski explained the radio call to Waters. "Moose gave them a heading of zero-seven-zero degrees into the bandits, who are eighteen nautical miles away and at three thousand feet." He didn't need to explain the "kill" order. Waters's face paled and her lips were compressed into a tight line. They waited.

"Tallyho," Leonard radioed. His voice was staccato sharp. "Fantans. Maybe twenty. We're engaged. Jake, shoot 'em in the face and blow on through. Head for the deck."

"Good thinking," Pontowski muttered to no one.

"I'm on the lead," Jake transmitted. He was yelling.

"Rog," Leonard answered, much calmer but still speaking very fast. "I'll stuff number three." They could hear a growl in the background when Leonard transmitted—the seeker head on his Sidewinder was tracking.

Almost simultaneously they heard a double-barreled "Fox Two. Fox Two." Both men had launched a missile at the oncoming bandits.

"Splash one!" Jake radioed. His Sidewinder had blown an A-5 Fantan out of the sky.

"Splash two," Tango added. "They're jettisoning their loads. Holy shit! They're on us. Jake, break left, take 'er down."

Pontowski was on the mike. "Tango, drag the fight over the base. We can nail some of the bastards." He was looking at the ceiling, trying to visualize the fight that was going on above them. He heard the sound of running feet. Waters was running up the stairs.

Anxiety and fear drove her outside and she ran through the sandbagged zig-zag that protected the bunker entry from bomb blasts. She burst into the open, her breath coming in ragged gasps. She was panting, not from the exertion but from the fear that was pounding at her. It was irrational but she had to be with him, to see him. By sheer willpower, she would keep the man she loved safe from harm.

An A-10 flew over her, so low that she fell to the ground. The jet blast blew dirt over her. She raised her head in time to see it climb sharply to the left and reverse course, still below a hundred feet. Its nose erupted in smoke and a loud growl washed over her as the pilot squeezed off a short burst of cannon fire at a Chinese fighter, a Fantan, maneuvering above him. He missed and the Fantan climbed skyward as the Warthog turned back to the right. Another Warthog flashed over the field, also below a hundred feet. Which one was Leonard?

Above her, she counted at least six, maybe seven Fantans, silhouetted below a thick cloud deck moving over the field. The Fantans were sandwiched below the clouds at two thousand feet, going in every direction. Now she realized the two Warthogs were on opposite sides of a big circle on the deck, daring the Fantans to come down and engage in their environment. She sucked in her breath as one rolled up on a wing and turned sharply. For a moment, she was certain its wingtip had brushed the ground. It accelerated straight ahead, breaking out of the circle.

A streak of smoke reached up from the ground toward the Fantans—a Stinger missile. A Fantan flared and tumbled to earth, exploding on the far side of the runway.

The Warthog that was going straight ahead pulled up and a Sidewinder leaped from under its wing. The speed of the missile surprised her as it homed on a Fantan. The Warthog twisted on its axis, diving for the ground, as the second Fantan exploded. Two more Stingers leaped skyward from their bunkered positions—positions she had helped site. A third Fantan disappeared in a fireball.

To her horror, a Fantan swooped down on one of the Warthogs in a hit-and-run attack. This time, she heard a machine gun-like rumble as the Fantan fired its twenty-three-millimeter cannon. The Warthog tumbled into the ground and exploded in a long trail of fire and smoke. She couldn't move—was it Leonard or his wingman, Jake Trisher? She didn't know.

The other Warthog turned into the escaping Fantan that was turning hard to the right at five hundred feet above the ground. This time, the fight was farther away and she saw smoke bloom from the Warthog's nose and the Fantan come apart before she heard the cannon fire.

Then it was over. The Warthog was alone in the sky.

The lone A-10 climbed to a thousand feet and circled to land. Waters fell to her knees as uncontrollable tremors wracked her body. An arm was around her, holding her tight. It was Pontowski. "Tango's okay," he said. He had followed the fight over the radios in the bunker.

She looked at him, relief flooding her eyes. "Not again," she whispered. "Please, God, not again." He held her tight, not saying a word.

Tango Leonard was standing in the bunker next to Pontowski. His flight suit was streaked with dark sweat lines and the marks left by his oxygen mask were imprinted in his face. He held a half-empty water bottle. He had flown less than fifteen minutes and fatigue weighed heavily on him, yet his voice was normal as he recounted the mission. "They don't want to come below a thousand feet," he said. "My best guess is that they don't train for low level." For a Warthog driver, flying low was a way of life. "Also, they didn't really rack up the gs in turns. I'd say they don't wear g-suits. Both give us an advantage, but I got to tell you, they are gutsy jocks."

"They'll learn fast," Pontowski replied. "We'll have to stay clear of them."

"We've done okay so far," Leonard said. "One for six is not a bad exchange. And they didn't get a single bomb off."

Waters wanted to shout at him. "That 'one' you mentioned," she finally said, "was Jake Trisher." No one answered her. The radios squawked as Maggot recovered from the first mission and four more Warthogs taxied out. The war was going on and they would have to grieve later for their lost comrade.

For Pontowski, the numbers were back: 45 pilots, 29 aircraft. Will there be more? he thought. He knew the answer. He scanned the boards, looking ahead. When would he send Leonard back into the maw of combat? When would he go? "Tango," he said, "take a break. I want you to lead the eleven hundred Go. Goat Gross will be on your wing."

"You bet, Boss," Leonard said, leaving the bunker. Waters followed him out, needing a fresh breath of air. "You okay?" he asked.

"No," she answered, "I'm not okay. I saw it and for a moment, I thought it was you."

"No way," he told her. Like all fighter pilots, he trusted his ability to get him through.

"But Jake . . ." Her voice trailed off.

"Jake had a very bad day," he said.

She stared at him, not understanding. She had heard his words but failed to understand the deep hurt they masked.

"John, I love you—" She bit her words off, not saying what she thought. She did love him, but she couldn't watch him die. He didn't need to hear that, only the first.

## Wednesday, October 16
## Near Jingxi, China

Lieutenant Colonel Sung Fu swore at the driver as the wheels of the truck spun in the mud. The paved road had ended less than fifty feet behind them and they were already stuck. He ordered the driver to stop before the wheels were buried up to the rear axle and climbed out of the cab to check on the road conditions for himself. The other eleven vehicles of his convoy were halted on the paved road.

He slogged down the road, the rain soaking through his cheap raincoat. He muttered the Chinese equivalent of "Bugger me" and returned to the convoy. As usual, his orders were crisp and clear. One squad of men was ordered back to the town of Jingxi to requisition tractors, and failing that, oxen or water buffalo. Another squad was sent to the nearby village to gather a work detail, and a scouting party was sent ahead to reconnoiter the road.

The scouting party returned first, with the good news that

the dirt road improved a half kilometer ahead when it started to climb into the hills. The drainage was better. The squad sent to the village returned with a hundred villagers and within moments, his lead truck was pushed out of the mud and was grinding forward.

Sung talked to the head villager, an old man named Li Jiyu, who swore the rain was unusual and normally they were well into the transition from the wet summer monsoon to the dry winter monsoon. Li Jiyu was very convincing and led Sung to believe the rains would soon pass. But Li Jiyu knew better. Li was Zhuang, not Han Chinese like Sung, and only wanted the foreigners out of his village. Unlike his granddaughter, Jin Chu, he could lie easily to foreigners.

When the lead truck was well clear of the mud, Sung motioned the next truck forward. It was one of the transporters, pulling a single thirty-five-foot Guideline missile. The tractor had no trouble pulling the five-thousand-pound missile through the mud and Sung was hopeful they could make up some lost time. They had only come eighty kilometers in twenty-four hours and the intelligence liaison officer sent from Kang's headquarters to spy on him was writing furiously in his notebook whenever he thought Sung was not looking. The fool, Sung thought, only knows how to criticize and shout slogans. Let him get his fine boots dirty.

He left three soldiers to wait for the squad sent to Jingxi to requisition tractors or oxen. They had orders to catch up with him as soon as possible, but no later than tomorrow morning. With the proper scowl to insure the three didn't desert, he ordered the convoy forward, into the mountains.

The convoy made good time until it hit the first of the switchbacks. Worried about the condition of the road, Sung sent the lead truck ahead. The sound of the truck's laboring engine as it ground up the steep road echoed over them. Then he heard it stop and the unmistakable sound of shifting gears as it tried to rock its way out of a mudhole. The engine revved and Sung heard shouting followed by a crashing sound.

The sound grew louder and the truck tumbled out of the heavy foliage, twisting and flattening everything in its path as it rolled down the hill. Sung watched in horror as it slammed into one of the transporters, knocking its valuable missile off the cradle. Before he could react, the truck burst into flame, engulfing the transporter in a wall of fire.

The men dived for cover as the missile's three-hundred-pound high-explosive warhead exploded and sent a shower of fragments into the transporters next to it in line, destroying them. The heat from the fire forced Sung back into the trees. The rain came down harder, and a cloud of steam rolled off the burning trucks and into the valley below them.

Sung's face was frozen granite hard as he watched his convoy burn. Of the six missiles he had started with, only two were left. As best as he could tell, the fuel truck and Fan Song radar van were undamaged. Through the smoke and steam, he caught a glimpse of the liaison officer from Kang's headquarters snapping a photo of the destruction.

"Bring the driver to me," he yelled. Men hurried up the road to do as he ordered. The liaison officer worked his way past the burning hulks and stood back, waiting to see what would happen next. Sung Fu was the most unfortunate man he had ever met.

Within minutes, the men were back, carrying the injured truck driver. "He was thrown out of the truck when it rolled over the edge," a sergeant explained. "But it crushed his legs."

Sung knelt beside the driver and questioned him, his voice flat and toneless. It had been a stupid thing. The driver was maneuvering around a tight hairpin turn and the truck had lost traction. He had tried to break free by shifting from reverse to forward, rocking the truck. He had started to move and gunned the engine. But the truck had slipped sideways and tumbled over the edge. Sung stood up and looked at his men. His eyes finally came to rest on the liaison officer. He pointed at the hapless driver on the ground. "Throw him in the cab of his truck," he ordered.

"It's still burning," a sergeant said.

"Do it now," Sung barked.

The driver's screams carried over the hillside as the men carried him over to his burning truck. Sung walked down to the liaison officer, drew his pistol, and shot him in the head. "Throw him in also," he commanded. "They both died in this unfortunate accident. Go to the village and bring every man, woman, and child who can work." He had two missiles left and they would complete his mission—no matter what.

## Wednesday, October 16
## Near Bose, China

The two men stood side by side outside the hilltop observation post, casually talking, gesturing at the wide, low valley below them, oblivious to the misting rain. They could have been surveyors measuring the land as one held a folded map and made constant reference to it. Their words were calm and relaxed and carried no hint of the tension swirling around them. They were the eye in the center of a typhoon.

Spread out on the valley floor was a scene reminiscent of the battlefields of World War I. Thousands of bodies were lying in grim contortions of death. Closer, on the slope in front of them, and entangled in rows of barbed wire, were hundreds more. "We first heard bugles," the commander of the First Battalion told Kamigami. "It was the signal to attack. They came from there." He pointed to a low ridge behind a village. "Nothing we did stopped them. They just kept coming, wave after wave. Then the Americans arrived with their Silent Guns." He made a chopping sign with his hand. His meaning was obvious, and the carnage in the valley was mute testimony to the effectiveness of CBU-58s against troops caught in the open.

Kamigami asked a few questions before returning to the four Humvees that made up his mobile command post. He huddled with his operations and intelligence officers, checking on the location of Kang's tanks and field guns. The intelligence officer keyed his radio and spoke directly to the J-STARS module at Bose Airfield. The tanks and heavy artillery were still well to the rear and not moving forward. The lowering weather explained why no enemy aircraft had been detected.

"This doesn't make sense," Kamigami said. "What is Kang up to?" He studied a chart before making his decision. "This is the most direct route to the bridge."

The First Battalion's commanding officer looked worried

as a lone bugle call sounded from across the valley. It was picked up by two others. "That is the way it started last time," he said.

Kamigami told his ASOC officer to call for A-10s. The man spoke into his radio and listened to the reply. He scribbled some numbers down, jerked off his headset, and ran over to Kamigami. "Two A-10s are launching now. Two more will follow and then two more." Panic spread across his face and he pointed to the sky. "The weather is a problem. Visibility is down to three miles and the ceiling is dropping." The dull whomp of outgoing mortar rounds silenced him. Kamigami nodded and headed for the battalion's observation post, his radio/telephone operator and operations officer right behind him.

He had to bend over in the low bunker to see through the observation ports. The scene stunned him. "My God," he said in English.

"Exactly," the First Battalion's CO replied.

A dark, moving mass was coming toward them. It was a tide of humanity flowing in their direction. He watched, fascinated, sure he was caught in a time warp. This was not modern warfare but right out of the history books. "Korea," he muttered, drawing the only analogy he could. The mortars laid a continuous mortar barrage, chewing up the attackers. But still the mass surged forward. This was not the way he fought.

His operations officer was glued to the radio and told him the first two Warthogs had checked in with the ASOC. In the distance, over the mortars and clatter of machine guns, he heard the jets. On cue, the mortars stopped as an A-10 swooped into the valley and pickled off two canisters of CBUs. Bright flashes sparked in the moving mass—the bomblets exploding. Still the mass moved forward.

The second Warthog rolled in and walked its entire load across the moving front. Did he see a pause in the mass of humanity? He wasn't sure. The first Warthog was back and pickled off the remainder of its ordnance. Accuracy didn't matter. A machine gun next to the observation post started to rattle as the first wave came into range. And still they came.

A Warthog made a strafing pass, its nose wrapped in smoke. Kamigami heard the sharp crack of the bullets breaking the sound barrier as they passed the observation post before he heard the cannon firing. The men on the receiving end of the cannon died before they heard either.

The second flight of Warthogs checked in and repeated the massacre. What was left of the first wave reached the barbed wire and tried to cut through it. The battalion's CO spoke into his own radio to organize his defenses as the first attackers broke through. Kamigami fought the urge to get involved in the fighting, to lead men into the maw of death. But that was not his job.

He detached himself from the actual fighting and forced himself to take the big view. A few Warthogs made the difference and as long as they were overhead, the attack was doomed to failure. So why do it?

He put the question aside and concentrated on the battle that was playing out before him. The defenders had wiped out the few men who made it through the wire and were regrouping for the second wave that was coming toward them. Kamigami hated being a spectator.

The attack was an hour old when a fourth flight of Warthogs flew overhead. The ceiling was so low that they barely cleared the hilltops as they dropped into the valley for the attack. One popped to roll in on a target and disappeared into the overcast.

Forward movement in the valley ground to a halt and small, narrow currents of movement started to flow in the opposite direction. The tide had turned and the attack was over.

What kind of general wastes his men like this? Kamigami thought. He tried to get into Kang's head, much as Trimler had taught him. "Why?" he muttered aloud, in English. He was also thinking in English.

The First Battalion's CO answered in the same language. "Kang drives them with fear. These are not his best soldiers, but cannon fodder he has dredged from the big cities— Canton, Shanghai."

Kamigami switched back to Cantonese. "Kang is a better general than this. He wants to focus our attention here." He checked his watch. "It took them ten hours to regroup and mount a second attack. I expect the third attack to come in ten to twelve hours, probably around two o'clock this morning."

"Can the A-10s fly close air support at night?" the colonel asked.

"Not in this weather," Kamigami answered.

"Without A-10s," the colonel answered, "I may not be able to stop them." Close air support had broken the momentum of the human wave Kang had thrown at them, but even then, it had been a narrow victory.

Kamigami raised his binoculars and swept the battlefield. "They have taken heavy casualties. How many men do they have to waste?" He dropped his binoculars and studied his map. "The next attack will probably be a heavy probing action to discover how weak we are. Resist and make them pay for every forward step they take. I'm almost certain the main attack will not be here."

"But where?" the colonel asked.

That is the question I can't answer, Kamigami thought. At least not yet. But I know the objective. In his mind's eye he saw the bridge of the angry dragons near Bose, the bridge that was the gateway to the west.

## Wednesday, October 16
## Bose Airfield

A persistent and very annoying drip of water kept banging on the table in front of Pontowski. He looked at the beams over his head and decided the Gopher Hole was amazingly dry. Rather than contend with the drip, he moved one space to his right, used his helmet as a catch basin, and ignored it.

He stood and stretched. It was almost midnight and he needed to get some rest. What am I missing? he thought. The numbers on the big status board were good. His twenty-nine Warthogs had flown 106 missions and stopped Kang's attack cold. Four Hogs had taken battle damage, two badly, and one would never fly again. He had gone out to check on it and wondered how Skid Malone ever got it on the ground. But he hadn't lost a single pilot, and that was the real story.

The weatherman posted the next day's forecast on the board. More rain. He walked over to the weatherman's desk for more details. "It's Typhoon Kewa," the young captain explained. "It's turning into the most destructive hurricane of the century. She leveled the Philippines." He traced the typhoon's path. "And it is headed straight for the Gulf of Tonkin. The weather we're getting is the leading edge. It's going to get worse, much worse. Thank God a hurricane dies quickly once it comes ashore. Just be glad we're not on the coast of Vietnam. Hanoi is going to get flooded."

"What about Cam Ranh Bay?" Pontowski asked.

"They're four hundred miles south of Kewa's track. They'll get a good drenching, like us. They should be okay."

"I hope they don't have to evacuate," Pontowski said, more to himself than the weatherman. He heard his name called and turned to see Mazie standing behind him.

"This," she said in a low voice, handing him a message, "just came in from Mr. Carroll."

Pontowski felt his face go hard as he read the message. He handed it to Waters. All he said was, "Call a staff meeting. Now."

The men and women who filed into the bunker were wet and tired. They sensed from the way Pontowski leaned against the edge of a table and stared at the message in his hands that something big was up. The Junkyard Dogs were the last to squeeze in. He came right to the point. "We've been put on alert to pull out of China. We'll have to move fast when the evacuation order comes down."

A voice came from the back of the bunker. "You mean we've got to run away with our tails tucked between our legs?" It was one of the Maintenance officers.

"What about the Chinese?" Charlie Marchioni shouted. "We all know what Kang will do to them. How the hell do they expect us to live with that?" Silence. No one knew how to answer his question.

Ray Byers chimed in. "Colonel, I got to tell you, pulling out sucks." The various comments from around the tent indicated most of his staff agreed with him.

"I don't like it either, Ray," Pontowski admitted. "But we don't have any choice," he added.

"Fuckin' A, Colonel," Byers shouted. "We volunteered to come here so we can fuckin' A decide when to unvolunteer."

Pontowski didn't answer for a few moments as he studied their faces. They had all volunteered to fight in a war far from their own country. But for what? Their country wasn't in danger. He knew what Maggot would say: "Hell, it's the only war we got." That wasn't the reason, not even for Maggot. So what motivated them to stay the course? Most had come to like the Chinese and some, like Marchioni, had found a home. Without exception, they all knew Kang would butcher the Chinese by the thousands if he won. Was that the motivation?

The truth was much more complicated. Like Pontowski, they had volunteered for a variety of reasons. Some were simply bored with their present life, others were looking for any well-paying job, and many needed the challenge. But underneath, Pontowski sensed an understanding. These people knew what was ultimately at stake: They were giving a few Chinese a chance at freedom and maybe, just maybe, they could stop a madman named Kang from setting Asia on fire. It would be a fire that would ultimately burn them all.

"I'm not about to disobey an order," he finally said. "But a commander never loses the right to protect his people." He looked around the room again. "With a little luck, we just might have to fight our way out of here." He hoped he had found the right words. "We've bugged out before, so you know how it's done. Start getting ready."

Mazie and Hazelton waited as the bunker emptied. "I talked to Mr. Carroll on the secure telephone," she said. "We need to talk." Pontowski found a corner and motioned for Waters to join them. "Congress is doing one of its preelection flip-flops," Mazie explained. "The leaders understand what's at stake here and what we're trying to do. But a congresswoman, Ann Nevers—"

"We all know who Nevers is," Pontowski grumbled, interrupting her.

"Anyway," Mazie continued, "Nevers is turning our commitment to the Chinese into a club to beat the administration with. The president is losing political support on this and Mr. Carroll is trying to salvage what he can."

"Do they know," Pontowski said, "how critical the situation is? We may only need a few more days."

"Mr. Carroll knows Kang has got to win now or Beijing will cut a deal with Zou. That will change the entire geopolitical map in the Far East. The problem is Nevers. She's turned Von Drexler into a martyr and has made his death a political issue."

Waters' sharp gasp for air stopped her. "They don't know . . . I mean Von Drexler was a . . ." she stammered. Then, "You need to see what I found in his quarters." She marched out of the bunker, leaving a very confused Pontowski behind.

"Another thing," Mazie said. "Went and I have been ordered back to Washington. Mr. Carroll is getting his ducks all lined up." Her face was pained. "It's all coming apart."

Pontowski shook his head. "We tried," he said. "Dark operations have never been our long suit."

Waters was back, carrying a video camera and three videocassettes. She slipped one into the camera and hit the play button. "Here," was all she said, handing the camera to Pontowski. "I don't need to see it again."

He looked in the eyepiece. His lips moved but no words came out. At one point he flinched. "No wonder," he muttered. He stopped the camera and paused before handing it to Mazie. "It's VD," he said. "Not pretty."

Mazie held the camera up and hit the play button. The image on the small LED screen inside the camera was sharp enough for her to make out a naked Von Drexler and two equally naked women. "He was a disturbed man," she said, turning the camera off, feeling very sick. "Mr. Carroll can use this to muzzle Nevers." She thought for a few moments. "Sara, since you were with Von Drexler when he committed suicide and found the tapes, you need to come with us."

"I've kept a war diary for the unit that might be useful," Waters said.

"You're going with them," Pontowski ordered. He scanned the status boards. A C-130 was inbound on a cargo run and the ceiling and visibility was still good enough for the Hercules to land. But it would be tight. "I want you all on that Hercules," he told them. Damn, he thought, it will take them at least twenty-four hours to get to Washington— if they were lucky. Maybe Mazie had enough ammunition to delay a withdrawal. Would those tapes and Sara's war diary do the trick?

"Sara," he said, capturing her attention by not using her nickname. "Don't plan on coming back. Get packed." He wasn't sure if the look on her face was relief or sadness. She hurried out of the bunker to say good-bye to Leonard.

## Thursday, October 17
## The bridge, near Bose, China

The four Humvees moved down the muddy road, their big V-8 engines pulling them through the mud. Their windshield wipers were on high speed, beating back and forth, barely keeping ahead of the pounding rain. The lead vehicle reached the paved road and turned westward, racing for the bridge, six miles away.

Kamigami sat in the passenger seat, his body a rigid spike. In the rear, the radios chattered, reporting a series of heavy probing actions along the southern flank. It was exactly 0200 hours and the sector in front of the First Battalion, the area he had reinforced, was quiet. Where will it be? he kept asking himself.

The driver slowed and worked his way through the bridge's defenses, allowing the other three vehicles to catch up. They were almost to the bridge. Ahead, he saw one of the dark Mercedeses Zou preferred as a staff car. He had reached his destination.

The rear door of the Mercedes swung open and Jin Chu climbed out. She stood in the rain, waiting for him. For a moment, Kamigami sat in the Humvee, a deep ache freezing him there. Then he got out and moved toward her. The rain beat on her bare head, plastering her dark hair to her back. And he knew he loved her, irrationally, uncaring, and without conditions. They were inches apart but did not touch.

"I got your message," he said. "This is a bad time. I'm needed there." He jerked his head to the east.

She lowered her eyes. "There is a woman you must hear," she said. She led him to the open door of the Mercedes. Inside, an old woman leaned forward and started talking. He had a hard time understanding her dialect but her meaning was clear. The main attack would thrust up the valley blocked by the First Battalion. This time, it would be led by tanks.

"Where did they come from?" he demanded, not believing her.

"They were moved one at a time and hidden in caves," the old woman explained. "My son says there are sixty-two tanks hidden behind our village." The look on Kamigami's face frightened the woman and she couldn't speak. Her throat contracted in spasms as she looked into the face of a demon.

"Please," Jin Chu said, "tell the rest. He won't hurt you."

She gulped hard. "The men who came in the tanks, they have taken our daughters. They say they will release them at dawn today because they will no longer need them."

"Is she telling the truth?" Kamigami asked. Jin Chu nodded, and he believed her. "Sixty-two tanks," he growled. "We can't stop them."

"But the Silent Guns have always stopped them before," Jin Chu said.

"They can't fly in this weather," he said.

"Is there nothing you can do?"

He nodded. "I must go. There isn't much time." He wanted to hold her, but she was no longer his. "Where will you be?"

"I am going to Kunming." She didn't say what they both knew—that she was going to Zou. "May May is with the Americans." She got into the car and Kamigami held the door open for a moment, searching for the right words. In the dark, reaching through the rain, her hand touched his face. "You are my love," she whispered.

He closed the car door and stood back. He would never see her again.

Kamigami listened on the radio as his Fourth Battalion reported bugle calls. "The beginning of a human wave attack," his operations officer said. More reports came in, confirming an attack was underway on the extreme southern flank.

Is Kang trying an end run? Kamigami thought. Or was the old woman right? It was still dark and he was standing beside his Humvee under a hastily rigged canvas canopy. The rain gushed off the low side of the tarp, reminding him of a curtain. What's behind the curtain? he thought. Should he reinforce the Fourth Battalion before it was too late? A gut instinct told him to wait. "Ask the Fourth," he told his operations officer, "if they need reinforcement."

The answer "Not at this time" was the clue he needed. The attack on the Fourth was a feint. He ordered every TOW missile team in his regiment to the First Battalion. They were going to take on tanks without A-10s.

He jumped into his Humvee and the driver gunned the engine, shooting through the curtain of water and skidding onto the muddy track that led to the First Battalion. The other three Humvees were right behind. His driver had memorized the road and hurtled the Humvee at forty-five miles an hour through the night. He was a microtactician and Kamigami trusted him to do his job. Within minutes, he was at the First Battalion and explaining the situation to the CO when four TOW missile teams from the Second Battalion arrived. He sent them back up the road, toward the bridge, and told them to dig in.

The first glow of approaching dawn lightened the heavy clouds in front of him as the low rumble of diesel engines drifted up the valley. "Are they moving?" his operations officer asked. "I don't hear the clank of tank tracks."

"The mud muffles the sound," Kamigami said. Two more TOW missile teams reported in. He sent them to the bridge. He gathered his small battle staff around him. His Cantonese was still heavily accented and he suffered from a limited vocabulary, but they understood him perfectly as he laid out how they would withdraw in force and fall back on the bridge. More TOW teams arrived and he sent them forward to reinforce the First Battalion.

He hurried to the observation post and arrived in time to see the lead tanks slogging up the valley toward them. He frowned—the rain and dark had allowed the tanks to close to within a thousand meters. A tank stopped and fired a round. Immediately, the smoke trail of a TOW missile streaked across the land and the tank disappeared in a flash of flame and smoke. The tank's round whistled harmlessly overhead. "They stop to fire," he told the men. "That's when we can kill them." The men cheered but he said nothing. There were too many tanks supported with infantry. And all were too close.

He needed a miracle and wasn't sure if the rain would give it to him.

# CHAPTER 22

Friday, October 18
Bose Airfield, China

"This place is a fuckin' swamp," Leonard groused to Pontowski as they waded across the low area between the mess tent and the command bunker. A light rain was still falling, the last of the deluge that had poured down on the base during the last twenty-four hours. "What's it like in the Gopher Hole?"

"Not too bad," Pontowski answered. "The Dogs got a pump working, Marchioni's villagers laid duckboards down and built a dike around the place. We're fairly dry."

"We need to build a dike around the runway," Leonard said.

"Mother Nature does swing a big bat," Pontowski said. "The weatherman says Kewa may have set a record."

"I can believe that," Leonard grumbled. The rain was the last of Typhoon Kewa, which had hit the coast of China two hundred miles southeast of Bose. Kewa had spent its fury on southern China, sending heavy rains and high winds far inland, making it impossible to fly. The wing had not turned a wheel in over twenty-four hours. But the same rain had also bogged the fighting down. "Is the evacuation still on hold?"

"Yep," Pontowski answered. "No official word yet. The C-130 was the last plane to take off and we got a few out on it."

"I'm glad Sara was one of them," Leonard mumbled. A sad undertone told Pontowski Leonard had mixed feelings about Waters' leaving. "Maybe it is time for us to cut and run."

"Not yet," Pontowski growled. "Not yet." Leonard's head jerked at the hard anger in Pontowski's reply. They waded through the water in silence and stepped over the sandbag dike surrounding the Gopher Hole. A pump chugged in the background, pumping water out of the bunker. Trimler was standing by the entrance, waiting for them. "G'morning, General," Pontowski called as they snapped a salute.

"Good morning, my ass," Trimler said, returning the salute. "Bad news all around. I've received orders to shut the MAAG down and get the hell out of China today. And some genius at Fort Fumble decided to place the AVG back under my command. That means you go with the MAAG."

"I wondered how they were going to solve the problem of command and control during the evacuation," Pontowski said. "Now I know." Trimler had a few choice words to say about the orders coming out of the National Military Command Center in the Pentagon. The Army general was articulate, competent, and hard-nosed. But more important, he responded quickly to changing situations and learned from his, and others', mistakes. Pontowski listened carefully, for Trimler was all that a general should be. And he was learning.

"It's official then?" Pontowski asked.

"Official as all hell," Trimler barked. He turned and looked over the airfield. "Our timing absolutely sucks. We're so damn close and we're blowing it at the last minute. Beijing has put out feelers to Zou and wants to talk accommodation."

"That doesn't make sense," Leonard protested. "Kang is Beijing's man and he's winning the war."

"Barely," Trimler replied. "Hell, Chinese politics change quicker than the weather. If Zou can hold on a little longer . . . who knows."

The three men walked down into the bunker. Pontowski was surprised to see Trimler's staff from the MAAG crowded around the walls. He raised an eyebrow. "You are serious about getting out," he said.

"The shooting's less than fifteen miles from here," Trimler observed. He stepped up to the situation map on the wall. "The rain and mud saved the New China Guard's ass. But Kang is still pushing hard. He knows he's running out of time and has forced the New China Guard up against the bridge. At last report, only Kamigami's First Regiment is on the eastern side. Once they're across, Kamigami will blow the bridge. That will force Kang to make an end run to the south. With the break in the weather, you can start flying again. That would slow him down. Maybe long enough for Zou to cut a deal with Beijing."

"Have you told Washington all this?" Pontowski asked.

"Repeatedly," Trimler grumbled. "Ah, shit." There was despair in his voice. "It's not going to happen that way," he moaned. "We were so damn close."

Pontowski's eyes narrowed as he stared at the map. "We're going to need airlift to get out of here. At least twelve to fifteen sorties by the C-130s. That will take a day or two. And we're going to need fuel for the Hogs. That means at least one KC-10 has to come in. No reason for those aircraft to come in empty, is there? A last-minute emergency resupply might keep the New China Guard fighting for a few more days."

Pontowski's transportation officer chimed in. "One problem, sir. All our loading equipment was destroyed. We need one forklift, and the KC-10 will have to fly in an on board loader."

"What the hell is an on board loader?" Leonard wondered.

"It's like a big erector set the KC-10 can carry," the transportation officer told him. "The load crew swings it out the cargo door on its own davit and they assemble it on the spot. It sorta looks like the skeleton of an elevator. Takes about four hours to assemble. Then they can off-load the jet in about forty-five minutes."

"Why don't they just push the pallets out the door?" Leonard asked.

"It's a seventeen-foot drop," the major explained. "It's

not easy, and it's asking for trouble, since a loaded pallet can weigh up to sixty-five hundred pounds."

Trimler shook his head. "I don't think Washington is going to buy it. They want us out. Now."

"An old friend helped once," Pontowski said. "Maybe he can help again." He picked up the phone and jabbed at the buttons. Six minutes later, he was talking to Cyrus Piccard, his grandfather's best friend and a former secretary of state. He explained what he wanted, listened, and hung up. "Pick isn't too hopeful," he said.

"Was that Cyrus Piccard?" Trimler asked, amazement in every word.

"Yep," Pontowski answered. "He said he'd do what he could, but Congress isn't in one of its braver moods right now. Too close to election."

"Don't you just love using political influence?" Trimler muttered.

"It's a beautiful thing," Pontowski shot back.

## Friday, October 18
## The Sino-Vietnamese border, China

Lieutenant Colonel Sung Fu stood on the edge of the road as the first truck crested the long uphill grade and headed into the narrow mountain pass. A swarm of villagers moved with the truck, carrying branches and brush to shove under the wheels at the first sign of slowing. They had learned the hard way that it was easier to keep the vehicles moving than to dig them out after they had mired down.

His eyes narrowed as a villager collapsed from exhaustion. Should he discipline the lazy dog to motivate the others? He held his temper when he saw his senior captain hurrying toward him. "Colonel Sung," the captain panted, "the road is dry through the pass and there is an excellent area for a missile site on the other side." He waited expectantly.

First things first, Sung thought, turning his attention back to the malingering villager. A kick in the ribs was warranted. He walked over to the prostrate man and gave him a

swift kick. Nothing. He bent over and examined the man.
He was dead. Sung stood up, angry with all the villagers.
They were nothing, beasts of burden to be used as he willed.
He walked, cooling his anger. When he reached the edge of
the road, he looked over the mountains. It struck him that
he had done the impossible to bring a surface-to-air missile
battery through those mountains. It had been a Herculean
task. Reluctantly, he ordered a break and told his men to
feed the villagers. They had earned it.

While his company and the villagers ate, the senior
captain escorted Sung through the pass and onto a broad
plateau. Sung checked his map and allowed a tight smile.
The plateau was right on the border. "Perfect," he said.
"Bring the trucks forward immediately." The captain hurried to carry out the order while Sung selected a site.

The work went smoothly and Sung's two remaining
Guideline missiles were moved into position and transferred from the transporters onto their launch pedestals.
While Sung's men worked on the missile site, the villagers
built a bivouac area. Finally, they were ready for an
operational check. The portable generator was fired up and
he waited inside the radar control van.

Sung was a commander, not a technician, but even he
realized something was wrong with the circuitry on his
number-two missile. His eyes narrowed into slits as he
listened to his men discuss the problem. Finally, the senior
captain approached him, fear written plainly on his face. He
gulped. "It's the battery in the number two-missile."

"So?" Sung replied.

"It has failed and must be replaced."

"Was it replaced during the last inspection?"

"Of course, sir," the captain said. There was indignation
in his voice. Sung couldn't believe it: His senior captain was
actually showing some backbone. "Moisture caused by the
rain reached the battery pack."

"Then replace it," Sung ordered.

"Our spares were destroyed in the fire. I have sent a
runner back to base for another one."

Sung fought down the urge to find and punish the person
responsible for the battery's failure. But an inner voice

warned him that it was not the fault of humans. It was his own bad luck. "You have done well," he said. He couldn't believe what he was saying. "Secure the system and take care of our men. They are tired and need a rest. Feed the villagers and send them home." He turned to leave but stopped. "Pay them well for their work." He walked out of the radar control van, ignoring the captain's reaction.

The rain had stopped falling and he removed his raincoat. When will my luck change? he wondered.

Less than thirty miles to the south of Lieutenant Colonel Sung's missile site, the orbiting AWACS reached the northern end of its orbit and turned away from the border, heading south, back into Vietnam. It flew at a leisurely speed, conserving fuel. When it reached the end of a ten-minute leg, it was 250 miles from Bose, at the extreme edge of its radar coverage.

The copilot, since the pilot was asleep, tweaked the autopilot and banked the aircraft into a gentle turn, reversing course and heading back to the north. The navigator cross-checked the AWACS' navigation system with the GPS, the satellite-based global positioning system. GPS satellite coverage was marginal over Vietnam and occasionally the navigator could not get a good reading. But it always cured itself in a few minutes. The navigator didn't worry about it as the inertial navigation system on board the AWACS was highly accurate and rarely required updating. The flight crew was bored silly.

In the back of the AWACS, the mission crew commander, Major Marissa LaGrange, was anything but bored. As usual, she was tethered by her long communications extension cord as she stalked the aisles behind the consoles. She was talking to the J-STARS aircraft on the secure radio as her ASO demanded her attention. "Major Mom," he shouted, "we have thirty-eight hostiles tagged up. All tracking for Bose."

"Say type," she snapped.

"Beagles, Fantans, and . . . and . . . holy shit! J-8s!" His announcement was electrifying. The Beagles and Fantans were light bombers but the J-8 was China's most sophisticated fighter. The Mach 2 aircraft was an enlarged version of the MiG-21 that had been updated with a modern avionics system supplied by the United States.

"Warn Bose that an attack is coming their way," LaGrange ordered. "The RO is talking to them on secure." The RO, or radio operator, actually smiled as he linked the ASO with the Americans at Bose. From his position, he monitored all transmissions and knew exactly what was going down.

"Moose," LaGrange said over net one of the intercom, "start talking to the F-15s. I want them in a CAP overhead in case those J-8s get interested in us."

The pilot on the flight deck came awake. "Major Mom, what's going on?"

LaGrange owed him an answer. Besides, it kept him awake and gave her time to think. "Trouble, big trouble. The J-STARS reports heavy ground traffic moving forward and we've tagged up beaucoup hostiles. Most of them are air-to-mud and headed for Bose. But we've got—" she looked over the shoulder of the ASO and counted the red upside-down Vs on his scope, "eight J-8s escorting them."

"Not good," the pilot replied. He remembered only too clearly when J-8s had forced them into a retrograde maneuver over the South China Sea. "We don't need them coming after us."

"Not to worry," LaGrange assured him.

## Friday, October 18
## Bose, China

Pontowski was on the flight line talking to the crew chiefs and wrench benders from Maintenance when the air raid siren began to wail. He jumped into his pickup truck, jammed on his helmet, and raced for the Gopher Hole. The heavy blast door at the entrance was still open when he reached the bunker. Where did that door come from? he wondered. He knew the answer—the Junkyard Dogs.

Leonard was sitting at the center console and gave him a quick update. "The AWACS reports thirty-eight bandits heading our way, seventeen minutes out. I'm scrambling as many Hogs as possible to get them airborne and away from the base."

"Who's up for air defense?" Pontowski asked, recalling how Leonard and Jake Trisher had broken up the last attack on the airfield.

Leonard shook his head. "They're escorted by J-8s. They'd eat us alive."

Pontowski's mouth compressed into a thin line. Leonard had made the right decision. But he didn't like it. They only had ten Stinger missiles, two Hawk missiles, and one antiquated thirty-seven-millimeter antiaircraft cannon for base defense. They were going to take a pounding.

But the Junkyard Dogs had other ideas. The four went into a well-rehearsed drill with Marchioni's villagers. Little Juan Alvarez, the Mexican-American who could have been a matador, and Big John Washington, the African-American built like a fireplug, worked with a group of villagers at the decoy airfield they had built a kilometer from the air base. They ripped camouflage netting off a weird collection of boxes, pipes, junked vehicles, and shacks. A specially equipped dump truck drove back and forth spreading a mixture of lime and dirt into a long strip that resembled a runway. Another truck raced around the area, setting up radar reflectors. The reflectors were arranged to create the pattern of an airfield on the inbound bombers' radar.

On the ground, the phony airfield looked like a surrealistic collection of junk that wouldn't fool anyone. But from the air, the Junkyard Dogs had created a very authentic-looking airfield.

While Alvarez and Washington labored to make the decoy field visible, Byers and Larry Tanaka worked with the Americans and fifty of the villagers to conceal the main base. They spread camouflage netting, moved trucks and vehicles out of sight, and spread brush and vegetation across the runway. They were still working when the first Fantans zoomed overhead, heading for the fake airfield.

Pontowski glanced upward at the heavy beams over his head when he heard the first bomb explode. No one had to tell him it had missed the base. He shot a look in the direction of Waters' desk, where she had sat running base defense. Her bank of telephones and radios were quiet.

There was no damage to report. The bombs continued to fall and still no damage reports came in. Finally, it was quiet and the all clear sounded.

He fought down the urge to go outside and check for himself. Instead, he took his cue from Trimler and waited. A sergeant handed him a message and he wished he had gone outside. The message was from the National Military Command Center in the Pentagon and ordered him to cease all operational flying. "The assholes," he muttered as he handed the message to Trimler. "This is hard to take right after getting the livin' bejesus bombed out of us."

"They missed, remember," Trimler said laconically as he read the message. "What's called for here is commonly called the 'Fuck you very much' answer. You need to send a message back asking, one, are you being denied the right to self-defense? two, where is the airlift and emergency resupply you requested earlier? and three, who is assuming responsibility for the evacuation? since they have taken it away from you."

"They haven't taken away my responsibility for evacuation," Pontowski protested.

Trimler nodded a reply. "True, but if you accuse them of it, they've got to scramble to prove they haven't. My guess is you'll be allowed to fly sorties in self-defense by—" he checked the master clock on the wall, "noon at the latest. Getting the airlift will take a little longer."

Pontowski sent the message and in less than twenty minutes he had authorization to fly all the sorties he needed for self-defense. There was no word about the airlift or emergency resupply. He still had much to learn from the general.


## Friday, October 18
## The White House, Washington, D.C.

Bill Carroll gulped his second cup of early morning coffee, grabbed his cane, and stormed around his office, venting his anger on Congresswoman Ann Nevers and her latest political ally, James Finlay, the chief of staff he had fired.

Mazie folded her hands and waited patiently. She was very much aware of Hazelton sitting next to her and the way he looked at her from time to time. It sent a warm feeling through her and she wanted to be alone with him. Pay attention to business, she told herself.

"Finlay knows exactly what information to feed her," Carroll groused, "and he'll give it the spin she wants."

"I was hoping," Mazie said, "that these tapes would bring her around."

"Videotapes don't carry much weight with Nevers," Carroll replied. "It didn't work the first time, remember?"

Of course, she remembered the time she had shown Nevers the videotape that documented Kang's brutality. Nevers had been reasonable at first and moderated her scathing criticism of the administration. It had been a total weather change to find Nevers dealing with the truth. Then she recruited James Finlay to her cause and resumed her crusade.

Carroll stopped in front of his desk and picked up one of the videocassettes. "Besides, this is pure pornography, and I'm not about to use it."

"Actually," Hazelton said, "it's sadomasochism. You need a psychologist to explain what is involved."

Carroll snorted, threw the cassette down, and lurched back to his chair. "Damn," he muttered. The pain in his leg was intense. He made a note to have a psychologist at the CIA analyze the tape.

"Is there any good news?" Hazelton asked.

"The worst appears to be over in Hong Kong," Carroll answered. "The British and UN cargo ships relieving Hong Kong have docked and as long as Kang is occupied with Zou in the west, the pressure is off."

"If Kang wins, he'll blockade Hong Kong," Mazie predicted.

Carroll's secretary buzzed and announced the arrival of Cyrus Piccard. Carroll came to his feet and hobbled to the door. He switched the cane to his left hand and shook the hand of the former secretary of state. Piccard was over six feet tall, lanky, hunch-shouldered, and with a full mane of gray hair. His gray-blue eyes were tired and he walked slowly, as befitted a senior statesman. "Sir," Carroll said, "thanks for coming over so early. May I introduce Mazie Kamigami and Wentworth Hazelton?"

Piccard was a gentleman of the old school and did not expect Mazie to rise as they shook hands. "My pleasure, Miss Kamigami. I have read your reports and your excellent monograph on Kang Xun." The old man's eyes twinkled as he held Mazie's hand. He still appreciated beautiful women, especially those with brains and talent. "Very insightful. I knew Kang's father—a terrible, vicious man."

"Ah, Wentworth," he said as Hazelton stood. "So good to see you again. Please give my regards to your mother."

"She doesn't know I'm in town," Hazelton replied.

Again, the sparkle was back in Piccard's eyes. "Perfectly understandable, my boy, perfectly understandable." He sat down, placed the tip of his black ebony cane on the floor between his shoes, and held it upright between his knees. It was a classic Piccard pose. "I am more than glad to be of help," Piccard said, coming to the business at hand. He didn't mention the phone call he had received an hour earlier from Matt Pontowski. "Perhaps you can bring me up to date on what is happening in China?" Piccard actually had an excellent understanding of the stakes they were playing for. Otherwise, he would not have been talking to them.

Carroll quickly recapped the situation and ended with, "It looks like Beijing is ready to deal with Zou if Kang can't win. That's why Kang is pushing so hard. He wins now or ends up in a trash can. The situation has gone critical and Zou has to hold on. Unfortunately, Congress is pressuring us to immediately withdraw our support."

"During a crisis or election year," Piccard observed, "your average congressman prefers an attack of amoebic dysentery to a display of intestinal fortitude. Dysentery is considered normal." The three waited for him to continue. Piccard was famous for his long, rolling speeches.

"Mr. Carroll," Piccard smiled, looking over the gold handle of his black ebony cane, "you are an idealist. Need I remind you that honesty and integrity are not the most efficient ways to deal with Congress? If one of these tapes should 'happen' to find its way into the hands of the right senator, it would become the 'in' scandal of the weekend, creating a lascivious interest in the back corridors of the Capitol.

"Of course, only the 'in' people will have seen the tape, which makes it desirable for everyone to possess a copy. If left to its own devices, Congress will keep the Honorable Ann Nevers fully occupied as she maneuvers to keep the tape out of the hands of the TV scandalmongers. Deals will be cut, promises made, and bets laid. After all, we cannot have the more tasteful scenes enlightening the electorate about the man the Honorable Ann Nevers calls 'a martyr to the American way of life.' What would it do to the image of Congress?" His bushy eyebrows raised expectantly.

"Can you make all that happen?" Carroll asked.

"Of course not," Piccard humphed. "Only Congress can do this to itself." He paused, thinking. "Tuesday I would say. Yes, you definitely have until Tuesday." He rose to leave. "May I have the tape, please?" Carroll handed it to him. "By the way, I mentioned wagers being made. Mrs. Nevers will be successful, you know. Do not bet against her." Then, almost as an afterthought, "Ultimately, she will have her pound of flesh." It was a warning. He smiled graciously and walked slowly out of the office.

Beneath Piccard's courtly southern manner beat the heart of a shark—a very polite, civilized, man-eating shark.

## Saturday, October 19
## Bose Airfield, China

The first C-130 entered the safe passage corridor leading to the airfield shortly after midnight. It slowed to 130 knots, turned on all its lights, and tried to look very friendly. The pilot didn't want a Stinger coming his way. The cargo plane was one mile out when the runway lights flicked on. The pilot slammed the Hercules down, reversed the props, and turned off at the first taxiway. The runway and taxipath lights snapped off, forcing him to stop. The field was totally blacked out. A Follow Me truck blinked its lights at the cockpit and the pilot taxied after the truck, trusting the driver to keep him on the taxiway.

The only spot of light on the parking apron was the C-130

as it prepared to off-load. The pilot kept the engines running while the cargo door at the rear swung up and the loading ramp lowered. A forklift rolled down the ramp, turned around and off-loaded the four remaining pallets of cargo. It wasn't much.

Pontowski's transportation officer spoke to the pilot while the first seventy passengers evacuating the air base climbed on board. The pilot told him that two more C-130s were right behind him and that one KC-10 was scheduled in with a load of fuel and twenty pallets of cargo before morning. The transportation officer gave him a thumbs-up and hopped off the plane. The taxi and takeoff drill went smoothly and the C-130 was airborne six minutes later, heading for Cam Ranh Bay.

The American Volunteer Group was pulling out of China.

"Gear down," Captain Rodrigo Murphy called as he angled his KC-10 into the safe passage corridor. "Where the hell is the field?" he asked. The copilot looked straight ahead, straining to see in the night. Nothing. "Flaps, slats," Murphy said, continuing with the before-landing checklist. Finally, he couldn't wait any longer. "Bose Tower, Prima. I need runway lights if you want me to land." Flying an aircraft weighing over 190 tons on a short approach into an eight-thousand-foot strip was not what the engineers at McDonnell Douglas had in mind when they designed the wide-bodied jet. But this particular twenty-seven-year-old captain was going to do it.

The runway lights came on and the flight engineer sitting behind the copilot gasped. They were high and fast on the glide slope. He solved the problem by concentrating on his panel. Murphy slowed the plane to 150 knots and touched down at 140. He slammed the throttles full aft, deploying the thrust reversers on the outboard engines. He came down heavy on the brakes as the heavy jet ate up the runway, slowly dragging the jet to a halt in six thousand feet.

"One-eighty, two hundred, two-twenty," the flight engineer called, reading the brake temperature gauge. Outside, an acrid-smelling smoke billowed off the main trucks. "Three hundred," the flight engineer said. "Damn, it's still going up." He was worried about a fire and blown tires. Finally, the needle stopped moving at 320 degrees centigrade. "Brake temp stabilized," he told the crew.

"Bose tower," Murphy transmitted over the UHF radio. "Where do you want me to park this puppy?"

"Do a one-eighty on the runway and taxi back to the first turnoff."

"I need 147 feet to turn around," Murphy answered.

"The runway is 150 feet wide," the tower replied.

"Get the Follow Me," Murphy said. "This is gonna be tight."

The Follow Me truck came out of the dark and a man jumped out with a pair of lighted wands to guide the pilot through the turn. He motioned the giant aircraft forward and to the side of the runway. When the right main tire was on the very edge, he motioned Murphy to start a hard left turn. Murphy cracked the throttles and the KC-10 swung around. The nose gear on the KC-10 is seventy-five feet behind the cockpit and the nose of the aircraft was well out over the dirt on the opposite side of the runway as they came through the turn. "Lookin' good," the copilot said.

The nose gear was two feet from the edge when the runway collapsed under the weight. Over the years, the concrete and substrata had decayed and the heavy footprint of the KC-10's nose gear buried the two tires in six feet of cement and gravel. The KC-10 nosed over and stopped, its tail in the air.

The flight engineer muttered, "Ah shit. There go all the atta boys." True to Air Force tradition, this one "Ah shit" incident was going to cancel out a lifetime's worth of "Atta boys," the pats on the back that meant promotion and a career. But promotion was the last thing on Murphy's mind. His jet had blocked the runway.

Pontowski walked around the nose gear of the KC-10, examining the damage. "Any ideas?" he asked Murphy.

The crew of the KC-10 gathered around Pontowski and they worked the problem. Ray Byers joined them and listened as they talked. This is turning into a dick dance, he thought. Somebody needs to take charge. He did. "Look, we got lots of labor here. I'll get all the bodies you need to dig a ramp in front of the nose gear while you offload as much cargo as you can. Then you can taxi it out of its hole."

The staff sergeant in charge of the load team that had flown in on the KC-10 explained how they had to erect the on board loader below the cargo hatch before they could offload the twenty pallets of cargo still on board. If they busted their butts, it would take about five hours. The KC-10's boom operator, who did double duty as a loadmaster, said, "Once we're offloaded, we can transfer fuel to the aft fuselage fuel tanks and make the Gucci Bird tail heavy. That will lighten the load on the nose gear."

Byers examined the concrete around the nose gear. "It's gonna take some time to break through all this shit and dig a ramp. Let's get to it."

Pontowski pulled Murphy and Byers aside. "Don't kill anybody but make it happen—quick."

## Saturday, October 19
## The bridge, near Bose, China

It was dawn when Kamigami climbed out of his Humvee and stood on the eastern approach to the bridge. A mass of refugees were pushing across the single-lane structure, trying to find safety on the other side. He watched impassively as a group of soldiers halted the civilians and cleared a path for his First Battalion. He hated to make the choice between civilians and his soldiers, but there was no alternative.

The PLA had thrown soldiers and then tanks at him, slowly wearing his regiment down. Only the heavy rains and mud had saved them. Thanks to the weather, the tanks had separated from their supporting infantry and had pressed ahead alone. Without enemy soldiers to contend with, his TOW missile teams had picked off the tanks one by one. But they hadn't been able to stop the slow, relentless advance of Kang's forces.

Why, Kamigami thought, am I best at retreating? He pulled into himself, thinking. When should he pull his rear guard across and blow the bridge? What about the refugees still streaming across, running from Kang? Could he condemn them to a certain death? He knew the answer. He gave orders to dig in on the eastern approaches and to rig the bridge with demolitions.

He looked up at the sky. The clouds were still dark and threatening but he could see breaks in the lower deck. He took his poncho off and carefully folded it before he handed it to his driver. The weather had again become neutral and the A-10s could start to fly.

Kamigami tried to gauge the condition of his men as they straggled by. Many were wounded and all were exhausted and dirty. He recognized the sergeant from Horse Company he had spoken to one night on the bank of the Pearl River. "Sergeant Wan," he called, motioning him over.

Wan Yan Fu pulled himself erect and saluted his general. There was a defiant pride in every gesture. "I see you are still looking after your men," Kamigami said.

"I've lost many of them, General," Wan replied. "But we are still fighting."

"What do your men say?" Kamigami asked.

"They talk about being safe on the other side of the bridge. It is rumored that Miss Li said the dragons will protect us if we destroy the bridge."

"Tell your men that is my intention."

"Thank you, sir." Wan saluted again and hurried to catch up with his men.

His small staff was clustered around the communications Humvee, shifting nervously as they waited for him. "Sir," his operations officer said, "the runway at Bose is closed. The A-10s cannot take off."

They had lost the close air support Kamigami had been counting on with the improvement in the weather. He grabbed the situation chart and jabbed a finger at the symbol for enemy tanks advancing toward them. "How current is this position?" he asked.

His intelligence officer answered. "It was reported ten minutes ago."

He turned to his logistics officer. "Do we have any more TOW missiles?"

"Fifteen arrived by airlift last night. I sent two trucks to pick them up. But the refugees . . ." he pointed to the clogged road.

"Get the TOWs here as quick as you can," Kamigami said. "I want all units but Ox Company across the bridge."

"Their captain is seriously wounded," his operations officer said.

"Is he still in command?" Kamigami asked. It was a pointless question. Ox Company was one of the original nine companies of the First Regiment and one of the best. The captain would only give up his command if he were totally incapacitated or dead. "I'm going to Ox Company," he told his staff. He climbed into his Humvee and ordered the driver back up the road. The refugees scattered like leaves in a wind as the Humvee plowed against the flow. He was going to command the rear guard and bring it across the bridge.

Ox Company was withdrawing in order and a mile short of reaching the bridge when three tanks burst out of a hiding place on their right, leveling shanties and a barn. The tanks paused as soldiers surged out of their hiding places and moved into the protective shadow of the tanks. Kamigami saw the developing threat on his flank and ordered a TOW team with their last missile into position while the rest of the company deployed into defensive positions. The wounded captain riding in his Humvee made a soft sound and Kamigami bent over him. "Use the Dragons," the captain whispered. The Dragon was a shoulder-fired, medium-range antitank missile, but it was only marginally effective against a main battle tank like the T-59s coming at them.

"They will have to get very close," Kamigami said. It was tantamount to a suicide mission.

"They will do it," the captain said. Kamigami gave the order to a runner and turned back to the captain. He was dead.

"Take the captain across the bridge," he told his driver. He scanned the advancing tanks and infantry with his binoculars. One of the tanks stopped and its turret traversed in his direction. A smoke trail streaked toward the tank. A Dragon. Before the tank could fire, the Dragon exploded. The smoke cleared and the tank fired as another Dragon homed on the tank. The round whistled harmlessly over Kamigami's head as the tank fireballed.

A mortar barrage rained down on the two remaining tanks, driving the soldiers to cover. Kamigami spoke into his radio and ordered Ox Company to pull back to the bridge in a series of leapfrog maneuvers. When he saw that most of the company was across, he ran for the bridge.

Most of the refugees still on the eastern side of the bridge had found cover when the tanks started shooting and the bridge was clear of traffic when Kamigami sprinted across. He was closely followed by a few soldiers. In the distance, a battered jeep and small truck raced for the bridge. The TOW team was in the jeep and the last of Ox Company was in the truck. Mortars laid a smoke barrage behind them, giving them a little cover as they dashed for the bridge.

Refugees surged across the bridge, desperate to reach safety. The driver of the jeep slowed but kept coming, pushing through the mass of humanity. A rage boiled in Kamigami. He couldn't blow the bridge with all these people still on it. But how could he stop them from pushing onto the bridge? "Lay smoke on the eastern approach," he ordered. Immediately, the mortar teams raised the elevation of their tubes and laid a barrage of smoke on the eastern approach. But it didn't work, and the refugees kept rushing forward, through the smoke, and jamming onto the bridge. The smoke blew away. The lead tank was a kilometer from the bridge.

His face hardened. "Fire one round of canister," he ordered. His stomach twisted into a knot as a single antipersonnel round was lobbed into the mass of refugees still pouring onto the bridge. It worked and the crowd on the eastern approach retreated while the people still on the bridge surged ahead, slowly clearing the bridge.

Kamigami forced himself to raise his binoculars and see the carnage he had ordered. It sickened him. I'm no better than Kang, he thought. These are the people I want to help. Now I'm killing them.

The bridge was almost clear of people as the lead tank clanked up the approach, running over anyone in its path, alive or dead. It advanced onto the bridge, its machine gun firing. *"Now!"* Kamigami shouted, ordering the bridge to be blown. The sergeant holding the detonator twisted the dial. Nothing. The man looked up in desperation and reset the detonator. Again he twisted and still no explosion. The tank was halfway across the bridge.

Kamigami pointed at the jeep-mounted TOW to take out the tank. The jeep maneuvered into position behind an abutment and the missile flashed out of its launcher, flying straight down the lane, directly at the tank, hitting the turret. The explosion blew the turret askew. Then an internal explosion sent the turret arcing over the side of the bridge into the gorge below. A hail of machine gun fire from both sides raked the bridge.

Again, the sergeant tried to detonate the explosives he had placed. No response. Four of Kang's soldiers raced onto the bridge and crawled over the railing, looking for the detonator leads. Kamigami borrowed an M-16 and picked one off, dropping him into the gorge. Then one of the soldiers hanging on the side of the bridge raised his fist, holding a severed wire. Kamigami shot him.

But it was too late. The bridge was still standing.

# CHAPTER 23

**Saturday, October 19**
**Bose Airfield, China**

Pontowski and Leonard stood well back from the KC-10. The huge plane looked even bigger in daylight and Pontowski seriously doubted if they could free the nose gear from the hole it had punched in the concrete. Slowly, he walked toward the load crew, who were still assembling the on board loader. "It does look like a huge erector set," he told Leonard.

The load crew had their shirts off and looked exhausted. "We should be finished in maybe another hour," the staff sergeant in charge of the crew told them.

"What happened to him?" Leonard asked, pointing to one member of the team who was hobbling around, bent over, but still working.

"He tried to do a Rambo and lift too heavy a beam by himself," the sergeant said. "Probably got a hernia."

"We'll take care of him," Pontowski said. He keyed his small radio and called for the flight surgeon. We owe these kids big time, he thought, and all I can do is watch. The oldest was twenty-three, two of them couldn't legally drink, and one was a woman. The irony of it struck home. Everything came down to them.

The pilot of the KC-10, Captain Rodrigo Murphy, joined them. "They're busting their butts, sir," he said. "And the

Chinese, can you believe it?" He gestured in the direction of Marchioni's villagers. Marchioni was with them as they chipped at the concrete with picks and hammers and chisels. They were carving out a long, sloping ramp down to the nose gear. It looked like an impossible task, but they were doing it.

"Are we blowing smoke here?" Leonard asked.

It was a fair question and Pontowski didn't answer at first. He measured the pace of the work going on around him. Should he evacuate by land and try to launch his Warthogs from the dirt? That wasn't an option. The roads were crowded with refugees and the dirt was too soft after all the rain. "Tango," he finally said, "we don't have a choice."

Maggot's voice crackled at him over his personal radio. "Bossman, we need you in the Gopher Hole big time." There was an unusual urgency in Maggot's voice. And Maggot would rather die than sound bad on a radio.

"Be right there," he answered. He turned to Murphy. "Captain, how many bodies can you shove on board the Ten?"

"Pack 'em in like sardines? Maybe five hundred," the pilot answered.

Pontowski called Marchioni over to him. "Charlie, we're taking your village with us. Every man, woman, and child."

"I can't take them back to Vietnam," Murphy protested.

"Fly them to Kunming," Pontowski said. "But I'll be damned if I'm going to leave them here for Kang." He jumped into his truck and raced for the Gopher Hole. The bunker was just as he had left it—a madhouse of activity. Maggot pointed to Trimler, who was standing in the communications section, talking on a radio. "The PLA is on the bridge," the general said.

"I thought Kamigami was going to blow it," Pontowski replied. "If the PLA takes the bridge intact, there's nothing to stop them from reaching the airfield." Panic brushed against his skin. It surprised him how real it felt. Stop that, he chided himself. You're getting tired.

Trimler shook his head. "He tried and failed. There's a destroyed tank on the center span and one hell of a firefight going on. Kamigami's not sure how long he can hold before they push across. Can you bomb the bridge?"

"We could if we could take off," Pontowski answered.

"I see," Trimler said. "Matt, I've rounded up almost a hundred advisors and a few of their Chinese buddies. They're all aching for a piece of the action. We're going to reinforce Kamigami." Pontowski caught the "we" and the quiet determination in the general's voice. "We'll hold until you can get some ordnance on the bridge."

Pontowski wanted to remind Trimler that they had been ordered to cease all combat operations. Instead, he said, "All for self-defense, right?"

"Wrong," Trimler growled. He spun and walked out of the bunker.

Maggot had overheard the conversation. "Boss, I want it. Get Marchioni to peak and tweak a LASTE and I'll drop that bridge faster than a flasher can drop his trou."

"You're the best with the gun," Pontowski answered, "but who's better on the pickle button?"

"Tango and Mako," Maggot grudgingly conceded.

"They got it. Set up a two-ship to go against the bridge as soon as the runway is open. Tango leads."

Maggot sulked until a colonel from the staff of the New China Guard entered the bunker and asked for Trimler. "He left about ten minutes ago," Pontowski told him. "Can we help?"

"Yes, you may," the colonel replied, his English very precise and formal. "Miss Li has information that may be helpful." He spread out a large-scale map of the city of Wuzhou and circled a school complex on the eastern side of the city next to the Pearl River. "Miss Li has learned that Kang has established a permanent headquarters in these buildings." He circled two nearby areas. "He is massing supplies in these areas." The Chinese colonel's face was impassive as he let the information sink in. "Miss Li requested that I tell you Kang will arrive there sometime tonight and will be there until noon. There are no students or faculty at the school." He folded the map, handed it to Pontowski, and walked out of the bunker.

"What do you make of that?" Maggot asked.

Pontowski stared at the scheduling boards. "I want you"—his words were slow, deliberate, and hard—"to plan an attack on that headquarters. Eight Hogs in two flights of four, launch at first light tomorrow morning."

Maggot was surprised at the anger in his commander. This man wanted to kill. "Let me do this one," Maggot pleaded.

"You lead the second flight."

"Who's leading the first four?"

"I am," Pontowski answered.


## Saturday, October 19
## The Sino-Vietnamese border, China

Lieutenant Colonel Sung Fu walked around his missile site. All was in order. His last operational Guideline missile was carefully concealed and protected from the weather. The control cables leading to the control van and the Fan Song radar were properly strung even though he had no intention of turning the radar on. His last experience had taught him how good the Americans were at air defense suppression, and an active radar was a beacon announcing his position and an invitation to an attack. He glanced at the makeshift cupola his men had mounted on top of the control van. Long dark green tubes, an optical tracking scope, stuck out both sides of the cupola, much like an insect's antenna. He could see the man inside watching him. Sergeant Lu is my best observer, Sung thought.

Sung climbed the two steps into the control van. The four men inside were waiting for him. "Good morning, sir," the on-duty captain said. The three other men remained at their consoles, sitting at attention and staring straight ahead.

"Status?" Sung asked in a normal voice.

"We are operational," the captain answered, a slight tremor in his voice.

Sung thought for a moment. Communications were his weakest link, so check that. "Initiate a radio check," he ordered. The captain barked a command and the communications operator ran through the check procedures. In order, the observation posts checked in. Sergeant Lu, the observer in the cupola on top of the van, was the last to acknowledge, completing the check.

Sung had replaced his search radar with a spiderweb of observation posts to serve as his early warning system. The observers scanned the sky and reported aircraft to the control van. Four of the observation posts were hidden well inside Vietnam to watch for the AWACS. It was enough information to turn the Guideline missile and the tracker in the cupola above Sung's head onto the AWACS should it stray within missile range.

Without the Fan Song radar, a backup system was needed to guide the missile. The observer in the cupola focused on the target with the optical tracking scope and called off range and azimuth. These inputs were manually dialed into the guidance computer in the control van. The guidance computer then broadcast steering commands to the missile over a UHF radio frequency. But the observer had to be very skillful at tracking the aircraft and keeping the optics precisely focused. If successful, he would be made a "Hero of the People." If the missile missed, Sung's company would witness punishment. It was a Chinese solution to a modern problem—primitive but effective.

## Saturday, October 19
## The bridge, near Bose, China

The corpsman was tired, dirty, and hungry as he sewed the gash on Kamigami's arm closed. Still, he tried to be as gentle as he could, admiring the way his commander bore the pain. "You were very fortunate, General. I was able to find all the fragments." Kamigami nodded. He had been lucky. An RPG-7 fired from across the gorge had corkscrewed all over the sky before it finally struck the Humvee he was standing beside. He had thrown his arm up in time to save his eyes. But his driver and radio/telephone operator had been killed. "Finished, sir." Kamigami thanked him and walked out of the mud hut the First Regiment was using for an aid station.

A familiar face was waiting outside. "Why are you here, Sergeant Wan?" he asked. "You should be with your company."

Wan Yan Fu stood at attention. "My men and I have volunteered to be at the bridge. My captain agreed. He said Horse Company should be there. There are forty of us."

A long convoy of trucks appeared around the bend of the road. "Wait here," Kamigami said. He walked over to the lead truck and flagged it down.

It was Trimler. "It occurred to me you might need some help," the general said.

"You weren't the only one," he replied. He waved for Wan to bring his men over to the trucks. "This is Sergeant Wan of Horse Company." Kamigami waited while Wan's men climbed on board the trucks. He motioned his Humvee up and swung on board. "Follow me," he told Trimler and headed for the bridge.

The convoy stopped a kilometer short of the bridge. The two generals spread a map on the hood of Kamigami's Humvee. "The problem," Kamigami told Trimler, "is the open space between us and the bridge. It's pretty much an open field of fire for the PLA on the other side. We have to lay down a barrage and smoke to move our wounded out or bring reinforcements forward to the bridge. And we still take a lot of casualties. They're wearing us down and can force their way across the bridge any time they're willing to pay the price."

It was a cold, bitter assessment of the situation, and Trimler understood what Kamigami was telling him. His First Regiment had fought a hard rear guard action and made the PLA pay for every foot of ground. But they had been chewed up in the process and had little left to give. Kamigami had done the impossible because he was a rarity, a true leader of men. Sergeant Wan and his volunteers proved that. Hell, Trimler thought, the fact I'm here proves it. But Kamigami was best at fighting a highly mobile, shoot and scoot type of warfare. Now they were going back to a much older method and Trimler didn't like what he had to do. They were going to dig in and hold, take their losses, and not let the PLA pass.

"The open area also works to our advantage," Trimler said. He quickly outlined his tactics. He would use his men, Sergeant Wan's volunteers, and the remainder of the First Regiment as a blocking force on this side. Kamigami had to hold the area on the southern side of the bridge. "When they come across the bridge, you're going to be on their left flank. They've got to keep moving to avoid stalling on the bridge. Your job is to force them to the north, into the open area, toward us. We'll turn it into a kill zone." Trimler swept the other side of the gorge with his binoculars. Tanks supported by infantry were moving out of concealment. "I think they've come up with a down payment."

Kamigami closed his flak vest and jammed his helmet on his head. His arm burned with pain but he ignored it. He paused for a moment. The two men shook hands. "Time to do it," Kamigami said.

The lead tank clanked onto the bridge and started pushing the destroyed tank ahead of it as a shield. Heavy gunfire raked both sides of the bridge, but the tank pushed relentlessly forward. The high bridge railings also provided a screen and Kamigami's defenders tried to knock the railings down with heavy gunfire. The steel railings resembled Swiss cheese but still prevented a clean missile shot with a TOW or Dragon antitank missile.

Three more tanks followed by six armored personnel carriers moved onto the bridge as the lead tank moved clear of the bridge. It pushed the destroyed tank off the road and moved beside it, still using it as a shield. Now it started to fire, pumping shell after shell into the defenders. A TOW missile flashed across the open area and destroyed the tank. But the bridge was still open as the second tank came across. It moved into position beside the two destroyed tanks and started to fire, only to suffer the same fate. The tactic was obvious. The PLA was building a shield of destroyed tanks to create a bridgehead and without close air support or artillery to reach behind it, the defenders couldn't stop it.

The PLA sacrificed fourteen tanks and three armored personnel carriers to build their shield. More tanks moved across the bridge. Only this time, infantry in the open moved with them. Kamigami's defenders on the southern flank of the bridge held to their contract and extracted a fearsome price from the attackers. But still they came. Now six tanks moved into formation and headed across the open area, directly into Trimler's field of fire. TOW and Dragon missiles stopped the tanks, but three more were off the bridge and forming up. Again, the process repeated itself, but this time the tanks made it halfway across the open area. And still they came.

Kamigami's defenders were coming under heavy attack and he was running low on ammunition. Slowly, he gave ground to the south. The third echelon of tanks were across the open area and into Trimler's defenders. It was man against tank but somehow, Trimler's men killed them. Armored personnel carriers were with the next wave and they all made it across the open area. Trimler and his defenders had fired their last TOW missile and were using captured RPGs to stop the APCs close in.

Kamigami's R/T operator handed him the handset. Brigadier General Robert Trimler had been killed. "Contact the AVG at Bose," Kamigami ordered.

Pontowski fought to control his emotions as he listened to the report of Trimler's death. The general had been more than a good friend. He had been a living example of all that was good in the profession of arms. Now he was gone and Pontowski felt the loss. "How long can you hold on?" he asked.

"Unknown," Kamigami answered. He broke contact.

"Maggot," Pontowski shouted, "I want Leonard and Mako in the cockpit, ready to launch as soon as the runway is open. I'll be on the runway." He ran out of the bunker for his pickup. When he reached the KC-10 he breathed easier. The last pallet was coming down the on board loader. Their one forklift quickly moved the pallet out of the way as a large group of Chinese pushed the OBL clear of the KC-10. The crew was on the flight deck and cranked engines.

Byers ran up to him. "They're transferring fuel to the tail now," he shouted. Pontowski waited as the flight engineer pumped fuel into the rear fuselage tanks, making the KC-10 tail heavy. Slowly the tail came down and the nose raised.

"The ramp is finished," Byers shouted, barely able to be heard over the engines.

Pontowski keyed the UHF radio in his truck. "Do it now, Murphy." The pilot cracked the throttles and felt the KC-10 shudder. The nose gear was still stuck. Murphy nudged the center throttle forward, increasing the power in the tail engine. It was enough. The aircraft moved forward, its nose gear coming up the ramp. With a rush, the KC-10 taxied free of the hole and onto the center of the runway. Murphy gave Pontowski a thumbs-up sign as he headed for the parking ramp to defuel. The tail of the KC-10 had barely cleared the runway as Leonard and Mako took off.

Pontowski drove over to the load crew, who were sitting on the ground, exhausted. "Hop in," he said. "You hungry?" He dropped them off at the KC-10 and called the mess tent to get a meal out to the plane. It was the least he could do.

A C-130 was in the pattern, approaching to land. "Good timing," he mumbled to himself. Two F-15s roared overhead—the C-130 had been escorted in. So that explains why we haven't heard from the Chinese air force, he reasoned. He keyed his radio and checked in with Maggot before heading for the C-130. The cargo plane slowed to a crawl as it taxied past the cargo area. The ramp at the rear of the aircraft lowered and six pallets came sliding out. A combat off-load. The Hercules stopped, its engines running, and a group of evacuees ran up the ramp. He was surprised to see a lone figure get off and walk away from the aircraft. The ramp came up and the cargo plane fast-taxied for the runway. It had been on the ground less than seven minutes.

Pontowski shook his head in resignation when he got a good look at the deplaning passenger. Sara Waters had returned.

The two Warthogs circled to the south of Bose and went through the arming sequence. The bridge was less than four minutes' flying time away from the airfield and they knew every landmark and high obstruction. But they had a problem—they couldn't raise any of the defenders on the radios. They circled again as Leonard cycled through every frequency they had been given. Still no contact.

"Let's go take a look," Mako said.

"Might as well," Leonard conceded. The two jets spread apart and headed for the bridge. They popped over a low ridge. In front of them was a scene of chaos, destruction, and death. "Holy shit!" Leonard shouted over the UHF. "Bug out! Rejoin to the south." The two Warthogs retreated to safety. "Where are the good guys?" he asked. Mako related what he had seen as Leonard constructed a mental map of the battle. "I think," Leonard transmitted, "the Gomers have a bridgehead on our side of the gorge and the good guys are holding to the south and on the far side of the open area."

"That checks with what I saw," Mako replied. "Not good."

Leonard agreed. To bomb the bridge they would have to run a gauntlet of fire from both sides of the gorge. "Cover-shooter," Leonard called. "I'll lead." He planned to ingress first and discourage any hostile fire while Mako went for the bridge. He called up a Maverick and turned toward the bridge. He firewalled the throttles and popped over the ridge. His eyes darted inside the cockpit to the TV monitor as his hands played the buttons on the stick and the right throttle. He locked the crosshairs on a tank and pickled off a Maverick. Eyes back outside in time to see rapid puffs of smoke from antiaircraft artillery and the smoke trail of a Grail surface-to-air missile. He jinked hard and sent a stream of flares into his slipstream, defeating the Grail. He rolled back in, locked on another tank, and sent his last Maverick on its way.

He was already set up for guns and raked the area where he had seen the Triple A fire. Leonard pulled off and turned hard back into another Grail missile. It missed and he was lined up on a tank and an armored personnel carrier racing across the open area. He killed them both. "Get the hell out of Dodge," he growled. But where was Mako?

On cue, he heard Mako call, "I'm off." Leonard was almost to the ridge and chanced a look back at the bridge. He saw Mako's Hog jinking wildly as it pulled out of its dive. A surface-to-air missile converged on the A-10 and exploded. The Warthog flared and came apart. There was no chute. Leonard dropped behind the ridge and then darted up for a quick look. Mako's bombs had missed and the bridge was still standing. "My turn," he muttered. He selected bombs on the armament control panel.

Leonard flew to the southeast, away from the bridge, before turning inbound. He intended to attack from a different direction. He ran in at one hundred feet and popped. He jinked the jet as he gained altitude. Luckily, the gunners had been expecting him to come back over the ridge and were slow to track him. He had rolled 135 degrees and his nose was on the bridge in a fifteen-degree dive before the first shell tore a hole in his left rudder.

Leonard was vaguely aware of the hell that surrounded him as he pressed the attack. His feet danced on the rudders as he flew down the wire. His thumb flicked on the pickle button and the Warthog shuddered as it shed its stick of six five-hundred-pound bombs. He pulled off hard to the right, over the far side of the bridge, away from most of the fighting. He slammed the big jet back onto the deck and turned north. Had he hit the bridge?

This time he climbed into the sky. The bridge was clearly silhouetted against the gorge and surrounding hills. It was still standing. His radio came to life. "Tango, how copy?" It was Kamigami.

"Where the hell you been?" Leonard rasped.

"We've been busy," Kamigami answered. It was a classic understatement. He had heard the earlier radio calls but had been fighting off a determined attack. Only the arrival of the Warthogs had saved them.

"Any sign of my number two?" Leonard asked.

"Negative." Kamigami's voice was dead calm. "A bomb on the first pass hit the bridge, punched a hole in the surface, but didn't explode. A dud. All were near misses on the second pass. One bomb hit the concrete footer on the western side or the steel girders underneath. I think it weakened the underside of the bridge." He scanned the bridge with his binoculars. "Tanks are moving onto the bridge and it looks like it's bending under the weight. I can see the girders working back and forth. One more bomb will drop it."

Leonard didn't have to look at his weapons status panel to check his armament. He only had his cannon and one

AIM-9 Sidewinder left. "I'll call for a second strike," he radioed.

"It had better be damned quick," Kamigami answered.

"Roger that," Leonard said. He dialed in the frequency for Gopher Hole and talked to Maggot, explaining the situation.

"We can have two on station in fifteen minutes," Maggot told him.

Did Kamigami have fifteen minutes? Leonard wondered. Probably not. But he still had a gun that could kill those tanks on the bridge. This time, he dropped down into the gorge, twisting and turning as he followed the river to the bridge. "Make 'em shoot down," he growled. He wasn't even aware he was talking to himself. Ahead of him the gorge narrowed and he rolled into a ninety-degree bank to knife-edge through. He rolled out in time to look up and see the underside of the bridge.

Then it came to him. "Yeah," he muttered. "I can do this." Rather than climb to strafe the tanks on top, he stayed low. He squeezed off a long burst of mixed high-explosive incendiary and armor-piercing incendiary into the underside of the bridge. He tapped the rudder pedals and for a brief second, moved the pipper over the concrete footing that had been weakened by his earlier bomb. Then he had to straighten out or hit the wall of the gorge. But it was long enough to send fifty rounds into the footing, cutting and ripping into the steel girders that supported the bridge.

Leonard flew under the bridge as it started to collapse. The Warthog shuddered as a long burst of twenty-three-millimeter antiaircraft rounds tore into its left side. The leading edge of the left wing shredded, peeling back like a banana skin, exposing hydraulic lines. At least twelve rounds bounced off the titanium tub that surrounded the cockpit. But the titanium held and saved Leonard's life. The gunner still had the hapless Warthog in his sights and sent a second burst into the jet. Over fifty rounds punctured the fuel tanks but the reticulated, fire-suppressant foam lining the tanks kept them from exploding. Six rounds hit the left engine and it chewed itself apart. The left rudder simply disappeared. And the Warthog was still flying.

* * *

Maggot looked at Pontowski in disbelief. "Tango says he's got hydraulics, one good engine, and the gear's down. He's gonna land it."

Pontowski pushed back from his console in the Gopher Hole and stood up. "We can bulldoze it off the runway if he crumps," he said. "Tell him to come on in." He looked at Sara Waters and gave her a gentle nudge. "I'm going outside. Want to come along?" She nodded and followed him.

They sat in his pickup and listened to the radio as Leonard brought the stricken Warthog down final. "He makes it look routine," Pontowski said, trying to break the tension that held the woman. They were silent as Leonard touched down. She gasped when the left main gear collapsed and the jet skidded to the left, leaving the runway. It kicked up a shower of dirt and mud as it spun around two times. The right wing lifted dangerously high into the air as the A-10 tried to flip onto its back. The wing came down and Waters breathed again.

Pontowski gunned the engine and raced for the jet, which was lying in the mud. Suddenly, the canopy blew back and up. Tango was a blur of motion as he climbed out of the cockpit, slid down the fuselage, and ran for safety. Pontowski slammed the truck to a stop just as he reached the runway. "What happened?" he yelled. "Canopy jammed?"

"Naw," Tango answered. "I've always wanted to do that."

Waters was out of the pickup and in his arms, crying. "Oh, my God," she whispered. "I thought I'd lost you."

He held her tight, not saying a word. Then, "Why did you come back?"

"When I got to Cam Ranh Bay, I knew I couldn't leave you." She pulled back. "John Leonard, I love you."

There was much he wanted to say, but it would have to keep until later. "Check out the Bossman," he said.

Pontowski was standing beside the truck, facing to the east, his gaze fixed on the horizon. His profile was lean and drawn and his hawklike nose, the trademark of the **Pontowskis, forged the profile of a raptor, a bird of prey.** He was going to fly one more mission.

# CHAPTER 24

Saturday, October 19
The White House, Washington, D.C.

I'm getting too old for this, Bill Carroll decided. His leg hurt and he could feel the twinges of a toothache at work in the back of his jaw. He ignored it and picked up a report from the CIA. It was a psychologist's analysis of the Von Drexler videotape. He flipped through the thin document, surprised the doctor had used layman's terms. Certain passages caught his attention:

"All acts were consensual. The male subject, identified as a Mark Von Drexler, and the two unidentified women were willing participants . . .

"At no time was duress of any type observed . . .

"The scene in which the male subject inserted his fists in the vaginas of the two women is referred to as 'fisting' and occurred when he was dominating the two female subjects . . .

"The episode in which the older of the two women inserted her fist in the male subject's anus while the younger female pierced the male's tongue and inserted a golden pin occurred when he was being dominated and not in control . . .

"The last scene was most unusual because of the use of the Ping-Pong ball. The male subject clenched the ball in his left hand while the women spread his legs and tacked his scrotum to the floor with at least eight tacks. The scrotum was spread to its maximum extent and bled profusely. The scene ends with the women taking turns licking his blood. It is assumed the male subject drops the Ping-Pong ball as a signal to stop should the pain become intolerable . . ."

The intercom on his desk buzzed.

"Mrs. Nevers is on your private line," his secretary said.

Well, well, he thought, here it is almost five o'clock Saturday afternoon and Piccard's ploy to distract Nevers is working. Then he reminded himself that the woman on the other end of the line had the power of the U.S. Congress behind her. But she was the one who had made a martyr out of a very disturbed, very sick, ego-driven man and tried to use his suicide as a club to gain her reelection. She didn't care what damage she caused as long as she continued in office. "I'll take the call," he said, picking up the phone.

"Who do you think you are?" Nevers snapped when she came on the line. She paused, expecting an answer.

"How can I help you?" Carroll answered.

"For your information," she continued, apparently satisfied with that answer, "I was elected by the people of the State of California to govern this country. You," she accused, "could not be elected dogcatcher." She paused, her case made.

"I'm confused. Are you urging me to run for dogcatcher?"

"Don't play silly-ass word games with me. You know what I mean."

"Please, Mrs. Nevers, what is the purpose of this call?"

"You know damn well what it's all about. It's about that goddamn fucking tape. The media has heard about it and is pressing me for a comment. If they see it . . ."

Carroll listened as Nevers ran through her working vocabulary of profanity. Grudgingly, he gave her an A plus for some of her more creative combinations. He let her blow. But instead of subsiding, her invective crescendoed to a startling climax that would have impressed the most grizzled gunny sergeant in the U.S. Marine Corps. Her conclusion was a snarling, but much more decorous, "Call off your dogs or I'll cut your fucking pecker off!"

He knew he should stall and try to calm the woman. "Didn't you say I couldn't even be elected dogcatcher?"

She banged her phone on the table, almost breaking his eardrum. "You're not listening, you cock-bite!" she screamed.

"Is that a sexist remark?" he calmly interrupted. More profanity from Nevers split the air. He waited for her to take a breath. "Have you seen the tape?" he asked.

Her answer was a high-pitched shriek. "Everyone's seen it!"

Carroll couldn't help himself. "He never dropped the ball, did he?" She slammed the phone down, hanging up. Does Piccard need a copy of this conversation? he wondered. Then he decided against it. He looked at the clock on his desk. It was 5:01 P.M. He made a quick time zone conversion. It's dawn in China, he thought. The beginning of a new day there. But not here.

# Sunday, October 20
# The Dragon's Teeth, near Guilin, China

An early morning mist hung over the fields and hid the verdant green of the rice paddies under a gossamer veil. A faint rumble in the west shattered the ghostly silence and grew into a gust of thunder as eight low-flying Warthogs passed over. Behind them, their jet wash cut long streaks of clear air in the mist and marked their path. Most of the visual checkpoints that Pontowski had come to rely on were obscured, but the few landmarks that he could see were enough. The land below him was an old friend.

Automatically, Pontowski's eyes scanned his instruments looking for the unusual, the telltale signs of trouble. Nothing to worry about. He scanned the horizon, looking for bandits. He knew they were out there. Pontowski twisted to his left and checked his formation. Again, all was well—his four jets were in a perfect box formation. Off to his right he could make out Maggot's flight of four flying above the early morning mist.

"Dragon's Teeth on the nose," Maggot called.

Maggot's got good eyeballs, Pontowski thought. Now he could just make out the beginnings of the karst buttes. It still amazed him how much the Dragon's Teeth did look like a string of huge fangs emerging from the earth. Ahead of him, he could see where the Luoqing River gushed out of the Gullet, the river gorge formed by the mountains to the west and the Dragon's Teeth to the east. As planned, Pontowski led his formation up the Luoqing River as Maggot's four jets fell into trail. "Entering the Gullet now," Pontowski transmitted as they entered the river valley. For six minutes, the Warthogs would twist and turn as they used the Dragon's Teeth for terrain masking.

The Luoqing flowed rapidly through the valley and the air was smooth and clear. This has got to be one of the most beautiful pieces of real estate on God's green earth, Pontowski thought. I wish Shoshana could've seen this. The old hurt flared. Stifle that, he warned himself, attend to business, don't get distracted.

A crisp radio call from Moose Penko demanded his full attention. "Bossman, Phoenix. Bandits zero-nine-zero at eighty, eighteen thousand." Established in orbit at thirty-two thousand feet, the AWACS could easily paint the bandits at eighteen thousand feet. Pontowski mentally ran the geometry—to the east of his position at eighty miles placed the bandits between him and Kang's headquarters. With Phoenix giving them vectors, they should be able to avoid them. That's a good thing, Pontowski decided, since the bandits had the sun advantage.

"Say number," Pontowski transmitted.

"Two-zero," Moose replied.

Twenty of them this fine morning, Pontowski thought.

"Correction," Moose transmitted. "Make that two-two. Two other bandits are in a race track pattern above the main formation at forty thousand feet."

Pontowski checked his RHAW gear for signs of hostile radar activity. Nothing. What the hell are those two doing up there? he thought. Are they the Chinese version of "eye-in-the-sky"? They're way too high to see anything. No threat, he decided.

## Sunday, October 20
## The Sino-Vietnamese border, China

"Colonel Sung," the communications operator shouted, "aircraft reported. Observation post sixteen reports an aircraft heading north." The operator paused, copying information down on his chalkboard while the plotter marked the reported location of the aircraft on the tracking chart tacked to the wall. The plotter then circled observation post sixteen, which was hidden on the Vietnamese side of the border.

"Is it the AWACS?" Sung asked. He immediately berated himself for interfering. His men were well-trained to identify aircraft and they knew why they were there.

"Yes, sir," the operator answered. "Altitude approximately ten thousand meters, heading due north."

Sung felt his body tense. The AWACS! And it was coming directly at them! He couldn't believe his good luck. He forced himself to remain quiet as his men plotted the course of the E-3 Sentry.

"I want you to destroy that aircraft," he told the on-duty captain. Then he added an ominous, "If you can."

Observation post twelve reported the aircraft. It was now in range but reversing course, quickly moving back out of range. "I'm sorry, Colonel Sung," the captain said. The relief in his voice was evident. He would not have to commit their last missile and suffer Sung's wrath if it missed.

More reports filtered in. "Sir," the captain's voice was almost a whisper, "the AWACS returns."

"What do you make of this?" Sung asked.

"I believe the AWACS is in a new orbit very close to the border," the captain answered. He was a very unhappy man. Why did this have to happen when he was on duty?

For the next few minutes, the men plotted the path of the AWACS. It was definitely established in a new orbit with its northernmost turn inside twenty miles—in range at that altitude. Sergeant Lu in the cupola reported a positive visual sighting through his powerful optical tracking tube, which was now fully extended and resembled a double-ended periscope laid on its side with the cupola in the middle.

Sung couldn't stand it any longer. This was his chance. "Initiate prelaunch," he ordered.

## Sunday, October 20
## The Dragon's Teeth, near Guilin, China

Pontowski hit the UHF transmit button on the throttle quadrant as they flew out of the Dragon's Teeth. "Ops check." The seven other pilots checked in with their remaining fuel. All but Maggot were within a hundred pounds of his own. The jet Maggot was flying had always been a hungry Hog. Fuel was the one constant that all fighter pilots lived with—they never had enough of it. And that includes those bandits in front of us, Pontowski reasoned. What to do about them?

Moose Penko's voice came over the UHF. "Bandits have been airborne thirty-three minutes." Pontowski grunted in satisfaction. Moose might have been trained as a weapons controller, but he thought like a fighter pilot and had keyed on the fuel check, giving Pontowski one more piece of information he needed.

"Boss," Maggot said over the secure radio, "if I use Bravo-North for an IP, your flight can use Alpha-North. No problem on separation then." It was a good suggestion. During the planning for the mission, Maggot had ringed the target with IPs, initial points, so they could alter their attack heading depending on circumstances. By altering course to the north and attacking from the northern initial points, they could continue their end run around the bandits. And Maggot was right about separation. His four Warthogs would take ninety seconds longer to reach their initial point, Bravo-North, before starting their attack run. They needed that time separation to stay clear of Pontowski's jets and the frag pattern from the first bombs.

Pontowski's decision was not a rational, easily reconstructed textbook process, but rather an instinctual weighing of the factors that determine success or failure for a fighter pilot, and in the extreme, life and death. The main objective was to get his bombs on target and then safely escape. Pontowski factored in fuel and distance, enemy defenses, the Warthog's capability, and finally, the men themselves. Were they as tired as he was? How could he compound the problem for the bandits? The answer was simple—avoid them and make them burn fuel. With a little luck, the bandits wouldn't have enough fuel remaining to search for them as they came off target. Don't count on it, he warned himself.

He made his decision and keyed the secure radio. "Phoenix, we're going north. Keep us clear of the bandits."

"A heading of zero-three-five," Moose radioed, "will take you twenty miles north of bandits." The noses of the eight Warthogs came around together as they headed into the mountainous terrain north of Kang's headquarters.

Damn! Pontowski thought. Maggot's IP will be a bitch for him to find. But on the other hand, no one's gonna find us rootin' around in the mountains. His fingers flew over the INS panel on the right console, punching in the coordinates of his flight's IP.

"Fence check," he told his flight. It was a hard reminder for his pilots to double-check all their switches to be sure their bombs were armed and they were configured for combat. Like him, they had all armed their cannons and AIM-9s shortly after takeoff. And like them, Pontowski rechecked all his switches. He punched up the station select buttons for stations three and nine and the green release/ready lights blinked on. He rotated a wafer switch and fused his six Mark-82 AIRs for nose/tail, high drag. He double-checked the ripple intervolometer—already set as planned to walk the six five-hundred-pound bombs across Kang's headquarters. He visually checked the master arm switch on the armament control panel for the third time, making sure it was in the up position. He was ready to pickle. Slow down, Pontowski told himself. Conserve fuel, use terrain masking—we're in no hurry. Avoid the bad guys.

Four minutes out of the IP, he split up his formation. As planned, his wingman, Buns Cox, was still off his left wing, slightly in trail. Ahead of him he could see his IP, a distinctive bend in the river.

"Six bandits, four o'clock, high," Maggot radioed.

Pontowski twisted to his right but couldn't see them.

"Say range," he demanded.

"Ten plus," came the answer.

Pontowski still couldn't see them. Maggot and his cosmic eyeballs, he concluded. But they were out there. The IP came under his nose. "Press," he transmitted, "bandits no factor. IP now." He firewalled the throttles.

## Sunday, October 20
## The Sino-Vietnamese border, China

The captain paled when Sung ordered him to start the sequence of actions that could lead to an actual missile launch. He looked sick as he sent out the first order to prepare the Guideline missile. Men sprang into action and ripped the camouflage away from the Guideline while two technicians fueled the missile's liquid propellant sustainer rocket as it swung up on its erector and its turntable slewed to the south.

The launch/guidance operator scanned his panel. "All circuits test yellow," he said. Every red light on the panel had gone out and had been replaced by a yellow light as each circuit was activated and tested positive for continuity.

The captain shot Sung another worried look. Sung nodded. "Activate launch circuits," the captain said.

The launch/guidance operator threw a series of toggle switches on the panel in front of him and then looked at the captain. "Ready for consent." The captain's hand moved, flicking open the guarded switch and shoving it forward. All the yellow lights but two flicked to green. The missile was hot and only needed its guidance system to come on line.

Now the launch/guidance operator's hands flew over his control panel in a series of well-practiced actions. The last two yellow lights blinked to green. "Internal gyro stabilized," he reported. "Automatic guidance in the green." For the first twenty seconds of flight, the Guideline was a ballistic missile that relied on its own internal guidance system. At twenty seconds, the solid-fuel booster separated, exposing the UHF radio antennas and allowing the liquid-fueled sustainer rocket to kick in. Normally, the missile would then rely on radio-command guidance from the Fan Song radar as it painted the target.

But this time, it would be a visual launch and there would be no telltale Fan Song radar transmissions to warn the AWACS that it was under attack by a surface-to-air missile.

# Sunday, October 20
## Wuzhou, China

The caret on the airspeed tape in the HUD refused to go beyond 330 knots. "Come on!" Pontowski shouted. But the Warthog was tired and 330 was all he was going to get hauling bombs at two hundred feet above the deck. Ahead of him, he could see the town of Wuzhou. Use the road as a pointer to the school, he reminded himself. The compound is on the northeastern edge of town, between the road and the river.

Again, he cursed his slow airspeed. Even though Pontowski was moving over the ground at 557 feet a second, fast by normal human standards, a determined gunner on the ground could track him, especially when he popped. He would have been much happier at twice the speed. But the Warthog had never been designed to go fast. However, if everything went according to plan, all eight aircraft would attack and be off target less than three minutes after Pontowski dropped his bombs.

Now Pontowski could see the road angling in on his left. But he still could not make out the school building Kang had turned into the center of his headquarters compound. He was almost to the pop point and still no target.

"Triple A coming from the river," Buns, his wingman, transmitted, his voice amazingly calm. Pontowski could see rapid puffs of smoke coming from a gun pit on the river levee. "I'm in on the left," Buns called as his nose turned toward the gun pit.

Ten seconds later Pontowski reached his pop point and

saw the school at his two o'clock position. Even at 330 knots, the attack was developing at a speed that defied normal thought and Pontowski's reactions were automatic. He honked back on the stick and climbed. At nine hundred feet he rolled 135 degrees, apexed at twelve hundred feet, and pulled the Warthog's nose to the target. He was vaguely aware of small black puffs flashing above him—Triple A coming from the gun pit. Not even close.

Now, he did have time to evaluate. He had apexed at exactly one mile from the target, the HUD's velocity vector symbol was beyond the target—marking the spot he would hit the ground if he didn't pull out. His dive angle of fifteen degrees was wired and his airspeed rooted on 325 knots. Perfect.

A flash of exploding bombs off to his left caught his attention. "I'm clear," Buns radioed. The puffs stopped. Buns had taken out the battery. Were there more?

The target was marching down the HUD's PIBL, the projected bomb impact line, toward the pipper. He could see dark figures running for cover—all soldiers. Subconsciously, he was thankful that Jin Chu had been right about the school being evacuated. Then he saw the unmistakable flash of an SA-7 being launched. The shoulder-held missile the Soviets called the Strela, or Arrow, streaked toward his wingman's jet. *"Break right!"* he yelled over the radio. The momentary distraction had taken his eyes out of the HUD. When he reacquired the target, it was still on the PIBL and almost to the pipper. LASTE had saved the bomb run. At 768 feet above the ground, the pipper reached the target and his thumb mashed the pickle button.

The six bombs rippled off and Pontowski pulled back on the stick, loading the Warthog with four *g*s in two seconds, the standard escape maneuver. He glanced back at the compound and saw his first bomb explode. He looked away.

Pontowski's first bomb hit seventy feet short of the main building and exploded in the midst of three communications vans and two trucks. The blast from the bomb blew in the building's outer wall while the frag pattern from the bomb and numerous secondary explosions from ammunition reached out over a thousand feet into a bivouac area. The second bomb hit short of the north wall of the building.

The blast collapsed the north wing and set it on fire. The third bomb landed in the building's center and penetrated to the basement before it exploded. The building was collapsing in on itself in a domino effect when the fourth bomb landed in the kitchen located in the south wing. The men at breakfast were vaporized by the succeeding blasts that built and fed on one another. The fifth bomb hit thirty feet south of the building and blasted a thirty-foot crater in the soft earth. A pillar of smoke, dirt, and debris rose into the air and then settled over the burning building. The sixth bomb's fusing malfunctioned and the bomb buried itself in over forty feet of soft earth. It would go undetected for six years until the vibration caused by a farmer's tractor set it off.

Two more Hogs dropped bombs on the compound, leveling the area while their wingmen provided cover and dropped canisters of CBU-58s on any air defenses foolish enough to announce their presence. The last two aircraft in Maggot's flight could not see the compound because of smoke and flames so they hit the supply dump and motor pool area on the other side of the river.

Kang's body would be found the next day under a ton of rubble. Charred, shrunk, and dismembered, his body was identifiable only by his distinctive bridgework. The soldiers dumped his remains into a common grave with 687 other bodies. A bulldozer sealed the grave.

Pontowski never saw the death and destruction his bombs created. Instead, he scanned the area and concentrated on finding Buns for a rejoin. Ideally, they would join and egress in a two-ship formation. He jinked to the left and saw a flash of flame engulf the tail section of a Warthog that was too far away to be Buns. "Shee-it," Maggot yelled over the radio, drawing the obscenity into two syllables, "I'm hit."

## Sunday, October 20
## The Sino-Vietnamese border, China

"Colonel Sung," the plotter sang out, "AWACS in range." Sung forced himself to remain calm. He desperately wanted to shoot down the intruder.

The tracker in the cupola, Sergeant Lu, announced he was tracking the AWACS.

"Permission to fire?" the captain asked. His voice was shaking.

"Granted," Sung said.

"Fire!"

The roar of the launching missile shook the control van and for the next twenty seconds an equally deafening silence ruled the men. Then from the launch/guidance operator, "Positive missile guidance."

The thirty-five-foot-long Guideline missile resembled a flying telephone pole as it arced onto the AWACS. The computer-activated commands transitioned its flight from a lead pursuit course to a pure collision course as it neared the unsuspecting AWACS. This particular Guideline missile was twenty-nine years old and had been manufactured in the Soviet Union. It had been carefully maintained against the ravages of time and the solid-fuel booster and guidance circuits worked perfectly throughout the launch. Even the liquid-fueled sustainer rocket functioned within design parameters, which meant the missile responded accurately to guidance commands.

Sergeant Lu could not believe his luck as the AWACS banked away from him, presenting him with a perfect plan form to track on. He watched in satisfaction as the missile closed on the aircraft. But without a radar signal to home on, the proximity fuse did not work and the missile struck the fuselage at the left wing root just as the AWACS rolled out of its turn. Because the missile hit at a low angle of incidence, it bounced off and the impact fuse malfunctioned. The self-destruct mechanism sensed the loss of stability and detonated the 288-pound high-explosive warhead as the missile tumbled. A huge fireball belched below the AWACS and Sergeant Lu reported a direct hit. Two observation posts confirmed his report.

But the high explosive in the missile's warhead had degraded over the years and the detonation was uneven, causing a much lower-order explosion.

The underside of the AWACS' fuselage took the brunt of the explosion as the high explosive ripped into the AWACS, shredding metal and peppering the control surfaces on the left wing and the number one and two engines. Shrapnel tore into the forward cargo and equipment hold, called the forward lobe. The high-velocity charged pieces of metal ripped into the wiring, junction boxes, and radios packed into the equipment racks.

Fire and smoke filled the forward lobe and poured into the main cabin.

## Sunday, October 20
## Near Wuzhou, China

"I think a Grail nailed you," Pontowski transmitted as he headed for Maggot. Where was Buns? He slid into a position below and behind Maggot to check the A-10 for battle damage. He could see hydraulic fluid streaking the ripped panels of the fuselage's underside.

"Shee-it," was the only reply. Maggot headed south and slowed while Pontowski joined on his right.

Behind them, Pontowski could see only smoke and flames. We did what we came for, he thought. Time to head home. It would be a gift if Maggot was the only one with battle damage and with a little help from the AWACS, they should be able to get Maggot safely home. He hit the transmit button, "Phoenix, say position of bandits."

Maggot drowned out any reply from the AWACS with, *"Bandits!* Two o'clock, high, eight miles."

Pontowski had no trouble finding the bandits this time. "Circle the Hogs," he ordered.

# CHAPTER 25

Sunday, October 20
Near the Sino-Vietnamese border, Vietnam

Major Marissa LaGrange was standing in the aisle beside her senior director when the explosion rocked the aircraft. Her next conscious thought was, Why am I lying on the deck? After that, her reactions were instinctive, honed by long hours of practice in the simulator. She jumped to her feet, jammed on her quick don oxygen mask and plugged into the intercom. *"Oxygen masks!"* she roared. "Oxygen on 100 percent. Sit down and strap in. Clear your consoles, shut up, and get your checklists out. And follow 'em!"

The heavy smoke pouring onto the main deck was blinding her. A crew member bolted past her heading to the rear of the aircraft. She grabbed him. *"Sit the fuck down and do your job!"* She pushed him into a seat.

She turned and pointed at Orly, the airborne radar technician sitting at the lone console aft of the wing. "Orly, pop the over-the-wing hatch. Vent this mutha." The sergeant leaped out of his seat and tore at the hatch. Within seconds, the smoke lessened and she could see through her tears. Now she had the source of the smoke. It was coming from the forward lobe.

Talk to the pilot first, she thought. "Buzz . . ."

"Stand by . . ." His voice was labored.

We're straight and level, LaGrange thought. He's handling the emergency up there. Put out the fire back here. On

451

net one of the intercom: "Fire fighters—Orly and Benny. Get ready . . . forward lobe . . . you're going down . . . fire fighters' masks . . . gloves . . . fire extinguishers." Much to her surprise, and without a word of protest, Orly rushed past her, giving a thumbs-up signal. The two men were at the hatch in the floor, waiting for her command.

The pilot's voice came over the intercom. "All fire lights are out, control checks okay, but we've lost our number two. Say status." Buzz had just told LaGrange that he had no indication of a fire and while he did have positive control of the aircraft, they were flying on three engines. And he wanted to know what was going on in the rear.

"I'm sending two fire fighters into the forward lobe now," LaGrange answered. "The smoke is venting." She motioned Orly and Benny down the hatch.

"Is the fire out?"

"How the hell would I know?" LaGrange snapped. "They just went down."

"Rog," the pilot replied. "We're heading for home."

LaGrange felt the E-3 turn gently onto a new course. She took a deep breath and forced herself to forget the fire and smoke for a moment. She had to regain situational awareness and called the senior director. "Say status."

"Radar and all communications out. Bossman last reported off target and bandits in area. The last radio call I heard was 'Circle the Hogs.' They're in trouble, Major."

Damn! she thought. The Warthogs needed help and the AWACS was heading in the wrong direction. Should she risk her crew again? They had taken one hit and had not observed antiaircraft fire. So it had to be a SAM. Would another one be waiting for them? Just one missile, she thought, with no radar warning. Then it came to her. They had been nailed by a single missile visually launched. But standard employment doctrine for surface-to-air missiles called for two missiles to be committed against a high-value target. And they were certainly that. Why only one? To insure success under such degraded conditions, a whole flock of missiles should have been barraged at them. Maybe that was the Last of the Mohicans. Her decision was almost made. But she had to get the fire out first.

"Moose!" she bellowed on net one. "Get your ass down into the forward lobe and sort those dumb dicks out."

"Hey," he answered, "I'm not a fire fighter!"

"You are now. Move!" The Monday morning quarterbacks are going to have fun with that decision, she thought, sending my best weapons controller down to fight a fire. But she had a very good reason for her decision. Moose hated her guts and could work miracles when he was pissed at her. She watched as he jammed a fire fighter's mask over his face and disappeared down the hatch.

"Major," one of the weapons controllers said, "checklist complete. What now?"

"Keep your thumb on the checklist," LaGrange replied.

"Why?"

"Better on the checklist than up your ass," she shot back. Things were returning to normal.

Moose's voice crackled over the intercom. "Orly and Benny bought it. They're dead!"

I sent them down too soon! she raged at herself. Worry about that later. Moose is still alive. "The fucking fire, Moose!"

"Workin' it," he grunted. "It's the power junction control box to the radios." She could hear the swoosh of a fire extinguisher over the intercom. "Nah, it's a couple of radios and the forced-air fan." Again, she heard the swoosh of the fire extinguisher. The smoke coming from the forward lobe started to dissipate. "Fire's out," Moose told her. Now she could hear a loud knocking sound coming over the intercom.

"What the hell's going on?" she asked, forcing her voice to be calm. No answer. To the pilot, "Buzz, the fire's out back here. Have I got four generators on line?"

"Rog," he answered.

"Return to orbit now," she ordered.

"You crazy?" He was shouting.

She stifled the urge to yell at him. Buzz was an emotional type and she had to explain things to him. "The Warthogs are tangling with a gaggle of J-8s and unless we do our job, they ain't nothing but dog meat."

The pilot's answer was a cool "Rog" as the aircraft

banked to the right, into the two good engines, and reversed course.

LaGrange thought about the situation. "If there are any clouds out there," she said, "stay above 'em or in 'em."

Again, the same cool and laconic "Rog" came back.

"Stalwart fellow," she mumbled into her mike, loud enough for everyone to hear. Time for another problem. She made sure she was on net one. "Everyone listen up. We're returning to station. Slovic, get the radar back on line. Mercer, sort out the radios. I want max com ASAP."

Mercer, the communications tech, looked puzzled. "What about Moose . . . Cap'n Penko?"

"Power 'em up sequentially. Talk to him and see what happens."

"Radar coming on line now," Slovic, the backup airborne radar tech, said.

"I've isolated the damaged circuits," Moose said over the intercom. "Turn 'em on, Mercer. I'll tell you if you need to shut a radio down."

Again, LaGrange could hear a loud knocking sound coming from the forward lobe. "What the hell you doing down there?"

"Trying," Moose grunted, "to get . . . the equipment rack . . . off the bodies."

So that's what happened, she reasoned. They got trapped. Probably cooked. "Leave 'em down there," she ordered. Moose's head appeared out of the hatch. He ripped off the fire fighter's mask and took a deep breath. Slowly he pulled himself out of the hatch. LaGrange plugged into her long communications cord and walked over to him. He was sitting on the deck, his skin still glowing from the heat and his flight suit smoldering. He reeked of smoke and a cooked-meat aroma. "You okay?" she asked.

"Yeah. I'm okay." He glared at her. "You want to know what happened?"

"Later."

Moose wasn't about to wait until later. He wanted her to know what he had been through. "You sent 'em down when the smoke was too thick. They couldn't see. The aft equipment rack cracked loose and fell on 'em—probably when the aircraft turned. It pinned Orly and cut Benny's oxygen hose. They didn't stand a chance, Major." There was condemnation in his voice.

But she wasn't about to respond to it. Not now. Perhaps later. When she was alone. "Get back to your station," she said, keeping her voice under tight control.

Moose wouldn't let it go. "What about Orly and Benny?"

LaGrange wanted to touch the distraught captain. Her voice was sad and very low. "They had a bad day, Moose." She let it sink in. "Let's get to work. We got some Warthogs to save." He shook his head and headed for his console.

## Sunday, October 20
## Near Wuzhou, China

Pontowski firewalled his throttles when he yelled "Circle the Hogs" and sideslipped away from Maggot. "Head south," he ordered.

Snake Bartlett, the lead for Pontowski's second element of two, saw the bandits and knew Maggot was a sitting duck. He led his wingman, Dirtbag, into a high-speed rejoin and fell in behind Pontowski, who was now turning in front of the much slower Maggot. Another element of two led by Skid Malone was right behind Dirtbag. "Skid's in," Malone transmitted. The five Warthogs were now flying in a circle around Maggot, who was heading south. Pontowski could see smoke coming from the secondary target but had lost his wingman. "Buns," he transmitted, "we're in a wheel around Maggot. Do you have us in sight?"

"Negative," came the reply.

"Head for home plate," Pontowski told him.

"Rog," Buns replied. "Tally on the bandits. They're on you. Expect company. I'm outa here."

Pontowski counted six bandits entering a CAP high above and to the west of the Warthogs. "What the hell are they doing?" Pontowski mumbled to himself. He estimated the bandits' altitude at twenty thousand feet. Time to use Maggot's eyeballs. "Maggot, say number of bandits."

Maggot's answer was immediate. "Six. Probably the same dudes we saw inbound to target."

"Same count," Snake chimed in, confirming Maggot's number. "Maybe," he added, "they haven't seen us."

"Or they're sorting us out," Skid said.

Pontowski wanted to know what had happened to the other bandits. He keyed his radio to call the AWACS. "Phoenix, say bandits." No reply.

"What the hell happened to Phoenix?" Snake asked.

Good question, Pontowski thought. Moose had originally called twenty-two bandits and now there were only six.

"Shee-it," Maggot radioed. "I got two more bandits stacked above the formation."

Maggot and his good old Mark One eyeballs, Pontowski thought. Then another thought came to him. Those must be the same two that had been playing Chinese "eye-in-the-sky." Something was different. "Maggot, how you doing?"

"Not too bad. I've lost right hydraulics but the left's okay. Controllability checks okay and I'm not losing fuel. I get a heavy vibration and start to shed skin when I push my airspeed above one-sixty."

"So how's the airplane doing?" Dirtbag asked. It was too good a line to pass up.

"Heads up," Snake called. "Here they come." The bandits were peeling out of their CAP and diving single file.

I'll be damned, Pontowski thought, just like a World War II movie. "Go for the weeds," he transmitted. It was an instinctive reaction for the six Warthogs—get as low as possible. The slow-moving Maggot dropped down to one hundred feet above the deck while the other five circled above him at two hundred feet. "Let's see how they like dodging rocks," Pontowski said to himself. He selected AIM-9 on the armament panel and called up the air-to-air mode on his head-up display. "Looks like a one-pass, haul-ass attack," he transmitted.

At altitude, the J-8s would have chewed the Warthogs apart in a sequential, high-speed hit-and-run attack. But Pontowski had significantly altered the odds by forcing the J-8s to engage in his environment. The Chinese pilots would have to contend with the A-10's turning capability while avoiding the ground.

Pontowski's jaw turned granite hard and his mouth compressed into a thin line as he watched the lead J-8 swoop down in a twenty-degree dive. He estimated its airspeed around six hundred knots, just below the Mach. "Too fast, you fucker!" he shouted to himself. The Chinese pilot had forced himself into early missile shot and pull out. It was that or hit the ground. Like most Warthog drivers, Pontowski wasn't proud and considered a kill a kill, even if his opponent did it to himself by digging his own grave in the ground.

The J-8 drivers were in for a nasty surprise.

Snake was in position when the first J-8 came inside three miles. He wrenched his Warthog's nose around onto the J-8 and brushed the trigger. The GAU-8 cannon belched and gunsmoke streamed from the nose, a very visible warning the cannon was firing. The Chinese pilot reacted instinctively and jinked to his right, destroying any chance to employ his air-to-air missiles. As expected, he zoomed out of the fight. Snake rejoined the wheel, which was now bigger because of his momentary turn onto the J-8. Skid was next and did the same to the second J-8 that was coming at them.

The result was the same. The Chinese pilots had not trained to engage so low and at such a high speed. And it was very disconcerting to be looking at the nose of a Warthog belching smoke when the ground was rushing up to meet them. But the third pilot was of a different cut than the first two. He throttled back and extended his speed brakes. At the same time, he increased his dive angle. He bottomed out of his dive five hundred feet above the ground, three miles from the Warthogs. Now he firewalled his throttles and angled in on the right rear quarter of the Warthog in front cf him—Pontowski. He had a clean shot and launched two of his missiles.

Much to his surprise, both Pontowski and the trailing Warthog turned on him. His missiles lost the heat signature they were homing on when Pontowski rotated his jet exhaust away. The two PL-2 missiles functioned as designed and went ballistic. The distinctive smoke trail of an AIM-9 Sidewinder missile streaked at him from the second Warthog as gunsmoke erupted from Pontowski's nose. The pilot reacted instinctively and jinked hard, fighting for his own survival. It was good enough to avoid the wild cannon shot coming from Pontowski but not the Sidewinder. Then he remembered: The American's AIM-9L was an all-aspect missile with a cooled infrared seeker head that could track head-on. It was his last coherent thought as the Sidewinder exploded in his left intake.

The last three J-8s aborted their run and pulled off high. They all returned to the CAP.

"Ops check," Pontowski called. "Lead has four thousand." Again, the Warthogs checked in with their fuel readings. Pontowski checked his INS and ran the numbers through his head—he had approximately forty minutes of fuel remaining at full throttle. They had to hit the tanker. "Phoenix, how read this frequency?" he transmitted. Nothing. He checked his knee board for the tanker's frequency.

"Bossman"—it was Moose's voice—"Phoenix reads you five-by. How me?"

"Five-by," Pontowski answered. It was hard to keep his voice cool and calm. He wanted to ask where the hell they had been. That could wait until later. "Bandits stacked above us and we need to rendezvous on Prima for refueling."

"Rog," Moose answered. "We've tagged the bandits and are talking to Prima now. Maintain your present heading. Can you push your airspeed up?"

"Negative, Phoenix. We're flying cover for a wounded Hog."


"Major," Moose Penko said over the AWACS intercom, "we've got something strange goin' on." Even though he disliked LaGrange, Moose knew who was in charge. As long as she was the MCC, he would be subordinate.

"Whatcha got, Moose?" LaGrange was plugged into her long communications extension cord and was leaning over his right shoulder.

"It's these two bandits stacked above the other five. They're established in a race track pattern at forty thousand."

LaGrange saw it immediately. The computer was marking the track of the two bandits stacked above the CAP with a dashed line. "Right. And the axis of the race track points straight at Bossman." She racked her brain, trying to recall everything she had read about the J-8. "It's like they're tracking Bossman flight on radar," she said.

"We sold the Chinese the AN/APG-66 radar for the J-8," Moose said. "Can it do that?" The relationship between the two officers would never be smooth and harmonious, but they made an effective team. "Oh, oh," he muttered. "Here they go."

He stomped his foot pedal to transmit. "Bossman, four bandits zero-four-five, at twelve, descending through ten thousand. On you." He studied his screen for a moment. The Chinese had broken up into flights of two flying line abreast and were descending fast. Again, he relayed the warning. Then he saw it. "Bossman!" he was yelling into his mike. "Bandits co-altitude. On the deck. Splitting apart. Pincers."

"Damn!" Pontowski yelled. This was the most aggressive bunch of Chinese pilots they had engaged. A pincers, he thought. Well, the wheel was still his best defensive maneuver. He cursed the Warthog's slow speed. "Heads up," he transmitted. "Make them come to us and engage." He was on the far side of the circle when the first two J-8s closed into firing range. He watched as Snake turned into the J-8 coming in on the right. Five seconds later, Dirtbag, Snake's wingman, turned into the J-8 closing from the left. Snake took the first shot with a Sidewinder, forcing the J-8 to jink wildly to avoid the missile. The missile missed and the J-8 headed straight for Maggot.

Dirtbag launched a Sidewinder on his bandit at the same time the J-8 fired a PL-2 at him. The missiles raced toward each other as the Warthogs and J-8 turned hard to avoid the missiles headed their way.

Pontowski pulled into the vertical when he saw the first J-8 heading for Maggot. He came across the top, well above Maggot. Sweat poured off his face, stinging his eyes as he grunted and pulled hard into a left turn. His airspeed rapidly bled off as his nose came around onto the J-8. He fought the *g*s, feeling his weight quadruple, then quintuple. The chopped stall warning tones bitched at him as the J-8 flashed in front and below him, turning hard away. The Chinese pilot had seen Pontowski's nose come onto him and rightly assumed that a Sidewinder would soon be coming his way if he persisted in the attack. He chose to live and for the moment, Maggot was safe.

But any cohesion the Warthogs might have had was gone. The first two J-8s had broken the wheel apart and turned it into a true furball. The second two J-8s were in firing range and exploited the confusion. Pontowski saw the first missile come off the rail of the J-8. *"Dirtbag!"* he radioed. *"Hard left!"* But it was too late. The missile fired at Dirtbag was not a PL-2 but a PL-7, a much more advanced version with a 180-degree acquisition angle. Its seeker head had no trouble following the heat signature of Dirtbag's A-10 as he turned into the threat. The missile curved in behind the doomed Warthog.

The rear of Dirtbag's jet exploded in a fireball and for a fraction of a second, only the A-10's nose was visible. *"Dirtbag! Eject! Eject!"* Pontowski called. It was too late. The aircraft tumbled into the ground. One of the J-8s flashed in front of Pontowski, barely missing him. Now they were gone.

The sequential pincers attack had been a tradeoff—one J-8 exchanged for one Warthog. Pontowski forced himself not to think of the pilot inside the A-10. He had liked the easygoing man called Dirtbag.

Would they come back? Pontowski mashed his transmit button, almost breaking it off. "Phoenix, say bandits."

"Disengaging," Moose answered. "Headed to the east." Fuel had finally forced the J-8s to disengage. "Two bandits are still at forty thousand, fifteen miles north of your position." Flying at loiter speed at forty thousand feet had conserved fuel for the two bandits hawking the fight.

"Ops check," Pontowski called to his flight. "Lead has three-point-two." Thirty-two hundred pounds of fuel remaining. The replies drove his next decision. The constant circling in the wheel around Maggot and the last engagement had eaten into their remaining fuel. All but Maggot were nearing bingo fuel. He had to get them to a tanker. "Snake, take 'em to Prima for refueling. I'll stay with Maggot. Those two bandits can't stay up there forever. Get

Prima headed my way when they go away. Phoenix, you copy?"

"Rog," Moose answered. "Snake, fly two-one-zero. Tanker on your nose at one-twenty."

A hundred and twenty miles to get a drink, Pontowski calculated. They should make it. He wasn't so sure about himself and Maggot.

Aboard the AWACS, Moose was grumbling at the ASO. "Those two Gomers keep hawking the fight. What the hell are they doing?"

"Beats the hell out of me," the ASO replied. "We're watching them."

LaGrange was studying Moose's monitor over his shoulder. A tickling at the back of her mind kept nagging her. Time to experiment. "Moose, the bandits are pointed at Snake. Tell Snake's flight to strangle their IFFs." Moose shot her a hard look. Without a radar transponder, the A-10s would be much more difficult for the AWACS to track.

He did as she ordered. "Snake, strangle squawks." The three dots in front of him changed color, telling him the AWACS' radar was now only receiving skin paints.

"Those two hawking the fight will look for Bossman now," she predicted.

"Sure," Moose replied, his doubt obvious. He watched as the computer traced the axis of the race track pattern. It moved and was pointed directly at Pontowski and Maggot. The J-8s were definitely tracking the two Warthogs. But how? Then it came to him. "I'll be," he whispered. He turned and stared at LaGrange with a new respect. How had she figured it out? "They're in a world of hurt," he said.

"Not if you do your job right," she replied. Again, she set the challenge for Moose. His jaw hardened. "Vector Bossman to the Dragon's Teeth," she said. "Fly 'em right into the Gullet and hide them."

"Rog," Moose answered. His blunt forefinger punched at a button labeled "Restricted Area." Moose had programmed the Dragon's Teeth into the system as a restricted area and now the DIODT, the drum initialize override data tape, was doing its magic. His monitor screen flickered and a red rectangular box appeared—the Dragon's Teeth.

"Bossman, snap two-niner-five for Dragon's Teeth." The two dots that were Pontowski and Maggot headed for the box, away from the tanker.

"They'll trust you," LaGrange told him.

Again, the computer trace for the bandits moved, still pointed at Pontowski and Maggot. Sweat poured off Moose, drenching his flight suit.

"You don't sweat much for a fat boy," LaGrange told him. It was her way of encouraging him.

## Sunday, October 20
## The Sino-Vietnamese border, China

Lieutenant Colonel Sung Fu was standing outside the control van enjoying a cigarette when the door opened and the captain said his presence was requested inside. From the quiver in his voice, Sung was certain that something had gone wrong. He took a last drag on his cigarette and exhaled slowly before he entered.

"Sir," the captain stammered, "the observation posts report another aircraft." Sung said nothing and waited. "It is established in the same orbit." The man was shaking.

"And," Sung said.

"Observation post sixteen—" he gulped, "claims it is the AWACS."

"But it was reported destroyed," Sung hissed. "How many AWACS do the Americans have?"

"I don't know, sir," the captain answered. He was shaking—hard.

"Then it must not be the AWACS," Sung shot at him. "Since you destroyed it," he added ominously. "The problem is easily solved," he continued. "As you shot the AWACS down, you only have to find the wreckage. Do so and report back here by twelve noon." A hard silence came down in the control van as the captain ran out the door.

"I want Sergeant Lu outside," Sung said into the silence, "standing at attention."

The plotter, the communications operator, and the launch/guidance operator exchanged knowing glances. A double execution would precede their midday meal.

**Sunday, October 20**
**Near the Sino-Vietnamese border, Vietnam**

LaGrange studied Moose's video monitor and verified that the two bandits were on Bossman and Maggot. "Moose, those two bandits hawking the fight might have a radar transponder . . ."

Moose completed the thought. "That can interrogate our IFFs."

"I misjudged you," LaGrange said. "You are a rocket scientist after all. I'm willing to bet half your sex life that those two jets are using our own IFFs to find us. When Snake strangled his squawk, they lost him. Notice how they are on opposite legs of the race track and how one always has its nose on Bossman?" She keyed her intercom to speak to the airborne radar technician. "Slovic, strangle our IFF interrogator." The AWACS would now have to rely only on radar skin paints to track the two A-10s.

Moose nodded. He and LaGrange were in sync. He tromped his foot pedal to talk to Pontowski. "Bossman, check your IFF panel and tell me when you've got an interrogation light." The hours Moose had spent studying the A-10 were now paying dividends. A green light on the A-10's IFF panel blinked whenever it replied to an interrogation by another radar. Most Warthog drivers considered the light a distraction and tweaked its lens closed. If LaGrange was right, the green light would blink when the Chinese interrogated Bossman's IFF.

"It's blinking at me about every ten seconds," Pontowski transmitted.

Moose looked at LaGrange. "Should I tell him it's not us interrogating him?" he asked.

LaGrange thought hard. What else have the Chinese got? Have they broken into our secure radio? We are so damn sure that it is secure that we don't even worry about communications security. Maybe it's time we do just that. "Negative," she said.

"Moose," LaGrange explained, "that's a pretty sophisticated capability for the Chinese to have developed on their own. And the APG-66 is a damn good pulse-Doppler radar. Have Bossman and Maggot strangle their IFFs now. Maybe that'll shake 'em off. When the Warthogs come out of the Gullet give them a vector south, ninety degrees to the bandits."

It all made sense to Moose. LaGrange was hedging her bet. If Bossman and Maggot turned their IFFs off, the J-8s would no longer be able to interrogate their transponders. At the same time, the Dragon's Teeth would offer them good terrain making from radar. Even the AWACS' radar had to rely on the Warthog's IFF squawks for tracking in the Dragon's Teeth. If they turned ninety degrees to the J-8s when they came out of the Gullet, they would be headed for the tanker and away from the J-8s. With a little luck, the J-8s might have overshot the Warthogs and be out in front of them.

The new respect Moose had been feeling for LaGrange turned to awe. Not only was she thinking tactically but she had countered the pulse-Doppler radar on the J-8s. On a heading of ninety degrees to the J-8s, the Warthog's relative motion would be zero and a pulse-Doppler radar could not detect them.

"Damn," Moose said in a rare outburst of profanity. The dots that represented the bandits on his monitor were no longer in a race track. "Bossman!" he barked over the radio. "Two bandits on you. Zero-seven-five at eighteen. Descending through three-five thousand feet."

"You got it, babes," LaGrange said, patting him on the shoulder and standing back. The situation was developing and changing so rapidly that she was in the way. She had to trust Moose to do it.

"Fucking lovely," Pontowski cursed under his breath. Moose's range and bearing call had clearly defined the threat: two bandits coming at him from the east, eighteen miles away, descending through thirty-five thousand feet. And going at the speed of smell, he thought.

"Bossman, Maggot," Moose ordered, "strangle squawks—now." Pontowski and Maggot flipped their IFFs to standby. The AWACS monitored a flurry of unknown interrogation signals. LaGrange had been right.

"Fly down the river and into the Gullet," Moose radioed. "Bandits now at your seven o'clock, co-altitude, twelve miles." Moose watched his monitor in satisfaction as the J-8s maintained their last heading as the Warthogs altered course and flew down the Luoqing River, into the Gullet. "Bandits east of Dragon's Teeth," he transmitted. He ran the intercept geometry and calculated where the J-8s would be when the Warthogs came out of the Gullet. Not good. Even without a radar, the J-8s would get a visual contact. He had to do something. "Bossman, say state," he radioed.

"Two heat, gun," Pontowski answered automatically. He had two AIM-9s and 1,100 cannon rounds. What the hell is Moose thinking of? he wondered. An engagement? I'm the one not thinking clearly, he warned himself.

"I think the boy's saying it's gonna get interesting," Maggot said over the UHF, "when we clear the Gullet."

It all made sense to Pontowski. They wouldn't be able to hide from the J-8s once they cleared the Dragon's Teeth. He considered the options.

Moose was doing the same. "Bossman," he transmitted, "at the Gap, vector zero-seven-zero for zero aspect. Bandits will be on your nose at six."

Pontowski understood immediately. The Gap was the one break in the Dragon's Teeth a Warthog could fly through. Moose had just told him that if he reversed course by turning through the Gap to a heading of seventy degrees, the bandits would be on his nose at six miles. Right in the AIM-9s' envelope for a head-on shot. With a little luck, he could get an AIM-9 shot off on each of the bandits. But he would have to be quick about it and not miss. And if Moose had the intercept geometry wrong, if he had miscalculated the closure rate between the bandits and the Warthogs, or misjudged the time it would take Pontowski to reverse course, the J-8s would eat his shorts in a close-in engagement. But it might give Maggot enough time to escape.

Pontowski made his decision. "I'll call the Gap," he told the AWACS. "Maggot, head for the tanker." He was almost to the break in the ridge line.

"Maggot," Moose radioed, "when clear of the Gullet, vector two-three-zero for rendezvous with Prima."

"Copy all," Maggot answered.

"Gap now," Pontowski transmitted. "In the turn." He firewalled the throttles and rolled left 135 degrees, knifing through the break in the ridge line. He caught a last glimpse of Maggot, still flying straight ahead down the Gullet. His left thumb hit the uncage switch on the throttle, freeing the AIM-9 seeker heads to search for a heat signature. He screamed out of the Gap still in a ninety-degree bank and saw the bandits. Exactly where Moose had predicted!

His earphones filled with the reassuring rattlesnake growl of an AIM-9 tracking. Automatically, he thumbed the weapons release, the pickle button, on the stick. Nothing happened! A missile should have come off the rail. He hit the button again. The firing circuit stepped over the first missile that had misfired and the second one leaped off the rail, accelerating with blinding speed.

The missile was homing on the bandit closest to him. Pontowski racked the Warthog to the right, looking for the second J-8. It was little more than a blur as it flashed in front of him. Pontowski mashed the trigger, sending a stream of thirty-millimeter cannon shells in the general direction of the J-8. He missed.

Pontowski thought for a moment that the Chinese pilot would not want to engage down on the deck and would shoot the moon, disengaging. He was wrong. The J-8's nose was coming back around onto him as a flash flickered in Pontowski's rear view mirrors. The Sidewinder had stuffed the first bandit in the face. But he knew the odds. Going one-on-one with a J-8 at low level put his chances of survival on a par with the proverbial snowball in hell.

He turned hard into the J-8 and his airspeed rapidly bled off. Bitching Betty bitched at him as he neared a stall. The two jets passed canopy to canopy with less than thirty feet separation. Neither was able to get off a shot.

Extend! Pontowski told himself. He had to regain some airspeed if he was to keep turning with the J-8. He check turned left twenty degrees, and twisted around, looking over his left shoulder for the bandit while his airspeed increased. He could see the J-8 using the vertical to pitch back onto him. There was no choice. He pulled back into the bandit, aching with fatigue from the long mission. The steady tone in his earphones told him he was max performing the jet and couldn't turn any faster. But the angles were all wrong. The J-8 had the advantage of speed and power and was using the vertical to maneuver on him. The Chinese pilot was herding him around the sky with ease, making him turn in the direction he wanted, not giving him a chance to disengage. "The bastard's good," Pontowski said to himself. The J-8 driver had a small but well-practiced repertoire of maneuvers. He was keeping his speed up while camping at Pontowski's eight o'clock by either barrel rolling or lag rolling behind the American. An F-15 or F-16 driver would have taken the fight into the vertical, forced the J-8 into a high-speed overshoot, and then converted to a rolling scissors to go on the offensive. But that was beyond the Warthog.

Pontowski watched the J-8 sweep down into his six o'clock, right into the envelope for a PL-2 shot. He keyed for the inevitable missile and kept his turn coming. His muscles screamed in protest as he fought the gs. Do something! he raged to himself. But there was nothing he could do—the angles were all wrong.

The J-8 was tracking Pontowski with ease as he fired his first missile. Pontowski mashed the flare button on his throttle quadrant, sending out a stream of flares for the PL-2 missile to home on. The Warthog's RHAW gear wailed at him. The high-pitched tone was warning that a J-band air-to-air radar was tracking him. Pontowski hit the chaff dispenser button to jam the radar. A burst of six chaff bundles mushroomed behind the A-10.

The Chinese pilot was momentarily confused by both the exploding flares and his radar breaking lock. He pulled off and barrel-rolled with ease behind the Warthog. He was surprised by the tenacity of the A-10 pilot in always turning into him. He glanced at his fuel gauge and decided he had fuel for one more pass before he had to disengage and return to base. He positioned for another pass, intending to launch two missiles and then close for a firing pass with his twin-barreled twenty-three-millimeter cannon. This time, he would do it visually and not lock on with his radar. One more pass would be enough.

Pontowski fought against the inevitable outcome and cursed loudly as he took the only course open to him. He dropped even lower, now turning at 235 knots barely fifty feet above the ground. He twisted in desperation as he watched the J-8 position. There was nothing he could do. He was low, slow, and out of ideas. The bitter, coppery taste of defeat flooded his mouth. He was going to die.

A flicker of motion caught at Pontowski's peripheral vision and then materialized into a Warthog. It was Maggot crawling along at 160 knots and coming into the fight. Maggot was inside the J-8's turn at its nine o'clock position. The Chinese pilot only had to look to his left and he would see the Warthog coming at him. But he had target fixation on Pontowski and had forgotten to check his six, or in this case, his nine o'clock position.

A new emotion surged through Pontowski—hope! The J-8 driver solved the intercept problem for Maggot by simply keeping his turn coming and flying right by Maggot's nose. With maddening slowness, Pontowski watched the Warthog's nose turn to point directly at the J-8's tail. The Chinese pilot never saw Maggot's Sidewinder leap off the rail and snake toward him. A second Sidewinder followed the first.

The J-8 disappeared in a fiery cloud as Maggot called, "Tallyho the fox!"

Moose Penko turned and looked at LaGrange. She stared back. "Bossman, Maggot," Penko transmitted. "Vector two-zero-zero to the tanker. No bandits in the area, Prima moving your way." Maggot, not Pontowski, acknowledged the call.

LaGrange cracked a smile. "Moose, if you ain't a weapons controller, you ain't shit."

He grinned back. He had never understood that strange phrase. But he agreed with the conviction behind it.

"Hey, Boss," Maggot radioed, "you still with me?" He was worried about the sudden silence.

Pontowski fought the emotions surging through him. Moments before he had tasted the bitterness of defeat and death. But he was still alive. Alive, he thought, if only Shoshana were alive. But there was no joy in killing Kang and avenging Shoshana's death—only a feeling of relief that it was over. He forced himself back to the moment. "Maggot, you were damn lucky he didn't see you."

"But he didn't," came the cheerful reply. "Like the man says, 'A kill is a kill.'"

"You were ordered to beat feet for the tanker."

"I said 'copied all.' Didn't say anything about doing it."

"I should court-martial you."

"You can't court-martial me," Maggot answered. "I'm a volunteer. Remember?"

"Then I'll fire your ass."

"That's all we need," Maggot laughed, "another homeless, unemployed aerial assassin on the streets."

# EPILOGUE

"The AVG is at Cam Ranh Bay," Mazie told Carroll, updating the national security advisor on the situation in China. "Apparently, Kang was killed when Pontowski bombed his headquarters."

"Strictly in self-defense," Hazelton added, his face serious.

"Of course," Carroll conceded.

Mazie wished they could be serious. But the two men were still enjoying the taste of victory. "What happens to the AVG now?" she asked.

"They fly back to Whiteman," Carroll replied, "and become the 303rd again."

"Are they still scheduled for deactivation?" Hazelton asked.

Carroll allowed a tight smile. "Not if I can help it." He changed the subject. "Any news of your father?"

Mazie shook her head. "The last I heard he was still with his regiment at Bose, rebuilding the New China Guard."

"We need to get word to him to stay there," Carroll said. "Nevers wants him arrested as a deserter and mercenary."

"She never gives up," Hazelton groused.

"We were warned she'd demand her pound of flesh," Carroll replied, recalling the words of Cyrus Piccard. "I think this may be it. She lost a heap of credibility and is scrambling to recover before the elections." He smiled. "But we did it. We pulled the dragon's teeth. Beijing is salvaging what it can and won't be much of a threat to its neighbors for quite a while. They've reached an understanding with Zou and the Republic of Southern China is now the Autonomous Republic of China and still part of China— sort of. Zou is a hero of the people for saving China from the evil warlord Kang, and Hong Kong is a self-governing international zone under the control of the UN."

"That will work for a while," Mazie said.

"You two did good," Carroll said. "Take a break and be back—say in two weeks?"

"After the election?" Mazie asked.

Carroll nodded as Mazie and Hazelton rose to leave. As they left his office, they heard him buzz his secretary and ask for the two Secret Service agents who ran with him to join him for a brewski.

"Two weeks sounds wonderful," Mazie said as they walked down the corridor of the White House. "I'm going to collapse into a hot bath for at least a day. Are you doing anything special?"

Hazelton thought for a moment. "I thought we could get married."

Mazie stopped, turned, and faced him. She almost told him to be serious. But she liked the idea and didn't want to discourage the thought. Instead, she asked, "What will your mother say?"

Hazelton pulled a face. He had been a major player in shaping events in China, killed a tank, and done things he still could hardly credit. Somewhere along the way, he had discovered who he was and didn't need his mother's approval. He needed Mazie. "She can say either yes or no when we invite her to the wedding."

"Went, this is one hell of a place to ask a girl."

He swooped her up in his arms. "What better place?" he said, gently kissing her and ending all her reservations. She threw her arms around his neck and kissed him back. The president of the United States walked by and shook his head. They hadn't even noticed him.

## Monday, November 4
## Nanning, China

The four Junkyard Dogs and May May stood in the center of the warehouse next to the train station. Outside, a freshly painted sign announced the central office of Southern China Enterprises. Inside, the building was a mess. "I've seen worse," Little Juan Alvarez allowed. "But I can't remember where." He brushed some debris off a chair and beckoned for May May to sit down. Instead, she looked at the large shadow filling the doorway.

It was Kamigami. He said a few words to her in Cantonese and she walked over to him. "Thank you," he said to the Dogs. "I owe you." Then they were gone.

"I'm going to miss her," Larry Tanaka said. "So what do we do now?"

"Make money," Byers answered. "We almost own the Hanoi-Nanning railroad, so let's use it."

"We're still expediters," Big John Washington intoned. "So who's our first customer?"

"Toragawa," Byers grinned. "Who else?"


## Wednesday, November 6
## Whiteman AFB, Missouri

The base chapel was filled to overflowing for the memorial service. Outside, four TV news crews held back at a respectable distance as the 303rd paid tribute to its fallen. The cameras came on when the doors opened and the people came slowly out and gathered on the lawn. A voice said "There" and they all looked to the east. Heading into the setting sun, four battle-scarred A-10s approached in a tight fingertip formation. The number-three man, Maggot, pulled up and away, leaving the three to overfly the chapel in a missing-man formation.

It was over.

"Melissa," Waters said to her daughter, "I'd like you to meet John Leonard."

The eleven-year-old girl looked up at the tall, lean pilot, remembering the first time she had seen him. "We've met," she announced. "But you looked like a teddy bear then. You look better now. I think you should marry my mom, don't you?"

Waters gave Leonard a weak smile. "I did warn you."

"That you did," he deadpanned. "Where did the Bossman go?" he asked. "We need to talk."

"Over there," she said. "But I think he needs to be alone."

Pontowski walked past the hangar and onto the deserted flight line. Across the runway, the moon was rising, casting a half-light down the long line of Warthogs parked neatly wingtip to wingtip. He stopped by the nose of the first jet and touched the scarred and pitted snout. The yellow-and-black nose art was chipped away and only the painted eyes were intact, still flashing with anger. His hand stroked the nose.

Another figure stepped out of a shadow. It was Maggot. "Kinda hard to let them go," he said. "I keep telling myself they're only machines."

Pontowski nodded. "It's the people who fly them," he said.

Maggot looked down the line of aircraft. "I know," he said. "But I hate to see them go to the boneyard."

"They're not," Pontowski replied. Maggot's head came up. "We're flying them to McClellan for rebuild."

"Who's getting them?"

Pontowski allowed a tight smile. Maggot hadn't heard. "Us."

"The 303rd?" Maggot was incredulous. "We're not getting the ax after all?"

"Nope. We picked up a new mission today—search and rescue."

Maggot smiled. "So we're going to be Sandies." Sandy was the traditional call sign for search and rescue aircraft. "Say, Boss, can we do that?"

"Oh, yeah. We can do that." The two men stood there, each lost in his own thoughts as a cool breeze washed over them. The part of Pontowski that belonged to Shoshana ached. I got most of them home, he told her.

An inner voice told him she heard.

# ACKNOWLEDGMENTS

The A-10 Thunderbolt II ranks as perhaps the ugliest aircraft ever flown by the United States Air Force. It offends the basic sensibilities of many pilots because it is not glamorous, does not have a pointy nose, and is unbelievably slow. But for those who have been on the receiving end of a "Warthog," it is a respected and feared weapons system. It was with good cause that Iraqi soldiers in the Persian Gulf War called the Warthog the "Silent Gun."

Since the A-10 is a single-seat aircraft and there are no two-seaters, I have never flown one. But thanks to Brigadier General John Bradley and the men and women of the 442nd Fighter Wing (AFRES) who care for and feed it, I have come to respect and understand the jet.

I am indebted to all the pilots of the 303rd Fighter Squadron. Major Don Slone and Captain Dave Graham were very helpful. A special note of appreciation is due to Majors Jim Preston and "Hampster" Brunke. Hampster never lost patience in making sure I understood A-10 pilots. Jim was unflagging in his support, was willing to spend long hours in answering dumb questions, kept me on track, and retaught me an old lesson—that love of flying and a challenge is what it's all about.

I owe a deep thanks to Captain Guy "Spike" Morley and the men and women of the 552nd Air Control Wing. They gave me a rare insight into the E-3 Sentry aircraft and the AWACS mission, proving again that people are still the key to high-tech warfare.

Others contributed significantly to the story that became

this book. Stephen Tse offered invaluable help with Chinese names. At McClellan Air Force Base, California, Don Zimmer and Mark Huntley shared their knowledge of the A-10. Lieutenant Colonel Mike Steffen and his Range Rats at Cannon Range in Missouri showed me the business end of bombs. At March Air Force Base, I was introduced to both ends of the KC-10 by the Seventy-ninth Air Refueling Squadron (AFRES). A crew from the Sixth Air Refueling Squadron (Twenty-second ARW), Captains Carlos Jensen and Wayne Cochran, Master Sergeant Duke Winder, and Staff Sergeant Jack Lemons, demonstrated what the "Gucci Bird" can do in a tight situation. But it was Major Mike Vitolo, Mr. Ron Trow, and Staff Sergeants Terry Contrell and Russ Taylor of the Twenty-second Transportation Squadron who acquainted me with the cargo-carrying capabilities of the Ten. It was impressive.

To all, again, thank you.

# GLOSSARY

**AFRES** Air Force Reserve.

**AIM** Air intercept missile, such as the infrared-guided Sidewinder AIM-9.

**ALO** Air liaison officer. The ground-based part of the forward air control team that directs fighters onto enemy troops.

**APC** Armored personnel carrier.

**ASO** Air surveillance officer. The officer on board the AWACS who is responsible for early identification and tracking of hostile aircraft.

**ASOC** Air support operations center. The section of a ground commander's battle staff that coordinates requests for close air support between various ALOs.

**AWACS** Airborne warning and command system. Provides surveillance command, control, and communications to commanders. Based on the E-3 Sentry aircraft, a much-modified Boeing 707 airframe, with a thirty-foot diameter radar dome on top.

**BAI** Battlefield interdiction. Sealing off the battlefield from resupply, reinforcement, and so forth.

**Bandit**  An aircraft positively identified as hostile.

**BDU**  Battle dress uniform. The latest name given to the uniform worn in battle.

**CAP**  Combat air patrol. A mission flown with the specific intention of finding and destroying enemy aircraft.

**CAS**  Close air support. The business of Warthogs. Involves killing tanks, bombing and strafing, and generally wreaking havoc on hostile attacking troops in contact with friendly forces. Dangerous but highly rewarding work.

**CBU-58**  Cluster bomb unit. The CBU-58 contains 650 baseball-sized bomblets, each of which explodes into 260 fragments. Inside each bomblet are two five-grain titanium incendiary pellets. It is much more effective than napalm, which was a squirrely weapon to deliver in the first place. CBU-58s are very effective against soft-skinned targets, such as enemy troops.

**DASR**  Directed assignment roster. The bureaucratic method of keeping track of, and paying, armed forces personnel who are engaged in covert operations.

**DCI**  The director of central intelligence. The individual in charge of all U.S. intelligence agencies and functions. Also heads the CIA.

**Dragon**  A man-portable, shoulder-fired, medium-range anti-tank missile.

**FAC**  Forward air controller. The pilot who, with the ALO, forms the airborne part of the forward air control team. Their job is to direct fighters, like the Warthog, onto enemy troops and tanks in contact with friendly troops.

Fantan    NATO code name for the Nanchang Q5/A5 twin-engined fighter-bomber. Similar in size and performance to the MiG-19 Farmer. China has an estimated six hundred.

Farmer    NATO code name for the MiG-19, a twin-engine Soviet-designed fighter-bomber. The Chinese variant is called the J-6.

Feng shui    The ancient Chinese belief that powerful spirits of dragons, tigers, and other beings occupy mountains, hills, rivers, trees, and so forth. Rather than incur their wrath, geomancers, men who know the will and desire of these spirits, should be consulted before doing anything to nature. Practitioners of *feng shui* do not come cheap in China.

Finback    NATO code name for the Shenjang J-8, an enlarged version of the Soviet-designed MiG-21. The U.S. sold the AN/APG-66 radar fire control system to the Chinese for the Finback, greatly improving its capability.

GAU-8    The thirty-millimeter, seven-barreled gun called the Avenger. The A-10 was designed around this gatling-type cannon, which was designed to kill tanks. Not to be trifled with when it is in the hands of a skilled pilot and you are a hostile tank driver in the immediate vicinity.

Grail    The NATO code name for the SA-7, a shoulder-held, Soviet-designed surface-to-air missile they call the Strela, or Arrow.

Have Quick    The name for the radio that uses rapid frequency hopping to defeat jamming and monitoring.

HUD    Head-up display. A transparent glass screen in front of the pilot on which tactical and flight information is displayed. Since the screen is in front of him, the pilot does not have to look down into the cockpit when he would much rather be looking at the bad guy.

IFF Identification friend or foe. A radar transponder used by interrogating radars for aircraft identification.

J-8 *See* Finback.

J-6 *See* Farmer.

J-STARS The Army/Air Force joint surveillance target attack radar system. The system is based on the E-8A, a Boeing 707 airframe, with a synthetic aperture/pulse Doppler radar. It can detect stationary targets, low-flying helicopters, slow-moving aircraft, tanks, and vehicles at ranges of two hundred kilometers or more. The information is downlinked to a mobile ground module and provides the ground commander with real-time intelligence about the disposition of enemy forces. Very cosmic.

LASTE Low-altitude safety and targeting enhancement. A weapons delivery system that makes the Warthog smart, not the bombs.

MAAG Military Assistance Advisory Group. A military mission that provides military aid to a foreign government.

Mark-82 AIR Air inflatable retarded. A five-hundred-pound bomb that is employed at low altitudes. Its fall is retarded by the ballute, an inflatable balloon/parachute, that deploys behind it and slows the bomb's descent, allowing the delivery aircraft time to scamper to safety and avoid the bomb's blast.

MCC Mission crew commander. The officer in charge of the working troops in the back of the AWACS. The MCC is responsible for mission accomplishment and must never lose situational awareness. The MCC takes the heat and is hanged first when anything goes wrong.

MRC   Major regional conflict. The emerging type of conflict that is large scale but limited to a specific region. The Persian Gulf War is a prime example. Not good, but better than total war.

PDB   President's Daily Brief. A summary of the best and most pertinent intelligence available to the United States. Strictly for the president's use. It is prepared daily by a committee at the CIA, is highly classified, and is read by a very limited number of high-ranking policy makers.

PLA   People's Liberation Army. The defense establishment of the People's Republic of China.

PL-2   The Chinese version of the Soviet Atoll air-to-air missile. The Atoll is a clone of an early version of the U.S. Sidewinder AIM-9 missile.

PRC   The People's Republic of China. The official name for China.

PRC-90   The small radio used for survival by aircrew members.

RHAW   Radar homing and warning. The equipment that alerts the pilot to hostile radar threats. A certified attention-getter.

RPG-7   Rocket-propelled grenade. A shoulder-held, Soviet-designed antitank rocket. It is an old weapon but still effective against older and medium tanks.

Sandy  The call sign for the close air support aircraft dedicated to search and rescue operations. Sandies hold off the enemy while helicopters extract downed aircrews. A very dangerous but satisfying job.

SA-7  *See* Grail.

SIB  Safety investigation board. The Air Force panel convened to investigate aircraft accidents. Its job is to determine the cause of the accident so corrective action can prevent it from occurring again. Its findings cannot be used for punishment or disciplinary action.

Sidewinder  An air-to-air missile. *See* AIM, PL-2.

SOF  Supervisor of flying. The officer who controls daily flying operations. Normally, the duty is rotated among experienced pilots.

Stinger  The U.S.-designed, shoulder-held, infrared-guided surface-to-air missile. An excellent short-range air defense weapon.

TOW  Tube-launched, optically tracked, wire-guided antitank missile. Bad news for enemy tanks.

A selection from

RICHARD HERMAN, Jr.'s

next thrilling novel

*IRON GATE*

Available in hardcover from
Simon & Schuster
February 1996

## Monday, January 19
## UN Headquarters, Constantia, Cape Town

Pontowski stood up from his desk, walked to the window of his office, and stretched. Outside, moonlight cast a gentle, soothing glow over the gardens and veranda. He watched as a tall figure, de Royer, walked slowly back and forth. His hands were clasped behind his back and his head bent, deep in thought. So you're frustrated too, Pontowski thought.

His frustration level moved up a notch as he considered the problems facing the UN. We've been here almost three weeks and haven't done a damn thing, he told himself. What we need is a concept of operations . . . some idea of how to go about this. He settled back into his chair and grabbed the UN manual on peacekeeping operations.

Twenty minutes later, Bouchard, de Royer's aide, appeared in his doorway. "General de Royer requests you join him in his office." Pontowski stood and they walked quickly down the hall. Bouchard spoke in French. "Madame Martine and the South African minister of defense, Joe Pendulo, are with the general. Be careful what you say. Pendulo remembers everything and understands nothing." Pontowski thanked him and entered de Royer's office.

As usual, the French general was wearing his dead-fish look. Only this time his cold stare was fixed on Joe Pendulo. What a pleasant change, Pontowski thought, glancing at the minister of defense. Pendulo was a short, wiry Xhosa whose beard was trimmed into a goatee. A diamond ring flashed on each hand and he wore a gold Rolex watch that hung loose on his wrist, much like a bracelet. His dark silk suit was tailored to his slender frame and his legs were crossed revealing expensive, hand-stitched shoes and white socks. What have we got here? Pontowski wondered.

Elena was sitting in the chair next to Pendulo, looking cool and beautiful in a white linen business suit. The coat clinched at her waist and gave the impression she was not wearing a blouse. It was both businesslike and provocative. How does she do it? Pontowski wondered. Her voice matched the image as she made the introductions. "We are discussing the UN's area of responsibility," she told him.

"The stability of my country," Pendulo said, "is being threatened by a small group of white fascists." His voice was in total contrast to his image and he spoke with an upper-class British accent. "Are you familiar with the AWB?" Pontowski nodded an answer. "Unfortunately, they have an army, the Iron Guard. We want you to destroy it."

"Why don't you use your own forces?" Pontowski asked.

"The leader of our defense forces are all white, and I cannot guarantee their loyalty if I order them to attack their white brothers. Better they remain in garrison than desert."

"The United Nations cannot do what you ask," Elena told him. "We are here in a peacekeeping function. You are asking us to take an active role in supporting the government against the AWB. That is peace enforcement, which is beyond our charter."

Pontowski expected Pendulo to explode in a temper tantrum. It didn't happen. "What do you intend to do?" the defense minister asked, his voice reasonable and calm.

"It is our intention," de Royer said, "to establish safe zones as we did in Bosnia."

This is the first I've heard about it, Pontowski thought.

Pendulo looked pleased. "That is acceptable to my government. As you know, many of my people are starving because of the instability caused by the AWB and its thugs. Will you use these safe zones for humanitarian relief?"

"That is our intention," de Royer replied.

No sign of emotion crossed Pendulo's face. "Then my government will provide protection, not your forces. If there is trouble, you must coordinate through my office."

What good will that do with the South Africans in garrison? Pontowski thought. But before he could object, Elena answered. "Agreed."

"You," Pontowski told them, "have just taken away our right of self-defense."

"How so?" Pendulo asked.

Pontowski decided to let his anger show. "If anyone starts shooting at us, we can't do squat all about it until we 'coordinate' through your office. We're sitting ducks."

"Then keep your aircraft on the ground," Pendulo replied, as if he was speaking to a child. He stood to leave. "It is late," he said. "I must go." Elena escorted him out and Pontowski gritted his teeth until the door was closed.

"General," Pontowski said, "that little shit is using us. We either do it his way, or we get the livin' crap shot out of us by any thug who wants some target practice. No way am I going to put my people in that kind of situation if . . ."

"The decision has been made," de Royer interrupted.

"Fuck me in the heart," Pontowski muttered, loud enough for de Royer to hear.

"Colonel," de Royer said, giving no indication that he had heard, "schedule a C-130 to fly a survey team around the country to identify safe zones. Madame Martine will be in charge of the team and you will accompany her. The worst food shortages are in Northern Cape Province, so we will start there."

"And the A-10s?"

"Keep them on the ground. That will be all." He turned to look out the window.

Pontowski stormed out of the office. Congress was right not to get us involved, he told himself. We got to get the hell out of here.

## Wednesday, January 21
## Northern Cape Province, South Africa

Pontowski shifted his weight, trying to find a comfortable position on the crew bunk that served as a bench at the back of the C-130's flight deck. He was bored and envied the pilots who were flying the C-130, caught up in the action of the survey mission. He shuffled through the notes on his clipboard and rank ordered the three airfields they had already surveyed as possible safe zones for UN relief centers. He handed his list to Elena Martine who was sitting beside him making her own choices. One more to go, he thought. Then we can go home.

"You sure that's it?" Captain Rob Nutting asked over the intercom. He was flying in the left seat of the C-130 as it approached the landing strip on the south side of the town of Mata Mata.

"Yeah, that's it," Lydia Kowalski answered. She was giving Rob Nutting an in-country check out and was playing copilot to his aircraft commander while he flew Pontowski and the survey team around. So far, he had done an outstanding job. She keyed the intercom and spoke to Elena and Pontowski. "This one doesn't look very promising," she told them. "Too isolated, not enough people. Do you want to land and check it out?"

Elena came forward and studied the land below her. Everything the pilot had said was true. But according to her notes, there was abundant water at this strip and that was a definite plus. "Let's land," she decided.

"Do you have enough runway?" Pontowski asked, not liking what he saw.

"No problem," Nutting assured him. "It's just a bit narrow. We'll do an assault landing on this one."

"Sounds good," Kowalski said. Rob was on top of it.

Pontowski scanned the field with his binoculars and focused on a group of villagers gathered on the left side of the landing strip. "Looks like we've got a reception committee," he said. He and Elena strapped in on the crew bunk while Rob flew a standard pattern and brought the C-130 down final, nose high in the air. "I got some kid standing on the right side of the runway," Kowalski said.

"Got him," Rob told her. "No problem."

The pilot slammed the big cargo plane down on the exact point he was aiming for. Just as he raked the throttles aft, Kowalski saw movement off to the right side. The kid she had seen moments before was running across the runway. "Look out!" she shouted. But it was too late. Rob had committed to the landing and had lifted the throttles over the detent, throwing the props into reverse. They felt a slight bump.

If a high-speed camera had filmed the landing, it would have recorded the main gear sinking into the surface and pushing up a small wave of dirt in front of the tires. As the wheels emerged from the depression, the dirt flowed back into place, leaving tread marks and some wrinkles to mark the C-130's touchdown point. The camera would have also recorded a ten-year-old boy being sucked under the right gear and disappearing into the depression before being thrown up against the underside of the fuselage like a flattened rag doll.

What the camera could not record was the fear that had driven the boy across the runway. The size and noise of the Hercules had totally overwhelmed him and the only refuge he could see was his father—standing on the other side.

The props threw a cloud of dust and debris out in front as the Hercules howled to a stop. Pontowski and the loadmaster were the first off, checking for damage. All they found were a few wet brown stains on the fuselage aft of the right main gear and a piece of cloth hanging on the gear door. Rob joined them and they were still inspecting the aircraft for damage when a group of villagers surrounded them. A man carried the mangled remains of his son and yelled while two women sent a loud keening lament over the crowd.

Elena Martine climbed off the Hercules and headed for the three Americans. A hand reached out and grabbed at her shirt, ripping it while another woman pushed her to the ground. The villagers had finally found scapegoats for all their troubles. Pontowski heard Elena scream and pushed through the crowd. But two men blocked his way, yelling and pointing at the dead child. Elena screamed again and Pontowski bulldozed his way through with Rob and the loadmaster right behind him.

Kowalski heard the shouting, jumped out of her seat and ran back through the cargo compartment. She reached the rear ramp in time to see Pontowski, Rob, and the loadmaster standing back to back as they were hit and kicked by the angry villagers. They were holding their own but not for long.

She ran back onto the flight deck and jumped in the left seat. "Starting three!" she yelled at the flight engineer as she cranked the right inboard engine. They quickly brought the left inboard engine on line. "Riley," she shouted at the flight engineer, "sit in the right seat and keep 'em revved up." She grabbed her helmet and ran for the rear of the aircraft.

"Follow me," she yelled at the three men from the UN survey team still standing in the cargo compartment. They didn't move. "Come on!" she roared. Still, they made no attempt to follow her. "Screw you!" She pulled her white helmet on, lowered the green visor, and picked up a tie down chain. She was going it alone.

Lydia Kowalski was a big woman, strong by any standard, and full of resolve. She jumped off the ramp and headed for the villagers, swinging the chain. A man saw her and froze. She had emerged out of the blowing dust like a demon from hell and the C-130's blaring engines were her war cry. The man wanted none of it and started to run. But he slipped and fell into his comrades, yelling incoherently. Now they saw her, and like him, they ran. The riot was over and only the Americans and Elena were left behind with a small body.

"What the hell happened?" Kowalski shouted as she picked Elena up off the ground. She was bruised and dirty, but okay.

Rob pointed at the body. "I hit the kid," he yelled.

"Let's get the hell out of here," Pontowski shouted. "Before they come back."


## Thursday, January 22
## UN Headquarters, Constantia, Cape Town

Piet van der Roos was waiting for Pontowski when he came to work an hour later than usual. It had been a long night sorting out the aftermath from the survey mission and Pontowski had waited for the results of the blood test before returning to his quarters. Both pilots had tested free of any drugs or alcohol, which for Pontowski ended the incident. He had told the pilots it was sad but not their fault. Now the aftershocks of the mission were reaching him.

"Pendulo was on TV last night," van der Roos told him. "He said the UN was responsible for the accident and the pilot will be held accountable. Whites can no longer kill blacks without fear of justice."

"Lovely," Pontowski grumbled. "Absolutely, fucking lovely." He filled a coffee cup and drank. He still needed one more cup to clear the cobwebs of sleep away. "He never asked for our version of what happened."

"Pendulo's turning it into an issue," van der Roos told him. "He wants to control the UN and make it do his bidding."

"What will he do next?"

Van der Roos shook his head. "I don't know. He's a very clever man and wants the presidency."

The answer came just before noon when Bouchard appeared in Pontowski's office. "The general wishes to see you," he said. "It is about the survey mission."

Pontowski took the few steps to de Royer's office and found him, as usual, standing at the window. Doesn't he ever sit down? Pontowski wondered. "I have spoken to Madame Martine," de Royer began, speaking in French. "Minister Pendulo has asked the minister of justice to swear out a warrant for the arrest of Captain Nutting, the pilot on yesterday's mission."

"Martine was there," Pontowski said, "and she knows what happened. Didn't she explain it to Pendulo? I thought that was her job. The kid ran in front of a landing C-130. What the hell did he expect Nutting to do?"

De Royer stared at him, unblinking. "The warrant is for Captain Nutting's arrest," de Royer repeated. He turned to look out the window and Pontowski assumed the meeting was over. De Royer's voice stopped him as he left. "You have a little time," the general said.

"Yes sir," Pontowski replied. Now what does that mean? he wondered. Then it came to him. De Royer was telling him that he had some time to act before the warrant was served. "I'll be damned," he muttered to himself. He grabbed his hat and ran to his car.

The operations building at Ysterplaat was all but deserted when Pontowski entered. The duty officer, Gorilla Moreno, looked up from his desk, glad to have someone to talk to. "I need to see Colonel Leonard and Colonel Kowalski—now," Pontowski said. "And get Rob Nutting in here ASAP."

"Colonel Leonard is flying," Gorilla told him. "Colonel Kowalski is in her office and Rob has the day off. I think he went down to Victoria Harbor with a couple of the guys."

"Gorilla, find Nutting. Get every warm body you got and search until you do. But get him here. Quick."

"Yes sir," Gorilla said as he reached for the phone.

Pontowski found Kowalski in her office wading through the inevitable paperwork that greeted her each morning. "The South Africans are swearing out a warrant for Nutting's arrest," he told her.

"That sucks, Colonel."

"Tell me," Pontowski replied. "There is no way I'm going to let one of my troops end up in foreign jail over this." He paced the floor, thinking. "Cut leave orders for Nutting. Back date them four days . . . before the survey mission. Lay on a C-130 to fly him out . . . anywhere but Africa."

"We came through St. Helena," she told him. "It's a British dependency. Will that do?"

"Perfect," Pontowski said. "Lydia, we haven't got much time to bring all this together. Maybe an hour. You better get some one to pack for him."

She gave him a worried look. "I gave him the day off."

"I know. Gorilla is organizing a search for him."

A South African army major and two MPs, one white and one black, walked into the COIC an hour later. First Lieutenant Lori Williams, Leonard's executive officer, was waiting and greeted them with a severe formality far beyond her normal manner. The sight of a tall and pretty black woman wearing the uniform of a U.S. Air Force officer wasn't what they expected.

"I have a warrant for the arrest of one of your pilots," the major said. He handed her a copy of the warrant.

Lori carefully read the warrant, which was in three languages, one of them English. "I'll present this to my superior," she told them. "Please wait here." She walked slowly down the hall to Kowalski's office. The stall was on.

Outside, Pontowski was waiting by a C-130, his personal radio in his hand. The aircraft was preflighted and the crew on board, ready to go. Even Nutting's suitcase was there. But no Nutting. His radio squawked at him. "Bossman, this is Groundhog. "We have a situation that requires your presence in the COIC. Over." The command post controller's rigid use of correct communicatios protocol warned him that someone was monitoring the radios and the warrant had arrived.

"Groundhog, this is Bossman, standby one. I have a problem with maintenance. Break, break. Gorilla Control, this is Bossman. Say status of parts. Over."

Gorilla's voice came over the radio, scratchy but readable. "Bossman, this is Gorilla Control. We have the parts and are delivering them to the aircraft. ETA fifteen minutes. Over."

Good work, Gorilla, Pontowski thought. "Roger, Gorilla

Control. Break, break. Groundhog, Bossman is inbound to the COIC. ETA five minutes. Over."

"Groundhog copies all. Over and out."

We just might pull this one off, Pontowski told himself. He told the crew to start engines in five minutes and call for clearance. He drove slowly to the COIC, arriving six minutes later. In the distance, the C-130's engines were spinning up.

Inside, he was introduced to the waiting major and presented a copy of the arrest warrant. He took his time reading the document. "This does appear to be in order," he said.

"Of course," the major replied.

"Unfortunately, it will have to be presented to our embassy."

"There is no diplomatic immunity involved," the major said, "We have jurisdiction in this matter."

Pontowski paused. He could hear the C-130 taxing out. "There is a problem . . . I believe Captain Nutting has left for the States on leave." He turned to Lori. "Lieutenant Williams, please verify the status of Captain Nutting."

Lori was into the game and she made a phone call. "We processed leave orders . . . ah . . . last week. He has signed out but we don't know if he has departed the base yet."

"We will seal the base and search for him," the major said.

"Please do," Pontowski said. "May I suggest you start at his quarters." Lori called for a sergeant to show them the way and ushered the three men out the door.

Gorilla came in with a big grin on his face. "We found him at Victoria Harbor sightseeing. He's on the plane." The sound of a C-130 taking off reached them.

Lydia Kowalski came out of the command post. "They're airborne," she said.

Lori started to laugh. "I have never heard so much rogering, overing, outing, and break-breaking in my life. This was like a Boy Scout camp. But you did skin and grin the man." It was the highest compliment she could pay them.

**Friday, January 23**
**The White House, Washington, D.C.**

The intercom on Carroll's desk buzzed. "Congresswoman Nevers is on line one," said his secretary, Midge.

Carroll picked up the phone, surprised that Nevers was calling him. The animosity between them was deep-seated and extended far beyond any political rivalry. "Carroll here," he said. As expected, he was talking to Nevers's secretary who put him through to the congresswoman. It was one of the minor irritating games played in Washington to establish who was top dog. But he was long past that.

"Bill," Nevers said, sounding cordial but businesslike. "I'm concerned about a report from South Africa that one of our airplanes was in an accident where a child was killed. I understand the South African government wants to arrest the pilot."

"That's basically correct," he told her. "It was a regrettable but unavoidable accident. A boy ran right in front of a C-130 when it was landing. There was nothing the pilot could do."

"Nevertheless," Nevers replied, "it raises many questions about what we're doing in South Africa."

"There's always questions," Carroll said. "Why don't I send you all the messages and reports we have on the accident and you can decide for yourself."

"That would be fine," she said. "As you said, it appears to be a regrettable but unavoidable accident. One of the facts of life we have to live with. Thanks for the help." She broke the connection.

What's that all about? he wondered. She actually sounded friendly. Has she changed her position on the UN? Probably not. Is she being reasonable for once? Or maybe she wants to declare a truce.

He lay back in his chair, willing to wait.

It was late afternoon and Carroll was clearing his desk to go home. His wife, Mary, had a family reunion planned over the weekend and many members of his family had flown in. Midge came to the door of his office and caught his attention. "CNN is interviewing Nevers on TV," she said. He nodded and she turned the TV on.

A reporter was standing with Nevers in the hall of the Capitol. "This is an outstanding example of why we should not be in South Africa," Nevers said. "Unfortunately, our pilot was the cause of the accident . . ."

So much for any truce, Carroll thought. "Turn it off," he said. He shuffled out of his office, determined to spend a pleasant weekend with his family. South Africa could go on a back burner.